TWOPENNY RAINBOWS

In 1863 Irish orphans Ismay and Mara are sent to Australia against their will. Worse, on arrival they're separated when Ismay is forced to take a job as a maid in the country and Mara must stay in the care of the Catholic mission.

Desperate to be reunited, Ismay flees her employers but runs into danger in the bush. She is saved by Malachi Firth, but although he's attracted to her, he doesn't want to be encumbered with a wife. Mara has also run away and though she finds shelter it is in a place with its own perils.

Meanwhile, elder sister Keara has not forgotten them. However, she has had her own struggles to face and by the time she reaches Melbourne she finds that the trail is cold.

Danger continues to threaten all three sisters as their desperate search takes them from one side of Australia to the other. Will they find one another again or will their old enemies triumph?

TWOPENNY RAINBOWS

Anna Jacobs

WINDSOR
PARAGON

First published 2004
by
Hodder and Stoughton
This Large Print edition published 2004
by
BBC Audiobooks Ltd
by arrangement with
Hodder and Stoughton Limited

ISBN 0 7540 9570 3   (Windsor Hardcover)
ISBN 0 7540 9585 1   (Paragon Softcover)

British Library Cataloguing in Publication Data available

Printed and bound in Great Britain by
Antony Rowe Ltd., Chippenham, Wiltshire

Dedication

To my long-time friend Sylvia Hope (nee Shore) who grew up in Lancashire like me, endured school alongside me and also emigrated to Australia. We've shared many good times over the years and its my pleasure now to make this 'her' book.

Part One

1863–1865

CHAPTER ONE

JULY 1863

The men had to drag the two girls on to the train. The older one fought and spat defiance every inch of the way and the younger one, more easily overpowered, wept loudly and bitterly.

Ismay Michaels saw one or two bystanders step towards them uncertainly and if there hadn't been a priest involved, she thought they might have helped her—but there was, so no one actually did anything.

Panting, the men shoved the girls into a compartment.

'This defiance will do you no good,' Father Cornelius warned.

As the train pulled away Ismay straightened her clothes and helped her sister Mara do the same, then sat as far away from their parish priest and his helper as she could. 'You've no right to do this! No right at all. We could manage on our own.'

The priest sighed and repeated, 'You're only just turned fifteen and your sister's eleven. There's no way you could earn a living and make a home for yourselves now your parents are dead. You know there isn't.'

'Keara promised she'd come back here to Ireland and we'd all live together.'

'Well, your sister is needed in England to help her mistress who's expecting a baby, so she can't do that now and—'

'I'll never forgive her for abandoning us, never!'

3

Ismay put her arm round Mara's shoulders. 'Neither of us will.'

'Keara's doing what she thinks is best for you. Why, Mr Mullane himself has arranged for the good Sisters of St Martha and St Zita to take you to Australia. You'll be able to make far better lives for yourselves there than you could if you stayed in the village.'

'I don't believe you. And anyway, we don't want to leave Ireland.'

When they got off the train, Ismay fought again, on principle, but once the big door of the convent thudded shut behind her she stopped struggling because what was the point? She became aware of Mara's trembling hand clutching hers and her little sister's tear-stained face, so put an arm round her. She didn't dare give way to tears, had to be strong now, so focused on her anger as she stared at the inside of the convent. Everything here was made of stone—big, square stones that seemed to press down on you—and the chill of the place made her shiver. Or perhaps it was fear of what was going to become of them now.

Two brisk young nuns in long black habits and white wimples came into the parlour.

'These men have kidnapped us!' Ismay announced at once.

After a startled look at the priest, the taller nun said quietly, 'Thank you, Father. We'll see to them now.' When the two men had left, she said, 'I'm Sister Catherine and I'll be going to Australia with you. If you'll come to the kitchen we'll find you something to eat. Everyone else is in bed, but we waited up for you.'

They trailed after her, Ismay still with one arm

4

round her little sister's shoulders. When the nun set some cake in front of them, Mara whispered, 'Will we eat it, Ismay?'

'I suppose so.' After finishing the cake and drinking a big glass of milk each, they followed the nuns to a long, narrow room whose walls were lined with shelves bearing piles of neatly folded clothes.

'Now, what size are you?' the tall one wondered, shaking out a skirt. 'I think this one will fit you, Ismay. Just try it on for me, will you?'

The girl shook her head. 'We don't want your horrid old clothes. We just want to go home.'

The nun's voice became steely. 'Either we do it by force or you take those clothes off this minute and try the skirt on.'

For a moment Ismay stared at them defiantly, then her shoulders drooped and she blinked furiously. 'I've got something in my eye,' she muttered as she saw Sister Catherine looking at her in concern. Taking off her clothes as slowly as she could, she tried on the ones she was given, then took them off again and donned the plain white cotton nightdress the nun handed her. She managed to hide the fact that she was amazed at having brand new clothes, or a long dress just for sleeping in. The shoes amazed her as well—two pairs each, plus a pair of slippers. What did you need two pairs of shoes for? You only had one pair of feet!

Sister Catherine and the other nun picked out a whole pile of clothes in their sizes. 'Right then. You two carry the shoes and we'll take you to your bedroom.'

The room was very simply furnished and

5

immaculately clean. Even the wood of the bedheads was polished. Ismay studied the two narrow beds and so far forgot herself as to go and finger the soft blankets and sheets. There were also two chairs, a small washstand with ewer and bowl, and two clean, neatly folded towels. The beds were high enough to show the plain white chamber pot underneath one, and at the foot of each stood a sturdy metal trunk, lid gaping open.

The nuns placed most of the clothes in the trunks, leaving out skirts, blouses and sets of underclothes for the next day.

Finally Sister Catherine stepped back and nodded in satisfaction. 'There, that's everything you'll need for your journey. You may as well go to bed now. The others went to sleep a while ago.'

'Others?' Ismay asked.

'The other orphans. We're taking a group of ten girls out to Australia.' She hesitated then said quietly, 'It won't be so bad, you know. You'll be well looked after.'

'They shouldn't be sending us to Australia at all! We have a sister in England working for the Mullanes and we should be going to her.'

'She must have given her permission or you wouldn't be here.' Because Sister Catherine could see how very unhappy they were, she added, 'None of us has a choice about going to Australia.' At their looks of surprise she added with a slight smile, 'I don't particularly want to leave Ireland, either, you know.'

The other nun cleared her throat and gave her companion a disapproving glance, so Catherine cut short what she was about to say and finished, 'Sleep well, girls.'

The two women left as quietly as they seemed to do everything else, taking the candle and locking the door behind them.

Ismay immediately got out of bed and sat very upright on the edge, swinging one leg. Mara hesitated but lay where she was, pulling the blanket up with a tired sigh. 'Shall we not go to sleep now?'

'Not yet, no.' When her eyes had adjusted Ismay found the moonlight bright enough for her to investigate the rest of the contents of the trunks. Underneath the clothes were all sorts of things: a prayer book, sewing materials, writing implements.

It was as she started to put the things back that the idea occurred to her. 'I'll show them what I think of their horrid clothes!' she muttered and took the scissors from the sewing kit. The idea was so monstrous that she hesitated for a moment, then with a toss of her head began to cut up their new clothes.

'Ismay! Ismay, what are you doing? Don't!' Mara whispered, horrified.

'Why not? Look what they're doing to us? You go to sleep. This'll take me a while.'

It took her a couple of hours to do the job properly, by which time her fingers were blistered. Once her little sister fell asleep she didn't even try to hold back her tears and the resultant pile of rags was well watered.

*　　　*　　　*

In the morning they were woken by bells. A short time later Sister Catherine came in, mouth open to say something, but stopped short and stared at the pile of shredded cloth beside each trunk, her

7

expression changing to one of shock, then horror. 'What have you *done,* child?'

'No worse than you've done to us,' Ismay repeated, expecting a slap. She was puzzled when the nun looked at her instead with compassion written clearly on her face.

'I'll have to tell Reverend Mother about this and she'll be furious. Oh, Ismay, can you not accept what's to happen to you?'

'No, I can't and I never will!'

An older nun was brought to see what the new girl had done and stood for a moment looking at the pile of ragged pieces of cloth and muttering under her breath a prayer for patience. Her voice grated with the effort it took her to say, calmly and evenly, 'If you do that again, Ismay Michaels, I'll separate the pair of you. Permanently. Send one to Australia and leave the other here.'

Mara gave a wail and flung her arms round her sister.

Ismay stared back at the grim-faced nun. 'You've no *right* to do this.'

'We have every right. You should be grateful that your landlord has paid for you to go to Australia. You'll have a far better chance of a decent life out there. They're crying out for decent young women as maids and wives.'

'Well, we're not—'

The old nun raised one finger in warning. 'Quiet! Just remember what I said if you want to stay together!'

If they separated her from Mara, Ismay didn't know what she'd do. She bit back an angry sob, looking at the hard, unyielding face that was not at all like Sister Catherine's whose expression was

8

kindly. 'I hate you!' she flung at the Mother Superior.

More clothes were found. When they were alone again, locked in the room even in the daytime, Ismay and her sister sat on one of the beds cuddled up close.

Mara made a sad sound in her throat and wiped away a tear with a corner of the new white pinafore. 'Do you think maybe Keara doesn't know about this?'

'Of course she does. How can she not be knowing? Didn't they send a letter to Father Cornelius to say she wanted us to go? She couldn't even be bothered to tell us herself or—' her voice faltered for a moment as she fought to control it '—come to Ballymullen to say goodbye. As far as I'm concerned, she's no sister of ours and I hope I never see her again as long as I live. If I ever do, I'll spit in her face, so I will.'

Mara continued to sob quietly.

A few tears escaped Ismay's control but she made no attempt to wipe them away, just hugged her sister close. She was the elder and she had to look after Mara now. If anything happened to separate them, she was sure she'd die of grief.

*   *   *

Malachi Firth crept into the house. He'd hoped his family would all be asleep by now, but there was a lamp still burning in the kitchen. Outside, the small Pennine village was blanketed in mist so thick he'd had trouble finding his way home, even the couple of hundred yards from the alehouse. Damned mist and rain! That's all they'd seen for weeks.

Lancashire must be the rainiest place on earth. Sometimes he longed for a sunny day.

As he closed the back door he saw his father rise up from the far end of the scrubbed wooden table, scowling at him as usual, and Malachi's heart sank.

'You've been with those louts again! What do you mean by staying out till this hour when you've a long day's work ahead of you tomorrow?'

Malachi scowled right back. He wasn't drunk or even tiddly, couldn't afford it on the meagre wages his father paid him. 'They're good lads and I only had a glass or two of ale! Where's the harm in that?'

'They're ne'er-do-wells and you shouldn't hang around with folk like them. Your brother shows a deal more sense in the friends *he* makes, and our Lemuel doesn't waste his time at a common alehouse, either.'

That was because Lemuel's wife hardly let him breathe without permission, but Malachi knew better than to criticise her to his father since she'd recently borne a son to carry on the family name. 'I do my work here and I'm entitled to a bit of fun in my spare time.' Besides, it'd been a singing evening tonight and Malachi, who had a good baritone voice, dearly loved a sing-song. He'd won five shillings for being the best singer, by popular acclaim, but his father thought singing in public below the dignity of a Firth and a master cooper's son. Malachi winced as the deep voice roared out its scorn.

'*Fun!* What's fun got to do with it when you've a trade to learn? You'd be better saving your pennies than wasting them on ale. How will you be able to set up your own cooperage when your time comes

10

if you don't save your pennies—aye, and your farthings too?' He gestured round him. 'This place must pass to the eldest son and don't think I'll split it between you.'

Suddenly the thoughts Malachi had been holding back for a while burst out. Coopering's a dying trade, Dad, and we all know it, even if *you* won't admit it!'

'Folk will always want barrels and buckets making.'

'I don't see any point in slaving through an apprenticeship when there's not enough work to go round.' Malachi never normally voiced his thoughts, but he agreed with those who said a galvanised bucket was better than a wooden one, and lighter too. Even before the Cotton Famine had impoverished so many in Lancashire, coopering had been losing custom to factory-made goods. But he didn't want to start that old argument again.

His father made angry noises in his throat at this rank heresy.

Fed up of the continual carping, Malachi turned to go up to his bedroom, then swung round in shock as a thud behind him shook the wooden floor. John Firth lay spread-eagled on the rag rug, motionless apart from one twitching foot. Alarmed, Malachi yelled for his mother to come quick.

But there was nothing she could do—or the doctor when he eventually came.

His father lay unmoving in his bed for two long days and nights, then died abruptly of another seizure.

Afterwards Malachi's elder brother cornered him in the kitchen. ' I hope you can live with

11

yourself!'

'What do you mean?'

'You drove Father to an early grave, worriting him with your boozing and not buckling down to learn the trade like you should have done. I'm telling you straight: I shan't be taking over your apprenticeship, you ungrateful pup! You can move out of here and find yourself another job—*if you can.* I don't even care what becomes of you.'

Defiance made Malachi shout, 'I was leaving anyway. Think I'd want to work with *you*!' He glared across at the brother who was both taller and stronger than he was and who had never scrupled to use his strength to get his own way. Lemuel took after their father's side, tall men with rock-hard muscles, while Malachi took after their mother, thin and dark-haired, full of nervous energy, with a mind that wouldn't be still but must always wonder at the world around him.

She came quietly into the kitchen to say reproachfully, 'Shame on you both to quarrel like this with your father lying unburied above you!'

Lemuel folded his arms and scowled. 'I meant what I said, Mam. He's not staying here when me and Patty move in and I'm not continuing with his apprenticeship.'

She looked from one to the other and sighed. 'No. It wouldn't work, not with you two so different.' They'd always quarrelled, right from the time they were little lads, to her great sorrow. 'But I'd be grateful if you'd keep the peace until after the funeral, then we'll decide together as a family what Malachi should do.' Her glance held both young men captive as she added loudly and clearly, 'And there will be no throwing him out of this

12

house, Lemuel, because if you do, you throw me out as well. Your brother has as much right to a decent start in life as you do and this is his home, too.'

Lemuel shuffled his feet, then shrugged acceptance of her edict.

*   *   *

That evening Malachi managed to snatch an hour with his mother after Lemuel and Patty had gone home. Everything was ready for the funeral. And afterwards—well, everything would change.

'I'm worried about you,' he said abruptly.

'About me? Why?'

'Because of how Father left everything. He ought to have left you a share.'

'He trusted Lemuel to look after me.'

'Lemuel, maybe, but not that spiteful bitch he's married to.'

Hannah Firth sighed. 'There was no changing your father. He was set in his ways when I wed him. He'd never leave the business or house to a woman.'

'Why did you mar—' He broke off, knowing he had no right to ask this question, especially now, when it seemed doubly disloyal to that still figure lying upstairs.

Hannah sighed. 'I had my reasons. It wasn't a love match, but he was good to me in his own way.'

'What shall you do now? You'll never be happy with Patty in charge here.'

His mother gave him a sad smile. 'What choice do I have?'

'You're young enough to do something else.

13

Why, you've hardly any grey in your hair, even, and you're still as active as a young woman. You could even marry again.'

She put one finger on his lips. 'Shh. Now isn't the time to discuss that sort of thing.'

But Malachi lay awake and worried about her. His sister-in-law Patty was already giving herself airs and looking round the house with a proprietorial air. Lemuel wouldn't stand up to her. He didn't dare breathe without his wife's permission.

*   *   *

The following day, after the funeral guests had left, Patty sat feeding her baby son in the kitchen while Hannah Firth led her sons back into the front parlour. 'Time to talk,' she said briskly, holding her own sadness at bay. 'Have you had any thoughts about what you want to do, Malachi?'

He hesitated, knowing it would hurt her, then said in a rush, 'Emigrate to Australia.' He looked out of the window at the rain that had fallen steadily all day. 'I'm sick of grey skies and damp air. They say it's sunny all the time in Australia.'

Lemuel let out a scornful snort. 'Nowhere's sunny all the time, you fool! And what are you going to do in Australia that you can't do here?'

'I don't know yet. Sell things, perhaps.' Dealing with customers, even if it was only a young couple buying a bucket, was the only side of the cooperage that Malachi enjoyed and he was good at it, too. He looked at his mother, pleading silently for her understanding. 'I've been thinking about going for a while, but I thought I might as well finish my

14

apprenticeship first. Now . . .' He shrugged. He watched her nod, could see the sadness in her eyes, but could do nothing to help her.

'I know you've been restless, son. But you'll do this properly, so until we have it all worked out, you're staying here. I'm not sending you out into the world penniless, not if I have to sell my wedding ring to fund you.' She looked at Lemuel as she said that and he shuffled his feet and avoided her eyes.

Patty came to the door of the parlour, rocking her baby in her arms and scowling at them. 'I don't think that's fair, Mother Firth. Your husband left the business to Lemuel, not Malachi. He has no right to any of the money.'

'What do you think about that, Lemuel? Is it fair that he gets nothing, not even a start in life?' Hannah stared at her elder son, knowing that although he was under his wife's thumb and had been even before they married a year ago, he was an honest soul, as like his father as any son could be. At twenty-two he was already set in his ways while Patty, three years younger, bade fair to become a shrew. Hannah was dreading living with them, absolutely dreading it. But she wouldn't burden Malachi with that. He, at least, should go free.

Lemuel looked from one to the other, then muttered, 'I'll give him a bit of a start, but I'm not depriving my child of his inheritance. If Dad had wanted Malachi to have owt, he'd have left him summat more than his watch.'

Hannah didn't say that there hadn't been as much to leave as John had hoped, for the coopering trade had been going downhill even

15

before these difficult times. She watched Patty toss her head and storm back to the kitchen. 'Tomorrow we'll start planning,' she told her sons, then went through into the kitchen to help her daughter-in-law clear up, biting her tongue when sharp orders were rapped out as if she didn't know how to run her own home. Patty was taking charge even before she moved in.

Not until Hannah was alone in bed that night, her last in the big front bedroom, did she give way to her grief—and if she was crying for the loss of her younger son, not her husband, no one else would know that from looking at her reddened eyes.

Tomorrow, when Lemuel and Patty moved into the house, she'd be taking the small room at the back of the kitchen where her own mother had ended her days. She wasn't looking forward to living in another woman's house, but that's what happened when your man died and there wasn't enough money to give you a separate home.

Almost she wished she could go out to Australia with Malachi. She was only forty-two, after all, not old in looks or ways. But she didn't dare suggest going because she knew Lemuel would kick up a fuss and refuse to give them any money for fares if she tried. For her younger son's sake, she must just accept her new role in life and be grateful she still had a roof over her head.

But it was going to be hard living with Patty. One of the hardest things she'd ever done.

*   *   *

A few days later the nuns took the orphans to the

16

docks and escorted them to the steamer which took them all across to Liverpool where they stayed in another convent. The porter from their own convent went with them to help keep an eye on the two rebels.

Ismay felt no excitement at her first sight of England, just dismay that they had found no opportunity to escape. They were closer to Keara than they'd ever be again, and here she was, helpless to find her older sister.

As they crossed the dock a few days later towards the much larger ship which would take them to Australia, the stern-faced nun who would be the Mother Superior in charge of the convent in Australia from now on held Mara's arm tightly, and the porter from the Irish convent held Ismay's arm even more firmly.

Sister Catherine, following with the rest of the orphans, felt her heart go out to the two Michaels sisters. Most of the other girls being sent out to Australia under the nuns' migration scheme were pleased to be going. She sent up a brief prayer that the two rebels would find happiness in their new life, then turned her thoughts firmly back to getting the other girls settled in their tiny four-berth cabins while the older nun and the Matron in charge of the single women's quarters made sure the Michaels sisters were safely locked up.

Not until the ship was under way were Ismay and Mara let out of the tiny cabin at the end of a row which the two nuns would occupy from then on because it was one of the few with a proper door, not a blanket hung across the entrance.

On deck the two girls joined the other orphans, all easily recognisable by their dark clothing. A few

17

were weeping as the ship moved slowly away from land. Sister Catherine moved among them offering quiet words of comfort, but like theirs her own eyes kept going back to the horizon.

Ismay stood with Mara by the rail and watched England fade into a misty outline, seeing nothing but a blur of colours through her unshed tears. Anger hummed within her and it helped her find the courage to continue looking after Mara and make the best of their present circumstances. At least she had one sister still. That was the most important thing.

Suddenly the clouds parted and shafts of sunlight shone down through them. There was an 'Oooh' from the passengers as a rainbow arched across the sky, perfect in every shimmering detail.

Mara stared up at it, entranced.

'A rainbow for hope,' Ismay said quickly. 'It's a sign, that's what it is.'

'Do you really think so?'

'I'm sure of it, yes.'

'Remember how Mam used to ask us to take her back a pennyworth of sunshine when we went to the shop?' Mara said wistfully.

'That rainbow's worth more than a penny,' Ismay declared. 'It's a twopenny rainbow, that one is. Ah, Mara darlin', we'll be all right, I'm sure we will. And every time we see a rainbow, we'll remember Mam, eh?'

Mara smiled and leaned her head against her sister's shoulder, comforted, but Ismay's expression was bleak and the colours of the rainbow ran one into the other as tears threatened again. She had to summon up more anger to keep them at bay and even then she was sure Sister Catherine knew how close she'd been to sobbing aloud.

*   *   *

Malachi continued to work with his brother so that no one could say he wasn't earning his keep, but the atmosphere in the house was full of tension.

Most of all he resented the way Patty treated his mother, who had until this time been mistress here but who was now ordered around and treated as a servant by her sharp-tongued daughter-in-law, and a rather stupid servant at that.

'Why do you put up with it, Mam?' he asked.

His mother shrugged. 'What else can I do, love? When your husband dies, you're dependent on your children.'

'Maybe you should come with me to Australia, then? I'd never treat you like that.'

'Don't be silly. I'm far too old for that sort of thing. And I have my own room here, with my favourite bits and pieces. That's a great comfort to me.'

He spent part of the last evening with his friends at the alehouse, to Lemuel's loudly expressed disgust. What did his brother's feelings matter, though? After tomorrow morning he'd not see Lemuel again, not miss him either.

At the alehouse people popped in all night long to wish Malachi well. An hour after his arrival, his closest friends began nudging one another and John Dean disappeared into the back room.

While he was gone the others sat Malachi on a chair and with much laughter blindfolded him. He sat straining his ears, wondering what they were planning, and heard a murmur which heralded the return of John.

'Hold thy arms out, lad,' his friend's deep voice said in front of him. 'We've got summat for thee, summat to remember us by.'

Resigned to them playing some sort of joke on him, Malachi did as they asked and found himself holding something quite large. When they whipped off the blindfold, he stared down at what was surely—it couldn't be, but yes, it was—a guitar in a sturdy canvas case.

'My uncle's had this in his attic for years,' John said, grinning. 'So we bought if off him as a going-away present.'

Malachi couldn't speak for a moment. John of all people had known how he'd longed for a musical instrument of his own, any instrument would have done. But of course his father wouldn't have one in the house. 'Eh, lads.' His voice was so husky with emotion he had to pause for a moment and swallow hard, then managed only, 'I don't know how to thank you enough.'

He undid the buckles holding the case shut and pulled out the guitar. Someone had polished it—he could smell the beeswax.

'My uncle fitted new strings,' John said. 'And we bought you some spares.'

Gently, Malachi ran his fingers across them. The notes came out sweet and soft.

'There's this, too.' John thrust a small book at him. 'It tells you how to play it.'

Malachi bowed his head and said hoarsely. 'Eh, lads, I'm going to miss you all that much!'

'Don't go, then!' someone shouted. 'Who'll sing to us now?'

He raised his head, aware that they must be able

20

to see the tears in his eyes. Well, to hell with that! 'I shall think of you every time I play this.'

He didn't stay much longer, wanting to spend a quiet hour with his mother.

Patty and Lemuel continued to sit up until well past their usual bedtime, with Patty making snippy little remarks about how she hoped he wouldn't be sorry about what he was doing—when he knew perfectly well she hoped he would fail in Australia.

In the end, Hannah said quietly, 'If you two want to stay up late tonight, Malachi and I can go into my room to chat.'

'I suppose we're not good enough to sit with you!' Patty snapped.

Lemuel shushed her and gave her a push in the direction of the stairs. As he turned to his brother, he hesitated then said, 'I wish you well, though I doubt you'll succeed out there. You're not steady enough to settle to any sort of work. But it'll be no use coming back to me for help. I must put my own family first.' After a brief hesitation he held out one hand.

Malachi breathed deeply, annoyed at his brother's words, but shook the hand and contented himself with saying, 'One day I'll make you eat those words.'

Lemuel turned to his mother. 'You allus did favour our Malachi, but I hope you'll remember from now on that I'm the man of the house and it's me who'll be looking after you, not him!'

When he'd gone upstairs after his wife, Malachi held out his arms to her. 'Come and give us a cuddle, Mam. A good big one. It'll have to last a long time.' He could feel her shaking with the effort of holding back her tears. Well, he felt like weeping like a babby himself, he did an' all.

They didn't even try to go to bed, neither wanting to waste a minute on sleep. Sometimes they talked, sometimes they sat quietly. Hannah held his hand most of the time and once she dozed for a while, her head on his shoulder.

He looked down at her dark hair, surprised to see how few grey threads there were in it. He was glad she looked younger than her age; young enough to remarry, he hoped, and escape from Patty. He blinked furiously. Hell, he hadn't thought it would hurt this much to leave her.

In the morning, when he heard his brother stirring upstairs, Malachi shook her awake and said urgently, 'I just wanted to say, Mam, that if you ever want to come out and join me in Australia, you'll be welcome. I'd walk through fire for you and don't you ever forget that.'

'Well, don't forget to write and let me know your address, then,' she said for the twentieth time.

'As if I would.' He had to have another hug as he spoke.

CHAPTER TWO

AUGUST 1863

As the voyage got under way, the ship's doctor arranged a programme of activities and entertainments for the passengers, with music provided for dancing two or three evenings a week by a group he called the ship's band, though it was made up of three men only, making thin music with a fiddle, concertina and penny whistle.

On the first dancing evening Ismay stood on deck with the rest of the steerage passengers watching the dancers, one foot tapping away, her body swaying in time to the music. 'I wish the nuns would let us join in,' she whispered to her little sister. 'They don't seem to approve of anyone having fun.'

'Reverend Mother says we should use the time on this voyage to improve ourselves.'

'We go to her reading classes in the daytime, don't we? And to Sister Catherine for arithmetic?' Ismay made a scornful sound in her throat. 'Ach, that old Mother Superior is just trying to persuade everyone to become a nun like her.'

'They must have a lovely peaceful life, though,' Mara said wistfully. 'I bet they never go hungry, either.'

Ismay shot her a startled glance. 'We've not gone hungry for a while. Do you still worry about that?'

Mara nodded. 'I do, yes. It was only when Keara went to work in the big house that we had plenty to eat. Now we haven't got her and I worry what'll happen to us in Australia.'

'I've told you and told you not to talk about *her*!' As she saw tears welling in Mara's eyes, Ismay forced the anger back and gave her little sister's hand a quick squeeze. 'Sorry. I didn't mean to shout at you.' She looked down at her dark, sensible clothes and sighed. 'Who'd want to dance with us anyway? Sure we look like a pair of dirty old crows in these things!' At fifteen she cared that her dark blue skirt was made with the minimum of material from a coarse, hard-wearing wool that was totally unsuited to the warmer weather. Each skirt

23

had a deep hem in case the girls grew taller and this made them hang badly. They wore grey blouses in a sensible cotton twill and had a tight dark jacket to match the skirt, though the Mother Superior had allowed them to leave off the jackets now it was warmer—not, Ismay suspected, because she cared about their comfort, but in case their sweat damaged the material at the armpits.

The old nun showed no signs of feeling the heat but moved through life with a calm expression which occasionally betrayed the briefest sign of irritation, quickly banished, as she dealt with her own small group. Sister Catherine, on the other hand, looked distinctly hot and bothered at times, and one day had exclaimed in delight over some flying fish, earning herself a reproving glance from her superior. The girls all liked Sister Catherine but were terrified of the Mother Superior.

Ismay watched a smiling Dr Greenham come towards them.

'Reverend Mother, why are your girls not joining in?'

The old nun greeted him with a frown. 'Because I don't approve of them dancing with strangers. That can lead to trouble.'

'Nonsense! It's when you don't allow girls rational exercise to tire them out that they get into trouble. I've seen it all too often on these long journeys. Anyway, by the time it's half over there will be no strangers on this ship.'

'Nonetheless, I shall not permit them to dance.' Her mouth was a tight line, her eyes hard as pebbles, her scrawny body held remorselessly upright.

He lowered his voice. 'I'm sorry to contradict

you there, my dear lady, but when it comes to the passengers' welfare during this voyage, I'm in charge—of everyone.'

After a moment of shock, she breathed deeply and fixed him with a look that normally cowed even the most rebellious girl.

Ismay saw with delight that he was not in the least intimidated, but his reply was so quietly spoken that only she and Sister Catherine were close enough to hear him.

'If I have to, Reverend Mother, I'll ask the Captain to enforce my command. As ship's doctor, I insist on *all* the passengers getting regular exercise. Even you should be walking round the decks regularly.'

Sister Catherine said, 'What harm can there be in the girls dancing in full view of everyone, Reverend Mother?'

Ismay saw a blush colour the younger nun's cheeks when she realised she had spoken her thoughts aloud and the girl didn't miss the angry glance the older nun threw at her.

'Spoken like a woman of sense,' the doctor said jovially. 'Now, let's see about finding partners for the older girls.' He turned to Ismay. 'Miss Michaels, I'm sure you'd like to dance, would you not?'

Ismay ignored the Mother Superior's glare and smiled up at the grey-haired man. 'Sure, I'd love to, Doctor.'

'Then wait there and I'll find you a partner.'

*　　　*　　　*

Malachi stood by the ship's rail, staring out across

25

the calm, moonlit sea. Behind him the three musicians scratched away, producing a rhythmic but not very melodious sound that grated on his nerves. It was impossible to ignore, though, because it was underpinned by the thump of feet on the deck as the dancers surged to and fro more or less in time with the music.

'Mr Firth—'

He jerked round to find the ship's doctor standing beside him, smiling genially.

'You're not dancing?'

Malachi shrugged. 'I was enjoying the sight of moonlight on the water.'

'Well, there'll be plenty of that during this voyage. At the moment there's a young lady over there who needs a partner. Let me introduce you.'

'I'd rather not dance tonight, if you don't mind.'

'We prefer our passengers to get some exercise.'

Although this was said mildly, there was an inflexible note to the doctor's voice that all the passengers had come to recognise. Dr Greenham was a stickler for cleanliness, fresh air and exercise, and he took his job of overseeing their health very seriously indeed, boasting that many of them would leave this ship in better physical condition than they had boarded it.

'Who?' Malachi asked in resignation.

'Ismay Michaels. She's travelling with the nuns.'

'I thought those lasses weren't allowed to dance. That old crow hardly allows them to breathe on their own.'

The doctor looked stern. 'They need rational exercise like any other human being, including yourself, so I've chosen to intervene.'

'Which one is she?'

'The dark-haired one at the end.'

Malachi looked across and saw a thin girl whose hair was as dark as his own, though his was straight and hers curled gently round her face. 'She's just a child!'

'Fifteen. A woman one minute, a child the next, but definitely old enough to dance with a young fellow of nineteen. I'm not suggesting you marry her, after all.' The doctor chuckled then lowered his voice to add, 'We can't have those nuns stifling the poor girls, so I'd really appreciate your help in this, Mr Firth.'

What could you say to that? Malachi followed him across the deck, hoping his partner wouldn't prove too empty-headed. The two men stopped once to let a couple of children twirl past as they tried to ape the dancers and he couldn't help smiling as he watched them.

*   *   *

Ismay had noticed the reluctance on the young man's face and felt embarrassed to think of anyone being forced to dance with her. If it weren't for the pleasure of doing something the Mother Superior didn't approve of, she'd have told him to go away again. As it was, when they were introduced she shook hands and allowed him to lead her into the end of the nearest set that was forming for the next dance.

As the music struck up again, he winced and she couldn't help smiling. 'They're not very good, are they?'

'Not good at all,' he agreed. 'You're musical then, Miss Michaels?'

'I like singing, but I don't know much about playing music.'

'You should join the ship's choir.'

'Mother Bernadette won't allow us to.' She sighed. 'I wouldn't be dancing now if it weren't for the doctor.'

'I wouldn't either—which is no reflection on you, but simply because I was enjoying having no one trying to talk to me for once.'

'It *is* always crowded on a ship, isn't it?'

He was pleased at how quickly she took his meaning. 'Yes, but it's much better than in the old days, apparently. They used to cram people in and take no interest in their welfare. Many died on the way to Australia, especially on bad ships. Nowadays there are laws about how passengers must be housed.' His mother had made him find out as much as possible about the long voyage to Australia, and while he'd fretted about having to remain in what was now Lemuel's house and keeping his tongue between his teeth whatever the provocation, he had seen the sense of that.

What's more, his mother had not only made his brother pay the fare but also give him a stake, then had slipped him a little extra money herself. They'd gone into Manchester by train and spent the day there choosing small items for re-sale in Australia: hairpins, combs, kitchen knives, scissors. People always needed those. They'd kept an eye open for bargains—looking particularly for things that wouldn't be damaged by sea water or rough handling.

He'd found some books of melodies with the guitar chords shown and bought those—a small extravagance which had paid off because learning the tunes helped pass the time. He had also learned to ignore the audience he inevitably collected when he practised on deck.

Malachi banished thoughts of his mother whom he was missing greatly. 'You and your sister are orphans, I believe?' He spoke more to make conversation than because he was interested.

'Yes.'

Her face reflected such stark anguish that he almost stopped dancing. What had happened to hurt her so?

The music swung them away from one another and he found himself with a new partner, then another: pleasant, smiling women of all ages. He did his best to keep up a conversation each time, but wished he could have stayed with his first partner and continued talking to her.

They had hardly got back together, however, than the dance ended and he had to lead Miss Ismay Michaels back to the scowling older nun. Sheer mischief made him whisper, 'Shall I ask your little sister to dance next?'

The glowing smile she turned on him made him realise how pretty she'd be if she were properly dressed and happy, though she seemed too thin at the moment, as if she hadn't been eating well.

'Oh, Mr Firth, please do. Mara would love that.'

So he turned to the slender child who looked so much like her sister, only smaller and even more delicately made, and asked for the pleasure of the next dance. He was rewarded by a shy smile as she moved forward to take his arm.

Sister Catherine moved over to stand beside Ismay and watch the young man showing Mara the steps. 'He seems a pleasant young fellow. Did you enjoy the dance?'

'Yes, very much.'

'I used to like dancing.'

Ismay stared at her. 'Did you really?'

Sister Catherine burst out laughing. 'I wasn't always a nun, you know.' Then she realised she'd been laughing again which would earn her a fresh reprimand. Reverend Mother had done a lot of scolding since they'd come on board. She had always been strict but never this bad-tempered. In fact, she didn't look very well, her face sallow and her eyes shadowed as if with pain. Perhaps that was what was causing her bad moods.

Whatever it was, it made her very hard to live with.

*   *   *

Those words she had spoken so carelessly to Ismay echoed in Sister Catherine's mind as she lay sleepless on the narrow bunk above her snoring fellow-nun that night, her belly growling with hunger.

I wasn't always a nun.

She had been born Eleanor Caldwell and her accent was still lightly marked by the Lancashire heritage she shared with young Mr Firth and a few of the other passengers. Sometimes she missed Lancashire dreadfully, even now, especially her own village—the slow voices of its people, the neat little houses of golden stone, the rolling moors, and her father, above all her father, the dearest friend and companion any girl could have had. She had turned down offers of marriage because she didn't want to leave him, believing there was plenty of

30

time for that later if she changed her mind. It was his sudden death that had sent her fleeing to a nunnery—for the wrong reasons, she now knew— but she had tried very hard to honour the commitment she had made to the religious life. She still had to make her final profession and the Mother Superior of the convent back in Ireland had had a serious talk with her about that before sending her to Australia.

'You sometimes seem—not fully committed,' she had said.

'Oh, but I am!' Catherine had protested.

'Well, the long voyage will give you time to think very seriously about your future. If you should have any doubts—any doubts at all—wait a little longer before you make your final profession.'

This advice was an error which only someone who hadn't made such a long voyage could make. After a few days on the ship, surrounded by people who were mostly not even Catholics, rebellious thoughts had started creeping into Catherine's mind. Here were a thousand things to remind her of the life she'd left, and there were babies and small children too. She'd forgotten how lovely they were and found herself watching them surreptitiously, longing to cuddle them as she'd once cuddled her cousin's children.

She lay still but her thoughts were in a tangle and memories would keep flooding back. In Ireland she had been busy but at peace in a familiar daily routine. This journey to their Australian convent had shattered her hard-won equilibrium already and she was beginning to realise that the calm on which she had prided herself was only a triumph of will over temperament, not a sign of true inner peace.

If only she hadn't had to travel with Mother Bernadette! Of all the unreasonable people, her present superior was the worst: narrow-minded, old-fashioned, utterly certain she knew best what her stern God required of her and her charges. And if Catherine made her final profession, it would be Mother Bernadette to whom she would answer in Australia until the day one of them died.

That shouldn't matter to a nun—but it had begun to matter to her.

Already, after a couple of weeks in that small cabin, the two of them were at odds. The bracing sea air was wonderful, the shipboard food plentiful if plain, but when Catherine began to eat more, her appetite sharpened by the hours spent on deck in the fresh air, Reverend Mother had chided her for the sin of gluttony and ordered her to eat less.

A protest had led to a direct order to abstain from the evening meal for a week as penance for her 'wilfulness and greed'.

Was it a sin even to fill your belly now? Catherine couldn't believe that, though she had obeyed her superior, naturally. Her stomach growled again and with a sigh she eased herself into another position on the narrow bunk, repeating a few prayers in a vain attempt to take her mind off her hunger.

But it didn't work. She still couldn't sleep.

*   *   *

Behind his joviality the ship's doctor was a shrewd observer of humankind and had been worried about the group of orphans from the minute he

32

encountered them. When he discovered that two of them had been brought on board forcibly and locked up until the ship set sail, he had disliked the sound of it intensely. He wouldn't have allowed that if it had been up to him.

The more Arthur Greenham watched the group, the more he worried about them. Most of the girls looked cowed and the Mother Superior was a self-righteous bully, nun or not. He put off doing anything about the situation, however, until he'd got the ship running smoothly, with plenty of activities and classes set up for the steerage passengers. Then there was a difficult birth which, if he said so himself, he'd handled well, saving both mother and child.

But he'd decided as a first step to persuade the sisters to allow their charges to dance at the evening hops, which took place on deck three times a week when the weather was fine. By the end of the evening he'd been pleased to see the girls with a bit of colour in their cheeks for once. He only wished he could do the same for the younger of the nuns, who was looking distinctly strained.

The following evening at supper time he made one of his inspections of the steerage areas to check the food and make sure the mess captains had shared it out fairly. As he passed the end of the long table in the single women's quarters, he saw the younger nun sitting without a plate in front of her and paused. Why wasn't she eating? Was she sickening for something? She did look a little pale today, with dark circles round her eyes. You had to keep a careful eye out for illness on a ship.

When the girl serving pudding offered the younger nun some, that damned old crow intervened.

'Sister Catherine is not eating this evening.'

'You didn't eat yesterday evening, either. Aren't you well?' the girl asked in all innocence.

'Mind your own business and get on with serving the food!' snapped the Mother Superior.

Arthur waited till the meal was over then sent for the younger nun. The older one came too, damn her.

'I believe I asked to see your colleague, not you,' he said, scowling at her.

'It wouldn't be fitting. You're a man.'

'I'm a doctor and hardly likely to ravish my patients within screaming distance of four hundred people!'

Colour flooded the old woman's cheeks, then receded, but she said nothing. Nor did she leave.

He turned to the younger woman. 'I was worried when I saw you weren't eating the evening meal, Sister. Are you not feeling well?'

'Sister Catherine is mortifying her flesh this week and will not be taking the evening meal,' the old woman said. 'We don't encourage ourselves to over-indulge in food.'

He studied her zealot's face, his eyes narrowed. 'Does this include water?'

'Yes, of course.'

'I'm afraid I can't allow that.'

She drew herself up. 'It's none of your business.'

'It's entirely my business. I'm responsible for the health of all the passengers, including you and Sister Catherine. In a warm climate it's dangerous not to drink enough water and ours is still sweet and pure.' He'd supervised the choosing and filling of the casks himself, and always encouraged the crew to trap rainwater whenever they could.

34

'I'm all right, Doctor, really I am,' Catherine said hastily, worried about being caught between two warring people. They'd all suffered today from the older woman's temper, presumably because the doctor had over-ridden her edict against dancing last night.

'Our religious practices are our own concern, Doctor,' the Mother Superior snapped and stood up. 'And I'll thank you not to bring us here again for no reason.'

He addressed the younger nun. 'If you continue not eating, Sister Catherine, I shall have you brought into the sick bay until you start again.' Which was overstepping his authority somewhat, but in a good cause.

Breath whistled into the older woman's mouth but she didn't let her anger out.

He looked at her, concerned about the unhealthy yellowish-white of her complexion, though her cheeks were tinged by a dark flush at the moment. 'Reverend Mother, life on board ship is different from normal life and I cannot allow passengers to make themselves ill by dangerous practices. You need to keep up your strength, not deplete it, on a long sea voyage, which has enough hazards without adding to them.'

Their eyes met in challenge and at length hers fell. 'Then I shall find another penance for my sister.'

'What has she done that you must punish her?'

'Been disobedient. Something even you should understand.'

'Please let the matter drop now, Dr Greenham,' Catherine murmured. 'I must obey my superior.'

'As long as you eat and drink adequately,

whatever else you do is your own business,' he said gently. 'But I care greatly about the welfare of each and every passenger and shall continue to oversee your health to the best of my ability.'

'If you've finished, Doctor?' the Mother Superior put in and when he nodded, led the way out, her expression stormy. 'Did you say anything to him about the penance I set?' she demanded once they were out of earshot.

'Of course not.'

'Well, you'd better start eating your evening meal again, but only to stop his officious interference in our ways. You can say a full rosary each night instead.'

Catherine tried to accept this edict in her heart, but couldn't, because the punishment would be tedious and was, she still felt, uncalled for. However, she had taken a vow of obedience so she followed the angular figure back to the part of the deck which their group had made their own, wondering yet again how she would endure life in Australia under this woman.

CHAPTER THREE

OCTOBER–NOVEMBER 1863

Although the two nuns weren't supposed to look at one another while getting dressed and undressed, a few mornings after their conversation with the doctor Catherine couldn't help noticing that her companion was having trouble getting out of bed. When the older nun fell back on the lower bunk, groaning, Catherine went to kneel beside her. 'Is something wrong?'

'Feel—unwell. You—see to b'fast. Make girls b'have.'

Reverend Mother had one arm across her face, but the side of her mouth seemed twisted. Was that with pain or with something else? Even her voice sounded different, slurred and not at all like her normal sharp tone. But Catherine knew better than to fuss over her.

After the meal she settled the girls on deck with one of them reading aloud, and went back to check on her Mother Superior, who this time seemed only half-aware of her presence and didn't answer her questions with more than a slow gesture of the hand, as if to dismiss her.

Seriously worried now, Catherine went to find the doctor.

He came at once and examined Mother Bernadette, ignoring her incoherent protests. Afterwards he beckoned Catherine outside the cabin and said in a low voice, 'She's had a seizure, quite minor as these things go, but she'll be a bit disoriented for a day or two. Can you look after her here or shall we take her into the sick bay?'

'She'd prefer to stay here and I'm sure I can manage, but I wonder—is there an older woman who'd keep an eye on the girls for me? We can pay her a small sum.'

'I'll find you someone.'

Gradually over the next few days Mother Bernadette regained control over her body, though she still walked with a slight limp and only slowly.

'It's a warning,' Dr Greenham told her, insisting on checking her progress every day. 'You really ought to take things more easily from now on.'

'I'll continue to do my duty, as I always have, until the Lord calls me to him.'

*   *   *

Ismay watched Sister Catherine grow very tired as she tended the sick woman. She didn't care about the Mother Superior, whom she blamed for forcing her and Mara on board this ship, but the younger nun was always pleasant and reasonable, and Ismay felt really sorry for her, having to care for that nasty old crow.

In an effort to keep the girls occupied, Sister Catherine gave them permission to join the choir, though only three of them sang well enough to be accepted. Under the guidance of the enthusiastic amateur choirmaster, Ismay, Mara and Jane enjoyed learning how to use their voices better, memorising the words and melodies of several new songs at their daily rehearsals.

Best of all, to Ismay, was listening to Mr Firth sing. He had a beautiful baritone voice and when she was chosen to sing a duet with him at the weekly Saturday concert she was so thrilled that for a moment she couldn't speak.

The night of the concert was the first time Mother Bernadette came up on deck after her seizure, leaning heavily on a walking stick the doctor had found for her. Her face was slightly drawn down on one side, but she looked much the same as ever.

As the three girls moved forward to join the group of singers the older woman turned to Sister Catherine. 'What are they doing in the choir?'

'I gave them permission to join because I felt it better for them to be supervised and kept busy while I was looking after you.'

'Well, now that I'm better they can leave. I'm not having those girls tainted with a taste for idling around or singing Methodist hymns.'

Sister Catherine bit her lip and stared down at her hands, noticing they were clenched into fists and unclenching them only with difficulty. Since her seizure Reverend Mother had become extremely unreasonable, far worse than before, criticising everything Catherine did and snapping at the girls, or even at other passengers when they stopped to express a hope that she was feeling better.

After some songs by the whole choir, which met with loud, enthusiastic applause even though everyone had heard them many times being rehearsed, Ismay and Mr Firth stepped forward and sang 'The Last Rose of Summer'. Catherine felt she had never heard it sung so well and could see tears on the cheeks of some of the people in the audience. She was surprised, too, at how lovely Ismay's singing voice was.

But when the concert was over and the singers had returned to their respective groups, Reverend Mother cut the congratulations short and told the three girls they would no longer be allowed to sing in the choir.

They stared at her in shock, but only Ismay dared ask, 'Why not?'

'Because I say so.'

'That's not a reason.'

'It is for me.'

Ismay spun on her heels and rushed off into the

darkness, desperate to find somewhere to be alone, but in the end could only stand at the rail with her back turned and let the tears run unchecked down her cheeks.

'What's wrong, Ismay?'

Malachi's voice behind her was gentle.

'She—Reverend Mother—says I'm not allowed to stay in the choir.'

'Why ever not?'

'She doesn't give reasons, just issues orders.' A sob escaped her and he moved forward to set his hands on her shoulders and shield her from passers-by. 'You won't be under her control for ever.'

'If it weren't for Mara, I'd run away as soon as we get there.' Her voice wobbled and she had to pause a moment before she could continue to speak. 'But even though I'm old enough to leave the convent and work as a maid, my sister will have to stay there. She's four years younger than me and I have to look after her.' She pressed her hand against her mouth to hold back the despair. 'But I don't know how I'm going to stand years of this.'

Sister Catherine's voice interrupted them. 'Mr Firth, it'll be better if I look after Ismay now.' She watched him walk away, hands thrust into his pockets, his whole body radiating anger, then turned to the girl. 'Reverend Mother sent me to find you. I think it'd be wisest for you to rejoin the group.'

'I hate her!'

'Hatred doesn't help.'

'It does. So does anger. They give me the strength to continue.'

Catherine sighed. What could she say? She too

40

felt the decision was unfair and would have liked to put her arms round the girl and offer her the comfort of an embrace, but her order's rules forbade her to touch others. When she sometimes forgot and patted someone who was in distress she got into trouble. She missed human contact dreadfully and had done right from the first day she entered the convent as a novice.

When Dr Greenham protested at the girls being forbidden to sing with the choir, the Mother Superior sought an interview with the Captain, who shrugged and said as long as health matters weren't involved, she must do as she saw best with her charges.

So Ismay sat listening to the choir rehearse each day with a stony face, and Mara sometimes had tears in her eyes as she watched the group gathering, while the other former member of the choir kept her eyes lowered, bit her lip and said nothing.

Watching the Michaels sisters, Catherine worried about how dependent on her older sister Mara was. The child didn't laugh and chatter like the other younger girls, but mostly sat solemn-eyed, listening rather than speaking. She only grew animated when she was with Ismay, who was very protective of her. What would the two of them do when she was found employment while Mara was left behind in the orphanage? Catherine ached to warn them about this, but knew it wasn't her place. And anyway, why make them unhappy before they needed to be?

When Ismay stopped work to listen to the rehearsal, Mother Bernadette told her to attend to her sewing. The girl gave her a look of scorn and

41

loathing. 'You can stop me singing aloud but you'll never be able to stop the music inside my head. Every song *they* sing, I learn.'

The other girls stopped work, frozen with terror at this defiance.

'If you answer me like that again, I'll send you below for the rest of the day.'

'I'll hear the singing down there, too.' The look Ismay gave her as she said this was in itself an act of insolence, then the girl bent her head to her sewing. A short time later she began swaying gently in time to the choir's singing.

'Stop moving your head like that, Ismay Michaels.'

'Like what? I didn't know I was moving it. How can I stop something when I don't know I'm doing it?'

Mara watched this wide-eyed and afterwards she occasionally let her head move in time to the music as well. She wished she were as brave as her sister, but somehow she couldn't bring herself to answer the Mother Superior back. She wanted to and often said things inside her own head, but couldn't force out any words of defiance.

Sometimes she would sit on the deck and stare across the water, thinking about their sister Keara, wondering why she had sent them to Australia. It seemed so unlike her. Mara had golden memories of the elder sister who had been more like a mother to her. She didn't mention this to Ismay, who got furiously angry at the mere sound of Keara's name, but Mara simply couldn't imagine their elder sister sending them so far away.

But if she hadn't done it, who had? And why?

When the luggage was brought up from the hold halfway to Australia it was a gala day, with people enjoying the break in their normal routine. Some people had several pieces of luggage, one for each stage of the journey, but the orphans had only one trunk each, so pulled out clean clothes and new books to read, packing away their dirty clothes to be washed on arrival.

Malachi took out some more of his merchandise and sold a few things to other passengers—all at a good profit, but not for extortionate prices. It didn't seem good business to him to upset a customer because you never knew when that person might want to buy something else from you.

After the trunks had been taken below again, Malachi was, as usual, the last to linger on deck. He spent a lot of time staring into the distance, thinking about his future. He had enough merchandise for sale to give him a start, but the money that he'd brought him must be used to finance a business of some sort. He'd come to the conclusion that it'd be hard to be successful if you didn't know how things were done in a new country, so had decided to try to find himself a job for a while, one where he would be able to learn as much as possible about shopkeeping before setting up on his own.

He lifted his head to the sun, enjoying its warmth on his skin. Thanks to Dr Greenham, some of the single men were allowed to sleep up here now that the weather was so warm. It was pure bliss to lie on your narrow straw mattress and look up at a sky full of bright stars, even if you had to get up very early to carry the mattress below again.

After a while, however, the weather began to grow cooler and they had to stay below deck, even during the day sometimes. At one point, they saw icebergs in the distance and it grew so cold that Malachi spread his coat over the blankets at night for extra warmth. The doctor had explained about Great Circles being the quickest way to get to Australia, which meant following the curve of the world's surface, instead of aiming for certain ports. Because of that, they had to go to the south before they made landfall, and here south meant colder. It was all very confusing for a chap who'd never left Lancashire before but he thought he understood it now.

If his mother had been here, they'd have discussed every new experience together and maybe asked the doctor some more questions. She and Malachi were so alike he often wondered how she'd put up with his father all those years—though he'd never treated her as strictly as he'd treated his sons. Malachi worried about whether she'd be happy living with Lemuel, who was a stolid fellow not given to wondering about the world they lived in and not really master in his own house. As for Patty, she was a shrew. There was no other way to describe her.

Eh, he'd be glad when this voyage was over, hadn't realised before how long three months could seem when you had no real aim in life but to pass the time. Even practising on his guitar palled after a while. You couldn't do it all day long. And although most of his fellow passengers were pleasant enough and the doctor was strict about keeping the ship clean, Malachi found it hard living

44

in such crowded conditions.

It also upset him to see the orphans, especially Ismay who was a nice lass, being bullied by that old harridan. He'd asked the doctor why the Mother Superior was so bad-tempered and Dr Greenham said it often happened after a seizure that people's behaviour changed, usually for the worse.

All very well if you were an ordinary individual, Malachi thought, but that woman had power over a group of other people. What harm could it possibly do anyone for a girl with a lovely voice to join the choir, for heaven's sake? And although the girls were allowed to join in the dancing when there was any, they had to go straight back to sit by the nuns after each dance, not even being allowed to chat to the other women and girls on board.

*   *   *

Just before the ship arrived in Melbourne, the trunks were brought up on deck again so that people could take out the clean clothes most had been saving for their arrival. There was great excitement as everyone speculated about which day they'd make landfall.

In the end, the voyage took seventy-eight days. A good run, the sailors said. And there'd been only one death, a baby who had been born on the journey and was sickly from the start. Eh, it'd been sad to see its little body consigned to the deep. It'd brought a lump into Malachi's throat and many had wept openly.

As the ship pulled into the dock he crowded against the ship's rail with the others, watching the chaos below them in fascination.

45

First of all the Medical Officer came on board and conferred with the Captain and ship's doctor. He left after a short time, escorted to the gap in the rails by the doctor. Both of them were smiling at something.

Almost immediately after that porters came on board and began to bring up the luggage from the hold, dumping it indiscriminately on the dock. Passengers complained at being kept on board when they were itching to step on dry land again, and grew angry at how roughly their luggage was being handled. Some of them could see relatives who'd come to greet them and waved or hallooed, which made Malachi wish he had someone to meet him.

He noticed a wagonette and cart waiting at one side of the quay with a nun standing quietly next to them, and felt glad the girls would be looked after.

As for himself, he'd persuaded a few other single men to stick together so that no one could take advantage of their ignorance about life here. There would surely be safety in numbers.

When at last they were allowed to disembark, the cabin passengers went first with their belongings carried off by obsequious porters. The steerage passengers staggered off laden with belongings and bundles, rushing to retrieve their larger pieces of luggage and find vehicles to take them into the city.

As they'd planned, one of Malachi's group was among the first off and ran across the dock to book one of the waiting vehicles, while the others carried his cabin luggage for him. The strategy paid off and they were among the first to pile their luggage into a cart and pull away from the dock.

As Malachi turned his head to look back at the ship, he saw the orphans walking sedately across to the waiting nun. Mentally, he wished them luck, but it was Ismay's face he pictured as he did this. Eh, he felt so sorry for that poor lass!

*   *   *

'I see they've sent someone to meet us,' Mother Bernadette said, standing by the rail. 'We'll wait until we can disembark without all this pushing.'

Even so, Catherine had to support her companion when a man bumped into them and made the older woman stumble. She let go as soon as she was sure Reverend Mother was steady again but was shocked at how thin the other woman's arm had felt beneath her hand, as if there was no flesh left on it.

The waiting nun came forward to greet them with a smile. 'Welcome to Australia, Reverend Mother. I'm Sister Hilda and I was in charge of the convent while we waited for them to send out a replacement for Mother Emmanuelle. I hope you had a good voyage?'

'We can discuss that later,' snapped Mother Bernadette. 'At the moment it's more important to get the girls into the vehicles and back to the convent.'

For a moment the plump sister's face reflected surprise at this curt and ungracious response, then she lowered her eyes and said, 'Certainly, Reverend Mother. You and I can ride ahead in the wagonette with the girls, if you like, with Mr Davies driving us. Mr Powell will collect and bring your luggage. He's our caretaker and gardener, and can be trusted absolutely.'

There was an awkward silence. The Mother Superior stood very still, as if she hadn't heard what had been said, and in the end Catherine said quietly, 'Should I stay and help Mr Powell since I know what our luggage looks like?' Once or twice she'd had to prompt her companion to do things and guessed that the seizure had affected her superior more than the old woman would admit.

'Very well. But don't gossip with him.'

Mother Bernadette moved slowly across to the wagonette, followed by the gaggle of dark-clad girls who were gaping around them and pointing things out to one another. Last of all came Ismay and Mara, together as always, with the older girl holding her sister's hand and talking to her quietly.

They all got into the back of the wagonette and sat pressed together, sweating in their woollen clothes.

'Do you think it's always this hot?' Mara whispered, fanning her face with one hand.

Sister Hilda turned round and smiled at them. 'This is the hottest part of the summer. It can be quite cold in winter, though we don't get snow.'

'Silence, girls!' snapped the Mother Superior.

Ismay noticed Sister Hilda give another quick, astonished glance sideways. You wait, she thought, that old woman is going to make your life miserable as well as ours. She tried to take in all the new sights as they jolted along, never having spent any time in a city even in Ireland. It amazed her to see how many people and vehicles there were, and how much noise, too. The convent, she gathered from listening to Sister Hilda's quiet responses to the Mother Superior's occasional

48

question, was just outside the city to the north, though houses were being built so fast it was already surrounded on one side by neighbours where there had been fields five years previously.

When the wagonette drew to a halt, everyone fell silent.

'This is our convent,' Sister Hilda said.

It wasn't made of stone like the one in Ireland, or even bricks. It was simply a large, two-storey house whose walls were made of wooden slats nailed sideways. And it had a tin roof on it, not tiles, with a few rusty patches where it had been nailed down. There was a veranda round the ground floor and another one above it running round the first storey. To the right there was a part that looked as if it had been built on separately, but even that sagged as if it were tired and expected the next strong wind to blow it away. In fact, the whole place looked in need of care and the woodwork desperately needed painting.

The convent stood on about an acre of land and Ismay glimpsed the roof of a small cottage at the rear. In the front garden were a few shrubs struggling in the heat and in the middle a small stone statue of Our Lady, standing with her back to the convent and staring down the street as if she weren't at all interested in the people who lived in the house behind her.

Mara leaned closer and whispered, 'I don't like this place.'

'Shh, love. We have to make the best of things.'

The girls hesitated to get out, having learned already that Reverend Mother didn't like them doing anything unless they had been told. The old nun allowed Sister Hilda and the driver to help her down, staggered and righted herself, then turned to frown at the girls.

'Get out, then, and line up at the door. What are you waiting for?'

They did so quietly. She looked exhausted, her face a dirty yellowish-white, and they knew from experience that when she was tired she was even more bad-tempered than normal.

Two nuns who had come out to greet them were introduced as Sister Elizabeth and Sister Veronica.

For a moment there was silence, with the old woman frowning round her as if she didn't like what she saw.

'Shall I take the girls up to their dormitory, Reverend Mother?' Sister Veronica prompted when the silence went on for too long.

'Yes. And tell them to sit quietly until they're sent for. Sister Hilda, please show me the chapel.' She walked off without waiting for an answer.

Watching the nuns, Ismay could see that they were surprised by the sharp orders and lack of a proper greeting, but they merely exchanged surprised glances and went about their business. She took hold of Mara's hand and followed the others inside and up the stairs. It smelled musty but was quite cool, thank goodness, even on a hot day like this.

'The older girls sleep in here,' Sister Veronica said with a smile, indicating a large room at the far end of the landing, 'and the younger girls here.' The two dormitories had bare, scrubbed floorboards and each had a dozen or so narrow beds separated from one another by small chests of drawers. 'You'll each have your own bed and you're not to sit on them during the day or get into bed with anyone else.'

'Please, Mara's my sister and we usually sleep together,' Ismay said.

'I'm sorry. No one sleeps with anyone else. It's a rule here.'

'Then can we have beds next to one another, please? We'd never slept apart in our lives till we went on the ship.'

The nun shook her head again. 'No, dear.'

'But—'

'You must learn to accept the rules and not question them. The younger girls sleep separately and that can't be changed.'

Ismay pressed her lips together. It was starting off as badly as she'd expected. She'd looked forward to sharing a bed with Mara again, after the narrow bunks on the ship, to cuddling up and whispering after dark as they always had. Already she could see her little sister's shoulders drooping and Mara had that frightened look on her face.

'Well, now, let's give you a bed each and then we'll kneel to offer thanks to the Lord for your safe arrival here.'

Ismay knelt as indicated but didn't even try to offer thanks—what was there to thank anyone for? She found it very hard to pray nowadays, because to her mind if the Lord had brought them to this place, then he couldn't possibly care about them.

Shortly afterwards a bell rang downstairs. 'That's for the evening meal,' Sister Veronica said. 'You can do your unpacking after the luggage arrives and tomorrow we'll have a big washday.'

The girls found a meal and a group of other girls waiting in the dining room. The four nuns ate at one table and the girls at two long tables set at

51

right angles to it, the older girls sitting at one and the younger ones at the other. Again the two sisters were separated.

After they'd eaten the plain but plentiful food, they were sent to sit in the schoolroom until their luggage arrived and Ismay was told to read to them, since she was the best reader now after all the hours of lessons on the ship. She smothered a sigh as she picked the book up and looked at the title. It was another one about saints and martyrs.

They were all glad when they heard the luggage cart drawing up outside. Ismay stopped reading and looked across at the nun sitting with them for permission to go out and meet it. Sister Veronica gave a quick shake of the head so Ismay continued reading in a flat voice, deliberately stumbling and making nonsense of some sentences.

*   *   *

When the wagonette left the docks for the convent, Mr Powell smiled at Sister Catherine. 'It'll take us a fair bit longer than them to get back. I borrowed this cart and the two horses from a neighbour and the poor things are getting on a bit, so they can only amble along.'

'I see.'

'She looks a stern one, that new Mother Superior. Mother Emmanuelle was a kind, gentle lady and we were all sorry when she died.'

Catherine could not hold back a sigh but did not comment.

'I'm the handyman and gardener. My wife helps out with the washing and anything else that needs doing. Gets your wimples up lovely, my Gwynneth does. We have a cottage at the rear end of the convent garden.'

She nodded, trying not to encourage him to gossip but interested nonetheless in finding out as much as she could about her new life.

By the time they arrived at the convent Catherine knew that Sister Hilda and Sister Elizabeth were both getting old now and rather stiff on cold mornings, while Sister Veronica was a little younger but not much.

'You'll be the youngest now,' he finished comfortably. 'Good thing, too. Those children need someone closer to their own age to look after them.'

She inclined her head.

'There it is!' He pointed.

She saw with dismay that it was a very shabby-looking house and quite small for a convent, then chided herself for caring about that.

'Father Henson should do something about repairs,' Mr Powell said, as if he could read her mind. 'But he cares more for that church of his than for our convent. He'll have to do something about the leaks soon, though, or you'll be sleeping in damp beds come winter.'

As he drew up in front of the house, a youth shambled out from the rear and stood waiting.

'That's my Barney,' Mr Powell confided. 'Poor soul, he's not right in the head. Very slow, he is, but strong. He wouldn't hurt a fly but he don't like folk shouting at him. Speak to him gently and he'll do anything for you. If you show me which trunks belong to you and the Mother Superior I'll take them upstairs first, then I'll put the rest in the girls' rooms over there.' He pointed to the side wing of the house. 'Good thing we sent a few of the older ones off to the country last month or there'd not be enough room.'

'Sent them to the country?' She hadn't heard about any other convents being set up.

'The Sisters train 'em up as maids—hard to get a good maid these days, you know—then they send them out to jobs in the country.'

Catherine got down without his help and went inside. The wooden floor of the veranda creaked under her feet and she shivered as she went through the front door because the house felt— unwelcoming. Chiding herself for her foolish thoughts, she went forward to greet Sister Hilda again and settle in.

CHAPTER FOUR

NOVEMBER 1863–JANUARY 1864

The morning after their arrival the older girls were roused at six o'clock and told to dress and say their morning prayers quickly. As soon as they had broken their fast they were set to work cleaning the dining room and schoolroom. Ismay didn't mind working because it helped pass the time and she was used to housework after helping out at the big house in Ballymullan so wound up organising the others. When Sister Veronica questioned them all about their previous experience Ismay was the only one who had already worked as a maid.

'We'll soon have you out at a job, then,' the nun told her with a smile. 'They're always looking for maids and our girls find employment easily.'

Ismay nodded, imagining she was to go out daily as she had back home in Ireland. She hated not having seen Mara and was only able to snatch a quick word with her sister at noon as they entered the dining room.

'Did you sleep all right?'

Mara shrugged and avoided her eyes so Ismay guessed her sister had lain awake. Well, she had herself. The beds were hard, the other girls made sounds during the night, and noises she couldn't always recognise echoed round the creaking old house.

The nuns kept all the girls very busy and there was little time for chatting or playing, even for the youngest children. On Saturday night they were told to wash themselves all over and put on clean blouses the next day so that they'd look tidy for early Mass. Even that seemed strange, for although the church they walked to in single file was built of brick, it was very small and new. It simply didn't feel like a real church to Ismay.

Again, she found it impossible to pray.

During Sunday afternoon the girls were given two hours of leisure, their only free time of the week, with instructions to stay in the rear garden or on the back veranda.

Ismay knew Mara was unhappy about their separation and could think of no way of cheering her up. They sat together on a bench away from the others and talked quietly about their week.

'I don't like it here,' Mara whispered.

'I don't either.' She tried to think of something positive about it but could only manage, 'At least we get enough to eat.'

Mara's bottom lip wobbled and she tried in vain to gulp back tears. 'I want to go ho-oome.'

'We can't.' Ismay looked out across the garden, her eyes filling with tears. She found her little sister's unhappiness even harder to deal with than her own. 'We just have to—' a word she'd seen in the book of martyrs came to her '—endure. But one day we'll get away, I promise you. Once we're twenty-one we'll be free to do whatever we want, and then we'll get jobs and live together, just as we always planned.'

Mara thought about that, then a loud sob escaped her control. 'That's nearly ten years away for me.'

'Shh now! Shh! They'll get angry if they see you crying.'

When they had to rejoin their groups and do some more of the interminable plain sewing and mending of the ragged garments given for the poor by the congregation, Ismay had a hard time holding in her anger at her little sister's unhappiness. It wasn't fair. Why should anyone have the right to kidnap them? This wasn't a better life, not at all. It was a loveless sort of existence, with no laughter or fun in it. She'd rather go hungry any day and be with people who cared about her.

That night she wept into her pillow for sheer helplessness. She couldn't do anything to make things better for Mara, couldn't even help herself. *I hate you, Keara,* she thought, bitterness filling her like acid. *It's all your fault.*

*   *   *

Malachi found some lodgings, arranged to have his

boxes of goods stored in his landlord's cellar and spent the first few days walking aimlessly round the city, getting to know it. He loved the warm weather and couldn't believe it could be so sunny day after day. From time to time he would stop walking to raise his face to the sun, relishing its warmth on his skin. Only rich women walking under the shelter of parasols had pale faces here.

In the city centre he admired the fine edifices, thinking there must be a lot of money to be made here if banks could afford such imposing buildings with marble columns and frontages. On Collins Street he peered into shop windows and stared through doorways at expensive merchandise. He didn't dare go inside among the elegant women who seemed to float along in their huge crinolines, and smiled wryly at himself for even wanting to. After all, he didn't intend to sell luxury goods to idle rich folk but life's necessities to ordinary men and women with whom you could have a cheerful word or two to brighten your day.

It was easy to find his way round the city centre because it was built on a grid system but when he got out into the suburbs he had to stop several times to ask his way. He saw some fine houses and more hovels than he'd expected in this land of promise, places where he wouldn't even have stabled a horse, where barefoot children with dirty faces stood staring out at him, and behind them ragged women who looked a hundred years old gave him barely a glance from eyes filled with hopelessness.

Well, he didn't intend to wind up like them. He'd show Lemuel whether he could succeed or not! And he wouldn't be like his brother, marrying young and then burdened down with children. He'd not marry till he'd made enough money to keep a family in comfort.

One day he rode out to Sandhurst on the new railway which was still something of a novelty in the colony though railways were commonplace in England now. After walking round the country town for a while, he decided he liked smaller places better. However there weren't many railways in Victoria yet so it wasn't going to be easy to explore his new country. He came back to study a map he'd bought and wonder yet again where and how he would fit in.

After a few days he decided it was time to find a job because he had done nothing but spend money since he got off the ship. But the time hadn't been wasted. He'd talked to many people met casually in the street and learned a great deal. He didn't want to work long hours inside a stuffy shop to make someone else rich, he decided, so that evening strolled round a smallish market not far from his lodging house, hoping to find a job there for the time being.

When two lads tried to pinch some scissors from a stall of household bits and pieces run by an old man, Malachi didn't think twice but grabbed the nearest one and shook him hard before dragging him over to the old fellow and making him hand back what he'd stolen.

'Thanks, my friend. I'm not so spry as I was.' The stall owner pressed a hand to his chest and sat down on a stool behind the stall. 'Eh, they did give me a turn.' He stared at the boy who wriggled uncomfortably in Malachi's grasp. 'Ah, let him go. He's nobbut a lad.'

'You sure?'

'Yes.' The old man fixed the youngster with a stern gaze. 'But if I even see you or your pal near my stall again, I'll cry theft whether you've touched anything or not.'

Malachi boxed the lad's ears for good measure, then bent to pick up the scattered goods. 'You need some help, grandad? You don't look well.'

The old man studied him thoughtfully. 'From the north of England, aren't you?'

'Aye. Like you, I think. I come from near Bolton.' He'd already found that his accent marked him out to other English folk though those born in Australia rarely commented on it.

'Well, I'm from Preston originally, so we're both northerners. And you're right, I could do with a bit of help. I'll give you five bob to stay for the rest of the day and help with the selling, then load up my things for me afterwards.'

'Done. I'm Malachi Firth, by the way.' He stuck his hand out and they shook on the bargain.

'Dan Reddings.'

The hand that grasped Malachi's briefly felt knotty, the joints swollen, and he glanced down at it in quick pity. He liked old chaps, had talked to many a one in the alehouse and understood the daily pain they often went through as their bodies grew older.

Dan glowered at him and drew the hand back. 'I'm not into my dotage yet and my fingers aren't too stiff to count out the right change. Any road, I reckon mysen lucky to be nearly seventy. There's not many as reach that age. But I'll tell you straight: I was transported out here for stealing, so if you don't fancy working with an ex-convict, say so

59

now.'

'You look to be earning an honest living to me,' Malachi said mildly.

'I am. You'll not find anyone as can say I've cheated 'em in this country.'

'Well, we all make mistakes.'

'I reckon you're a bit young to have made many.'

Malachi grinned. 'I'm trying not to.'

He enjoyed working on the stall and quickly learned about what they were selling: stuff rather like his own bits and pieces, both new and second-hand, ranging from sewing implements and thread to cutlery and fire irons. He was soon calling out to passers-by, beckoning them over and persuading them to look at the wares. At one stage—just after he'd made a sale to a woman who'd been walking past without intending to buy anything—he winked at Dan, who gave him a nod of approval.

By ten o'clock at night, customers had thinned out and stall owners began to pack away their goods. Malachi worked quickly to pack up for the old man and pile the boxes on a hand cart. 'I'll give you a push home, if you like?'

'I can't pay you more nor the five shillin'.'

'I'm not asking for it.'

As they walked along, Malachi slowing his pace to suit his companion, Dan said suddenly, 'Looking for a job, are you?'

'Aye. I've brought a few goods out from England to start me off, a bit like your stuff, but I'm not sure where best to sell 'em or what to do afterwards.'

'Hmm.' Dan stumped along for a minute or two, then said brusquely, 'Come and have a bite of supper with me. Happen I've got a suggestion as'll suit you.'

60

'All right.'

Malachi helped Dan stack the boxes along one side of his cluttered room then accompanied him to an eating house that stayed open late to accommodate the market crowds. He let his companion lead the conversation until they'd finished eating, then leaned his elbows on the table and rested his chin on his linked hands. 'Out with it.'

'All reet, then. How'd you like to help me run a travelling shop?'

'Not sure what you mean by that?'

'We buy a wagon and take goods out to the country. It'll be a while afore the railways reach most of the country towns and there's good money to be made in the meantime. Folk there can't come into the towns very often, but they still need to buy things. Later, when the railways come, it'll be time to buy a shop and settle down.' He grinned at some memory, then looked at Malachi. 'I should ha' done that afore I grew too old, but I didn't because I like the travelling. There's allus summat new to see. But when I fell ill, I couldn't manage the horses or the heavy lifting, an' now I've been reduced to that bloody stall on the market.'

'Have you no family?'

'Nay, not me. Had a wife in England but when they sent me out here, that were that. She told me she'd done with me. After I'd done my time, I were determined not to go back to prison, though, so I worked hard—damned hard. It took me a while to build up to owning me own wagon. I used to go round on foot pushing a handcart at first.' He looked into the distance, then shook the memories away. 'I've nobbut a few year left to me, I know

61

that, but if you can do the heavy work an' you'll not desert me if I get ill, why, I can show you the ropes an' help you make some brass, so we'll both benefit.'

Malachi sat frowning. To him travelling round sounded little better than being a tinker, nothing to write home about with pride.

'I've got enough money to buy a wagon and my share of the stock, but I think it's only fair if you buy the horses so if you've nowt to put in, well, you'd better say so.'

Malachi watched the bright look of hope fade from the old man's face and suddenly something inside him told him to take the chance. 'I do have a bit of money—enough for two horses, I should think—and I brought a couple of boxes of goods with me from England. We'd have to be careful, though. Not much leeway there. Still, what's life if you can't take a chance now and then, eh?'

Dan took out his handkerchief and blew his nose loudly, imperfectly disguising the tears in his eyes. He had a bit more money saved but wanted to keep some back just in case. At his age you never knew what was going to happen to you. And anyway, it was only fair for both partners to contribute. 'All reet, then. We'll start getting things together tomorrow. I know where there's a good cart, though it needs a bit of work doing—but we s'll have to take care choosing the horses. They need to be strong buggers in the winter, with all the mud.'

'I know a bit about horses. And about woodworking. I was apprenticed to a cooper before I left England.'

'Was that one of your mistakes?'

62

Malachi shook his head. 'No. It was my father's. He was the cooper but I never did want to do that sort of work and I told him so. I had no choice, though. Had to do as he said. You know how it is for lads. When he died, the business went to my brother. He and I don't get on, so I left. I don't miss him, but I do miss my mother and worry about her, being dependent on our Lemuel. His wife's a right nasty bitch.' It suddenly occurred to Malachi that if he made enough money he could invite his mother to come out to Australia and live with him, pay her fare out here. Yet another reason for not getting wed for a few years yet.

Dan grinned at him. 'And you're not nasty?'

Malachi smiled back. 'Only if folk try to cheat me. Mostly I'm too easy-going for my own good. I prefer to use this,' he tapped his forehead, 'rather than these.' He brandished his fists in the air. When he looked round, he saw that the eating house was nearly empty. 'Time to get you home again, Dan lad.' He helped the old man to his feet and escorted him back to his room. 'I'll come round first thing in the morning and we'll set it all down on paper, do our sums proper.'

Lost in thought, Malachi walked slowly home along the street which was deserted now. When he thought he heard footsteps behind him he set off running, arriving at his lodgings breathless but safe, laughing at his own fears. He didn't reckon himself a coward and could give a fair account of himself if pushed, but he wasn't the sort of fellow to get into fights when they could be avoided, never had been.

*   *   *

The following morning Malachi woke full of energy and excitement. As soon as he'd finished breakfast with the other lodgers, he hurried round to see Dan, who was a bit grumpy and stiff this morning, complaining of his 'rheumatiz'. But the old man soon cheered up once Malachi had made him a cup of tea and a slice of bread and jam.

Together they went to inspect the cart which, although it needed a few things doing to it, was basically sound. Malachi reckoned he was a good enough craftsman to fix it himself.

'Leave the bargaining to me,' Dan whispered.

Malachi stood back and hid a grin as Dan pleaded poverty, groaned at the seller's counter-offer and gradually knocked the price down. When he grudgingly agreed to buy it, Malachi stepped in and said it'd be no good to buy it as it was. 'Can we keep it here for a week or two so that I can work on it?'

The owner rolled his eyes. 'Two weeks, no more.'

Once they were out of sight of the harness shop, Malachi stopped and offered his hand. 'You're a terror at bargaining, old man!'

Dan smiled smugly. 'Told you I'd be worth working with, young fellow, even if I have lost my strength. And you didn't do so badly yoursen. Now, if you're after horses, I have a good friend we can visit when the time comes, but that's enough for me for today.' He patted his chest.

Malachi looked at him in concern because his companion's face was pale and he was struggling to keep up. 'I'll walk home with you and see you've something decent to eat. Bread and jam won't build up your strength again.'

While Dan rested, Malachi went out and bought some roast beef clapped between slices of crusty new bread from a nearby alehouse, purchasing a few apples from a street vendor on his way back. He stood over Dan until his friend had eaten half the beef sandwich, then wrapped the rest in a cloth and set it aside for the following morning. 'My mother believes good food is the best medicine there is, so you're to eat an apple as well before you go to bed.'

'*An apple a day keeps the doctor away,*' Dan mocked. 'Aye, well, I can do without them thieving bastards, taking a man's money when he's not hissen. They got their hooks into me when I were ill.'

'What did they say about you?'

'To take it easy.' He spat to emphasise his words. 'I'd as soon cock my toes up now as sit around all day doing nowt.'

Malachi let the silence drift around them for a minute or two then looked at the fire and the long metal toasting fork and smiled. 'You could roast an apple on this, you know. They taste sweeter when they're softened and they're easier on the teeth.' Before he left he looked round the small, cluttered room. 'We're going to need somewhere else to store our stock until we leave.'

'Got a friend who lends me his back room when I've too much to fit in here. Charges me five bob a week.'

'Sounds all right to me. We'll take my things round there tomorrow and you can tell me what you think of them.'

Their final task was to purchase two sturdy young horses, not beautiful, since they were a mixture of breeds, but sound in wind and limb.

Then they left Melbourne on a cart fully equipped for them to camp out on the road. It had a hood over the back to protect them and their merchandise from the weather and was heavily laden with the many small items they'd bought. Malachi walked beside it to ease the burden on the horses, going through their goods in his head, hoping they hadn't left out something essential.

Galvanised buckets hung from the sides of the cart, plus a couple of tubs for laundry work. Tea kettles, frying pans and saucepans clanked and jangled as they bumped along—all wound on with wire through the handles so they couldn't be snatched by thieves. Inside the cart were boxes containing lamps and spare fitments for them like glass shades, chimneys and burners, which Dan said always sold steadily. These were packed carefully in straw. There was everything for laundry work: possers, flat irons, even a modern box mangle. Other crates contained kitchen tools, some of them brought out from England by Malachi: choppers with wooden handles, graters made of tinplated iron, whisks, sieves, colanders, toasting forks and sharp knives. There was plenty of sewing equipment for the ladies: threads, cotton and embroidery silks, needles, tape measures and scissors, as well as hair pins, brushes and combs, little hand mirrors and even a bottle or two of lavender water.

Once they'd left the city Malachi felt he could breathe properly again. Throwing his head back, he burst into song.

When he stopped, Dan looked at him thoughtfully. 'That voice o' yourn's worth money, lad.'

'What?'

'Can you play that guitar as well as you sing?'

Malachi shrugged. 'Not quite as well, but I do all right.'

'We could put on little shows, then. We'd make money from them, too. You've got a right lovely voice, lad.'

It seemed incredible to think of anyone paying good money to hear him sing when Malachi's father had complained all his life about him wasting his time warbling like a bird!

*　　　*　　　*

Christmas was celebrated in the convent as a religious festival only. The one attempt to make the girls' day brighter was a special plum cake served with their evening meal.

A month later, on a sunny day in late January, Ismay was summoned to the Mother Superior's office, something she'd rather have avoided. Sister Veronica escorted her there and took a seat at the side of the big mahogany desk, folding her arms and tucking her hands into the sleeves of her habit then sitting with eyes downcast.

Ismay, left standing alone in front of the desk, held her head up high, determined not to show any weakness in front of the woman she hated.

'Since you're already trained as a maid we've found you a job. You're to pack your things this afternoon and set off tomorrow.'

'Pack my things?' Ismay was puzzled.

'The job's in the country, about a hundred miles from Melbourne.'

Chill fear struck Ismay and she stared at Mother Bernadette's wrinkled face in horror. 'Please, Reverend Mother, can you not find me another job nearby? I don't want to leave Mara.'

The old nun scowled at her. 'She'll be quite safe with us.'

'But I won't be able to see her. She's the only family I have now.'

'If the Lord has chosen a path elsewhere for you, then that's where you'll go.'

After a minute's silence, punctuated by the impatient tapping of the old nun's fingers on the desk, Ismay looked across at her and said flatly, 'I won't do it.'

'*What did you say?*'

'I said, I won't go.'

'You'll do as you're told, young woman.'

'How will you make me?'

'We can, if necessary, invoke the force of the law on you because you still owe us money for your passage out here. If you refuse to work and pay us back, we can have you arrested.'

'I don't believe you!' But the Mother Superior's face was so calmly confident that Ismay felt something crumpling inside her. Nevertheless defiance made her say, 'I'm *not* going away from Mara.'

'I have better things to do than waste my time arguing with you. Go to your room and think about it.' She looked at the clock. 'I'll give you one hour to consider whether you can do most for your sister by working or by being in jail.'

Sister Veronica stood up and gave Ismay a nudge so she moved towards the door. In the middle of the hall she stopped walking to repeat, 'I'm not

68

going to the country.'

'You should think it over very carefully, Ismay.'

'I don't need to. How can she even ask me to leave Mara?'

'Reverend Mother knows what's best for us all.'

'She doesn't even care what happens to us!'

'God has placed her in charge of us, so we must obey.' Sister Veronica sighed. 'Go up to the dormitory, child. It'll be deserted at this time of day. Think about this and pray for acceptance of what's been decided. I doubt Reverend Mother will change her mind.'

Without a word Ismay climbed the stairs. In the dormitory she did the unthinkable and sat on her bed, heedless of whether she wrinkled the bedspread or not. She tried not to cry but tears would escape. When she heard footsteps coming up the stairs and along the landing, she wiped them hastily away and turned with a scowl to face the door.

Sister Catherine came in, putting one finger to her lips. 'I shouldn't be here,' she said in a low voice, 'but I wanted to talk to you.' She would confess her sin to the priest after the girl had left, but felt this was a cruel decision and wanted to try and help.

'How can that woman ask me to leave Mara?' Ismay's voice broke on the words and the tears betrayed her.

'She's in charge of the convent and does as she sees fit.'

'She said she'd have me put in jail if I didn't take this job, said I owed the nuns money for the voyage out. How can that be possible when we didn't even ask to come here?'

Catherine sucked in her breath at this news, disgusted by what her Mother Superior was doing. Then she realised she was not only being disobedient but sitting in judgement on her superior, and tried to put herself in a more obedient frame of mind. But she couldn't. In her opinion Mother Bernadette was acting in a distinctly cruel fashion. In fact, since her seizure the older nun had behaved very strangely at times. There was nothing Catherine could prove, but she couldn't help wondering if it had changed something inside Reverend Mother's brain. The old nun had always been strict and joyless, but never deliberately cruel like this.

'Ismay, you have no choice. If you take this job, at least you'll be able to save some of your wages and when Mara is old enough, you can make a new start together. And you'll have two weeks' holiday every year, so you'll be able to come and visit her then.'

'Not see her for a year!' With a wail, Ismay flung herself into the young nun's arms and wept bitterly on her shoulder.

Catherine couldn't repulse her, though this would be another sin to add to her list. She let the girl weep for a while, patting her shoulder and making soothing noises, then held her at arm's length. 'You'll have to do as she says, Ismay.'

After a struggle, the girl stopped weeping and looked at her, heaving a sigh. 'Thank you for coming to see me.'

Catherine shrugged. 'I can't really help you.'

'You were kind. No one else has been kind to me for a long time—except for Mr Firth on the ship.'

'I'd better go now.'

70

'Will you be in trouble for coming to talk to me?'
'A little. It doesn't matter.'

*   *   *

As Catherine reached the bottom of the stairs, Reverend Mother came out of her office. She looked at the young nun. 'Where have you been?'

'Speaking to Ismay. I think I've persuaded her to accept your will.'

'I didn't give you permission to do this.'

'I didn't think . . . just wanted to help.'

'She'll do as we ask?'

'Yes, Reverend Mother.'

'You will say ten Hail Marys as a penance for disobedience to our rules.'

The younger woman bowed her head in acceptance.

'And you're not to speak to her again.'

'No, Reverend Mother.'

*   *   *

When Sister Veronica came up to fetch her, Ismay was sitting on her bed staring down at her clasped hands.

'Have you decided to obey Reverend Mother?'

'Yes. But only if I can say a proper goodbye to my sister.'

Sister Veronica didn't answer for a minute. She suspected her superior wouldn't even grant this request, though it was perfectly reasonable. In fact, she too was upset that Ismay was to be sent so far away from her sister when there were undoubtedly jobs available in nearby suburbs. Mother

Bernadette must have some reason for this decision, but Sister Veronica couldn't think what it was.

She thought fast, knowing she would have to confess to what she'd done later. 'I'll see you get some time together after the evening meal. Now, you'd better start your packing. Come up to the attic with me and we'll find your trunk.'

*   *   *

Ismay found herself unable to swallow a mouthful of the evening meal, stirring the food round her plate and pretending to eat. As usual she sat so that she could watch Mara and wondered what her little sister would say when told she was leaving. Tears filled her eyes even at the thought.

'What's the matter?' the girl next to her asked.

'They're sending me away.'

'I wish they'd send me away. I hate it here.'

After the meal, Sister Veronica asked Ismay to come to the store-cupboard and help tidy the sewing materials. The girl did as asked and when she got there the nun said quietly, 'Mara's waiting for you on the back veranda. Keep your voices down.'

When Ismay told her sister that she had to leave and explained that she had no choice but to go, the child froze and stared at her, eyes huge with fear.

'But I won't be able to see you!' she whispered at last.

'I don't want to go, you know I don't. But *she* says she'll put me in prison if I don't.' Ismay hugged the younger girl to her and fought back more tears because she had to make this as

72

bearable as possible for Mara. 'So this is what I've been thinking. I'll save up my wages and as soon as I have a few pounds, we'll run away together. Two years at most, I promise you.'

'It's still a long time.'

'Well, I'll write to you often, I promise. Let's sit down on the bench for a little while.'

They sat staring across the back garden, saying little, just wanting to be close. A shower of rain stopped and the sun came from behind a cloud. Suddenly a rainbow arched across the sky, shimmering and beautiful.

'A twopenny rainbow,' Mara said softly. 'I'll think about you every time I see a rainbow, Ismay, even if it's only a penny one. I'll pretend I'm at one end and you're at the other, joined by it.'

'Yes.' Ismay couldn't say another word or she'd have burst into tears. Here she was trying to comfort her sister, but it was Mara who was finding something to comfort her with.

When Sister Veronica came to fetch them they looked at her in mute misery, gave one another a hug, and then Mara walked away slowly.

'It won't be that bad,' the nun said gently.

'It will so. It'll feel wrong every minute I'm away from my sister. We've never been separated in our lives before.' Ismay stared bleakly across the garden. 'I don't know how you people can live with your consciences, sending me away like this.'

*   *   *

In the morning, Ismay broke the rules by rushing into the younger girls' dormitory and flinging her arms round her sister. They stood weeping

73

together until Sister Hilda separated them and sternly ordered Ismay back to her own room.

She refused to go down to breakfast and after she had finished packing the last things into her bag, sat on her bed weeping until the other girls were occupied with lessons or housework. When Sister Veronica came to fetch her, she didn't try to hide the tears that were streaming down her face.

Father Henson was waiting at the front of the convent, sitting at the reins of his little gig. Ismay's trunk was already strapped on the back.

'The good father will take you to your employers who are waiting to leave for the country,' Sister Veronica said.

Ismay didn't reply, just cast her a look of loathing and climbed up beside the priest.

When they'd been driving for a minute or two he said, 'The Mother Superior tells me you're reluctant to work for Mr and Mrs Berlow.'

'It's nothing to do with them. I don't want to leave my little sister. Surely there are jobs in the city?'

He looked at her sternly. 'We prefer to send our girls to the country because we think they'll be safer there. In the city there are temptations and unscrupulous people. You should be grateful for the care that's being taken of you.'

She looked at him, scorn on her face. 'I'm not and never will be grateful for being separated from my sister. I'm not even sure I believe in your God any more. If he cared about us, he'd not do this to me and Mara.'

He was so aghast at this, he couldn't speak for a moment. 'How *dare* you say such a thing?'

'Why should I not? You can't do anything to me

that's worse than this.' She wondered if lightning might strike her dead for speaking to a priest like this, but nothing happened, which seemed a further sign that she had right on her side.

'I shall make allowances for your grief at leaving your sister and pray that you see the error of your ways. You are to pray every night to accept the Lord's will.'

Ismay's voice was tired. 'I can't pray any more, not after what those nuns have done to me. I haven't been able to pray properly since they forced us to leave Ireland.' She ignored his hiss of shock, folded her hands on her lap and stared stonily ahead.

For some reason he found himself unable to scold her as she deserved and not for the first time he too wondered about this situation. The girl was right after all. There were plenty of jobs nearby and it was a sad thing to separate two young sisters. But the Mother Superior had said Ismay was a bad influence on her sister Mara, and if she had indeed lost her faith, one had to think of protecting the younger child.

*   *   *

In Melbourne Father Henson stopped outside a small family hotel. The stableman helped him lift the trunk down, then took the horse and gig away round the back.

'Wait in the hall while I have a quick word with Mr and Mrs Berlow.'

A few minutes later he opened the door of the guests' sitting room and beckoned Ismay inside.

She studied Mrs Berlow as openly as the woman

75

was studying her: tall and middle-aged, just a little on the plump side but with no softness to her body or face, as if she had led a hard life. Mr Berlow was a little shorter, balding and thin, and winked at Ismay as he shook hands. She tried to smile back at him, grateful for the kind gesture, but couldn't manage it.

'I hope you're a good girl and a hard worker?' Mrs Berlow frowned at her, as if she doubted that.

Ismay shrugged.

Mrs Berlow's lips tightened.

'She's a little upset at leaving her sister, as I told you,' Father Henson put in quickly.

'I'm *very* upset,' Ismay corrected him. 'It's a dreadful thing to be doing to us.'

'Well, you can be as upset as you like so long as it doesn't affect your work,' Mrs Berlow snapped.

When they set off, Ismay rode in the back of their cart, her eyes glazed. She'd hardly slept the night before and finally stopped resisting the urge to sleep. When they stopped she woke with a jolt, jerking upright, unable for a minute to work out where she was.

'We've stopped to eat,' Mr Berlow called. 'Come and join us, Ismay.'

She climbed down and accepted a cup of cold tea from the large bottle Mrs Berlow pulled out of the picnic basket, forcing a sandwich down because she hadn't eaten since noon the previous day and her stomach was growling.

'Tell me more about your experience as a maid,' Mrs Berlow commanded once they'd finished eating.

Ismay started telling them about Ballymullan and working at the big house there, but this

76

brought tears welling in her eyes and her voice choked to a halt.

'The child's upset, Peggy. Let her be till she gets used to us,' Mr Berlow said.

His wife shrugged. 'As long as she's a hard worker.'

'I'm a hard worker as long as I'm treated fairly,' Ismay warned.

She saw Mr Berlow shake his head at his wife to stop her replying sharply to this impudence, but she didn't care, didn't seem to care about anything, kept seeing Mara's face and wanting to weep— managed not to only by a huge effort.

CHAPTER FIVE

JANUARY–FEBRUARY 1864

When Mara heard the priest's horse trot off into the distance, she knew her sister really had left and began weeping. The more Sister Hilda tried to shush her, the harder she wept. In the end, they took her up to the dormitory and left her there, sobbing into her pillow.

'I wish I could give her a cuddle,' Sister Catherine said softly as the two nuns left the big room.

'You know that's forbidden!' Sister Hilda exclaimed, looking horrified.

'Yes, I do know. But what she really needs is someone to hold her.' She walked off before she said anything else that would upset her fellow nun.

Alone in the big, echoing dormitory Mara wept

77

herself to a standstill then lay with one arm across her eyes, exhausted and miserable.

When Sister Hilda came up later and ordered her to get up and wash her face, she did so. But she couldn't force any food down at lunchtime or even at teatime. By then she was so pale that Sister Catherine went to see Reverend Mother.

'I'm worried about Mara Michaels.'

'What's the matter with her?'

'She's upset about her sister leaving.'

'Is that all? Well, there's no sauce like hunger. I doubt she'll refuse her breakfast.'

Mara stumbled up to bed with the other girls, who had been ordered by the Mother Superior to leave her alone until she pulled herself together. By this time she was light-headed and although she knelt to pray with the others, nothing came into her head. As she lay in bed her mind felt as if it were floating above her body.

She didn't consciously decide not to eat breakfast, but was unable to do more than drink a few sips of milk. In class, when it was her turn to stand up and read, she gasped and slid to the ground in a faint.

'She's cut her head, Sister!'

'Look how white she is, Sister!'

'Let me through.' Sister Veronica clucked her tongue in exasperation and lifted Mara up, so that she was sitting on the bench again, leaning limply against Janey who sat next to her. 'Keep hold of her and someone go and fetch Sister Catherine. She's good with sick people.'

The girls watched in silence as the two nuns exchanged worried glances, then Sister Catherine said, 'I'll take Mara out on the veranda and see if I can persuade her to eat.' She looked round. 'When she's better, it'd help if you girls were kind to her. She's very upset about Ismay leaving.'

'But Reverend Mother said—'

The girl next to the speaker jabbed an elbow in her ribs and as Mara stirred just then, everyone's attention switched to her.

Catherine turned to Janey, who was almost the same age. 'Could you help me get her outside, please?'

On the veranda she propped Mara up on a chair and then turned to Janey. 'What did Reverend Mother say?'

The girl avoided her eyes.

'Tell me.'

'She said Mara was wrong to feel sorry for herself and we were to ignore her foolishness.'

Catherine felt sick at this further example of her superior's spite towards the Michaels sisters, but didn't comment. She left Janey to watch Mara then went to the kitchen where Sister Hilda was cooking the midday meal with the help of two older girls.

When she returned with a tray of food, she found Mara staring blindly out across the garden. The girl didn't even turn round to see who it was.

'Thank you, Janey. You may return to your lessons now.' Catherine put the tray down on a small table nearby and sat beside Mara. 'You need to eat and stay strong, child.'

'It's too long.'

'What is?'

'The years till we can run away.'

Catherine looked at her in both shock and compassion. So they'd been making plans, had they? Well, she didn't blame them. 'You mustn't tell anyone about that. Just work hard, learn all we can teach you,' her voice became gentler, 'and one day, I promise, you'll be together again.'

Mara stared at her. '*She* wants to separate us for ever, I know she does. She hates Ismay.'

Catherine had no need to ask who *she* was. She chose her words with great care. 'No one can take away your memories or the knowledge of who your sister is.' She tapped her own forehead. 'You'll always have that inside your head. I never had a sister and I envy you. I know you're unhappy now and I can't change that, but you can't give in, can you? I'm sure Ismay won't.'

There was silence, then Mara surprised her by asking, 'Do *you* think our other sister sent us out here to Australia? Keara was always so loving that I just—well, I can't imagine her doing it. Ismay says she hates her, but until I hear it from Keara's own lips I won't believe she'd send us away.'

'If she's anything like you two, I'd not believe it either.'

Mara gave her a grateful look and smoothed down her pinafore, tracing the line of the hemmed edge with great care. 'I wish I could write her a letter. I could send it to the big house in Ballymullan. They'd send it on to her in England. Mr and Mrs Mullane live there most of the time. Keara had to go with them because the mistres liked having her for a maid.'

'I don't think Reverend Mother would allow that. She feels it would be better for you to make a completely new life for yourselves here.'

After a few moments of thoughtful silence Mara looked up at her. 'I thought you might—send a letter for me?'

'It'd be breaking my vows to do that.' And besides she had no money for postage, which was expensive to England.

Mara sighed. 'I will try—to be brave, I mean. If I don't, *she* will have won, won't she?'

'I'm sure it's the right thing to do. Now eat this food then go back to your class.'

As she watched the girl walk slowly away, sadness in every line of her skinny child's body, Catherine shook her head. She could never accept that it was right to separate two such loving sisters. And suddenly the decision she had to make in a few weeks' time became very clear to her. Squaring her shoulders she walked back to her work, saying nothing to anyone, not yet.

She'd encouraged the child to be brave and now she could do no less herself than face what was to come with dignity and courage.

*   *   *

As they travelled on, Ismay was horrified to realise how far away from Melbourne the Berlows' farm was. It might not be very far in miles, especially if you had a railway line nearby, but it took them six days at the slow pace of the heavily laden wagon.

At night they stayed with families because it seemed to be the rule out here in the bush that anyone passing by should be offered hospitality. On the final night of the journey, however, there were no houses nearby so they all slept underneath the wagon, where Mrs Berlow's snorting breaths seemed even louder in the confined space.

'How often do you go into Melbourne?' Ismay asked Mr Berlow as they set off the next day.

'I go in twice a year. Mrs Berlow comes with me once.'

'Usually we leave our maid at home, but this year she insisted on going home to her mother, said she didn't like living in the bush.' Mrs Berlow gave Ismay a possessive glance. 'That won't apply with you, though, because the Mother Superior signed you over to us until you're twenty-one. If you try to leave before then, I'll report you to the magistrate and have you brought back. You wouldn't get far on your own anyway. We'd easily find you.'

Ismay stared at her in shock. *'Till I'm twenty-one!* What do you mean?'

'You're in the nuns' charge until then.'

'Unless you marry,' Mr Berlow put in.

'Which we'll make sure you don't,' his wife snapped. 'Anyway, who is there for you to marry out in Upley where there are only half a dozen houses?'

Ismay felt as if the world were whirling round her. 'Surely she can't do such a dreadful thing?'

Mrs Berlow looked at her in surprise, 'I thought you'd know about it?'

'Well, I didn't. They never told me a thing. And I have a little sister at the convent. I have to go and see her sometimes. She's all I've got left in the world.'

Mr Berlow raised one hand to quieten his wife. 'The nuns didn't tell you anything, you say?'

'No.'

He looked at his wife. 'That wasn't fair, Peggy.'

She shrugged. 'Fair or not, she's bound to us now.'

'I didn't want to leave my sister but they said—' a sob escaped Ismay '—no, Sister Catherine said I could go and see her when I had my annual holidays. Two weeks every year, she said.'

Mrs Berlow sniffed. 'You'd only get to Melbourne and back in that time with tracks like these.' She gestured to the ruts and as if to emphasise what she was saying, the wagon lurched on the edge of another dip in the ground and then jolted down into it. 'And we're not going to make a special journey to take you there, either, or give you more than two weeks' holiday, so you'd better resign yourself to the situation: you're legally bound to us for the next six years and that's that.'

Ismay bent her head, unable to prevent tears running down her face. Neither of her employers said anything. ,

When they stopped Mr Berlow brought her some food but she shook her head.

'You have to eat, child,' he said quietly. 'You'll do yourself no good fretting like this.'

'I wish I were dead!' she sobbed. 'What if they send Mara away as well and I never find her again?'

'Perhaps she can come and work for us when she's old enough,' he offered.

'She's only eleven.'

'Well, in three years, she could—'

'*Three years!* Didn't we sleep in the same bed all our lives, till the nuns kidnapped us and forced us to come to Australia?'

'Don't speak about the good nuns like that, young woman,' Mrs Berlow began.

'Hold your tongue, Peggy!' her husband snapped. 'Have you no compassion?'

She looked shamefaced but muttered, 'We've paid those nuns a year's wages in advance and I

83

mean to get value for it.'

Ismay raised her head, puzzled. 'Paid *them* a year's wages? I don't understand. Surely those are *my* wages?'

'You owe them money for your passage out here,' Mrs Berlow said. 'It'll take you three years to work it off. After that your wages will be your own, but you'll still be bound to us.'

Ismay was so shocked she couldn't utter a sound for a moment or two, then said bitterly, 'They treat slaves better than I've been treated.'

And at that moment she knew she'd not stay with the Berlows a second longer than she had to. She'd run away and if she died trying to get back to Melbourne, then so be it. She couldn't believe how the nuns had tricked her.

Had Sister Catherine known about this? She remembered the nun's steady gaze and shook her head. Surely not. But she was quite sure Mother Bernadette had.

There were two people she hated in the world now, really hated—her sister Keara and the Mother Superior. That hatred helped her continue, somehow. The only praying she'd do from now on would be for them to get their just desserts.

She picked up the plate which Mr Berlow had left beside her and forced the food down. She had to be strong and learn as much as she could about life in this part of the country—ready for the day she ran away.

* * *

In March Mother Bernadette summoned Catherine to her office after breakfast. 'It's almost time for you to make your final profession.'

The younger nun took a deep breath and stared at her lap for a few moments. She had been expecting this and had tried to prepare herself for it, but her stomach was churning with nervousness because not making the final vows that bound her for life to be a nun was almost unheard of. She raised her eyes and said quietly, 'I can't do it. I've decided that I'm not suited to a nun's life.'

Reverend Mother's face turned a dusky red and for a moment Catherine thought the old woman was about to have another seizure. She watched her fight for self-control, reining back the anger and breathing deeply.

'Why?'

'I've come to realise that I entered the convent because I was grieving for my father and was unable to face life without him. The religious life irks me in many ways. I can't obey orders mindlessly, I just can't, and I hate not being able to touch people. So it's better if I make a new life for myself—outside.'

'This is some foolish whim.'

'No, it definitely isn't. I've given it long and serious consideration.'

For over an hour, the older nun harangued and hectored her, using every argument she could muster to make her reconsider. Catherine felt shaky inside as the other woman attacked her powers of understanding and decried her foolishness in not talking about this before, then went on to say she'd be shunned by other Catholics if she took such a step.

When all other arguments had failed, she said, 'You *owe* it to the order to stay. They've looked

85

after you for years.'

And Catherine was at last driven to shout, to drown out that harsh voice, because the Reverend Mother wouldn't even allow her to finish a sentence, let alone listen to what she was trying to explain. 'I brought a good dowry with me. When I leave, the order will owe *me* something, not the other way round.'

At last Mother Bernadette stood up and pointed one quivering finger at the door. 'Go to your room at once and stay there, praying for guidance. I'll send for Father Henson and we'll see if *he* can talk some sense into you. You are not to tell anyone about this whim of yours. In fact, I forbid you to speak to anyone.'

Catherine bowed her head and walked quietly up the stairs. The tiny, separate rooms the nuns occupied had been made by partitioning a large bedroom into four and she had always found hers claustrophobic. She stood for a moment with her back against the closed door, breathing deeply, finding the confined space even more airless than usual, then she went to kneel by the bed and pray. But she couldn't. Instead she kept seeing images from the past few months, the pieces which had fallen together to make her realise she wasn't suited to staying in the order, most especially in a convent controlled by a woman like that.

Eventually she grew stiff, her knees too painful for her to continue kneeling, and stood up. As she went to the window to look across the front garden, Father Henson's gig drew up outside and she watched Mr Powell come from the side of the house and lead away the horse and small vehicle to the rear, talking to the animal in the kindly way he

86

had. Catherine smiled. She liked Mr Powell and his wife, and had no trouble dealing with Barney who was a hard worker when he knew a task, as long as you spoke to him gently. But the lad always avoided Mother Bernadette, hiding from her if he could.

She was still standing by the window when Sister Hilda knocked on the door.

'You're wanted in the chapel. Father Henson's here to see you.'

Suddenly the spirit of rebelliousness overflowed again in Catherine. 'He's here because I'm not going to make my final profession.'

Sister Hilda's mouth dropped open in shock.

'Reverend Mother has probably told you not to speak to me and she told me not to mention this to anyone, but I want to be sure you—and everyone else—understand that I've thought very deeply about this decision and prayed many times for guidance. My decision has not been lightly made, I promise you.'

Sister Hilda gave her a sideways glance and a quick nod, but didn't say anything else. Catherine moved forward with a sigh. 'I'll go down, then.'

In the chapel Father Henson was waiting for her. She paused for a moment then moved towards him, head held high, hands tucked into the long sleeves that were so unsuitable in the hot Australian summers. She had expected him to be angry but his voice was gentle.

'We'll sit here in front of the altar and talk quietly. But first we'll say a prayer for help at this difficult time.'

Afterward she explained her reasons once more, ending, 'It'd be wrong to take my final vows, I know it would.'

'Your Mother Superior is very—upset.'

'Yes.'

They discussed the matter at length and in the end the priest sighed and said, 'I can see that you haven't made the decision lightly, but your order is small and we've no way of dealing with this in Australia. I'll speak to the Bishop, but I think he'll agree with my recommendation that we send you back to Ireland. Once you're there, they'll be able to help you as you should be helped.'

She sat with bowed head, grateful when he didn't try to hurry her into speech. She'd thought about what she wanted to do afterwards, of course she had. And she'd known that wouldn't please them, either, but since she was nearly thirty and wasn't breaking any secular laws, there was no way they could prevent her. Unbidden, the memory of Ismay's misery came back to her and she thought of how quiet Mara was nowadays. She looked up again. 'Thank you for your patience, Father. This isn't easy for any of us, I know, but I'm afraid I don't want to go back to Ireland. In fact, I shall refuse to do so.'

'Ah. That does complicate matters somewhat.'

'Can the church not advance me a little money, just a very little, to tide me over until I can find employment and regain my dowry from the order?'

'That would be for your Mother Superior to decide.'

'We both know she won't do that. In fact, she doesn't always make the most rational decisions. I think the seizure she had on the ship coming to Australia affected her mind and—'

'Seizure? What do you mean? She's said nothing

to me of a seizure.'

'The ship's doctor said it was a relatively mild one, but still, it seemed to me to change her personality for the worse. I cannot submit myself to her decision about this. I just—cannot!'

It was his turn to bow his head in thought. When he at last looked up, he asked, 'Could you take a week to think about it, go on retreat and pray for guidance?'

She nodded. She could give them that, at least, though she already knew it wouldn't make any difference. She had done little but think about her future lately.

'Then I'll tell Mother Bernadette what we've decided and I'll explain to the Bishop.' He stood up and she followed suit.

*   *   *

The next day Sister Veronica stopped Mara as she was leaving the dining room. 'Reverend Mother wishes to see you.'

Mara stared at her in shock. The mere thought of going to that big, dark office to be shouted at terrified her. It terrified them all. 'Are you coming with me?'

'No. She wants to see you alone. Run along.'

But Mara couldn't move. She shook her head and backed away. 'I don't want to. I'm frightened of her.'

'She's in charge here, so you have no choice, child.'

'What if she sends me away like she did Ismay?'

'You're not old enough to be sent out to work, for heaven's sake. You're still at school.'

89

'I want to see Sister Catherine.'

'You know she's on retreat. She's not speaking to anyone this week.' She frowned at the girl. 'Come along now. You're being foolish.'

Dragging her feet, Mara followed the nun along to the big office in the new wing of the house, standing only just inside the door, surprised to see a man and woman sitting with Reverend Mother.

Mother Bernadette beckoned to Mara, who moved reluctantly forward. 'These people are Mr and Mrs Hannon.'

Mara nodded her head in greeting to them and they both stared at her.

'She's very pretty,' the lady said. 'And she's got dark hair, like our Briony had.'

The man looked quickly at his wife. 'She's not our Briony, though.'

'I know that.'

Mara was surprised to see tears welling in the lady's eyes.

Mother Bernadette said, 'Mr and Mrs Hannon would like to see the garden and chapel. I said you'd show them round.'

Puzzled, Mara watched the lady smile at her and stand up. She led the way out and showed them the back garden, where Mr Powell grew vegetables and a rose bush for his wife, then the front garden and the statue of Our Lady.

'Let's sit on this nice bench and chat,' Mrs Hannon said, taking Mara's hand and pulling her to sit down beside her.

Mara watched Mr Hannon sit at the other end of the bench, arms folded. He had hardly said a word to her and seemed angry.

'Tell me about yourself, dear,' Mrs Hannon said

in her gentle voice. 'I believe you only arrived here a few months ago. How are you enjoying life in Australia?'

Mara stared down at her shoes, not sure what to say.

'Well?' the man asked, an edge of impatience in his voice.

So she told them how she and Ismay had been forced to come here and how much she missed her big sister. By the time she'd finished she was in the lady's arms, sobbing.

When she'd calmed down, Mrs Hannon stood up and looked at her husband. 'I'd like to talk to you about Mara, Charles.'

'I'm still not sure about this, Barbara.'

'Well, I am. I think it was meant to be.' She took Mara's hand again and led the way back inside. 'Would you wait for us in the chapel, please, dear?'

Bewildered, but glad to have some time to herself, Mara went to sit at the back of the tiny chapel, wishing Ismay were here. With a sigh she abandoned herself to her memories of her sisters.

'There you are, Mara! I've been calling you.'

She jerked to her feet. 'Sorry, Sister Hilda. I didn't hear you.'

'Reverend Mother wants to see you in her office again.' She saw the fear on the child's face and said encouragingly, 'It's good news.'

'Ismay's coming back?'

'No, of course not. *Other* good news.'

Mara sighed and followed her back to the office. There was no other good news as far as she was concerned.

Mother Bernadette frowned at her across the desk. 'You're a very lucky girl, Mara. You're going

91

to live with Mr and Mrs Hannon from now on. Go up and pack your things. I'll send Mr Powell to fetch your trunk down from the attic.'

Mara gaped at her in surprise.

'Well? Do as you're told.'

Mrs Hannon stood up. 'I'll come and help you, dear, shall I?'

Mara looked desperately from one woman to the other. 'I'm sorry, Mrs Hannon. You're very kind, but I can't leave here or Ismay won't know where to find me.'

'The nuns will be able to tell her where we live.'

Mara looked at the sour-faced Mother Superior and shook her head. She didn't trust this woman to help her in any way. 'No. I daren't leave here. I have to be *sure* Ismay can find me.'

The man looked impatiently at his wife. 'You see. She's too old, has too many memories.'

Barbara looked back at him. 'Charles, my mind is made up.' She looked at the old nun. 'Can the child not write a letter to her sister and leave it with you? Then if Ismay comes back, she'll know where to find us.'

The nun pursed her lips, then nodded reluctantly.

Barbara took Mara's hand. 'There you are. We'll make sure your sister is able to find you. I'll explain the rest to you as we pack your things.'

Mara gave her a shy smile. 'Thank you.'

When they'd gone, the Mother Superior looked at Mr Hannon and shook her head. 'Mara is young enough to re-educate, but her sister was a disobedient and wilful girl, *not* a good influence. It's better to separate them. Permanently.'

'Hmm.' He looked towards the door, then back

again.

'And it must be clearly understood that once you've taken Mara away, there'll be no bringing her back. It unsettles them and they never fit in again.'

He frowned. 'Surely there could be a trial period?'

'No. You must be committed to the course of action, for the child's sake.' She paused, head on one side. 'Don't you want to adopt her?'

He shrugged. 'I'm indifferent, to tell you the truth. But when our daughter died, I thought my wife would die of grief. It was only when our priest suggested adopting a child—Barbara can't have any more herself, you see—that she started to get better. I thought we'd be looking for a younger child, but our daughter was the same age as Mara and if Barbara wants *her*, well, I'll agree to it.'

His voice grew harsher as he added, almost to himself, 'Barbara's good with children. She'll help the girl settle down. But I will make sure the child isn't spoiled, I promise you.'

'Very wise, Mr Hannon.'

*   *   *

After they'd gone, the Mother Superior took the child's letter to her sister and put it in the bottom drawer of her desk. When the weather grew colder and she had a fire lit in here, she'd burn it.

'I'll make absolutely sure that Thy will be done,' she told the crucifix hanging above the hearth.

She was sure she saw Him nod in approval as she took out another piece of paper and began drafting her letter to the Bishop, recommending that Sister Catherine be denied permission to leave the order and kept in Australia until she'd had time to see sense.

CHAPTER SIX

MARCH–JULY 1864

Dan perked up as soon as they left Melbourne and the fresh air seemed to do him good. But sometimes he grew very tired for no reason and his complexion turned sallow. Then he would look as if he could barely hold himself upright and allow his young companion to look after him without protest.

Each morning Malachi got up early and made a small fire, setting the billy on it and watching the first dawn light filter through the gum trees as he waited for the water to boil. When a kangaroo hopped into sight one day, a female with a joey peeking out of its pouch, he reached for the rifle they always kept ready. Then his hand stilled and he set it down again. It'd be good to have some fresh meat, but if he killed the mother, the joey would die too.

'Y're a softie,' Dan said from his roll of blankets under the wagon.

As the kangaroo hopped away, Malachi turned to smile at him. 'Aye, well, why kill two when you only need to eat one?'

'They're nobbut vermin.' Slowly, Dan unwrapped the blankets and stumbled away to relieve himself.

Malachi felt a pang of pity at the old man's

stiffness and the obvious pain he was in from his 'rheumatiz', especially in the mornings, but Dan never complained.

By the time he returned and eased himself down on a log, Malachi had the tin pint pots of steaming tea ready and was toasting some stale bread on the fire. They still had jam left from the tin they'd opened a few days ago because Malachi always scraped it into a screw-top jar to prevent ants getting at it. He sometimes smiled wryly at what a fussy housekeeper he had become. His mother would be proud of him.

When they'd finished eating Dan said, 'I were too tired to explain the next stretch of road last night, but there's a nice little farm just a mile or two further on, or there used to be—you can never be quite sure who'll succeed an' who'll fail—then beyond that a new settlement. It's not bad land round here so some of 'em will have stayed on. They hadn't got a shop last time I passed through but if they have one now we'll move straight on. There's allus another place being settled further out in the bush. We'll travel round for a year or two till we've saved up for a shop an' then we'll find a place to open one.'

Malachi nodded patiently. The old man liked to emphasise their future together, though he did tend to repeat himself. But Dan was teaching him a lot and was good company, with a fund of stories to share, so why not stay together? They neither of them had anyone else in Australia. In the meantime Malachi was enjoying the trip and was in no hurry to settle anywhere.

As they set off he sat on the driving seat, enjoying the scenery. Victoria was tamed in parts

95

and sometimes resembled English countryside—
well, it did if you half-closed your eyes and ignored
the greyish-green of the gum trees' foliage. When
he passed a meadow full of sleepy cows, he would
occasionally feel a pang of homesickness, but it
soon passed. It was only really his mother he
missed. He hoped there'd be a letter from her
waiting for him when he arrived back in
Melbourne. He'd written to her before he left,
telling her all his plans.

A flash of vivid red caught his eye, then
another—rosellas. He still marvelled at the fact
that parrots were common wild birds in Australia.

'If we can't buy any bread today, we'll need to
bake some damper tonight,' he said a little later.
Dan didn't eat much but this outdoor life gave
Malachi a hearty appetite.

'Ah, they'll have some in the settlement. And we
might try out your singing tonight.'

Malachi flushed. 'That feels more like begging
to me.'

'Nay, if you work to entertain someone, it's only
fair they pay you for it. Leave that part of it to me.
That guitar of yours sounds nice. It's softer on the
ears than a fiddle.'

And indeed, the settlers seized the opportunity
to hold an impromptu party and were quite happy
to hold a collection to pay Malachi for entertaining
them.

As they rolled along the next morning Dan
grinned and said, 'Told you they'd enjoy your
singing! And pay for it.'

Malachi smiled back at him. 'I was a bit nervous,
but it went well, didn't it? When I write to my
mother next I'll ask her to tell the lads what a good

present they bought me.'

*　　　*　　　*

Catherine emerged from her week of solitude, prayer and meditation even more convinced that she was not cut out to be a nun and told Reverend Mother so firmly.

The old woman gave her a baleful look. 'Well, we can do nothing about that here. You'll have to go back to Ireland and since we can't do without you, you can't leave until we get a replacement. I'll mention it in my next letter home. You can rejoin the normal life of the convent from tomorrow onwards.'

Catherine didn't argue with her, but when she returned to her bedroom to get her dark working apron stood staring out of the window, unable to suppress a feeling of resentment and rebellion. She didn't belong here any more, whatever anyone said.

She watched Mr Powell working in the back garden with his son, smiling with real love at the young boy locked in a lumbering man's body. She had never heard him be less than patient with Barney, even when the poor chap made mistakes. If she didn't wait too long, she might still be able to marry and have children herself. A stab of sheer joy went through her at that thought, then she frowned. Waiting for a replacement and going back to Ireland would take a year or two, and she was already thirty. It seemed so silly to go back when she didn't even want to return.

But if she just left the order, she would be cut off from the few people she did know in Australia because everyone would be horrified at what she'd

97

done. She guessed that the congregation of the local church would avoid her too and if she did take the decision into her own hands it'd be better to move away from here. She might or might not get her dowry back, or part of it. She would certainly try because it had been a substantial sum and it would be good to have some money behind her. In the meantime she intended to find a job, however menial.

But how to escape? Not only did she have no money, she didn't have any normal clothes and her head was shaven in accordance with the order's rules.

She didn't find out until the following day that Mara had left. None of the other nuns knew exactly where the girl had gone, only that a couple had come to the convent several days ago and the child had left with them.

'Who were they? Did the Rev—um, did they force Mara to go with them?'

'No, she went willingly,' Sister Hilda insisted. 'But we weren't told their name.'

Catherine went to see Reverend Mother. 'I'd like to know where Mara has gone, please? I've grown fond of the child and would like permission to write to her.'

Her superior raised one eyebrow. 'You'll be told what you need to know and as you're still a nun, you won't be writing to anyone.'

'I'm not really a nun any more.'

'You are as far as I'm concerned.'

Catherine didn't intend to let the matter drop. 'But how will Ismay find her sister again if no one knows where she is?'

'I know where she is and am satisfied that she's

in good hands. Ismay was a bad influence on that child. Mara is better off without her.'

'She was not a bad influence. They loved one another.'

'How dare you argue with me?' Suddenly Mother Bernadette's face turned dark red and she began to have difficulty breathing. Alarmed, Catherine called for help and they persuaded the old nun to rest.

That evening Catherine walked up and down the garden, feeling angry and upset. She didn't dare pursue the matter of where Mara was for fear of causing the old nun to have another seizure, but her heart was sore for the child—and for Ismay when she found out what had happened.

Her own state of mind was, to her, further proof that she wasn't fit to be a nun. One by one the disciplines she had thought engrained were slipping away and she was reverting to the woman she had been before her father's death. Lively. She had definitely been lively. And surrounded by love, not only from her father but from the servants who had been with them for years and from neighbours too, some of whom had tried to talk her out of entering the convent. She'd been fond of some of them and still missed them and her old life dreadfully. All she had lacked then was a mother, but since hers had died when she was born, it wasn't something she had missed greatly, especially as she'd had such a wonderful father.

'I'm not going back to Ireland,' she vowed suddenly. 'I'm not.'

'Are you all right, Sister?'

She swung round to see Mr Powell standing watching her. She was about to reassure   but

99

changed her mind. 'No, I'm not all right. I've decided to stop being a nun. I haven't made my final profession yet, and it's been a difficult decision, but I'm sure it's the right one for me.'

He looked at her gravely, his eyes filled with simple kindness. 'You never did seem like the others.'

'I feel even less like them now. Um—you don't know where Mara has gone, do you, Mr Powell? You must have looked after the couple's horse while they were with Reverend Mother.'

He shook his head. 'They never said. He gave me a good tip so they're not short of money. The man was—' he searched for a word '—on edge. The woman had a kind face and you could see that the little lass had taken to her. Oh, and I think the husband called her Barbara.' He frowned in an effort to remember then nodded. 'Yes, Barbara. Definitely.'

Catherine felt a sense of relief. As long as there was someone to be kind to that child, she would feel easier. 'Thank you for telling me about them.' She didn't move away because she always enjoyed chatting to him. Why should that simple pleasure be forbidden, especially now?

'So you'll be leaving us, then? Me and the wife will miss you and so will the girls. Do you know when you're going?'

She shook her head. 'No. They want me to go back to Ireland, but I'd rather stay in Australia.'

He glanced round to check that no one was near. 'Well, if we can help you in any way, you know where to find us.' With a nod he went back to his work and Catherine went inside to the evening meal.

To her relief Mother Bernadette wasn't there. From the looks the other three nuns gave her, they were wary of her now. She picked at her meal in silence, not feeling hungry, just numb and unlike herself. Disoriented, that was the word, she decided as she got up from table.

The feeling of strangeness didn't go away. It was one thing to consider leaving, another entirely to think of doing it in a way that contravened the instructions she'd received from both Reverend Mother and the Bishop. She wasn't sure she could be so blatantly disobedient.

*   *   *

Ismay worked hard, not because Peggy Berlow nagged her but because it wasn't in her nature to be slipshod or lazy.

One day her mistress said, 'Those nuns have trained you well, I'll give them that. And you're not afraid of hard work, either.'

'They didn't train me. I was already working as a maid in the big house back home in Ballymullan when they kidnapped me.' She had to pause for a moment to swallow the tide of grief that suddenly welled up inside her at the thought of her village and home.

'Well, all credit to whoever taught you the work. But we'll have no more of that talk of kidnapping, if you please.'

'I'm sorry, but they did kidnap us and I won't say any differently.'

Although her mistress had become less grumpy as she proved herself a competent worker, and now chatted away to her as they worked, this hadn't changed Ismay's mind about running away. It was how to do it that was going to be the difficulty. The only thing she could think of was to wait until the following year when her employers would both be in Melbourne on their annual trip. That would give her time to lull their suspicions.

It was hard to stay cheerful, though, when quarter day came and the two labourers were given their wages while she got nothing.

Mr Berlow must have noticed that she had tears in her eyes because later that afternoon he slipped her a few coins. 'It's not fair if you don't get anything for all your hard work, lass. Here. Next time a peddlar comes through, you'll be able to buy yourself a trinket or two.'

She looked down to see two shiny half-crown pieces lying in her hand. 'Thank you.' Five shillings wouldn't go far when she ran away, but it was a start at least. She sewed them into her petticoat that very night.

She didn't need trinkets, she needed her sister.

A few days later she saw another opportunity to earn a bit when one of the farm hands wanted a letter writing to his mother. Ismay offered to do it for him for a penny, and added that she'd do his mending as well if he'd pay her. She earned a few more pennies that way, not much but everything counted.

The other farm hand leered at her and hinted at much bigger payments if she let him have his way with her. She slapped his face for him and told Mrs Berlow what he had said. But that only got her into trouble about the money.

'I'll see he doesn't make such an offer again,' the mistress said grimly. 'But you'll give the money you earn to me to look after. I'm not having you running off.'

'I won't give it to you,' Ismay said at once. 'Those nuns have stolen my other money, but this is mine and I'm keeping it.'

'Impudence!'

It was only Mr Berlow's intervention that saved the day. 'What can she do with a few pence, Peggy?'

His wife rounded on him. 'You know how hard it is to get good help out here. Do you *want* to lose her?'

'If she runs away, I'll be the first to go after her,' he said quietly, turning to fix Ismay with a steady gaze. 'You can be quite sure of that, lass.'

'To run away, you have to have somewhere to go,' she threw back at him, her voice breaking on the words. 'I don't know a soul in Australia except you and the nuns so I'm trapped here! But one day I'll be free and then I'll need every penny I can get. It *comforts* me to have the money, even if it's not much, and I won't give it to you or anyone else.'

'You'll mind how you answer me back in future, though, miss!' was all Mrs Berlow said.

After a struggle, Ismay managed to apologise for how she had spoken, though the words stuck in her throat.

But they let her keep the money, which was what counted. And she thought they'd believed her when she said she had nowhere to go. Of course she had somewhere. She'd be going to the convent to find Mara and then they'd both get as far away from it as they could.

*   *   *

Mara tried to watch where the Hannons were taking her so that she could find her way back to the convent if necessary but soon lost track of the twists and turns in the road. In the end she fell asleep with her head in Barbara Hannon's lap.

Charles looked sideways to see his wife looking down with a fond smile. 'Don't get too attached to her till we see what she's like.'

'I know what she's like. She's a little girl who's lost her family, as we lost Briony. Our finding Mara was meant to be. Besides, didn't the Mother Superior tell us we couldn't give her back? She's ours now, and I'm glad of it.'

He was pleased to see some colour in Barbara's cheeks again and a smile on her face, but he couldn't feel the same about a stranger as he had about his own daughter, just couldn't. He didn't tell Barbara that, though. He was doing this for her sake, not the child's.

When they arrived home Barbara shook Mara gently awake. 'We're here.'

She rubbed her eyes and stretched, then sat upright. 'Have I been asleep for long?'

'An hour or two.'

'I wanted to see where we went.'

'Why?' Charles asked harshly. 'You'll not be going back to the convent again. This is your home now.'

Barbara nudged him and shook her head warningly. 'Come on inside, dear.'

'It's a fine big house,' Mara said. 'Ours at home wasn't this big.'

Barbara put an arm round her shoulders. 'Come and see your bedroom. We'll give you a nice bath before you go to bed and you can wear some prettier clothes than those dark, ugly things.'

Mara looked down at herself and for a moment her mouth wobbled. 'Ismay always hated them too.'

Charles's lips tightened. He intended to stop her mentioning that sister of hers after what Mother Bernadette had told them.

That night, when she snuggled down into the soft bed that had once belonged to another little girl, Mara shed a few tears. Then she remembered the letter she had left at the convent for Ismay and cheered up. Her sister would find out where she was and come to see her, she was sure. Or at least write her a letter.

If only the Hannons had wanted two girls, not one, she and Ismay could have stayed together. She still felt strange on her own here. She liked Mrs Hannon, but she wasn't sure about Mr Hannon, who spoke quite sharply to her and frowned at her sometimes. Would he hit her if she did something he didn't like, as her own father had? She hoped not. She hated quarrels and loud voices and people being unkind to one another.

In the morning, Barbara woke her and told her to wash and put on the prettiest dress Mara had ever seen.

'Just for everyday?' she whispered. 'Sure, it's too fine for that.'

Barbara held it up against her and sighed. 'I suppose so. I always liked to see Briony wearing pretty things.'

Mara said without thinking, 'But I'm not Briony.'

The woman blinked and tried not to cry, but a tear rolled down one cheek, than another. Without thinking Mara put her arms round her, surprised at how thin she was, and rocked her a little. 'Shh, now. Shh. I can't bring your daughter back, but we could talk about her if you like. And I'll be company for you, so you won't miss her as much.'

The woman looked at the girl and managed a faint smile. 'You're kind. I like that. And you're right: I mustn't try to pretend you're Briony. No one can ever take her place. But I would like another daughter. I can't have any more babies, which is why we went to find you, why we brought you back here. Will you stay and let me love you?'

Mara looked at her sadly. 'I'll stay till Ismay comes for me. I miss her dreadfully. She always looked after me and was kind to me. No one could have a better sister than Ismay. But the Mother Superior hated her and sent her away. She's very bad-tempered and she shouts at people.' Almost as an afterthought, she added, 'But one day Ismay will come back for me. I know she will. She promised. That was why I had to leave the note for her.' She brightened. 'But maybe she could live here too, or get a job nearby. Then we could all be happy together.'

Barbara didn't say anything to mar that illusion, but she intended to talk to Charles when he came home from the shop and ask him to try to find out where the other sister was. They could make inquiries, find out if Ismay was as bad as the old nun had painted her, perhaps even let Mara write to her.

In the meantime she'd do her best to make the girl happy here. Already she was drawn to the child who had such clear eyes and a gentle nature.

Charles would grow to love Mara too, she was sure. Barbara was feeling happier already for

106

having company every day, not just servants. The better the shop did, it seemed, the less time her husband had to spend with her.

CHAPTER SEVEN

OCTOBER 1864–JANUARY 1865

Catherine looked out of the window and sighed. It would soon be summer but there was no sign of anything being done about her leaving the order, something she was still reluctant to do without permission. But she couldn't go on like this, either—just couldn't. Mother Bernadette was picking on her, giving her all the most menial jobs, making sharp comments aimed at her and refusing to discuss her future at all. The old nun would only say that she'd written to the mother house and they would all have to wait for a decision and a replacement to be sent out.

The other nuns regarded Catherine askance these days, as if they felt she was no longer one of them, and indeed she felt increasingly ill-at-ease in the long flowing robes and wimple, as if they didn't belong to her and she had no right even to borrow them.

But there were practical considerations which made it hard to leave. She had no money, no proper clothes, nowhere to go and no experience of life in Australia outside the convent walls except for a little shopping and tales she'd heard from the girls. She had stopped shaving her head, not wanting to face the world looking so ugly, but

107

luckily the wimple came down low on her forehead and hid the new growth of hair.

At the very least she'd need some sort of employment, so after serious thought she decided to see what she could find out about this. One day she slipped out into the back garden when she was supposed to be cleaning the chapel, and as she'd expected Mr Powell was kneeling in his vegetable garden, humming to himself. She went to stand nearby, hoping he wouldn't realise she was taking advantage of a large shrub to shield herself from the rear windows of the convent.

'I wonder—do you ever buy a newspaper, Mr Powell?'

He stood up and wiped the soil from his hands, his expression puzzled. 'I do, Sister.'

She hesitated then said in a burst, 'Then might I borrow one now and then? They expect me to wait another year or more before I leave the order and they say I'll have to go back to Ireland. I don't want to do that so I thought I'd look at the jobs being offered and see what I might expect if I just— walked out.' She flushed as she looked at him, hoping desperately that he would understand and reassured by his gentle smile as he answered.

'I could leave my newspaper in the shed, on the shelf to the left of the door, then you could come out when convenient and study it. Ladies are always looking for maids, that I do know because a friend of my wife's left a job she didn't like and easily found herself another one. But maybe you'd want something better than that—governess, perhaps?'

'I'd take any job that was honest.' A sigh escaped her. 'You must think I'm being foolish.'

'No.' It was his turn to glance round to make sure they weren't being overheard. 'I think you're doing the right thing. I hope you'll excuse me saying it, but you're too young and pretty to shut yourself away from the world.'

Catherine swallowed hard, feeling near to tears at this, the only support she'd experienced. 'Thank you. I'm so grateful to find someone who agrees with my decision. I'd better get back to my work now.'

It was only later that she realised he'd called her 'pretty'. That shouldn't have mattered but it did. So there was another sin surfacing—vanity.

*   *   *

Over the next two months Catherine learned a great deal about what sort of jobs were available and decided she'd try for a housemaid's job first, because ladies seeking governesses always insisted they needed 'excellent references'. It made her smile wryly to think of the former Miss Caldwell of Netherbeck House working as a maid, but what choice did she have? Presumably the order would pay back her dowry eventually, or some of it, but in the meantime she wasn't afraid of menial work— they made sure of that when you entered the novitiate.

But she had no references and if she told potential employers the truth about her background, might it make them reluctant to give her a job? After some thought it occurred to her that she could pretend to be a widow. They wouldn't expect a recently widowed woman to have references, surely? Especially if she'd come up to

Melbourne from the country.

She pressed her hands against her cheeks as a hot flush swept across her face. Now she was thinking of telling outright lies. As she let her hands fall again, she looked down at her left hand and frowned. If she were a widow, she'd need a wedding ring. How would she obtain one without money? Her order didn't give the nuns wedding rings.

At her next confession, she would make one last effort to get the priest to help her stay in in Australia then she wouldn't need to run away—though she'd asked him before and he'd said the Bishop preferred her to wait and do things 'properly'. When she'd asked to see the Bishop herself she'd been told she must apply through Reverend Mother, who had refused to let her do so and had insisted yet again that this was just a phase she was going through and that she'd come to her senses soon.

In the meantime the days seemed to drag by as she was suspended in a kind of earthly limbo.

And then, suddenly it seemed, Christmas was upon them, with its holy services and rituals, and she couldn't help cheering up a bit. This was her favourite time of year, even though to celebrate the festival in hot summer weather seemed strange.

I'll wait till Christmas is over, Catherine told herself as she helped the girls set up a crib, enjoying their delight in arranging things just so. She said a special prayer that those girls who had left the convent recently would have a good Christmas, especially Ismay and Mara.

*   *   *

110

The Berlows planned to give everyone an easy day and celebrate Christmas with a newly killed lamb and a big plum cake. When they were discussing it, Ismay risked asking them again if she could send a letter to Mara when Mr Berlow went to the post.

'Why will you not accept that it'd do no good?' Peggy asked in exasperation. 'That Mother Superior said she wouldn't allow your sister to receive letters from you. I've told you so several times now.'

Ismay put down her head and wept, because the approach of Christmas was making her feel desperately sad. 'How can she call herself a nun and do this to me?'

Irritated, Peggy revealed something Fred had told her not to. 'Because you're a bad influence on the child and they want to see she grows up happy and obedient, unlike you.'

Ismay raised her head to stare in shock at her mistress. *Bad influence?* How have I been a bad influence on her? Haven't Keara and I looked after her for most of her life, right from when she was a baby, because Mam was always ill and Da was useless? I love Mara, and without her it's like a part of me has been cut off!'

Standing in the doorway, Fred shook his head. He couldn't believe a nun would lie about something, but neither he nor his wife had seen signs of deviousness or cunning in the girl, let alone laziness, faults of which Ismay had been accused and which they'd thought explained why they'd got her services so cheaply. What he had seen instead was a hard-working girl who sometimes had eyes puffy from weeping, and that continued to upset him because he prided himself on being a good employer and didn't like to see people under his responsibility so unhappy.

'Sometimes, Ismay, you just have to accept things,' he said gently.

She rounded on him and shrieked, '*How have I been a bad influence? Tell me!* Don't I love her more than anyone in the world? Don't I think about her every hour of every day, worry about her, wonder if she's happy?'

'We can't go against what the Mother Superior has ordered.'

'Why not? She's just a nasty old woman who delights in making people miserable. She wouldn't even let me be in the choir on the ship, though it was very respectable and well thought of by the doctor and captain. She was unkind to Sister Catherine all the time. She's horrible!'

'Shame on you to speak like that of a holy nun!' Peggy exclaimed, shocked.

For answer Ismay made an inarticulate noise, pushed past them and ran out of the house across the paddock, disappearing into the hollow channel of the billabong at the far end. This had run with water during the winter but was now almost dry and she went there sometimes to get away from everyone.

She lay on the dusty ground weeping until she could weep no more, then stayed there, quiescent, aware only of the sorrow that ran so deep within her. Some time later she heard footsteps and looked up reluctantly to see Fred standing next to her.

'Come back now, Ismay. This will do no good to you or Mara.'

She pulled herself to her feet and looked at him resentfully. 'I don't know how you can live with your conscience, keeping me a prisoner like this and not letting me see the only relative I have left in the world.'

He didn't answer because in truth he did feel somewhat guilty, especially when he saw her so distraught. And Peggy felt the same.

Ismay began to walk alongside him, everything about her drooping. When they got back, Peggy tried to be particularly kind to her, but the girl didn't notice, going about her work listlessly.

After that there was no more humming to herself or singing as she pegged out the washing. Fred found himself listening for her tuneful voice and missing it. Even Peggy was beginning to worry about the poor girl.

*   *   *

On Christmas Day Ismay went back to bed after she had finished her chores and refused to join in the festivities in any way. 'If it's a holiday, I can do what I want.'

'You can't spend Christmas like this, child,' Fred said from the doorway of her room.

Her voice was thickened by tears. 'Why not?'

'That girl's getting thinner by the day,' he worried when he went back into the kitchen.

Peggy shook her head. 'She does her work but the heart's gone out of her. Is it possible—could that old nun really have been telling lies about her?'

They exchanged glances and shook their heads in bafflement. But the knowledge that someone

113

was lying weeping just beyond their kitchen seemed to put a damper on the festivities and even the two farmhands kept glancing in the direction of Ismay's room.

The older one said bluntly as he was going back to check on the stock, 'That's the unhappiest girl I've ever seen, missus.'

After Christmas Fred said abruptly, 'I think I should go to Melbourne earlier than usual, Peggy. I want to go and see that Mother Superior, ask for proof of what she claims about Ismay.'

'Yes, you do that, but I'll keep a careful eye on her while you're away. I don't want her running off.'

'Can you not persuade her to eat a bit more? She's still losing weight.'

'I've tried. No one can say I don't set a good table and the servants eat the same as we do.' She sighed. 'I don't think she even notices if you try to be kind to her.'

When they told Ismay that Fred was going to Melbourne, she looked at him pleadingly. 'Take me too, I beg you. If I don't see Mara, something inside me will die, I know it will.'

'Don't exaggerate! I'll go and see your sister and make sure she's all right. You can write her a letter and I'll give it to her myself, whatever that nun says. You'll be all right here with Peggy and the Harpers will be coming round to help out a bit, so you'll have some company to cheer you up.'

'You're as cruel as the nuns.' A tear ran down her cheek and Ismay continued to weep silently as she went about her work.

'Should we both go and take her with us?' Fred worried in bed that night. 'She's making herself ill.'

'No. You find out how things stand first. It'd be cruel indeed to raise false hopes.'

*   *   *

The early January night was hot—it had been a fierce summer this year. Catherine lay in her tiny cell of a room, bathed in sweat under her voluminous nightgown. At one point she got up to stand by the window, hoping for a breath of cooler air. But the breeze outside seemed just as hot as the air inside. Below her she could see light coming from Reverend Mother's office, revealing the shrubs and dusty earth in nearby parts of the garden, and she wondered what the old nun was doing up at this hour.

After a few minutes she went back to bed, but still couldn't get to sleep. She envied the other three nuns who always slept heavily. Indeed, Sister Hilda had a particularly penetrating snore that the girls giggled about.

*   *   *

Below her Mother Bernadette was sitting in her office, wire-rimmed spectacles perched on the end of her bony nose, doing the accounts. There never seemed to be quite enough money however careful they were and she didn't want to ask Father Henson for extra help again. She would have to find some way of reducing their expenses. Going back a few months, she began going over the figures. So much went on food. Those girls ate like horses! The sooner the older ones were sent out to work, the better for the order's purse.

115

The lamp flickered and she looked up at it, clicking her tongue in annoyance when she realised how low the flame was. An examination of the cut-glass font showed that it was running out of oil. As shadows chased one another round the room she glanced across at the clock and was surprised to find that she'd been sitting there for three hours. She should leave this now and go to bed.

The trouble was she didn't feel at all sleepy and it was hard to concentrate in the daytime with people disturbing her and so many duties to be fulfilled. No, she'd light a candle and refill the lamp herself, instead of waiting for Mr Powell to do it in the morning. Taking the globe and chimney off the lamp, she lit a spill and used it to light the candle, then blew out the lamp. She made her way to the back kitchen, where the paraffin was kept in its big square can under a special table used only for the dirty, smelly task of cleaning and filling the household lamps each day.

She hesitated. Should she bring the lamp through here to fill it? No, the meagre light shed by this one candle wasn't enough for her to work with; the older you got the more light your eyes seemed to need. There was a three-branch candelabrum in her office and she'd be able to see better if she lit that. She'd been filling oil lamps for years and knew how to be careful.

She was determined to finish her accounts and work out ways of reducing their expenditure.

Taking the special pouring jug into which Mr Powell drew off paraffin from the big can, she half-filled it and carried it slowly and carefully back into her office. Bringing the candelabrum across from the mantelpiece she lit all three of its candles. Ah,

116

that was better! She could see properly now. As she reached for the jug with its long spout to fill the glass font, pain stabbed through her head so strongly she cried out. It stabbed again and this time she crumpled where she sat, beyond crying out, beyond anything more in this life.

As she slumped forward the pourer fell from her hands and paraffin spilled across the papers on the desk top, dripping over the edge on to the rug. Her head hit the desk and the candelabrum rocked for a moment, then fell sideways. One of the candles winked out immediately but the other two didn't. In seconds the oil-soaked papers caught fire and flames began licking across the desk.

The dead woman felt nothing as the flames leaped rapidly from one piece of furniture to the next until the whole room was ablaze.

*　　　*　　　*

Catherine was dozing and the sound of the flames below woke her even before she smelled the smoke: loud cracking sounds, horribly out of place on a dark night in summer. As she sat up in bed she saw a glow through her window and rushed across to see what it was, gasping in shock as she realised that the flickering light below her could only be a fire.

Even as she watched, the window of Reverend Mother's office exploded outwards and the hungry flames followed it on to the veranda.

She yelled out at the top of her voice, calling to the other sisters and girls to waken quickly. Thrusting her bare feet into her shoes and snatching her dressing gown, she ran out of her room, still shouting.

Sister Hilda came stumbling out of her room, still half-asleep. 'What's wrong?'

'Reverend Mother's office is on fire! Get everyone out of the house as quickly as you can.' A wooden house would burn easily Catherine was sure, especially one so old and warped dry by years of hot summers. Pulling her dressing gown round her, heedless of the fact that everyone would see that her hair was growing, she ran down the stairs and tried to make her way to the office. But although the door was half-open, it showed her such a burning inferno that she knew she would die if she tried to go inside. And in the centre of the inferno she could see a black figure slumped unmoving at a desk ringed in flames.

Even as she heard the first girls coming down the stairs, a ball of flame erupted through the doorway and within seconds the corridor was on fire.

Girls clattered down, their faces lit into grotesque masks by the flames and their shadows jerking wildly along beside them on the wall. Some were sobbing, some silent, and one was screaming until Sister Hilda slapped her.

Catherine couldn't believe a fire would spread so fast!

Someone tugged her arm and Sister Veronica said, 'Where's Reverend Mother?'

'I saw what looked like a body in her office before the flames drove me back. She must be dead.'

Sister Veronica crossed herself and muttered something under her breath.

Catherine pulled her towards the door. 'Come on! You can't stand here.'

'We should go and save what we can from the chapel.'

But with another roar the flames leaped closer to the foot of the stairs and they didn't need telling that they'd be saving nothing and should get outside as quickly as possible.

Mr Powell joined them just as the upstairs balcony caught fire.

'There's nothing we can do, ladies,' he said gruffly. 'Have you counted the girls?'

Sister Hilda nodded. 'Yes. There's only Reverend Mother missing. Sister Catherine thinks she saw her body among the flames.'

He crossed himself and bowed his head for a moment, then looked round. 'You'd better all come down to our house. You should be safe there. I've got Mary and Barney filling buckets and the washtub, in case our roof catches fire.' He looked up. 'Though I don't think it will, unless the wind changes direction.'

But Catherine lingered to watch the fire and then neighbours gathered and she had to talk to them. She knew they were staring at her short hair, an inch long all over her head now, showing it was still a pretty light brown in colour. She had been proud of her hair when she was younger, was starting to be proud of it again for she had stolen glances at it in the girls' mirror.

Someone had already sent for the local volunteer fire brigade, but by the time the horses drawing the pumping engine came to a halt outside, it was too late to save anything.

Father Henson arrived soon afterwards and stared at Catherine. 'Shouldn't you be with the other nuns, Sister?' he asked pointedly. 'And why is

119

your head not shaven? You should cover it out of modesty.'

'I'll join them in a minute. And I have nothing to cover it with.'

'Join them immediately, if you please.'

She breathed deeply, but managed not to shout at him that she was tired of people telling her what to do.

'Where shall we go now, Father?' Sister Hilda asked when the priest came down to the Powells' house.

'The church hall. It's only small, but we can borrow beds and bedding from the parishioners. After that, I don't know yet. As the eldest, you'll be in charge, Sister Hilda.' He looked at them. 'The first thing is to get you all some proper clothes.'

Mrs Powell came in just then. 'I've been sorting through the clothing we keep for the poor. How lucky we store it in the shed! I've found some clothes and sunbonnets for the sisters to wear—just until they can get you something more suitable— and afterwards we'll see what we can find for the girls.'

Catherine was given a threadbare petticoat, a faded blue skirt and a white blouse, plus an old-fashioned sunbonnet to hide her hair. It felt strange to be wearing normal clothes again and she couldn't help running her fingers down the skirt which was a pretty colour still. She felt much cooler in this warm weather and suddenly hated the thought of donning the heavy black habit again.

They walked to the church hall, arriving just as dawn was breaking. It was very small, built recently by volunteers, but there was a separate room where the nuns could sleep and the girls could use the main hall. Parishioners had already started turning up with blankets and food for them.

The girls were a woebegone group, still streaked with smoke and dirt. They clustered together in the hall, looking to the nuns for guidance.

'As soon as you have enough bedding, you must try to get some sleep,' Sister Hilda told them.

One of the overwrought girls burst into tears and Catherine couldn't bear to stand and watch, but went and took her in her arms, making soothing sounds and rocking her slightly.

'Sister Catherine! You forget yourself.'

She turned to look at Sister Hilda. 'The girl needs comforting.'

'Not by you!'

Reluctantly she allowed one of the older girls to take her place.

It was two hours before they had enough bedding and by then it was fully light. The exhausted girls huddled down on the blankets and mattresses that had been brought in and the nuns went into their tiny, claustrophobic little room which had been built to house a kitchen though nothing had yet been installed.

'They'll never sleep,' Catherine said, lingering at the half-open door to watch the girls whispering to one another. 'I don't think I will, either.'

'Then you can just lie down and let others sleep,' Sister Hilda snapped. 'The girls will stay there until they're told to get up.'

With a sigh, Catherine lay down on her own makeshift bed. Soon Sister Hilda was snoring and the other two nuns were breathing deeply.

What now? she wondered. Where would they be sent? And would this allow them to expedite her release from the order?

Somehow she didn't think so. She'd already realised that the church authorities considered it shameful for a nun to renounce her vows.

No, it would be up to her to do something and she had no more excuses for procrastinating.

CHAPTER EIGHT

JANUARY–FEBRUARY 1865

Father Henson came to the little church hall two days after the fire, bringing habits for the four nuns—not quite like their own, but near enough.

'What a relief!' said Sister Hilda in her comfortable voice. 'I've felt bad about wearing these other clothes.'

Catherine looked down at her bright blue skirt. 'I've enjoyed wearing them. They've reminded me of what I'm missing.' She looked at the elderly priest. 'I think I'll keep these on. I'm not entitled to wear a habit because I don't feel like a nun any more.'

The three other women stared at her in shock. 'You can't do that!' Sister Hilda gasped. 'I absolutely forbid it.'

'What will you do, dress me forcibly in a habit?'

'If necessary,' said Sister Hilda, bright red spots burning in her sallow cheeks.

Catherine folded her arms and stared them out, though her heart was thumping in her chest. She still couldn't disobey orders without a great deal of effort and heart searching afterwards.

122

'I will remind you, Sister Catherine,' Father Henson exclaimed, 'that you took vows of obedience to holy rule.'

'My name is Catherine now.' It had, after all, been her own second name once and she felt more like a Catherine than an Eleanor now. She was not going to back down about this because it was more than time to take steps towards a different future. 'I asked to be released from my vows several months ago. Mother Bernadette refused to act quickly so I requested an interview with the Bishop, but she refused to grant me permission for that. I begged *you to* ask the Bishop to see me anyway, Father, and you wouldn't. So you've left me no choice but to take my future into my own hands.'

'I'll see what I can do with the Bishop,' he muttered, 'as long as you give me your word that you'll stay here, not do anything foolish.'

'I'll stay until I hear from you again, but I won't wear a habit any more. Ever.'

After that the other nuns only spoke to her when they had to and the girls whispered in corners, looking at her in shocked fascination. In such close quarters word had soon got out that she was leaving the order.

*   *   *

Two days later Father Henson returned and asked to speak to Catherine alone. 'I've seen the Bishop. He's displeased by your behaviour—very displeased indeed—and has ordered you to go to the Convent of the Little Grey Sisters where you are to stay in seclusion until we hear from your mother house in Ireland. He's concerned for your

123

safety *and* your state of mind—as am I.'

She could see his genuine concern so didn't try to argue with him. The Bishop was probably equally well-meaning. But what they were asking would be purgatory for her. She had gone through her period of doubt and made her decision after much agonising. She didn't intend to waste any more of her life. 'When must I go?'

'You're to return with me now.'

She stared at him in shock, then lowered her eyes to cover the anger that followed it. 'I'll need to pack my things.'

'Do so. I'll wait here.' He smiled encouragingly at her. 'It's for the best, Sister Catherine. You really must allow others with more experience to guide you in such a momentous decision.'

Guide her, indeed! What they wanted was to make her change her mind. Well, she wasn't going to! She went into the crowded bedroom and zigzagged her way through the mattresses laid on the floor to hers at the end. Making sure her sunbonnet was firmly tied to hide her short hair, she dumped her few possessions into a pillowcase for lack of a bag, then found herself still nun enough to feel a need to bow her head and ask forgiveness for what she was about to do.

She left the church hall with the priest, head down as if ashamed, but anger fuelled still higher by his smug expression. So *he* knew best what was right for her, did he? So she was to wait around for months, if not years for a decision, was she? They'd see about that.

Not until he had unhitched his horse and was fully occupied manoeuvring it and the trap back on to the road did she move, running away down the

124

side of the church hall where he couldn't follow in the trap. She ignored his shouts for her to come back. It was years since she had run anywhere and she was soon panting, but something wild was fluttering inside her, joyous, hopeful, reaching out greedily now for freedom.

When she risked a quick glance over her shoulder, the priest was still standing holding the horse and staring after her open-mouthed, with girls and nuns gathering round him, gesticulating. No one was attempting to follow her and thank goodness for that! After years of never even hurrying, she didn't think she could outrun some of those girls.

She rounded the corner and slowed immediately to a rapid walk, not wanting to draw too much attention to herself. She had no money, hardly any possessions, didn't know where she'd be spending the night, and yet she had not felt so exhilarated and happy for a good many years.

It was as if she had come fully back to life again. She was sure her father would be pleased about that.

*   *   *

Ismay waited until Fred Berlow had been gone for two days then put her plan into operation, creeping out of the house as soon as everyone was asleep. Since it was almost a full moon, she planned to keep walking through the night and go into hiding by day. She took some bread and cold meat, and a tin canteen of water which she had prepared the previous day. If they charged her with theft for that, so be it. She was a prisoner here anyway. They

125

might as well lock her in a real jail.

Since it was summer many of the streams wouldn't be running, but there would be some water to be found, she knew that from hearing men talk about their travels. If men could go on the tramp, working here and there, why couldn't she? She was sixteen now, strong enough to cope with most women's work.

It was an eerie world into which she strode and at first she kept jumping in fright as shadows flitted across her path and sounds startled her. To give herself the courage to continue she kept reminding herself that at last she was going to find Mara and mustn't be faint-hearted.

As soon as the sky started to pale she moved off the dusty road, taking great care to hide her tracks, but she marked her trail through the trees in ways she hoped others wouldn't notice. When she found a spring, she sobbed in relief but didn't stay near it once she had filled her canteen.

In the end she huddled down between the roots of a tree and was soon asleep.

When she awoke, she stared round in shock until she remembered where she was. She ate some of her provisions, wishing there were more because she was ravenously hungry, then before it grew fully dark again, she retraced her way to the road, letting out a low groan of relief when she found it. Her biggest fear had been getting lost in the bush. You heard such tales of travellers wandering for days and dying only a few hundred yards away from help.

Again she walked all night, though she was feeling tireder now and had a blister on one foot, which she was trying to ignore. She knew she would

126

have to walk for several nights before she dared try to beg a ride on a cart so kept going doggedly until it grew light again. She had only enough food for one more scant meal and knew it would grow harder after that, travelling on an empty belly. But she would manage. She would do anything to find Mara again.

When she left the road at dawn she didn't find a spring and found to her horror that she was close to a farm. She stayed on the uncleared land nearby, huddling down between some trees but tired though she was, it took her a long time to fall asleep.

A few hours later she woke with a start as someone shook her and looked up into the eyes of their neighbour, Alan Harper. Disappointment slammed through her.

'It was quite easy to find you, Ismay,' he said quietly, indicating the native tracker standing slightly behind him. 'You put yourself in danger for nothing. Come on. You can ride pillion. We'll be back at the Berlows' farm in a few hours.'

She burst into tears and pleaded with him to leave her alone, trying to make him see that she'd go mad if she didn't find her sister again.

'It's a sad situation,' he agreed, 'but you're contracted to work for the Berlows until you're twenty-one and the law will punish you if you try to leave.'

She refused to move and they had to carry her to the horse and then tie her behind him because she tried to throw herself off again, heedless of whether she injured herself or not.

He grew angry at this and, as they set off, demanded, 'What good does this defiance do?'

'What good does keeping me prisoner do? *I* didn't agree to work for the Berlows, I was forced into slavery. And I *will* find another way to escape, you see if I don't.'

When they got back to the farm, the native helped get her down from the horse but the two men had to drag her into the house. It reminded her of the time in Ireland when the priest had done the same thing. She hated men, hated the way they were so much stronger than she was.

Peggy stood waiting at the door, arms akimbo, expression grim. She grasped Ismay's arm as the men thrust her forward, shaking her as she demanded, 'What do you mean by this, young woman?'

Ismay stared at her bleakly. 'You know what I mean by it. And I promise you now: I *will* get away or die in the attempt.'

It made a shiver run through Peggy to see the determination on the girl's face, and the sadness behind it touched her heart, even though she tried not to let it.

'You could have had both of us,' Ismay said, 'Mara and I would have worked willingly for you. But that Mother Superior wanted to separate us and told you lies about me. She's an evil woman, nun or not. They didn't even tell me I'd be going so far away, or that I'd get no wages, or that I'd have to stay here till I was twenty-one. Is that fair? Is it?'

Alan Harper looked at Peggy. 'Is that true? Did she really not know what the contract involved?'

'She says not.'

'It's true,' Ismay said quietly. 'I swear it.'

He stared down at his feet. 'Well, if that's the case I won't go after her again, Peggy. We don't

128

allow slavery in British colonies.'

'She's a minor. The nuns were her guardians.'

'Such guardians are worse than none.' He looked at Ismay. 'But you should remember how dangerous it can be for a young girl travelling on her own. This isn't Ireland. It's an untamed country.'

'I have to find my sister again one day,' she said quietly, 'or die trying.'

Peggy shook her head and pushed the girl into the house.

From then on Ismay did only the work she was told to, never initiating a task herself and always working more slowly than necessary.

But what really made Peggy realise she was beaten was watching the girl picking at her food and staring into the distance like someone not really there. She didn't want to be responsible for anyone dying of heartbreak. When Fred came home again, they'd have to see what they could do. Perhaps once Mara was old enough to leave school, she too could come here to work for them? Why not? That would solve everyone's problem. She said nothing about that to Ismay, however. She'd need to speak to her husband first and they'd have to make sure the old nun didn't stop them reuniting the two sisters.

*　　　*　　　*

Fred Berlow had an uneventful drive to Melbourne. He hesitated as to whether to go to the convent first or purchase the supplies they needed, but decided to go to the convent and get it over with, for he was not looking forward to the coming meeting with the Mother Superior.

As he turned into the street he frowned in puzzlement because something looked different, he couldn't quite work out what. The trees hid what it was until he was almost outside the place where the convent had stood.

'Dear God!' he muttered as he reined in his horses. 'How did this happen?' To his relief he saw the roof of the caretaker's cottage to the rear, still looking whole, so left the horses standing patiently with nosebags on to go and hammer on the door.

'What happened to the convent?' he blurted out as soon as Mrs Powell opened it.

'It burned down two weeks ago.' She stepped outside and pointed to the side of the garden with one floury hand. 'My husband's down there. He'll tell you what happened. I'm in the middle of kneading my bread.'

Owen Powell explained that no one knew how the convent had caught fire. 'The flames spread so quickly we weren't able to do anything. It was just good luck that Sister Catherine was still awake and noticed the fire.'

'Where are they now, then? The sisters and the orphans, I mean? I need to speak to the Mother Superior.'

'They're in the church hall. But I'm afraid Mother Bernadette died in the fire, God rest her soul. We think she might have knocked over a lamp as the remains of one were found on the floor near where the desk stood, next to her charred body.'

'Who's in charge now, then?'

'Sister Hilda—and Father Henson.'

'I'd better go and speak to them, then.'

Fred took off the nosebags and gave the horses

130

some water, then set off again, still shaking his head in amazement at this tragedy.

He found the church hall easily enough and was taken to see Sister Hilda. He didn't waste much time on civilities but said bluntly, 'We have Ismay Michaels working for us and she's anxious for news of her sister. In fact, I have a letter for Mara.' He half-pulled it out of his pocket but stopped when he saw the expression of dismay on the nun's face. 'What's wrong?'

'I'm afraid we don't know where Mara is. All our records were burned in the fire. Perhaps Father Henson will know or the Bishop.'

But neither of them knew anything about the adoption of Mara Michaels, which the Mother Superior must have arranged by herself. They both looked disapproving about this, but it was too late to do anything.

'How am I going to tell Ismay?' Fred asked the priest afterwards as they walked slowly away from the Bishop's residence.

Father Henson could not offer any suggestions.

'That girl is so desperate for news of her sister she's pining away.' He swallowed hard and added in a whisper, 'It was wrong to part them, very wrong. Are you *sure* it wasn't someone from this parish who adopted the girl?'

'Certain. The nuns have a lot of contacts with people in the country. That's how they placed their girls in service. But their records have all been burnt.'

With a heavy heart Fred made the purchases his wife had listed then set off home. If he had felt sorry for Ismay before, he felt doubly sorry for her now and couldn't think how to make this up to her.

Catherine hid in someone's garden until after dark when she made her way back to the grounds of the burned-out convent.

When Mr Powell opened the door he looked at her for a minute, then gestured to her to come inside.

She didn't move, but studied him, trying to assess his mood, prepared to flee again if necessary. 'You said once you'd help me if you could, Mr Powell. I need help now. They want to send me to another convent and if they do, it'll be years before I can leave the order. So . . .' she had to take a deep breath to say it aloud '. . . I'm going to run away. It's not against the law, just against the church's rules. But I have no money and only these clothes. I wondered—you said you'd help. Are there any other clothes left in the poor chest? And—could you lend me some money, just a little, until I can find work? You know I'll pay you back.'

Her words seemed to echo in her own ears and she looked at him, waiting desperately for his answer.

Instead it came from behind him.

'Of course we'll help you.' Gwynneth Powell stepped forward and put an arm round her shoulders. 'My Owen's told me about you and your problem, and I've seen for myself how you didn't fit in. You were always smiling, touching the girls when you didn't think about it, then looking guilty. And that last Mother Superior was sour and spiteful, treated our Barney like an animal, she did, and him as kind and willing a lad in his own way as you'd ever meet.'

Catherine closed her eyes in sheer relief, then opened them to give Gwynneth a tremulous smile. 'I don't know how to thank you.'

'Help someone else in trouble one day. My mam always said kindness should be passed on. Aw, don't cry, *cariad*. Come into the house and we'll work out what you need.' She turned to her husband. 'Owen, you'll not tell anyone she's here.'

'As if I would!'

It was the arm round her shoulders that was Catherine's undoing, someone touching her. She burst into tears and sobbed for a long time against Gwynneth's plump shoulder while Mr Powell and Barney made themselves scarce.

*   *   *

Mara sat quietly on the back veranda, listening to the Hannons arguing. They argued a lot but at least *he* didn't hit his wife as her father had hit her mother. When Barbara—Mara could never think of her as Mama—started sobbing, tears came into the girl's eyes too. It was all her fault. She'd made too much noise when she was playing in the garden and *he* said that sort of thing disgraced them in front of the neighbours.

When he slammed out of the house, she hesitated then went to peep into the parlour. Barbara beckoned to her, trying to hide her tears, but Mara could see traces of them on her cheeks.

She hesitated before asking the question she'd been wanting to ask for a while. 'Why doesn't he like me?'

Barbara's eyes welled with tears. 'Oh, Mara!'

133

But she didn't deny it.

'You should send me back to the nuns. You're not well and the arguments upset you.'

'Do you want to go back?'

'I'd like to stay with *you,* but . . .' The words trailed away. Ismay wasn't at the convent any more, so there was nothing at all for her there now.

'I want you to stay here, dear. I really enjoy your company. Charles is upset about business at the moment. There are a few problems with one of the nearby shopkeepers. When all that settles down, I'm sure he'll stop being so bad-tempered. He was never like this before.'

'I don't mind eating my tea in the kitchen,' Mara volunteered.

The tears welled again. 'I'd wanted us to be a real family again.'

The girl didn't say that Mr Hannon would never feel like family, never, but she saw from Barbara's face that she didn't need to. They both knew it.

'Just eat there for a little while then. I asked Cook and she doesn't mind.'

Mara didn't say that Cook took her tone from the master and treated the newcomer scornfully when the mistress wasn't around.

'We'll have to send you to school soon. You should have gone before now.'

'I've never been to a proper school.'

'Haven't you, dear? How did you learn to read and write, then?'

'Father Cornelius had classes for the village children sometimes. And Ismay helped me with the reading after Arla, who kept the village shop, taught her. Then the nuns gave us some more lessons on the ship and at the convent. I like reading, but I'm not so good at sums.'

'You're a clever girl and read really well.' Barbara's face brightened. 'We'll go out later and buy you a nice story book and I'll help you read it.'

But the outing exhausted Barbara and she had to take to her bed to recover. Mara went to sit quietly in the garden with the new book and stayed there until the maid came to the kitchen door to call her in for tea.

The next day the doctor came to see Mrs Hannon and spent a long time with her husband afterwards. When he left the house he was looking so solemn that Mara took fright. The doctor in Ballymullan had looked just like that when he'd come to see her mother before she died.

As she ate her evening meal she heard Cook and the housemaid whispering together and pretended she couldn't hear what they were saying, but of course she could. *'Not got long for this world, poor soul,'* was what Cook whispered.

In bed that night Mara wept for her benefactress, the woman who was so ready to love her and whom she loved in return. She didn't want such a lovely woman to die and couldn't help worrying about what would happen to her afterwards.

Two days later, Mr Hannon left to go to Melbourne, saying he'd be away only for one night and forbidding them to let their mistress lift a finger.

'You are to fetch and carry for her,' he told Mara. 'It's the least you can do.'

As if she needed telling.

But Barbara spent most of the time staring into space. She usually chatted when they were alone

135

together, but this time she hardly said a word.

*   *   *

Charles reined in his horse with a muttered curse when he saw that the damned convent had burned down. Dismounting, he tied the animal to a section of fence that had somehow survived the fire before making his way down to the back of the garden where the caretaker's cottage still stood.

'What happened?'

Owen Powell found himself explaining yet again to this scowling stranger who had refused to give his name.

'Are the nuns still looking after the orphans?' Charles asked.

'I did hear that they'd sent some of them to another order of nuns and they're trying to find places in service for the older girls. They've kept me on at reduced wages to keep an eye on things here till the Bishop decides what to do with this place.'

Charles let out a growl of exasperation and slipped him a shilling.

'Did you want to see the nuns, sir? Sister Hilda is in charge now. You can find them at the church hall—that's where they're living for the time being.'

Charles shook his head. Given the sudden deterioration in her health, Barbara might have accepted the need to return Mara to the nuns if everything had been all right, but she wouldn't now. Only what the hell was he going to do about the brat once his wife died? He was damned if he was keeping Mara, hadn't wanted her in the first place, had only done it at Barbara's pleading.

136

No one could take the place of his own daughter.

Or of his wife.

He went back to his gig and got up on the driving seat, but didn't move off for quite some time, sitting frowning into space as he contemplated a future without Barbara. Why was he worrying about the brat now, anyway? When his wife was no longer there to defend Mara, he could do what he wanted with her—send her back to the nuns or find someone to employ her. That appealed most of all to him. Get rid of her where he'd never have to see her again, never have to be reminded of how fond his wife had become of a stupid Irish child.

They didn't bother much about a girl's age when they wanted a maid out in the bush. He'd simply find someone to take Mara and hand her over to them.

In the meantime she could make herself useful helping Barbara.

*   *   *

Fred Berlow arrived home from Melbourne one hot day in February. For once he left one of his men to unharness the horses and give them the food and water they had more than earned, and went straight towards the house, thinking once again: *Best get it over with.*

Before he had even reached it, the door was flung open and Ismay stood there, a damp cloth clasped to her bosom. 'Did you see her? Is she all right?'

He sighed. 'Come inside, lass.' Over her head he

137

saw that his wife was also regarding him anxiously.

'Tell me!' Ismay didn't move.

He guided her gently but inexorably inside. 'There was a fire at the convent.' He saw the look of terror on her face and added hurriedly, 'It was after Mara left so she wasn't harmed.'

'Left? Where did she go?'

Peggy pulled her down on a chair by the table and sat beside her. 'Let him finish before you panic.'

'Mara left soon after you did, apparently. A couple wanted to adopt a girl. They'd lost a daughter of the same age, you see, and—'

'Dear heaven, she's fainted clean away.' Peggy grabbed Ismay just in time to stop her falling off the bench.

'There's worse,' he said in a low voice. 'The Mother Superior who arranged Mara's adoption died in the fire, the nuns lost all the records and no one knows where the girl is now. They were people from outside the parish is all the priest knows.'

They roused Ismay and explained what had happened.

'She's alive,' Peggy kept repeating. 'You hold on to that, girl. Your sister is alive and well somewhere. That's the most important thing.'

'We'll take you with us next time we go to Melbourne for supplies,' Fred offered. 'Maybe by then that priest will have found someone who knows where Mara is. Father Henson has promised me he'll keep his eyes and ears open.'

After a few moments' silence Ismay said quietly, 'The only good thing is that *that woman* is dead and won't be able to hurt anyone else as she's hurt us.'

And Peggy didn't contradict her, though she'd

138

never expected to think ill of a nun.

The following morning Ismay got up as normal and went about her work, even though it was a stifling day with an oppressive humidity that had sweat starting on people's brows every time they moved. She said little and they had to bully her into eating.

In the afternoon there was a sudden thunderstorm and Peggy said loudly, 'Well, thank heavens for that!'

Rain pelted down, surrounding the farmhouse with a wall of water.

'We'll go out on the veranda and watch it,' Peggy decided. 'You too, Ismay.'

The rain went on for another few minutes then stopped as suddenly as it had started. As they stood there, enjoying the cooler air, a rainbow arched suddenly across the lower pastures.

As Ismay stared at it, her eyes filled with tears. It was a great soaring arch of colour, a real 'twopenny rainbow'. Surely that meant she would find Mara again one day? It must do.

PART TWO

1865–1867

CHAPTER NINE

FEBRUARY–MARCH 1865

Keara and Theo stood at the rail of the coastal steamer which had become a favourite place for them to chat during their two-week voyage from Western Australia to Melbourne. Behind them their friend Maggie sat beside the cradle of their four-month-old daughter, and both looked drowsy and content.

'For a woman who claims to have no skill with small children, Maggie's coping very well with looking after Nell,' Keara murmured with a smile. She hadn't felt she needed a nursemaid—no one from her village in Ireland had ever had that luxury—but her lover was a gentleman and had insisted on a nursemaid for his child, just as he had assumed that when they settled somewhere permanently they'd have servants. When she protested, Theo told her it was because he wanted her to himself some of the time but she had worried about how she'd deal with servants, she who had been a housemaid herself once. Fortunately, so far they only had a native girl to help at home because servants were hard to find. All the decent housemaids seemed to get married within months, sometimes within mere days, of arriving in Australia.

'I think Mrs Jenner's been giving Maggie lessons.' Theo glanced behind them with an equally fond smile. He had waited so long for a healthy child. The one baby his wife Lavinia had carried to term had lived only a few short months and poor little Richard had ailed the whole time. For many years Theo had been bitterly aware that the money Lavinia had brought him couldn't buy health, heirs or happiness, and had regretted the match his father had forced him into. After little Richard died, he'd arranged to live separately from his wife and hoped never to see her again.

But Nell, his love-child, was thriving, as was this glowing, vibrant woman by his side. Every single day he wished he was free to marry Keara, the girl who'd once been his wife's maid. But he wasn't.

She glanced sideways and nudged him, sighing as he followed her gaze in the other direction. 'Poor Mark looks so lonely. He often stands on his own, staring out across the water. See how sad his expression is.'

'He cheers up when he's with his daughter,' Theo murmured.

She smiled. 'Yes. He's almost as besotted with Amy as you are with Nell.' Then her smile faded and she sighed again.

Theo put his arm round her, realising what that look on her face meant. Mark Gibson wasn't the only one to have a lingering sadness. 'We'll find your sisters, I promise you, my darling.' It was his damned wife who'd sent all three of the Michaels sisters forcibly to Australia, and then Keara on her own to the western side of a continent so vast it took two weeks by coastal steamer to get to the eastern side where the other two sisters were. Even if he weren't searching for the two girls for Keara's sake, he'd be checking that they were all right, out of a need to right the wrongs Lavinia had done from sheer spite. 'Ismay and Mara can't have

144

disappeared into thin air,' he added as Keara's expression remained sad.

She nodded. They both said that to one another regularly and if anyone could find her sisters, it would be Theo, she was sure. He was a very determined man when he wanted something, which was why she was with him now. She hadn't wanted to live in sin, knowing her mother would have been horrified, because although they'd been dirt poor they'd always been respectable. But Theo had come all the way to Australia to find her after Lavinia and her old nurse had had her kidnapped and sent here. He adored their little daughter and being with him felt so right to Keara. She knew he loved her as deeply as she loved him. 'I shall be glad to get to Melbourne. The voyage has been very pleasant, but . . .'

'But you're worried about your sisters?'

She nodded. They must have believed their older sister had known and approved of them being sent away to the other side of the world, when in fact it was Lavinia's doing. That woman had caused so much unhappiness. The thought that they might blame or even hate her haunted Keara's nights and made her wake sometimes with tears on her cheeks.

But at least she and Theo were on their way to find Mara and Ismay now.

*   *   *

Mark watched his two friends for a while then turned back towards the water, wondering why he'd never loved anyone as Theo loved Keara. He'd been fond of his wife, of course he had, but his

145

marriage had been a pale affair compared to the vibrant love these two shared. He sometimes thought he'd married Patience out of sheer loneliness. He'd missed his family so much since he'd come to Australia.

When Patience had died in childbirth, her father had begun trying to take the child. As Alex Jenner was a religious bigot who made his family's lives unbearable, Mark had been determined not to let him near Amy and in the end had run away to Western Australia with his daughter rather than outface the man. Keara and Maggie had worked for him there until Theo arrived to claim his love.

Mark admitted to himself that he was good at running away. He'd fled from England, too, rather than marry the woman he'd got with child there. But he wasn't going to run away from anything ever again, he'd promised himself that. He was not only going back to Melbourne but to Rossall Springs, where he'd briefly been happy. There he hoped to exorcise all the old ghosts before moving on to another small town that needed an eating house and starting up a new business. That was one thing he knew how to do properly, at least, feed people. And his mother-in-law Nan didn't mind where they lived now that her husband was dead, as long as she could look after her beloved grand-daughter.

It had taken him till he was thirty to grow up completely, Mark sometimes felt. If he had grown up now. He hoped he had.

He turned and smiled at Nan as she stopped beside him, holding tightly to Amy's leading reins, as you needed to do on a ship. At two, his daughter was such a lively little imp. 'She's woken up, then?'

'Yes. And had a nice drink of water.' Nan smiled

up at him and reached out to pat his arm. 'Are you all right, love? You look a bit sad.'

He shrugged. 'I was just thinking about what brought us here.'

'You dwell too much on the past, Mark. It's the future that counts. You can't bring the dead back, but you can certainly raise your own daughter to be happy.'

'And try to keep my mother-in-law in order,' he teased.

She gave him a pretend slap. 'Don't be cheeky.'

He gave her a sudden hug. 'You're wonderful, Nan. You can always cheer me up.'

'Well, you cheer me up, too, Mark love.'

*　　　*　　　*

When they arrived in Melbourne Theo whisked them all off to a good hotel. Mark had intended to take Nan and his daughter to a more modest establishment, but Theo insisted on paying for them all because he didn't know Melbourne and needed Mark's help in tracing the nuns.

The very next day Theo ordered a carriage to take him and Mark out to the convent. Keara got up with him and it wasn't until he saw her putting on her hat that he realised she intended to come too.

'Don't you think it'd be better if you stayed here and let me—'

'No. You're not leaving me out of this.' If they were very lucky, they'd find her sisters and she wanted to be there when they did.

But they weren't lucky. She sat staring in horror at the burnt-out convent while Theo and Mark

147

talked to the caretaker. Then she got angry with herself for letting the sight of the devastation upset her and jumped nimbly down from the carriage to join the men.

After Mr Powell had explained what had happened, she had a question of her own. 'Did you meet my sisters, Ismay and Mara?'

'Yes, I did. A fine pair of girls they were, too, devoted to one another.'

She swayed suddenly and Theo put his arm round her.

'Sorry.' She blinked away a tear. 'It's just such a relief to hear that they're safe.'

'We'll go and see the priest next,' Theo decided.

To their horror, no one knew what had happened to Mara, but the priest could at least tell them where Ismay had gone and assure them that he'd seen her employer only a week or two previously. 'She was fretting for her sister, I'm afraid, but otherwise she was well.'

'How soon can we leave for the country, Theo?' Keara demanded as they were driving back into the city.

He was frowning, chewing the side of his lip in a way he had when thinking about a problem.

'Theo?'

'I want you to let me go after them on my own, Keara.'

'No!'

'Be sensible, darlin'. It'll be much quicker if I ride.'

'I'm coming with you. If you try to leave me here, I'll follow you.'

But when she woke the next morning she was sick, so her secret was out and there was no way

148

Theo would let her risk her life and that of their unborn child on a rough journey into the bush. He brought Mark in to back up his arguments and since their friend knew so much more than they did about how rough travelling in the bush could be, she had to give in.

The main thing which convinced her was the thought of how much more quickly the two men could ride to this farm where Ismay was employed—and of course a reluctance to expose Nell to danger. Keara wasn't really worried about her own safety. She was a strong woman and had carried her first child easily, apart from a little nausea in the early stages. She hoped her lover didn't intend to fuss over her this time or the two of them would soon be quarrelling.

'So you'll stay at the hotel, darlin', and behave yourself,' he coaxed.

'It seems I have no choice.'

But then Nell fell ill and the men's departure was delayed for a few days while Theo agonised over his little daughter.

'She's only got a touch of diarrhoea,' Keara insisted.

But he didn't dare leave until the baby was well again.

*   *   *

It was Ismay who saw the huge cart first as it trundled slowly along the track that led to the farm. She rushed to tell Peggy because visitors were so rare that this was quite an event, even shaking her out of her sadness.

By the time the visitors reached the house, Fred

149

had recognised the man sitting beside the driver. 'It's Dan Reddings! I thought the old devil had died. Haven't seen him for two or three years.' He stepped forward, beaming.

Standing in the shade of the veranda, Ismay gasped as the driver reined in his horses and jumped down. 'It's Malachi Firth!'

Peggy glanced at her. 'You know the young fellow?'

'He came out on the ship with us.'

'Well, we'd better go and get that kettle boiling. Dan dearly loves his cups of tea and I dare say your friend won't say no to one, either.'

'What are they doing with all those things?' Ismay pointed to the wagon whose shape was half-hidden beneath the various goods attached to the outside.

'Selling them. It's a travelling shop. I'll be able to buy a few things I need. I do miss having shops nearby.'

Malachi turned to help Dan descend more slowly. The old man walked stiffly towards the veranda, settling down at the table there with a sigh of pleasure while Malachi saw to the horses.

It wasn't till the two women came out of the house again with laden trays that Malachi realised who the girl was. Even then he had to look twice to recognise her. 'Ismay,' he said, stepping forward. 'Is it really you, lass?'

She nodded.

He moved to take the heavy tray from her, setting it down carelessly on the table with one corner sticking off the edge, so that Dan had to give it a push to safety. But like the Berlows,he was watching the two young people who now seemed

150

unaware of the rest of them.

'You've grown so thin. Have you been ill?' Malachi asked gently.

Tears welled in her eyes. 'No. Just—unhappy.' He looked round.

'Where's Mara?'

'They separated us.'

Suddenly she was sobbing and his arms were around her instinctively. With a suspicious glance at his hosts, he guided her along the veranda. 'Tell me.'

He was surprised at how angry he felt at the way she'd been treated. The sight of her looking so wan and dispirited made something inside him clench tightly and want to help her. 'The only consolation is that you know she's not dead,' he said gently.

'That's what I try to tell myself.' Ismay stared out across the paddock, her face setting into grim lines that gave a brief foretaste of what she'd look like as a much older woman. 'I'll find her again one day, though. I swear I will.'

'What's happened to that lass?' Dan demanded when the two young people were out of earshot. 'She looks dragged down by grief.'

Peggy made an irritated sound in her throat and left it to her husband to explain.

'That's a downright shame,' Dan said. 'Eh, to separate two sisters like that, for no good reason. It don't bear thinking of.' They'd separated him from his family when they'd transported him and he'd never seen them again. He'd written, but his wife had never replied and he'd only had one letter from his sister when his mother died. He'd been paying the penalty for theft, but what had that lass done to deserve it?

151

Later, Peggy spent an enjoyable hour or two looking through the stock on the cart with Malachi in close attendance. She made some purchases, more than she'd expected to, but as he said, she wouldn't find anything better in Melbourne and they had a nice range of goods. She invited Ismay to see if there was anything she wanted, knowing the girl had a little money saved.

'No, thank you. I'll manage with what I have. I might need my money. You never know.'

'Don't you try running away again, young woman.'

Ismay didn't answer, just threw her an angry look.

Malachi looked from one to the other but said nothing.

It was taken for granted that the two men would stay the night and share the family's meal so when he found himself sitting opposite Ismay, he tried to cheer her up. And he did rouse her from her lethargy a little with his tales of their travels.

'You've seen a lot of Victoria already. I'd like to travel one day and—' she said, then the words seemed to echo in her brain and she couldn't finish the sentence. She stared at him for a moment then finished lamely '—see more of the country.'

When the meal was over, Dan said, 'Fetch your guitar, lad, and give us all a song.'

'You've still got it?' Ismay asked. 'Oh, I remember so well you playing it on the ship.'

'What *I* remember is that wicked old woman stopping you singing.' He turned to his hosts. 'Ismay has a really beautiful voice but the Mother Superior wouldn't let her join the choir.'

'The old biddy sounds to have been a nasty piece

152

of work to me, nun or not,' Dan said. 'Where's the harm in singing in a choir?'

Malachi brought out the guitar and Ismay went to run her fingertips over the polished wood. As she touched the strings a soft chord shivered through the room. 'I wish I could play.'

Malachi sang several simple folk songs then turned to Ismay. 'Do you still remember "The Last Rose of Summer?"?'

She felt warmth rising in her cheeks. 'Yes, but I'm out of practice.'

'That doesn't matter with a voice as lovely as yours.'

So they sang it together and when they'd finished, Dan wiped a tear from his eye and Peggy stared at Ismay in amazement.

'Why did you never tell us you could sing like that? You used to hum as you worked, but you never sang so—' she waved her arms around searching for words and finished lamely '—so beautifully.'

Ismay shrugged. 'I didn't feel like singing. I was too unhappy.'

'Let's try another,' Malachi said, hating to see the droop returning to her shoulders.

'I don't think I can,' she said in a choked voice, and rushed inside to her bedroom.

He looked at his hosts, who shrugged their shoulders and said nothing. When Dan muttered something about getting some shut-eye, Malachi began to pack away the guitar and took his bedroll round to the back veranda where the two men were to sleep.

Peggy began to clear up, not bothering to call Ismay out to help.

Dan cocked one eye at his host. 'Are you going to keep that girl prisoner here?'

Fred shook his head helplessly. 'What else can we do? We don't know where to begin looking for the sister, and besides, Ismay's contracted to us till she's twenty-one.'

'What crime did she commit to deserve that?'

A sigh was his only answer from Fred.

When he and Malachi were lying together on the veranda, Dan said, 'I know you're awake.'

'So?'

'We can't leave that girl here, eating her heart out.'

'We haven't the right to take her with us, Dan. They'd only come after her and the law would back them up.'

A short time later Ismay crept along the veranda towards them, a white ghost of a figure. 'Can I speak to you, Malachi?'

He sat up and Dan rolled over to watch them. She was beautiful in the moonlight, her dark hair curling gently down over her shoulders against the white of the simple cotton nightgown, with a faded shawl round her shoulders.

'You shouldn't be out here dressed like that.'

She looked down at herself and pulled a face. 'What does that matter? Malachi, when you leave tomorrow will you take me with you? I could creep out after dark tomorrow night and catch up with you before dawn if you'll tell me where you're going.'

So he repeated what he had told Dan. 'Ismay, it wouldn't do any good. They'll just come after you. You're legally bound to them till you're twenty-one.'

154

She tried and failed to hold back a sob. 'Well, I'm not staying here. *I'm not!* I'll keep running away till they stop chasing me. They sent a neighbour with a native tracker after me last time, but when he found out how I'd been brought here against my will, he said it wasn't fair and told them he wouldn't come after me again. So if I came with you, I'm sure I'd get away.'

Dan looked from one to the other but said nothing. He'd have taken the girl with them like a shot, but his partner was over-fussy about doing things properly and obeying the law.

She waited but Malachi remained stubbornly silent. *'Oh, please* take me with you! I'll work hard, help you, do anything you like. When we were talking I suddenly realised that if I could travel with you, I'd see lots of places and that'd give me my best chance of finding Mara again. I promise you wouldn't regret taking me.'

When nothing she said would persuade him to change his mind, she began to unbutton her nightdress.

'What the hell are you doing?' He threw back the blanket and stood up hastily.

Dan hid a grin and stayed out of it.

'I'll give myself to you if you'll only let me come,' she whispered. 'I'll let you do anything you like. Please, Malachi.'

Shocked at his own body's reaction to the slender beauty of hers, he reached out and pulled her nightdress together again with an angry gesture. 'Fasten this at once! I don't want your body. What sort of man do you think I am?' As tears welled in her eyes, he added desperately, 'Ismay, we *can't* take you with us, but I will keep my

155

eyes open for Mara, I promise, and—'

But with a sob she had run off into the night.

'You should've agreed to take her,' Dan said from behind him.

Malachi swung round. 'How can I?'

'Easy. If you married her, no one would worry at all.'

'Marry her! You must be mad! She's only sixteen and I'm barely twenty-one.'

'Old enough to wed. And she's bonny, too, or would be if she weren't so unhappy.'

'You haven't been sneaking a drink of rum, have you?'

'No. And it's you who's mad not to consider what I've suggested seriously. Decent lasses are scarce here in Australia. Pretty lasses with voices like that are even scarcer. Think how folk would pay to hear you two sing. We'd double our earnings.'

'As if I'd take her for that reason!'

'It's not the only reason. You can't deny you care about her. I've seen the way you are with her. You told me yourself you were upset at how thin she'd grown.' After a pause, he added slyly, 'What reason would you take her for, then?'

'None! It's just—not possible. The last thing I intend to do is marry. You're tied down with a wife and then the babies start coming and it gets worse. I'm not marrying anyone till I've the money to look after a family properly.'

'Then more fool you. I married a good lass and my biggest regret in life is how badly I treated her. I let her down. Don't let this one down.' He played his last card. 'If someone doesn't help her, she'll pine away.'

156

But Malachi still shook his head. Much as he wanted to do something to help Ismay, he had to be sensible.

CHAPTER TEN

MARCH 1865

Catherine looked down at the metal band on her finger—not gold, but some cheap imitation. To the world it marked her out as a married woman, now widowed, but to herself it marked her out as a liar. Only what choice did she have? She stared at herself in the broken fragment of a larger mirror, which was the only looking glass the Powells had, and her solemn face stared back, wisps of reddish-brown hair showing under the bonnet, blue-grey eyes looking apprehensive. It seemed a stranger's face after her years without mirrors for it had changed so much, not only grown older but sadder too.

Another lie would explain both the short hair and her husband's death. She and Mrs Powell had worked it all out together. A fever had killed her husband and nearly killed her so the doctor had cut off her hair to stop it draining her strength. She crossed herself and muttered a quick prayer for forgiveness at the thought of this extra falsehood, then grew angry with herself. She had to stop crossing herself, except in church, but she kept forgetting. She shouldn't do it even there, probably, because she didn't think she'd dare attend a Catholic place of worship for fear of someone recognising her.

She turned and spread her arms wide as Gwynneth Powell came back in. 'How do I look?'

'Respectable but poor, which is what we want. Are you ready?'

'Yes.' Squaring her shoulders she followed Gwynneth outside. They walked only a few streets, but her nerves were on edge the whole time in case someone recognised her.

The house looked well-maintained though no larger than its neighbours, and when Gwynneth knocked on the front door it was opened by the mistress herself, who beamed at the sight of her friend.

'Nesta love, I found someone to help your sister.' Gwynneth lowered her voice. 'If I can just have a word privately?'

They left Catherine on the front veranda while Gwynneth explained about her 'second cousin' being widowed and then falling ill herself, so that 'the poor thing' was now destitute with almost no possessions left after selling them to buy food.

'Proper shame that, isn't it?' Nesta said. 'But it'll be a godsend for our Olwen. She's not been well all year and I don't think that second husband of hers understands how hard it can be for women of that age. I didn't take to him anyway, but what's done is done. Your cousin will have to work hard, mind.'

'She's a hard worker, Katie is. Better educated than the rest of the family, too. Her mother was a governess, see.'

'She's not too proud to do menial work, though?' It came out sharply.

'The only thing she's too proud to do is take charity.'

158

'I'd be exactly the same. I'll have a quick word with her, though the fact that she's your cousin is enough for me, really.'

'She'll only agree to three months' work, mind, with a half-day off each week. She wants time to get on her feet a bit before she takes anything permanent.'

'Not even a year?'

'No. Sorry. She might stay on a bit longer, though, if she's happy there.'

This cursory interview resulted in plans for 'Katie' to leave in a few days' time for the small settlement in the country about fifteen miles away from a town called Rossall Springs. In Welbin, she would work as general maid to Olwen Bevan.

The evening before she left Catherine thanked the Powells with tears in her eyes. 'I can't tell you how grateful I am for all you've done. Be sure you'll be in my prayers from now on and one day I'll pay you back, I promise.' She knew how short of money they were with Mr Powell on reduced wages after the fire, and yet they'd still found a little to share with her.

Gwynneth waved one hand dismissively. 'We don't want money from you. We have some saved so you don't need to worry about us.' After a moment's hesitation, she gave Catherine a cracking hug. 'If this doesn't work out, you can always come back to us, mind! I've met Nesta's sister and she's a nice woman, though not very strong, but I haven't met the second husband. Her first died two years ago and she remarried quite quickly. Well, when you're left with a farm you need a man to run it, don't you? Anyway, if things don't work out, remember that three months is all you've agreed to

159

work for. And you be sure you stick up for your rights. Some folk try to work their servants all the hours there are and that's not fair.'

Catherine nodded, but knew she'd only come back if she were utterly desperate. She intended to manage on her own from now on, becoming 'Katie' in every way possible, working hard and saving her money. And surely if she lived in the country she wouldn't meet anyone she had known in her former life? Though Gwynneth Powell insisted that no one would recognise her without her nun's habit, especially once her hair had grown.

*   *   *

In the morning Malachi and Dan were ready to leave just after dawn. Ismay came out on the veranda and stood there, her eyes pleading with them to take her.

Malachi tried to ignore her but began to feel guilty and before they set off he went across to say softly, 'It wouldn't work, you coming with us, but I will keep my eyes open for Mara, I promise. Dan and I'll be back in a few months so look after yourself till then. It'll do no good to anyone, least of all Mara, if you pine away.'

She swung round and went into the house, to refuse breakfast. When Peggy urged her to be sensible, she burst into tears.

'What are we going to do with you, girl? You can't go on like this.'

'You can let me leave, that's what you can do.' Her sobbing redoubled.

'It'd be like looking for a pin in a forest searching for your sister. You'd not even know where to begin. And anyway, you're needed here.'

But Peggy didn't say that with as much conviction as previously. How could she when she saw Ismay looking unhappy all the time? She wasn't a cruel woman and if there'd been any chance of finding the other sister, she would not only have given the girl permission to leave but sent Fred with her to make sure she didn't come to any harm. It was a hard world, as Peggy herself had discovered when young. She'd been lucky to find a husband like Fred and that's what this girl needed, too. Since Ismay had lost the rest of her family she needed a husband to look after her, someone of her own to take her thoughts from those she had lost.

Peggy grew thoughtful. That Malachi would make a good husband for any girl because he was hard-working and clever. He seemed fond of Ismay, too. A smile crept over her plump features. He was coming back in a few months and it'd do no harm to try a little nudging with the pair of them. Sometimes folk didn't know what was best for them till you showed them, especially young men of marriageable age.

*   *   *

As the big cart trundled along, Dan said loudly. 'Some of you young fellows don't have the sense you were born with.'

'Mind your own business, old man.'

'How can I when I see a lass as unhappy as that one? We could easy have brought her with us. She'd have fitted in well.'

'Look, it's not my fault she's unhappy and what

161

good would it do her to drive round the country districts with us? Mara could be anywhere by now—in Sydney or Perth, even.'

'Just looking would give Ismay hope. She needs that or she's going to fade away and die. Must have loved that sister of hers very much.'

Malachi remembered the two of them and his voice softened. 'Aye, she did. Everyone on the ship commented on how close they were. Did your heart good to see them.'

'There you are, then.'

'She's still not our responsibility.' He remembered the pain on Ismay's face and guilt speared through him, but he pushed it aside. He wouldn't *let* Dan make him feel guilty. He'd nothing to be guilty about. He wasn't the one who'd been so cruel to her after all.

They drove along in silence and for once Dan didn't gossip. But however hard Malachi tried to keep his thoughts busy, they kept going back to Ismay and he wondered what would become of her. He *would* definitely keep an eye open for Mara everywhere they went, and ask after her. That at least he could do.

But he doubted he'd find her. It was a big country, most of it uncharted even after eighty or so years of settlement. People disappeared all the time.

*   *   *

As soon as everyone was in bed, Ismay crept out of the house and set off after the cart, her expression grimly determined. A half-moon guided her footsteps for the first mile or two before it set, but

162

her eyes were accustomed to the dark by then, so she carried on walking. And she didn't fall very often.

The only way they'd stop her running away, she vowed, would be to chain her down. If this attempt failed, she'd try again and then again until she succeeded. And one day she'd find Mara. She had to believe that.

It seemed a very long night and she wished she'd brought some food and water. But she'd been terrified of making a noise in the kitchen, so had simply climbed out of her bedroom window on to the veranda and slipped away.

The most important thing now was to catch up with Malachi and Dan before they set off again in the morning. Surely if she did, he'd not refuse to take her with them? Dan was on her side, she could tell. But even if she didn't catch them up, she'd keep going somehow. She had to.

If only her head didn't ache so. She should have eaten her tea and supper. She had to start thinking more clearly, being practical. Weeping did no good. It was action that was needed. She was giving in to her miseries and that wouldn't do.

*   *   *

As dawn was breaking Malachi got up and stretched, yawning and making little grunting noises as he eased his body into action. He blew some life into the embers of the fire and poked a few twigs and dry leaves into the faint glow. You could usually get it burning again quite easily and a pot of tea made a good start to the day.

He glanced towards the horses, saw they were all

163

right, then went to relieve himself behind some trees. When he went to give the horses a drink, however, he saw a figure lying on the ground just beyond them. He stopped short, realised it was a woman and ran forward.

It was Ismay! Eh, she must have walked all night. Why the hell hadn't she woken them up when she arrived? Why had she just lain down there on the damp ground? Well, if she'd go to this length to look for her sister, she might get herself into real trouble and he didn't even like to think of that. They'd have to let her ride with them. The decision had been taken for him.

He went to shake her awake and tell her she'd won, but he couldn't rouse her. She groaned and murmured something under her breath. He couldn't understand what she was saying so shook her again, but she still didn't open her eyes. She looked flushed and when he felt it, her forehead was burning hot.

He swung her up into his arms, amazed at how light she was, and as he carried her over to the wagon he called, 'Wake up, old man. *Wake up, dammit!* I need some help.'

Dan crawled out from his blankets, blinking in shock at this rude awakening. But when he saw the limp figure in Malachi's arms and realised that Ismay was unconscious not asleep, he too began to worry. 'Wrap her in a blanket, lad. She's shivering and we've got to get her warm again.'

'She was burning hot a minute ago.'

'It's a fever, then!' He gently brushed her hair off her face. 'Eh, look how thin her arm is! She's not been eating properly for a long time, if you ask me. We mun feed her up a bit.' He risked a quick

164

glance sideways as he added, 'Brave lass, isn't she?'

'Pig stubborn, I'd call it.'

'You're not going to send her back, though?'

No answer.

Hiding a grin, Dan set about making some tea, fetching a brand-new pint pot from the stock and thinking: *That'll be hers from now on.*

But although Ismay did rouse enough to recognise Malachi and murmur, 'Thank goodness!' she didn't seem capable of stringing any other words together and soon closed her eyes again.

'I don't like the looks of her,' Dan said frankly. 'She's not at all well.'

They set about making her comfortable with a makeshift bed on the floor of the wagon. When she began to sweat and mutter, 'Too hot!' they tried to drip water into her mouth and wiped her face with a damp cloth.

Nothing seemed to help. One minute she was delirious and trying to throw off her covers, speaking gibberish in which the only recognisable word was 'Mara'. A few minutes later she was shivering and huddling down under the blankets, moaning.

'What are we going to do?' Malachi whispered an hour later when nothing seemed to have helped. He looked down: her hair was damp with sweat, her skin flushed, and her body was so thin you could see the bones beneath the delicate skin. 'How did she find the strength to catch up with us?' he wondered yet again. 'She must have walked all night long.'

'Desperation.'

Dan went back to the fire and stood frowning down at it for a few moments, then looked sideways at Malachi. 'I know a fellow as lives round here—well, he does if he's still alive. Jack's half-native and that isn't his real name, but I can't get my tongue around that. He's a good bloke for all he's a bit dark. His wife's a native too, one of their healers. They call her Wilya. She doctored me once when no one expected me to live. Saved my life, she did. I usually stop by to see them and let them have a few things—well, I do when I'm on my own. But they prefer to keep themselves to themselves and I thought you wouldn't want to see them. Now . . . well, mebbe the wife can help Ismay.'

'Why should I not want to see them if they're friends of yours?'

'I told you: they're *black.* Some folk treat the natives bad, but I don't reckon they're much different from you or me.' Another pause, then, 'If I take you to see them, you mun promise not to tell anyone where they live.'

'Is that necessary?'

'Aye, it is. There are some sods as kill black folk for sport.' He spat to one side to show what he thought of that. 'Same sort of buggers as like to torment convicts, I reckon, an' I know what that feels like, by hell I do.'

'Well, I'm not that sort of person and if you think this woman really can help Ismay . . .' Malachi cast another anxious glance at her,

'If anyone can, it's Wilya. But we'll have to hide our tracks when we leave the road. Don't want passers-by turning off and stealing what little my friends do have.' He grinned, then added, 'Besides, it's my land and my hut they live in, so that's another reason to protect it.'

'Yours?'

166

'Aye. When they gave me my ticket of leave, I worked hard and fell a bit lucky so later I bought some land off a fellow as wanted to go back to England. I'd thought to live out here, away from folk as looked down on me, but when it come to it, I didn't like it. Too lonely and I'm a chap as likes company. But if I keep the place occupied, well, one day I might be able to sell it. An' if I die afore then, it'll be yours.'

'You can't give it to me!'

'Why not?'

'Because I'm not a relative. You hardly know me. You must have some family left in England.'

'I don't even know if I have. They said they never wanted to see me again, only wrote once when Mam died. Terrible respectable, my family.'

'You should have got married, then, Dan, made a new family for yourself.'

'I were married already. Even if I didn't know where she was, even if she didn't want to see me again, I never wanted another wife than my Pam. No, I never did. I didn't do right by her, got in with a bad crowd, but I still thought the world of her.' After a pause, he added, 'I'd better get it written down proper that you're to have everything if I die, though. I'll do that next time we're in Melbourne. We don't want anyone cheating you.'

Malachi didn't know what to say to that. 'We'd better load up, then. I'll ride in the back and keep an eye on her. You drive.' The only way he could fit into the loaded wagon was to sit with Ismay's head on his lap and he found himself stroking her cheek, patting her hand, anything to soothe her. And for some reason it worked.

'I reckon she knows and trusts you, even through

167

the fever,' Dan observed at one point.

Malachi didn't reply, not wanting to encourage him to pursue that point.

They turned off the road an hour later and after about fifty yards Dan drew to a halt.

'Why are you stopping?'

'To hide our tracks. You'll have to do it, though. I'm noan so nimble these days. Go and stamp on them ruts we made turning off, an' then use this piece of wood to make the ruts look as if they go on with the rest.'

'Is this really necessary?'

'Aye, it is. After you've flattened the ruts, go back and scatter some of them fallen leaves over the ground, too. A native tracker would still find us easy, but most white folk won't notice owt.'

By the time Malachi swung up into the wagon again, Ismay had tossed the covers off. He dampened the cloth and used it to wipe her face, talking to her in a low voice. Once more she calmed down.

Dan chuckled. 'See. She knows you. You should definitely wed her.'

'Will you shut up about that, old man!'

After jolting through the woods along a faint track, they drew up at a small slab hut with a bark roof. There was smoke rising from a cooking fire to one side, with a small cauldron still hanging over the flames and emitting a savoury smell, but there was no sign of anyone.

'Don't get down yet,' Dan whispered to Malachi. 'They'll come out in a minute when they see who it is.' He cupped his hands to his mouth and yelled, 'Hoy, Jack lad! It's only me. I've getten mysen a new wagon and partner.'

A couple of minutes later a tall, thin man with coffee-coloured skin and a tousled mass of greying hair stepped out from behind some trees and came across to the wagon. He reached up to clasp Dan's hand in the European manner, then allowed him to introduce Malachi.

'Your wife around?' Dan asked. 'Got a sick woman here who needs help.'

A woman followed Jack, shorter and much darker-skinned. She was wearing a ragged skirt and bodice but her feet were bare. With the merest nod to Dan, she went round to the rear of the wagon, climbed lightly up the step and studied Ismay, bending to feel her forehead. Muttering something to her husband in her own language, she got down and hurried off into the forest.

'She's gone to gather some plants,' Jack said. 'Wants us to take the girl into the house.'

Malachi looked at Dan. 'You're sure about this woman?'

'Aye. I'd trust Wilya with my life. She's allus clean, too, unlike that sod as called hissen the prison surgeon. Filthy, drunken devil that one was, killed more folk than he cured.' He spat to emphasise his disgust.

Malachi picked Ismay up gently, looking down at the pale face resting against his chest. Eh, she had been so bonny but now she looked like a skull, with damp hair plastered against her sweaty skin.

The house was so spotlessly clean it surprised him, then he felt ashamed for assuming that natives would be dirty. There was a strong smell of eucalyptus leaves—a clean, pleasant sort of smell. When the native healer came in, she was carrying some branches and plants, and immediately

169

gestured to the men to leave.

'They don't like men seeing women's business,' Dan muttered and gave the younger man a push. 'Come on, lad. Out of here.'

Malachi busied himself making camp, then fidgeted around, wondering what was happening inside the house. Once or twice the woman came to the door and passed them a bucket, asking for more water.

Dan and the Aboriginal man sat and smoked peacefully. A little later their host gave them some of the savoury kangaroo stew which had herbs in it that Malachi didn't recognise but which tasted good. He and Dan supplied some bread which Mrs Berlow had given them.

'Should we go and check on Ismay?' he asked Dan as the moon rose.

'Nay, Wilya will let us know if she wants owt. Leave her to do her work.'

In the end they went to bed with nothing resolved. Malachi slept badly and every time he looked towards the house he could see that the lamp was still burning. So he reckoned Wilya wasn't sleeping too well, either.

He hoped Dan was right and this woman was a good healer. Ismay couldn't die, she just couldn't!

*   *   *

It took Theo and Mark four long, hard days' riding to get to the Berlows' farm because summer was coming to an end and the roads were starting to get muddy. Heavy rain fell throughout the second day, soaking them to the skin. They were rewarded with a few tantalising glimpses of the sun the morning

170

after that, then it clouded over and more rain fell.

The men were as exhausted as the horses, because although they'd found shelter with a farmer and his family on the first night, they'd pushed on till darkness fell on the second day and had had to camp out. The rain had woken them several times.

'I must be getting soft in my old age,' Theo complained as they huddled under a large tree for shelter. Water dripped down on them and although they had groundsheets, it was impossible to stay dry or sleep properly.

'This reminds me of the goldfields,' Mark said as he felt under his groundsheet to pull out yet another rock, only to find it far smaller than he had expected. 'Discomfort piled on discomfort.'

'But you found gold?'

'Just a moderate amount till we found a big nugget—and I lost that within the day. My partner hit me over the head and stole it, but it didn't do him much good, either, because someone murdered him for it. After that I went back to my old trade and shall do so again once everything's settled.' Only this time he wanted to run somewhere he could offer people overnight lodgings as well as meals. He knew from experience that good, comfortable accommodation wasn't easy to find. Out in the bush most families took in travellers passing through, but in small country towns folk had to accept what accommodation there was. 'Are you really going to settle permanently in Australia?'

'I hope so,' Theo admitted. 'Especially the way things are between me and Keara. I've bought land near my cousin Caley and we're breeding horses

171

together. He's overseeing my place while I'm away. What worries me is: if we can't find her sisters, I don't think Keara will agree to leave Victoria—and she can be an extremely stubborn woman.'

'Brothers and sisters can be very close. You missed something not having any.'

'I have a half-brother, Dick, but I only found out we were related a year or two ago. He's helping to mind the estate in Ballymullan until I decide whether to sell it.'

'I have eight brothers and sisters, and I really miss my family.' Mark stared blindly into the distance, thinking of them and wishing he could go back for a visit. At least he was in touch with them now, though their letters were following him around Australia and taking a while to catch up with him.

He loved Australia, but you paid a heavy price for going so far away from your family, as he'd found to his cost.

*   *   *

As daylight began to fade on the fourth afternoon Theo and Mark arrived in the small settlement of Upley and were directed onwards to the Berlows' farm, arriving just as the first stars began to twinkle down from a now cloudless sky.

Dogs began to bark and a man came to the door with a shotgun in his hand. 'Who are you?'

'Theo Mullane, looking for the Berlows.'

'What for? I'm Fred Berlow and I've never heard of you.'

'I'm Ismay's brother-in-law.'

Silence, then: 'Come forward where we can see

172

you. Who's your companion?'

When Fred was satisfied that they were respectable travellers, he called for one of his farm hands to come and stable his guests' horses then invited them into the house.

Theo looked round eagerly, expecting to see Ismay, but there was only Mrs Berlow who was bustling about getting them some food. 'Is Ismay not here?'

Fred came back in time to hear this and gestured to the table. 'Sit down and I'll tell you what's happened. You've only missed her by a few days.'

'Missed her?'

'Yes. She ran away.'

After a moment's shocked silence, Theo burst out, 'And you didn't go after her?'

'Of course I did. What sort of fellow do you think I am? But there was no sign of her.'

*   *   *

Mara gradually became Barbara Hannon's nurse, fetching and carrying for her, even helping her with intimate tasks.

'You don't mind doing all this, do you?' Barbara said wonderingly.

'Me and Ismay helped our Mam when she was ill. Why should I mind? You've been kind to me. I'm happy to help you.'

'Well, today I want you to fetch me a pen and paper. You know where they're kept. It's time I wrote a letter to my friend.'

The effort exhausted Barbara and as the days passed she seemed on edge, asking every day if there wasn't a reply for her. When it finally arrived over a week later than expected, Mara carried it along to the bedroom, pleased to see the thin face brighten at the sight of the envelope.

'Don't tell Charles about this, dear. It's a secret. You go out and play for a while now while I read it.'

She was very thoughtful for the rest of the day.

The next morning she wrote another letter and sent Mara off to post it secretly.

The child didn't question any of this. She knew Mr Hannon could be very bad-tempered and her only concern was to keep Barbara happy, so if that meant hiding things from him, she'd do it.

Two days later, Barbara patted the bed and when Mara was sitting beside her said quietly, 'When I die—'

Mara stared at her in dismay and couldn't help bursting into tears.

'Come now, dear, shh. We both know I won't get better and I'm concerned about what'll happen to you —afterwards. So listen carefully. When I die, this is what you are to do . . .'

CHAPTER ELEVEN

LATE MARCH 1865

The two men were offered beds in the barn, but in spite of the comfort of a pile of hay and shelter from the weather, Theo slept badly, lying awake worrying about Ismay. Why had she run away to follow a couple of itinerant traders? Was it really in the vague hope of finding her little sister or was there some other reason?

The thought of what might happen to her travelling on her own made him shudder. The Australian countryside was so different from Ireland. He'd discovered that already for himself, both back in Western Australia and over here in Victoria. Mark's tales of gold mining had only reinforced the evidence of his own eyes. This was not a soft country, but a harsh and magnificent land.

Hell, to miss Ismay by only a couple of days! It was so unfair. He dreaded telling Keara of how close they'd come to finding her. And Mara could be anywhere now, anywhere at all. It was so foolish to rush around searching for her blindly. Ismay might pass within a mile of her sister and not even know it.

And he might never find either of them!

Well, he'd give the search for Keara's sisters the best effort he could, but afterwards, whatever the outcome, he'd settle down again. He gave a wry smile. He wasn't ambitious to win a great fortune for himself, just to earn a decent living and enjoy raising his family. This trip had given him plenty of thinking time and he'd decided to sell his small estate in Ireland, because all that he loved was here: Keara, his little daughter, his cousins and some grand horses to breed.

He'd leave his estranged wife living in Lancashire with Nancy, her old nurse, and hoped he'd never see Lavinia again.

He tossed around and couldn't seem to get to sleep. Even after this short time apart he was missing Keara greatly for she was like the other half of him. He had never realised before that a woman could be a friend as well as a lover. He ought to be with her at this time, looking after her and his unborn child, not wandering round the countryside on a wild goose chase.

The thought of the new baby that was growing in her belly brought a fleeting smile to his face as he lay there watching dawn slowly brighten the sky and listening to Mark's even breathing.

In the morning, Mrs Berlow provided a hearty breakfast then Fred rode out with the two men because he knew where the traders had been heading. He'd already searched this road, but it was obvious the others wouldn't be satisfied unless they searched it themselves. But after several days of hard riding and hunting everywhere that the travelling shop might have gone, it became clear that Dan Reddings must have changed his plans. He definitely hadn't arrived at the settlement he'd spoken of as their next destination and although a couple of people had seen him and his wagon the day he'd set off from the Berlows' farm, no other sighting had been reported, not a single one.

After a while, even Theo admitted defeat and the two men set off back to Melbourne.

'How could a big wagon full of goods simply disappear like that?' he asked yet again as they rode along.

'People and wagons disappear regularly in Australia,' Mark replied sombrely. 'Sometimes on purpose, sometimes because people die out in the bush and no one finds them again. I heard of one sad case where the driver died and the horses couldn't get free, so pulled the wagon along until an axle broke. Then they had to stay where they were and the poor things died in harness. No one

176

found them for months.'

When his friend made no response to this gloomy tale, he prompted, 'What are you going to do next?'

Theo had already thought about this. 'I'll have posters printed and distributed far and wide, offering a reward for anyone who can help us find the girls. I'll see if the police can help me trace them and I'll speak to that parish priest again. Any other suggestions?'

Mark shook his head. A little later he said, 'If you do go back to Western Australia, you can leave word with the police to contact me. You know I'll do anything I can to help.'

But he didn't feel optimistic.

*   *   *

In Melbourne Keara listened to what the men had to tell her, then burst into tears. 'How can we get so close, then lose her?'

'It's hard luck,' Theo agreed. 'But at least we know she's alive.'

She sobbed a little longer then wiped her eyes determinedly. 'What next? There must be something else we can do.'

'I thought of getting some posters printed and offering a decent reward for anyone finding your sisters.'

She squeezed his hand gratefully. 'Yes. Yes, we can do that, can't we? Oh, if only I had a photograph of them!'

'Well, I was thinking—if we got an artist in, maybe he could draw portraits of them based on you. You all three look so much alike. That should give us a better chance of finding them.'

In bed that night, she nestled against him and sighed. 'What will we do after we've tried everything, Theo?'

'I don't know. We'll decide that together. But we won't give up hope yet.'

She reached out to stroke his cheek. 'You want to settle permanently over there in the west, don't you?'

'Yes, my darling, you know I do. But only as long as you're with me. I'd settle on the moon itself if you wanted to go there.'

'Oh, Theo.' She snuggled up closer. 'Once we've tried everything we can think, we'll go back to Western Australia. But—not yet, please?'

'Of course not. We won't leave until we find them or you're sure we've done everything we can.'

She put her arm round him and sighed. 'I can't stay awake any longer. I was never so sleepy when I was carrying Nell. Perhaps this one's a boy.'

He closed his eyes and prayed briefly that she was right. He was getting greedy now, greedy for both sons and daughters, he who'd once have sold his soul for one healthy child of either sex.

*   *   *

Ismay became aware of feeling warm and comfortable. She opened her eyes slowly to see a woman bending over her, a woman with brown skin and eyes so dark they seemed like deep caverns. Yet in their depths lay peace and kindness, she knew that instinctively and was not afraid.

'You been ill. You need to rest and eat good tucker. 'Ere.'

178

Her accent was different from anything Ismay had heard before and she guessed that English was a foreign language for her. She ate what tasted like a strong meat soup, which was spooned carefully into her mouth. It was good, but after only a few spoonfuls, the woman stopped.

'Not too much at first. You sleep again now, eh?'

Ismay wasn't aware of how much time passed, but she seemed to wake only to take some more soup, drink an astringent herbal brew or relieve herself. Each time she couldn't wait to sink back into that deep, restful sleep.

Then one day she woke fully to find her clothes laid out beside her, washed and ready to wear. When she got up she felt weak but her head no longer spun and best of all she felt more hopeful about the future.

The woman returned as she was finishing dressing.

'Good. You're up. Your fellow, 'e's worryin' 'bout you.'

'My fellow?'

'Malachi. 'E's a good man. Make a good 'usband.'

'He's just a friend,' Ismay protested, blushing.

The woman gave her a knowing smile and led the way outside.

Malachi rushed over to Ismay as soon as she appeared in the doorway and put his arm round her shoulders. 'Are you all right? Wilya wouldn't let us in to see you.'

'Women's healing,' the dark-skinned woman told him severely, 'is not men's business.'

'I'm a lot better and I feel more optimistic somehow,' Ismay said. 'How long have I been ill?'

179

'Over a week.'

She stared at him in shock.

Dan ambled over to join them. 'Nice to see you with some colour in your cheeks again, lass.'

'Have I kept you here for a whole week? I'm so sorry!'

'We wanted you to get better. But Wilya told us last night that we could leave today so we got everything ready to go.' He turned to gesture towards the wagon.

Ismay turned to the healer. 'I can't thank you enough.'

'No need. But don't give in to grief. Watch out for them rainbows. You'll find your sisters again one day.'

'I only have one sister now,' Ismay corrected.

'You got two. And you'll find 'em both.'

The woman was gone before she could protest.

'She's like that, Wilya,' Dan said. 'Helps you when you need it, then gets on with her own business. She's a good healer, though. Saw me right once when I thought I was done for.'

'Let's get you up on the wagon then, Ismay,' Malachi said. 'Dan reckons we can reach the next settlement before nightfall.'

But they didn't manage that. A chance stop at a lonely farm allowed them to sell some goods and they decided to stay there overnight because Ismay was looking exhausted, in spite of dozing on a blanket in the back as they drove along.

*   *   *

There were few railways yet in Australia so Catherine travelled by stage coach to the small

180

town of Rossall Springs, which was the nearest staging post to her new employers' farm and a few hours' drive north-west of Melbourne. A letter had already been sent by Mrs Powell's friend, telling her sister to expect her, and although there had been no reply, they assured her that the Bevans would be there to meet her.

She had to hope they were right.

She studied the countryside they were passing through with great interest, amazed at how few towns there were once they'd left Melbourne, especially after they turned off the main highway to Ballarat. They stopped occasionally at settlements consisting of only a few houses to deliver parcels or pick them up, once to put down another passenger.

Rossall Springs was larger than most of the places they'd passed through, but very unlike an English or Irish country town. Indeed, it seemed more like a village to Catherine, and would have been considered one in Lancashire because there couldn't have been more than a few hundred people living there, if that. As in most Australian country towns, there was a central street lined with shops and businesses, and not much else. This street rose slightly at one end, curving round to the right so that a narrower street running off it formed a Y-shape. There were a few short lanes or alleys leading off those two thoroughfares.

A man and woman were waiting for her at the livery stables where the coach stopped. He was of medium height with grizzled hair. As he stepped forward, his eyes raked her face and body in a way she found impertinent. She had forgotten how some men looked at you because of course that sort of thing had stopped once she became a nun.

'Katie Caldwell?' His voice had a rasping tone to it.

'Yes.'

The woman stepped forward, holding out her hand. 'I'm Olwen Bevan and this is my husband Albert. I'm so glad to see you. I do hope—'

He interrupted without a word of apology. 'Where's your luggage?'

'I have only the one bag.' She indicated it and he picked it up.

'Come on. I don't want to waste all day.'

'I'm sorry Albert's a bit curt. He's got a cow due to calf and wants to get back to keep an eye on it.' Mrs Bevan whispered as they followed him outside. She spoke with just a hint of her sister's Welsh accent. 'He's not one for chatting at the best of times, mind.'

Catherine studied her new mistress as they drove out of town. Mrs Bevan looked gaunt, with an unhealthy tinge to her complexion, and indeed everything about her seemed to droop tiredly.

The farm was more isolated than Catherine had expected, surrounded by bush and with no neighbouring habitation within sight. There were two men working in the yard and they stopped to stare at her appraisingly.

'How's that cow, Sam?' Mr Bevan yelled.

'She's all right. Not started to have the calf yet.'

'I hope you're a hard worker,' he said to Catherine as he pulled her bag off the back of the wagon and tossed it on to the veranda. 'I don't employ people who don't earn their wages.'

Surprised at this churlish remark, she watched as he drove off towards the rear of the farm buildings. He paused to yell something at one man, which sent him hurrying away, then vanished round the corner of the house. Catherine turned at the sound of Mrs Bevan's voice which again sounded faintly apologetic.

'I'll show you to your room, Katie, then we'd better start cooking the meal. Albert is always very hungry when he comes in at night. And you can take out a cup of tea to the men as soon as it's ready. We have some tin mugs we use for that. No use risking the good china outside, is it?'

Within minutes, Catherine was working, determined to show herself capable and willing because even the most menial of jobs could be done well.

At first she found the hard physical work very tiring and was glad of that because it made it easier to sleep. It didn't take her long to realise that this wasn't a happy place to work. Mr Bevan was always chivvying his men and seemed suspicious of everything Catherine said or did, though once Olwen had shown her what needed doing, her mistress was soon leaving many things to her, snatching a little rest each afternoon while her husband was away from the house.

When Catherine first asked which day was to be her half-day, Albert glared at her. 'You're hardly here but you're trying to get out of working!'

'A half-day off every week is part of our agreement.'

'Well, save them up and take a full day later, when it's more convenient.'

'I'd rather take a half-day each week, thank you. Everyone needs to rest and I have some urgent sewing to do as I'm short of clothes.'

Their eyes met for a moment; then he turned to

183

his wife and snapped, 'You arrange it, Olwen. But see she only takes the time off she's due and make sure the chores get done first. I've no patience with people who try to get out of working and I don't intend to sit around waiting for a meal while her ladyship takes a rest.'

Once he'd gone out again, Olwen glanced over her shoulder then apologised in a low voice. 'I'm sorry. He's so strong he forgets other people need a rest sometimes.'

'I really must have time to do my sewing,' Catherine repeated quietly. She and Mrs Powell had sorted through the poor-box clothes before she left and found several garments which could be altered to fit her, plus a few undergarments, but they'd take quite a bit of work. 'And I'll expect an hour off each evening, too. Your sister said she'd mentioned that in her letter.'

'She did, she did. But *he* conveniently forgets such things. It'd be best if you didn't press matters at first.'

'It'll be best, Mrs Bevan, if I start as I mean to go on.' You had to stand up to bullies, everyone knew that, or you wound up as cowed as this poor woman. Though Catherine suspected Olwen saw more than she admitted about her husband, including the way he ogled the new help.

Not a good start to this job, she thought sadly as she got ready for bed that night. Already she doubted she'd be staying longer than the three months agreed upon. No wonder the Bevans found it hard to get help.

*   *   *

184

Ismay sat by the camp fire, exhausted after her second day up but feeling content. Malachi, who had been playing and singing softly, set his guitar aside and looked across at her.

'Do you still want to travel with us?'

'You know I do.'

'You do realise that there's no guarantee you'll find your sister?'

'I definitely won't find her staying with the Berlows, and besides, I never wanted to live out in the middle of nowhere. I like to have other people around, things to see and do. I think that's why I got so down-hearted about it all. No one to talk to.' After a pause she added in a wobbly voice, 'I still miss Mara dreadfully.'

'I know.' They sat in silence for a few moments, then he said abruptly, 'Dan and I have been talking. We thought we'd give it a try with you for a week or two, see how we all get on together. He thinks people would enjoy our singing and it'd bring in extra money so that we could pay you a small wage.' Ismay's face came alight as he spoke and suddenly she was the pretty girl he'd seen on the ship, the one full of energy.

'Oh, Malachi, you won't regret it, I promise you. I'll work so hard.'

'We'll have to sort out the sleeping arrangements. If you could manage on the floor of the wagon, Dan and I could sleep under it—except when it's raining hard and then we'll all have to cram inside.'

She laughed. 'I'll sleep under it, too, if you like. Perhaps Dan needs a bit more comfort than I do. I'm not fussy, Malachi. I grew up in very poor conditions. The three of us just had a straw mattress on the floor and we used to huddle together for warmth in winter. Our father drank, you see, so we were always short of money till Keara . . .' She broke off.

'Your elder sister?'

She nodded and said in a voice which grated with suppressed anger, 'I hate her. She let them send us to Australia, after she'd promised we'd all live together.'

'Who told you that?'

'The nuns.'

'They can be as mistaken as the next person. And that Mother Superior was a nasty old hag.'

Which gave Ismay something to think about.

He couldn't be right, could he? But she didn't dare let go of her anger. Sometimes it was all that kept her going.

*   *   *

Mark and Nan walked slowly along the street, each holding one of Amy's hands. The child toddled along, smiling at the world.

'Eh, she's a dear little soul,' Nan said fondly, 'and she does love to go out walking. It's not good for her, living in a hotel. When we settle somewhere, I hope there'll be a garden for her to play out in and other children nearby. They shouldn't grow up on their own.' A shadow of sadness crossed her face. 'Alex would never allow our two to play out on the street. He was so strict. And I was too afraid of him to go against his wishes. I shall always regret that.'

'Well, Alex is dead now and you're happy looking after Amy for me, aren't you?'

She looked at her tall son-in-law with another fond smile. 'You know I am. I can't thank you enough, Mark lad.'

'We help one another. I couldn't manage without you.' He hesitated, then said in his quiet way, 'Once Theo and Keara have gone back to Western Australia, I want to go back to Rossall Springs on my own just to say goodbye properly. I'll take you another time to see Patience's grave, but this time—well, I need to lay some ghosts.'

She nodded, disappointed but keeping that to herself.

'After that I'm going to look for somewhere to open a small hotel with an eating house attached. I don't want to go back to the west. I feel more at home here in Victoria. Is that all right with you?'

'Eh, I don't mind where we live as long as I'm with you two.'

Mark smiled down at Amy, then across at Nan. 'I'll start making plans. As soon as Theo and Keara decide what they're going to do, as soon as I'm sure they don't need my help any longer, we'll make a start on our new life.'

'And maybe,' his mother-in-law said with a sigh, 'if I'm very lucky, one day I'll see my son again. The only thing that worries me is how Harry would ever find us.' Nan hoped her runaway lad was still alive somewhere and prayed for him every night. He'd left the family shortly after their arrival in Australia, unable to bear his father's strictness and religious bigotry.

'We could go back to the place where you were living when he ran away and ask them to pass on a message if he ever turns up. We could leave a letter for him at the central post office, too. We could

187

even go back to your husband's church and leave a message there.'

She shuddered.

'I'll do that for you,' Mark said quickly. 'Trust me, Nan. If it's at all possible, we'll make sure Harry can find you again.'

She looked at him, her eyes welling with tears and yet with a smile on her face. 'You're a lovely man, Mark Gibson. I hope you meet another woman and get married again one day. You deserve to be happy.'

It was his turn to shudder. 'Two women have died because of bearing my children and I've sworn never to marry again. I haven't even met my daughter who lives in England, though I've promised myself that one day I'll go back to find her.'

What a waste of a good man that'd be! she thought, but didn't say it. People often vowed not to marry and yet it only took a meeting or two with the right person for them to change their minds. She'd seen it happen many a time, and would add a plea to her prayers that one day it would happen to Mark.

CHAPTER TWELVE

APRIL–MAY 1865

As the days passed in a round of household chores, Catherine's main feelings were of loneliness and boredom. Olwen had such a struggle to keep up with the work that she seemed to have no breath to

188

spare for talking, and although Catherine had lost the habit of idle chat during her years as a nun, now she wanted to talk to people occasionally and see something other than the same few trees and fields.

'I'd like to come into town to market with you when I get paid,' she said towards the end of the first month. 'Is that all right?'

'I'm not sure Albert will approve. What do you need to go into town for? Couldn't I get you whatever you need?'

'I'd enjoy an outing and I want to see if I can buy something to read. You couldn't choose that for me.'

Mr Bevan came in just then and scowled at them. 'Reading's a waste of time. You're not using our candles for that sort of thing.'

'Then I'll buy myself a candle or two while I'm at it,' Catherine snapped. 'I didn't realise you were so short of money here that you'd have to limit my candles. Mrs Powell and your sister-in-law will be surprised when I tell them that.'

'A servant has no right corresponding with my wife's sister! You mind your lip, my girl, and don't twist my words to suit yourself.'

Catherine set her hands on her hips and faced him. 'I'm not a girl, Mr Bevan. I'm a woman who works very hard for you and I won't be spoken to in that carping tone.'

He stared at her in shock, but she stared right back at him. Behind him, Olwen had her hands tightly clasped at her bosom and looked utterly terrified. He had his fist clenched and for a moment Catherine thought he was going to hit her, but slowly the fist unclenched and with a mutter

189

that sounded like a curse, he swung on his heel and went back out.

Olwen let out her breath in a long, shaky sound and looked at Catherine. 'It doesn't do to get on his wrong side. I soon found that out.'

'Does he hit you?'

A blush was her only answer.

'Well, if he hits me—even once!—I'll leave immediately.'

She didn't know whether Olwen repeated her words to him, because her mistress kept most of her thoughts to herself, but from then on the looks Albert gave Catherine were less than friendly and he was always finding fault with her work.

When she received her first wages of one pound a few days later she looked at the coins lying on her outstretched palm with a wry smile. Before she'd entered the nunnery, this would have been small change to her, not even worth counting. Now, it was almost all she had in the world. Did she dare spend some of it on reading material? She had to or she'd go mad. Surely there would be cheap, second-hand books to be found in Rossall? When asked, Olwen said there was a stall that sold all sorts of bits and pieces and she reckoned she'd seen books there. Catherine decided she could spare a few pence to keep herself sane.

A few days later Olwen said quietly, 'I'm very happy with your work, Katie, and would like you to stay and work for us after the three months are up. Albert says it's all right to ask you.' She gave a timid smile as she added, 'Even with the half-days off. He can get a bit grumpy sometimes, but he doesn't mean anything by it.'

Catherine hesitated, but Mr Bevan's attitude was

more than merely 'grumpy' and he still eyed her in a way that disturbed her. 'I'll have to think about it. I didn't realise you were so far away from everything when I took the job.'

The other woman frowned. 'You were surely told that we lived out in the bush?'

'Yes, but I'd never been to the bush before so I didn't realise what it would be like. I only arrived from England last year, you see.'

Olwen looked at her sympathetically. 'And in that time you've lost your husband and most of your possessions? It must have been awful for you, having to sell them to keep yourself alive till you got better. I remember when my first husband died, I was so upset and didn't know how I was to manage.' She sighed. 'That's why I married Albert. He'd lost his wife just a week or two before I lost my husband and we both needed help. But my Paul was far easier to live with—and kinder. I wish . . .' Her voice trailed away and she wiped a tear from her cheek. 'No use dwelling on that, is there? You have to make the best of what you've got. Please stay on, Katie.'

After a moment's thought, Catherine said, 'I'll decide by the end of next month, but it's only fair to warn you that I'll probably be leaving.'

Mr Bevan was in a foul mood the following morning and found fault with everything Catherine did, so she assumed his wife had told him what she'd said. Well, his attitude and general grumpiness only made her more eager to leave, however sorry she felt for his poor wife.

As they all three drove into Rossall, he told Catherine, 'This'll count as your half-day, you know.'

191

'Yes. You said so. Several times.'

He breathed deeply and scowled at her. She looked calmly back, tired of his moods.

The market was held at one end of the town and was a lively affair with stalls and handcarts full of food mainly, but also other items. Clearly people came in for it from all over the district and there was a festive atmosphere.

To her delight Catherine was able to pick up a couple of dog-eared novels for threepence each at a stall full of odds and ends, but she resisted offers of refreshment, not wanting to spend more of her precious coins than necessary.

She wandered along the main street while Olwen finished making her purchases and studied the shops which included a grocery store, looking as if it was thriving, an eating house, looking a little tired, two low-class alehouses, and what she'd have called a decent public house but which here was called a hotel. There was also an ironmonger's, a smithy, a livery stables and a dressmaker, whose sign looked very new.

She was sorry when it was time to return to the farm.

*   *   *

The following month after she'd been paid Catherine went into town with her employers again and called into the grocery store. She'd noticed last time that it had some little cards in the window offering services or items for sale. Mentioning to the owner Mr Grove that she was looking for work, she produced a card on which she'd written her details. Well, it wasn't actually a card but the

192

endpaper from one of her books, and she'd had to write it secretly while the Bevans were out at market the previous week, but it would do the job.

'I thought I might put this in your window.' She proffered the piece of paper.

The owner studied her, read it, then asked, 'What sort of work are you wanting?'

'Anything respectable.' She explained her so-called situation, hating the necessity to tell more lies.

'Have you got any references?'

She pulled a wry face. 'No. And Mr Bevan's angry that I want to leave so he's not likely to give me good references, is he?'

Mr Grove winked. 'He's always angry, that fellow, and is well known for his bad temper.' After another minute spent chewing the inside of one cheek, he seemed to come to a decision. 'Come and talk to my wife. She needs someone to help out in the eating house next door. She's not been well lately and it's all a bit much for her. The woman who used to do a lot of the organising has moved out of the district and my Sally can't find anyone to take over. You seem a capable sort to me.'

'I like to think I am.'

They went next door and half an hour later Catherine walked out of the eating house with a job which was to start in a month's time. She could have started work immediately, but had insisted she must keep her word to the Bevans and stay with them for the promised three months. She was to have an attic bedroom above the eating house— tiny, but no smaller than the one she'd occupied as a nun—and all her aprons would be provided. Best of all, such work would bring her into daily contact

193

with other people, lots of people. She was really looking forward to that.

Sally Grove was another woman who looked worn out and in poor health, but she had a kindly husband who was clearly fond of her so didn't have the harried look of Olwen Bevan.

'I never thought it'd be such hard work running an eating house,' Sally confided during their talk. 'There's so much to think of. Mr Gibson, who sold it to us, made it all seem easy but I'm not as clever as he is. It seemed a good idea to buy it off him, it being next door, because Samuel's always been very ambitious, but I soon wished we hadn't.' She gave a self-deprecating shrug. 'I'm not as clever as he is. Are you any good at keeping accounts?'

'I think so.'

A heartfelt sigh of relief was the answer to that.

*   *   *

As they were driving home, Catherine said to the Bevans, 'I need to give you notice that I'll be leaving at the end of next month.'

'I knew it!' Mr Bevan snapped. 'That's downright ungrateful, I reckon, when we paid your fare out here.'

'Well, *I* think I've given you good value for your money,' she retorted. 'And you more than made up for the fare by paying me extremely low wages.' The new job would be paying her double what she earned at the farm, plus providing accommodation.

'You've been paid on time and fed well. What more do you want?'

'Company and politeness,' she snapped back.

During the afternoon he came inside the house

194

several times to grumble at her and chivvy her around. She set herself to endure it without comment.

At noon the next day, when Catherine went for her midday meal, she found Albert waiting for her in the kitchen. He greeted her with a triumphant smile and Olwen stood behind him, looking as if she'd been crying. 'I've decided we can do without help like yours. You can pack your things and leave today. I want you off this place within the hour.'

Catherine stared at him in shock.

'Albert, please,' his wife bleated.

'I told you not to interfere. I'll see this one off my land before I set about my work today and it'll give me great satisfaction to get rid of such an ungrateful bitch.'

He gave Catherine another of his triumphant smiles and her heart sank as she realised that he didn't even intend to drive her into town. Well, she wasn't going to beg him. She didn't think she could reach Rossall today, though she had always been a good walker, but if necessary she'd sleep rough or walk all through the night. Without a word she stood up and went into her room.

He followed her and stood in the doorway. 'I want to make sure you're taking nothing of ours with you.'

To her intense embarrassment he stood watching as she packed her underwear and other personal items. She said nothing, not wanting to make him angrier than he already was. She had finished in a few minutes, so picked up her bag and moved to the door. He didn't move aside to let her pass.

As she stood there looking at him, he suddenly

reached out and grabbed her breast, squeezing it painfully. 'Yes,' he muttered in a throaty voice. 'Yes, you've got nice, full titties.'

She swung her arm and cracked him across the cheek, making him yelp and then look at her with an ugly expression on her face.

'You'll be sorry for that,' he said in a low voice. 'I can catch up with you quite easily. You'll not get to Rossall without paying for that slap in the only way a woman can. If ever one needed taking down a peg or two, it's you, you uppity bitch.'

Only then did he step aside.

She knew it was no use appealing for Olwen's help so set off walking, not looking back until she was off the farm.

*　　　*　　　*

After a week of travelling with Malachi and Dan, Ismay felt happier than she had since her arrival in Australia. There was something about the free and easy life on the road that appealed to her and for the first time she began to enjoy this new country, in spite of her underlying sadness about Mara. Although it was autumn now, there were still sunny days when the whole world seemed beautiful. The nights were a bit nippy, but they had warm blankets and in her cosy nest in between the rows of shelves she felt secure and able to sleep well. She was eating better, too, and the small mirror told her she'd put on weight and regained her rosy cheeks.

It fascinated her to see the houses of the newer settlers, some of them built of wood, with roofs of bark held down by wooden planks. She wondered how well they'd keep out the rain and how warm

196

they'd be in the winter. She was growing used to the Australian landscape now. The leaves were so different from the vivid Irish greens: grey-green, dull dark green, grey, and only occasionally a brighter green. Some of the trees had light-coloured trunks and sparse foliage, some were so huge they took her breath away. She liked it better out here in the countryside than she had close to the city, she decided.

One day it began to rain so heavily that when they stopped for the night they made do with bread and jam, lighting a small fire only to boil the water for their nightly pots of tea which they drank sitting in the wagon. The rain showed no sign of letting up and since neither of the men had said anything, Ismay said it for them. 'We'll all have to sleep in here tonight.'

'There isn't room,' Malachi said shortly.

'Of course there is. You've sold quite a few things so there's more room than there would have been when you first set out. We can half-sit with our backs against the lower shelves of blankets and clothes.' She giggled suddenly. 'Like three spoons in a drawer.' She couldn't suppress a yawn. 'I don't know about you, but I'm tired enough to sleep standing up, so I am.'

Malachi smiled. He loved it when her voice twisted into an Irish lilt, which it did more strongly when she was tired.

Dan insisted on sleeping at the outer end of the wagon, because he usually needed to get up during the night to relieve himself. Ismay was already sitting behind the driving seat, which acted like a shelter, keeping off most of the rain. She slid down and began to arrange her blankets and pillow in the

197

light of the flickering lamp.

Malachi waited until she was nestled down, then covered her and himself with a tarpaulin before extinguishing the lamp. He tried not to touch her and failed because there wasn't much room. The warmth of her body made him feel uncomfortable. It was a dark night, the moon hidden behind the clouds that were bringing so much rain, but the wagon seemed charged with hidden currents of feeling.

He was conscious of even her slightest move. It was one thing to drive around with Ismay, quite another to lie beside her in the darkness, hearing her gentle breathing. He bit back a curse. He was a young man and hadn't been near a woman since he left England, had thought his sexual urges under control, but suddenly the need flared up, a need fuelled to white heat by the pretty lass lying beside him and even more by the fact that it was Ismay. He could only be grateful that the darkness hid his physical reaction to her closeness.

'We'll go back to Melbourne for the worst of the winter,' Dan said from the darkness at the end of the wagon. 'We've made enough money to take a month or two off, and we can always make some money there if you two do a bit of singing.' He yawned loudly. 'Eh, I'm ready for my sleep, me.'

Within a couple of minutes he was snoring.

Ismay giggled in the darkness. 'Doesn't he keep you awake?' she whispered.

Malachi smiled. 'You get used to it and I'm usually so tired I fall asleep as soon as I lie down.'

'Me, too.'

He didn't want to stop chatting. 'You're feeling all right now?'

'I am, yes. Better than I have for ages. Wilya was so kind, wasn't she? Er—Malachi?'

'Yes?'

'I *am* earning my keep, aren't I?'

'Of course you are. The women we meet prefer dealing with you for their personal items.'

'I like dealing with them, trying to help them. I've got all sorts of ideas for items for women we could bring on the next trip.' There was a pregnant silence before she added, 'If you'll let me stay with you. You will, won't you?'

'We'll talk about that when we get back to Melbourne.' He didn't know why he was so reluctant to commit himself.

'You don't want me.' Her voice was flat, with just a hitch at the end, as if she was upset.

'It's not that. I'm not even sure what I want for myself, let alone taking responsibility for your future.'

'I can always find myself another job as a maid.'

He heard her sniff and felt her move her arm, guessed she was wiping away a tear. 'Don't cry, Issy. We won't abandon you whatever happens, I promise.'

She stretched out her hand and found his. 'Thank you, Malachi.'

He gave her hand a quick squeeze. 'It's all right. Now get to sleep.'

'Yes, Malachi.'

After another silence, she said, 'You called me Issy.'

'Did I?'

'Yes. No one's ever called me that before. I like it. Hasn't anyone ever shortened *your* name?'

'My mother wouldn't allow it. And I prefer

199

Malachi now.'

'It suits you. I've never met anyone called that before.' She yawned and soon was breathing softly and slowly.

It was a long time before he got to sleep and when he woke during the night to find her cuddled up to him, he felt too uncomfortably aware of her female curves to do more than doze from then on.

In the morning she came awake suddenly, blinked at him and realised how close she was. Blushing furiously she pulled back. 'I'm sorry. I'm so used to cuddling up to Mara at night, I just did it in my sleep.'

He managed to speak calmly, or at least hoped he did. 'That's all right. No harm done.'

But it wasn't all right, really. The memory of how she had felt nestled against him stayed with him all day.

*   *   *

Catherine walked briskly along the road, trying to pace herself, trying not to keep looking behind to see whether someone was pursuing her. It was about twenty miles into Rossall Springs by this track and she didn't think she could make it by nightfall on such muddy, rough terrain. Before it grew dark she'd better try to find a hiding place for the night.

She wondered if she should turn off the road to one of the farms that were signposted, but she didn't know if the owners were close friends of the Bevans or not. They might just tell her to be on her way and then she'd have lost time. Besides, pride made her want to manage on her own.

But as she continued on her way she grew worried. There had been regular rain lately and the ground was soft so her footprints showed all too clearly when she looked behind her. If Albert did carry out his threat to pursue her—and something told her he would—he'd follow her tracks easily and be able to tell when she left the road. Unless . . .

As the sun began to drop towards the horizon she walked along for a while on the hardest earth she could find, jumping from one patch to another so that footprints didn't show. Then, when she came to a place where she thought she might find a resting place for the night, she took even more care as she moved away from the road into the woods, using a leafy branch to smooth out her footprints. Eventually she found a tree with big roots and set her bag down between them. She'd have to wear most of her clothes to keep warm. However, after a few minutes of lying there tensely, it occurred to her suddenly that she'd better arm herself, just in case, and she got up again. She found a stick that was big enough to use in self-defence and took a couple of hand-sized rocks back to her hiding place as well. If he attacked her, she'd fight back. Definitely.

She had never before prayed as fervently as she did that night. *Dear God, if he follows, please let him pass by without finding me!*

As dusk fell she watched entranced as a female kangaroo hopped across the clearing. It was grey against the foliage darkened by the fading light and was only about as tall as her elbow. A baby was peeping out of its pouch. What did they call them here? Joeys, that was it. She kept very still and after a minute or two, the little creature eased itself out of the pouch in a tangle of arms and legs, then began to hop around, always keeping an eye on its mother.

Then she heard the sound of a horse's hoofbeats, a dull thudding on the soft earth. It had to be him. No one else would be out at this time of night. He must have set off after her well before it grew dark, following her footprints no doubt, though there was only one road to Rossall Springs, so he'd know exactly where to find her. Her heart began to thud in her chest. She had never felt so alone in her life or so helpless. She should have gone further into the bush, only she'd been afraid of getting lost.

The kangaroo heard the rider too and froze in place, its head up as if listening. She didn't know whether it had given some sort of signal but suddenly the joey bounded across the clearing and dived head first into its mother's pouch. Immediately the mother hopped away, the little one's rear legs still protruding.

The hoofbeats passed on the road and then stopped. Catherine put one hand across her mouth, feeling as if she were holding in all her fears, not to mention the whimpering noise she might make if she let herself be overwhelmed by fear.

Sounds seemed to carry so far in the moist air that she could hear quite clearly when the horse stopped. The sound of its hooves grew louder again as it returned and one whimper of fear did escape her.

He rode past the place where she had left the road. Had she fooled him?

But just as she was beginning to hope she had,

he turned and came back.

She heard quite clearly the triumphant laugh as he found the place where she had left the road. The fact that he should laugh made her angry. Laughing when he was chasing her with the intention of harming her!

She picked up the stick in her right hand. With her left hand she picked up one of the small rocks and stuffed it in the pocket of her skirt as she stood up.

'Katie! Where are you?' He laughed again. 'You won't escape, you know. The minute you move I'll hear you and I'm used to the bush. You're not. Come on, Katie. Stop trying to hide. I won't hurt you. I only want a taste of what others have had.'

Was he trying to goad her into moving? she wondered. She kept very still, but shuddered as she heard him dismount and come closer. Further away the horse's harness jingled and she heard it moving restlessly.

Just as he reached the clearing the moon chose to come out from behind the clouds and she almost groaned aloud.

He laughed again. 'Even the moon is on my side. You're not going to get away, you know.'

She tried to pray, but the words wouldn't come, so she concentrated on standing perfectly still. She wasn't going to give him the satisfaction of seeing her run away. And anyway, she didn't think she could outrun him. He was a very strong man.

The moon vanished behind the clouds again and he chuckled. He sounded horribly close now.

'I only have to wait for the moon to come out again and I'll be able to follow your footprints,' he said. 'You can't get away from me.'

He wasn't moving now, just waiting. Her heart was in her throat, pounding, sending blood roaring past her ears. It was as if all her senses were magnified and she could hear him, the way he moved from one foot to another, the way he sighed impatiently.

Then the moon came out again and he walked across the clearing, yelling in triumph as he saw her standing behind the tree. Well, the leaves were so sparse on this sort of gum tree that they didn't even cast enough shadow to hide in.

She stood very still, watching him, her hands behind her to conceal her makeshift weapons.

'I'll fight you every inch of the way, Albert Bevan,' she said. 'I'm not your wife to cower away and do as you say. I'm tall enough and strong enough to hold my own against you.'

'A woman, best me? You'll have to prove that.' With another of those hateful laughs, he lunged across the clearing.

CHAPTER THIRTEEN

MAY–JUNE 1865

Barbara Hannon died one night in the last month of autumn, passing away so quietly that when Mara went into the bedroom in the morning with a cup of tea, she found her dear friend lying there already stiff and cold. No stranger to death, Mara set down the cup carefully, then bent to kiss the pale cheek and close the eyes that seemed to be staring far into the distance.

Taking a deep breath, because she was nervous of him, she went to find Charles Hannon. He opened his bedroom door to her timid knock and when she stammered that his wife was dead, pushed her out of the way and rushed along the landing into the bedroom he hadn't shared with Barbara for several weeks.

As Mara heard the sound of a man's strangled sobbing she leaned her head against the wall and shed a few more tears of her own. He couldn't be completely bad if he had loved his wife so much, but he'd never treated Mara well and she would be glad to get away from him.

When he came out of the bedroom again, his face was grim and cold, even though his eyes were reddened. 'What are you doing hanging around here? Go to the kitchen and send Cook to me.'

She did as he asked, explaining what had happened and taking over without being asked the stirring of the servants' porridge as Cook exclaimed and ran out.

When she came back, she said to Mara, 'You're to stay in the kitchen and help out. He'll find you somewhere else to live after the funeral. And you're to move out of that bedroom up to one of the attics before tonight.' Lips pressed close together, she sent the maid running for the doctor and then continued with her work, stopping every now and then to shake her head as if disapproving of something.

She was kinder to Mara that day than she had been before which for some reason filled the girl with apprehension. What had the master said to Cook?

The funeral was set for two days later and immediately after breakfast on that day Charles summoned Mara into the parlour. He looked at her scornfully. '*You* will not be attending today. You're no longer part of this family and never were as far as I was concerned. I don't want to be shamed in front of our friends by the presence of such as you at *her* farewell.'

Mara stared at him in horror. 'Please let me go with Cook and Min! I promise I'll stay out of sight and—'

'*I said no!*'

'But I loved her, too!'

He gave a scornful sniff 'You mean, you knew which side your bread was buttered on.'

She saw his lips set in that bloodless line they had when his mind was made up. Even so, she tried again to plead with him to let her be there when they buried the woman who had been so kind to her.

He stood up, saying slowly and distinctly, 'If you give me *any* trouble about this, I'll lock you in the store cupboard till we come home again. Now, get back to the kitchen where you belong. *She* might have thought you were special, but no one else does. You're nothing but Irish scum.'

Mara backed away from him, then ran sobbing out of the room and back to the kitchen.

Cook greeted her with, 'There you are, Mara! Hurry up and get ready, do! The cabs will be here in a few minutes.'

'I'm not to go.' As Mara controlled her sobs, she saw the two women exchange startled glances, but

206

kept her mouth closed because if she'd opened it, she'd have burst out crying all over again.

She was still sitting there, staring down at her clasped hands, when they all drove off and left her alone in the big house.

It took a minute or two for it to sink in that she must act now, then she went along to the bedroom that had once belonged to Barbara's daughter and, for a short time, to her. Standing at the end of the bed, she turned slowly round, willing herself to remember it because it was the prettiest place she'd ever lived in. One day, somehow, she was going to have another room just as pretty, she vowed.

Next she went into Barbara's room and walked over to the bed to run her fingers over the ruched silk counterpane and say a prayer of her own for her benefactress.

Half an hour later she left the house by the back door, slipping along the rear lane and walking away quickly. In her pocket was the money Barbara had given her and the carefully written instructions. She was carrying only the things she had brought with her from the convent, because she didn't want him to accuse her of stealing. But before she did as Barbara had asked and went to her friend's house, she intended to go to the churchyard. As soon as the mourners had left she would lay a rose on Barbara's grave. It wouldn't be right not to say a proper farewell.

The boys from down the road jeered at her as she passed their garden. She didn't even hear them. The old woman at the end house looked at her through the window, not recognising the Hannons' protégée in the dark, stiff clothes provided by the convent. Further along, a shopkeeper came to his door to watch her pass. She didn't notice any of them.

At the church she waited behind some bushes as the last mourners dispersed, then went to lay her rose on the new grave and bend her head for a moment in her own silent farewell. The men hadn't finished filling the hole in and the sight of a corner of the coffin brought tears welling into her eyes. 'The Lord bless and keep you,' she murmured, crossing herself.

It was as she was leaving the churchyard by the rear gate that the boys pounced on her and stole her purse. With a shout of glee at what it contained, they ran off down the lane at the back, taking with them the piece of paper with the instructions on it as well as her bag of clothes.

She stood frozen with shock, then began to weep. It was the final straw. She didn't know what she'd do with herself now.

She didn't even see anyone approaching until someone said, 'What's the matter?'

Gasping, afraid someone else was going to attack her, she put one hand up to her mouth and tried to stop the sobs.

'Ah, leave her to it,' one of the men said.

'She's upset,' the other said in a much softer voice.

'So what? She's no concern of ours.'

'Ah, we can spare a minute. Tell us what's wrong, child?'

She sobbed out her tale of robbery.

'The young divils! And you have nowhere to go now, you say?'

'No.' She gulped, but more sobs came out. 'They even took my spare clothes.'

The man frowned at her, then said slowly, 'We could take her back with us.'

'What the hell for? She's too young and scraggy to be of use to a man.'

'Not for that, you fool. Dolly's been saying she could do with some help in the house and this lass is old enough to do housework.'

'Do you think?' The bad-tempered one scowled at her.

'I do, yes. And I think it'd put Dolly in a good mood.'

'Would you be interested in a job as a maid?' the kind man asked. 'It's our sister who needs help.'

Mara stared at him, then nodded. 'Yes. Oh, yes, please!'

They found her bag further down the lane with clothes scattered around it. It seemed like an omen to the girl that she was doing the right thing. Though what else she could have done, she didn't know.

*   *   *

Charles Hannon said goodbye to the last of the guests who'd been invited to the funeral then went to sit in the parlour with a glass of port. He had closed the shop for the morning and his employees had all been instructed to attend the funeral. The decorous line of bent heads at the rear of the church had pleased him.

Only Mara hadn't been there. He felt suddenly guilty about that. The girl had obviously been fond of Barbara, whatever he thought of her. Perhaps he'd been too harsh?

He took a large swallow of port. Why the hell

should he feel guilty about an Irish gutter brat? Only the faint hope that adopting a child might help Barbara get better had made him even consider taking someone like that into his home. The sight of Mara's skinny child's body, so like his own daughter's before she fell ill, had done nothing but exacerbate the agony of his loss. He'd hated the Irish girl's rosy face, her laughter, the very sound of her breathing. Why should someone brought up in abject poverty look so healthy when his own daughter, brought up with all the care and love a child could ever be given, had died?

Well, he'd drive into Melbourne tomorrow after he'd reopened the shop, and go and see those blasted nuns. If they'd sent the other orphans elsewhere, they could send Mara too.

He became aware of a knocking on the door. 'Come in!'

Cook entered, her eyes reddened, twisting her apron in her hands. 'I didn't like to disturb you before, sir, what with the visitors and everything, but we can't find Mara.'

He thumped the glass down on the nearest table. 'What do you mean, can't find her?'

'She's not in the house or garden, sir. And her things have gone. I think she's run away.'

He went up to the attic to check for himself, then to the room she'd occupied while Barbara was alive. Some of her things had indeed gone, the ones she'd brought with her from the damned convent, but the pretty dresses and delicate underwear Barbara had bought her were all there.

He stood frowning, not sure what to do, then it came to him. Nothing. He need do nothing. Wherever she'd gone, good riddance to her!

'I'll make inquiries,' he said. 'Let the authorities know.'

'But—'

'I said I'll make inquiries. She's probably run back to those nuns. That will be all, Cook.'

He poured another glass of port with an unsteady hand. With a bit of luck he was rid of the brat for good, and without lifting a finger.

It was meant to be.

He wished he could shrug off his grief so easily.

*   *   *

Catherine waited in the darkness until Albert Bevan was close to her before lashing out with the stick. He yelled as it made contact with his head, then roared in anger and ripped it out of her hand. Before she had realised what he was doing, he had grabbed her by the front of her dress and slammed her back hard against a nearby tree trunk. Breath whistled out of her at the impact and although she struggled, he slammed her back against the tree again. The pain of bumping against the hard trunk made her head spin and she sagged against him.

He thrust his knee between her legs and with a hoarse laugh, ripped the front of her blouse open, making buttons pop off and cloth tear.

The shock of that made her start fighting again but as she began to scream and beat at him with her hands, he clouted her hard across the head and knocked her to the ground.

She rolled over, but he caught her by her blouse and pulled her back. As she curled up to avoid him, he lifted her skirts above her head and she cried out in shock and fear, her voice muffled by the

211

layers of cloth which he held down across her face, leaning the weight of his upper body on her.

With his other hand he grabbed her most private parts and tore at her skin, thrusting his fingers inside her. Shock froze her rigid, for no one had even seen her body for years, let alone touched it. He was making free with it in the most humiliating way possible. She couldn't hold back a sob, then another.

'Tears won't soften me, you bitch!' he muttered, removing the intrusive hand. She managed to twitch enough of her skirts off her face to see him fumbling with his trouser buttons.

It was as she tried again to pull away that she became aware of the stone she'd thrust into her skirt pocket. 'Don't hurt me,' she begged in an effort to gain time. 'Please don't hurt me.'

Laughing, he straddled her to hold her down. 'Women were made to be hurt by men. Has no one taught you that yet? If not, you're about to learn. Uppity bitches like you don't know their place.'

'Don't! In God's name, don't!' She fumbled with the opening of the skirt pocket with one hand, but the weight of his body made it impossible for her to pull the stone out.

'*Please don't!*' he mocked, mimicking her breathless tone. '*Oh, dearie me, please don't.*'

Again he thrust his fingers into her and she bucked against the painful invasion, retaining enough sense to continue her efforts to pull the stone out. She was touching it, but his body was too heavy.

'You're nice and tight. Must have been a while,' he muttered, pausing again to slip one of his braces off his left shoulder.

She stopped struggling and pretended to weep, but it turned into real weeping as he laughed and eased himself sideways to remove the other brace.

At that moment her scrabbling fingers grasped the stone and she managed to pull it out of the pocket. Without thinking she slammed it against the side of his head with all her might. He gave a bull-like roar, so she hit him a second time, as quickly as she could manage it, and he grunted and sagged sideways. As his weight rolled off her, she slammed the stone against his head for a third time and he fell to the ground, not stirring.

Dear God, had she killed him?

She couldn't move for a moment, so shocked was she at what she'd done, then forced herself to kneel beside him and feel for a pulse. There was one. He was alive! She groaned in relief, then realised that she must make the most of this opportunity so went to pick up her bag of possessions.

When she looked back across the clearing he hadn't moved.

She found his horse tied up by the roadside and almost borrowed it. But much as she'd have liked to ride the rest of the way to Rossall, the horse would link her with him. He might even claim she'd stolen it. Instead, she untied it and gave it a slap across its rump that sent it cantering off down the road towards its warm stable.

Only later, when the clouds passed over and the moon came out to shine steadily down, did she realise she was still wearing the torn blouse, that one of her breasts was bare and her chest covered in scratch marks made by Albert's rough fingers. Shaking with nervousness, she stopped to fumble in

213

the bag for another blouse and put it on, stuffing the torn garment in anyhow, then setting off again. She'd have liked to stop and wash herself, because she felt dirty in her most intimate places from his touch. But she didn't dare do that, either.

When she tripped and fell, she lay there for a minute, holding her breath and listening with her ear to the ground in case he was pursuing her. But she could hear nothing. She could have been the only person alive in the whole world.

She reached Rossall just as dawn was about to break. Without even stopping to tidy her hair or put on a bonnet, she made her way to the grocer's shop and went round the back. After hesitating for a minute, she knocked on the door, and when no one answered, hammered on it harder— hammering, hammering until it swung open and she fell through it into the arms of Mr Grove, sobbing hysterically.

'Katie? What's wrong?' When she didn't answer, he raised his voice to yell, 'Sally! Sally, come quickly!'

They sat her down and she sobbed out her story, hiding her face in her hands, so embarrassed she could have curled up and died.

'Look at the scratches on her,' Sally whispered. 'And the bruises.'

'He's a mean devil, but I'd never have thought him capable of this.'

'She wouldn't have made up a story like that. No woman would. I'll help her wash herself. She'll feel better then. You go into the shop for a few minutes.'

When he came back, his wife went to whisper to him that there were scratches on Katie's most

214

intimate places as well. 'I thought it best to check, in case he tries to claim differently. She definitely wasn't willing.'

Samuel sighed. 'I suppose I'd better ride back and check that he's all right. She sounds to have hit him hard.'

'Serve him right!'

'Did he . . . have his way with her?'

'I don't think so. It sounds like he just touched her.' She shuddered. 'Any decent woman would sympathise with another who'd been assaulted like that.'

He growled something that sounded angry. 'Unfortunately, she's best keeping quiet about the attack.'

Sally knew he was right. Complaining to the law would cause too much trouble and Albert Bevan would only deny it, so it'd be Catherine's word against his. But it seemed wrong, so very wrong, for him to get away with his cowardly attack. 'I know what I'd like to do to him and all men like him,' she muttered.

Now that he knew their new employee hadn't been raped, Samuel was more concerned about the interruption to his own busy life. 'As if I haven't enough to do! I dare say this'll take the whole morning. Can you manage here?'

'Yes. As long as *he* doesn't come after her.'

'He wouldn't dare do that. Anyway, Tom will soon be at work. You won't be alone in the shop or the eating house.'

But nowhere along the road to the Bevans' farm did Samuel find any sign of Albert, though he found the place where a horse had been tied up and then walked into the woods a little way to find

215

a clearing exactly like the one she'd described. There was even a stone lying on the ground. He grinned. Good for her!

When he got near the farm he saw Bevan working in the field so knew the fellow was all right, though he could see the bruise on the man's forehead quite clearly. Serve the bugger right!

Samuel didn't go to the house. But he believed what his new employee had told him, especially after what his wife had seen. Anyway, Katie had been too distressed to be making it up. He had never liked Albert Bevan, but would not have believed him capable of such outrageous behaviour.

When he got back he went next door and found Catherine chopping vegetables in the kitchen of the eating house, looking pale and tear-stained.

'Is he all right?' she asked at once.

'Yes. He's out working in the fields. Must have a head made of iron if you hit him as hard as you said. He's badly bruised and serve him right.'

She let out a shuddering sigh of relief. 'I was afraid I'd killed him.'

Something else was worrying Catherine. 'What do I do if he comes into the eating house?'

'You'll serve him as you would any other customer.'

She looked at him in dismay. 'Surely not?'

'Do you want the whole town to guess that something happened between you?'

She shuddered. 'No.'

'If he comes in, I'll deal with him,' Sally said. 'And believe me, he won't get friendly service in *my* eating house.' She didn't say anything to the others, but had decided to reveal something of what had

216

happened to a few of her friends. The women of the town had their own ways of dealing with men like him. This wasn't a lawless goldfield town any more, but a respectable farming centre and women needed to know they were safe from molestation.

*   *   *

The two men took Mara with them, walking so briskly that after a while she was out of breath. She had spent so much time indoors at the Hannons', not allowed to play or run, that she tired more easily now. When they stopped to knock at the door of a tall, narrow house in a back street, she felt exhausted.

A plump woman in a crumpled house gown threw open the door, curly black hair tumbling over her shoulders. 'Where the hell have you two been?'

'Aren't you going to let us in, Doll?'

She flung the door open without really registering the girl's presence behind her younger brother Gil. Mick had to poke Mara in the back before the girl stumbled inside.

In a big, untidy kitchen at the rear of the house, Dolly pulled the lid off the main cook hole in the stove and shoved the kettle over it, then adjusted the damper to make the wood fire inside blaze up. 'I'm gasping for a cup of tea. And while I think of it, you did well with that bloody madman who tried to attack Lily last night. Good thing you were there to keep him from hurting her.'

Gil grinned. 'Good thing you got those emergency bells installed. Anyways, I don't like men who beat women up, never have.'

'How about something stronger than tea?' Mick

217

asked impatiently.

'Not at this hour, with a night's work ahead. I know you two. One drink becomes two and before I know it, you're useless to me.'

'Ah, Dolly. Such hard words when we've brought you back a present from our little walk.'

'Oh, yes? And why would you do something like that?'

'You said you needed help in the kitchen. I thought this girl would be just the thing. We found her behind the church. Some lads had robbed her and she has nowhere to go.' He gave Mara a push that sent her stumbling forward.

For the first time Dolly studied the girl properly. Poor little bugger! she thought. Another one too weak to keep out of trouble. 'You all right, love?'

'I am now.'

Irish, Dolly realised at once, and feeling for a fellow countrywoman made her put one arm round the narrow, childish shoulders and give the girl a hug. 'Where are your family, pet?'

'There's only my sisters. I don't know where Keara is and the nuns sent Ismay away to the country, but they wouldn't tell me where.'

Bloody nuns again, thought Dolly. She'd suffered from their attentions herself when younger and had only sour memories of her own meagre education, most of which had involved a heavy wooden ruler that hurt when it whacked down on your hand. 'Right then, I'll send these two off to do some work—we have a door to repair, *if* it's not too much trouble, boys?—then you and me will have a little chat. Irish, aren't you?'

Mara nodded.

When the men had gone Dolly settled her at the

218

table with a mug of tea and a piece of bread and butter, then proceeded to find out exactly what her situation was. After all, she did need some help and not many would come to work in a brothel.

'What are you like at housework?'

'I know how to do it. The nuns were teaching us to be housemaids.'

'Then why don't you stay here and help me? The girls who work here can be real lazy sluts sometimes and I like to keep things tidy. We get the evening meal sent in, so there's not a lot of cooking, but there's breakfast to make, cups of tea and other things.' Her voice became coaxing, 'Stay a bit and see how we go on. Us Irish have to stick together.'

Mara looked at her uncertainly. The woman was plump and blowsy, but kindness shone from her. 'What is this place?'

Dolly hesitated, then shrugged and said, 'A brothel.'

After some frowning thought, Mara asked, 'What's that?'

With a great roar of laughter, Dolly gathered the girl in her arms and gave her a big hug—and felt the thin body suddenly relax against hers. She held Mara at arm's length, her eyes warmly sympathetic. 'No one's hugged you for a while, have they?'

'No.'

'Well, no one's hugged me, either, not for free. We'll be giving it a try, eh? You working for me, I mean. I'll be payin' you wages every week.'

Mara nodded, eager now. If she was earning money, she'd be able to save some, surely. And if she had money, eventually she could go and look for Ismay.

219

CHAPTER FOURTEEN

JUNE–JULY 1865

In Melbourne, Theo was having no luck with his search. The priest still insisted he couldn't help them find Mara, while Ismay seemed to have vanished from the face of the earth. Even the nun who had been particularly friendly with the two of them had run away, one of the other girls revealed. What sort of a convent had it been if everyone ran away from it and its connections?

Keara tried to keep cheerful, not feeling it fair to burden Theo with her sadness when he was so excited about the baby she was carrying, but sometimes her thoughts would turn to her sisters and she would weep in secret.

One day he came back to their hotel room unexpectedly and found her staring out of the window, so lost in thought she hadn't even noticed him come in. He put his arm round her shoulders, startling her.

'You were miles away.' He kissed her cheek and looked at her very seriously. 'There's not much else we can do now, darling, not once the posters have been printed. We'll wait a week or two, then we'll leave it in my agent's hands. And Mark's.' He put his arms round her and she leaned back against him with a sigh.

'I suppose we'd better start planning to go back to Western Australia, then, Theo. There's nothing for us here and you're not the only one who doesn't enjoy city life. But if Mark weren't here to answer any enquiries, I might feel differently. And if anything turns up, anything at all, then I'm coming back, child or no child.'

'Thank you.' He knew what that had cost her.

'And we will leave enough money, won't we, so that if—' her voice wobbled for a minute then she forced herself to continue. '—they're found, they can be sent to join us?'

'Yes, darling. I've already done that.'

'I shall miss Mark and Nan, little Amy too.'

His hands settled on the swell of her belly, almost invisible except to him who knew her so well. 'Not for long. What with Nell and this one, you'll have plenty to keep you busy. And after the new baby's been born, I intend to teach you to ride. We can't have the wife of a horse breeder not knowing one end of the animal from the other.'

She turned her head slightly to give him a faint smile. 'I love you, Theo Mullane.'

'I love you too, Keara Mullane.'

She sighed. 'That's not really my name. We aren't married, whatever we say to other people.' She still felt guilty about living in sin. It would have upset her mother so much.

'It's how I always think of you. As my true wife.'

*   *   *

When they started packing, Maggie came to see Keara. 'I want to stay here, love. I like Melbourne and I—I've found myself a job. At least, I have if Theo will speak for me, tell them I'm respectable.' She looked at her friend hesitantly. 'Was it all right to give them his name?'

Keara looked at her, feeling sad. She and

Maggie had sailed to Australia together, looked after one another through some hard times and she'd hoped her friend would eventually settle near her and Theo. But if this was what Maggie wanted, then that was what mattered. 'Of course it was right to give Theo's name. Tell me about the job. You look excited.'

'It's one of those new jobs in a hotel—they call it being a barmaid. And it's a place where they'll only take respectable women who dress nicely.' She looked down at herself. 'These clothes you've given me helped me get the job, but so did the fact that I look attractive.' She tried to suppress her pride in this, but couldn't. 'It's all thanks to you and Theo and Mark. You've taught me so much, from table manners to—well,' she twirled round and dipped a mock curtsey, 'how to behave in polite company.'

'You're a hard worker, Maggie love. You deserve a chance to make something of yourself.'

'I haven't told you the best yet.' She paused expectantly.

'What's that?'

'The wages. They're to pay me thirty shillings a week, plus a room, plus I keep any tips from customers.' She threw back her head and laughed. 'To think of me earning so much, all for myself, when I used to be hard put to find the cost of a loaf of bread!' She let out a long sigh of pure ecstasy, then went on, 'There were a lot of women went for the job, but they chose me. I'll be standing behind a counter, pulling beer and serving drinks and food—they do sandwiches and cakes, easy things like that. And I'll be called Miss Brett, not Maggie. Oh, it'll be so much more interesting than being a servant.'

222

Keara pulled her into her arms and gave her a hug. 'I'm delighted for you. You've been wonderful with Nell but I know your heart's not in being a nursemaid. Besides, you need to make a new life for yourself and it's very quiet where we live.'

Maggie let out her breath in a long groan of sheer relief. 'I couldn't sleep last night for thinking how to tell you. Only . . . what do you think Theo will say? He'll give me a reference, won't he?'

'You leave Theo to me. Have you enough money to tide you over?'

Maggie grinned cheekily. 'I will have once you've paid me.'

*   *   *

Dan sniffed and said grumpily, 'We need to return to Melbourne. It's no pleasure travelling during the worst of the winter months. You get bogged down an' you're allus shiverin', let alone the goods get damp. And any road, we're running out of stock.'

Malachi looked at Ismay dubiously. One of the reasons he'd delayed their return was because of the problem of where she would live.

As if he'd read his young friend's mind, Dan said, 'She can share our room.' He smiled at her. 'You know you'll be safe with us, lass, don't you?'

Ismay smiled warmly back at him. 'Yes.'

'She can't do that. She's a woman, not a child! It'd not be decent.'

'It'd be as decent as we choose to keep it,' Dan snapped. 'Any road, it's easy enough to hang a sheet across a corner for her.'

Malachi bit back a sharp reply. During the past few weeks he'd had a few unintended glimpses of

223

Ismay's body as she washed in streams and they hadn't left him unaffected. She might be slender, but she had the sort of curves men dreamed of and he'd not been able to forget how she looked with that mass of dark, wavy hair rippling across her bare shoulders. There'd be no hiding his reactions to her if they were all three in one room.

Maybe they could find two rooms. No, he didn't want the extra expense. It'd been a good season's selling, but they were still building their capital and needed all their money for new and better stock.

'I could maybe get a live-in job for a few months in Melbourne,' Ismay volunteered. 'In an alehouse or something.'

'No.' Dan's voice was flat and very definite. 'You'd be safer with us.' He looked sideways at the younger man. 'We're not risking her safety. Without references she'd not get a decent job.'

Malachi shrugged. 'All right.'

A little later Ismay asked in a hesitant voice, 'Do we have to go back the same way we came?'

'It's the only way I know to get to Melbourne,' Dan said. 'Why?'

She bit the corner of her lip and stared from one to the other. 'We'll be going near the Berlows' farm if we do that. They might see me, or—or someone might tell them I'm with you. What if they try to force me to return to them?'

'You can keep out of sight while we're near them, stay in the back of the wagon,' Malachi said impatiently. 'It'll only be for a day or two.'

'I suppose so.'

But as they got closer to Upley she became nervous, jerking in shock if someone approached the wagon without her seeing them, whipping round at the slightest sound.

'They drove her to desperation so it's only natural she'll be worried,' Dan told Malachi when he grumbled at her edginess. 'Have a bit of consideration for her feelings, lad.'

Malachi shrugged and went off to feed the horses. Since Ismay had joined them he didn't feel in control of things any more. Dan sided with her more often than not, looking after her fondly as if he were her grandfather. And she—well, there was no denying she was a loving lass, teasing the old man, giving him the most tender bits of meat since he had few teeth left and those in bad order, making sure his blankets were warmed by the fire each night.

She tried to fuss over Malachi too and he didn't know why he was so surly with her. He didn't understand his own feelings about her—and didn't want to. Bad enough the way he reacted to her body. This wasn't a time in his life to be getting interested in women; this was a time to be making his fortune. Or so he kept reminding himself.

But it upset him more than he liked to admit to see how nervous she became as they approached Upley. She refused to sing in the evenings and kept her head down while serving customers. At night she would sit staring into the flames of the camp fire and sigh as if she had the cares of the world on her shoulders.

Surely the Berlows would have lost interest in her by now?

*   *   *

They were still about two days away from Upley,

225

given their circuitous route from buyer to buyer, when they drew up outside a farm Dan had visited before. Not until they pulled up did they see that the man talking to the owner was Fred Berlow.

Before they could do anything, he looked towards the wagon, gaped for a moment then strode across to them and shouted at Ismay, 'Where the hell have you been, girl? Peggy and I've been worried out of our minds about you.'

She clutched Malachi's arm and he could feel how she was trembling.

'No need to shout at her,' Dan said mildly. 'There's nowt wrong with her hearing.'

'Get down this minute, Ismay Michaels!' Fred ordered. 'You're coming back to us. It's not decent, a lass your age travelling round with two men who're not related to her. Besides—' He bit off the words he'd been going to say. Better not to tell her about her brother-in-law's visit until he had her safe under his roof. She'd always been adamant that she didn't want to see her older sister again.

Ismay looked pleadingly at Malachi, her face white and twisted with anxiety.

'Stay where you are,' he said quietly, looking down at Fred. 'What you were doing with Ismay was as near slavery as anything I've seen or heard of—and in a British colony, too. You should be ashamed of yourself.'

'And what *you're* doing is immoral, as well as against the law.'

Malachi jumped down before anyone could stop him and went to stand in front of Berlow, hands on hips, whole body radiating anger. 'No one's been doing anything immoral! You can't know Ismay very well if you think she's like that. What's more,

226

when she ran away to join us she was so ill we nearly lost her. *That's* how well you and your wife were looking after her!'

Fred swelled with indignation. 'She's legally bonded to us!'

'Legal slavery!' Dan said, echoing Malachi's words.

Before he could stop her, Ismay clambered down to tug Malachi back a little. 'You'll only get in trouble with the law if you quarrel with him, and— and I won't be responsible for bringing harm to you or Dan.'

Instead of moving away, Malachi put his arm round her and looked at the heavily built older man. 'She's not coming back to you, Mr Berlow. If you force her, she'll pine away like she did last time. She was so worn down by it she nearly died.'

Dan climbed down from the wagon and went to stand beside them.

Fred stared at Ismay. 'Well, maybe we can make some new arrangements. But Peggy will want to see her before we decide anything. She's been worried sick about you, Ismay. How about we call a truce and all go back to the farm? We can talk better there.'

Dan put his hand on Malachi's shoulder just in time to stop another angry response. 'It's on our route, lad, so no skin off our noses.' He looked at Fred. 'But before we do anything, I want your promise that you won't force her to stay with you. We saved her life this time when she ran off, but it was a close thing for several days. Who'll save her next time?'

Fred could see for himself how Ismay had changed since she'd left them, grown plumper, with

227

roses in her cheeks again. He also saw that her eyes were bright with tears, though she held her head high and tried to blink them away as she faced him.

'I shall definitely run away again if you try to make me stay with you,' she said quietly. 'I need to find my little sister, Mr Berlow. That's the only thing I really care about now.'

The farmer and his wife, who had been watching all this with great interest, intervened to suggest the travellers at least stay long enough to open their shop and sell them some things they needed.

'Come on, Ismay,' Malachi said gently. 'Let's do that. Mr Berlow will just have to wait for us.'

As they worked together, he whispered, 'We won't let them keep you at the farm, I promise.'

When she looked at him her eyes were almost luminous with gratitude and she looked so soft and beautiful, his heart flipped in his chest. He cleared his throat and began to work twice as fast, avoiding her gaze.

Fred watched as Ismay helped find and sell the items the woman wanted. She always had been a good little worker but she seemed to be thoroughly enjoying this task, taking great pains to help the woman.

Afterwards, when the travellers had packed everything up and set off, he fell in behind them on his horse. Peggy would know what to do. She always found an answer to a problem. But a young unmarried girl travelling and living with two men wasn't right, whatever they said. Even if nothing immoral had happened so far, it would in the end because human nature couldn't be denied. He'd seen the way she looked at that young fellow and he at her.

As they drew up at the Berlows' farm a few hours later, having taken the most direct route, Malachi heard Ismay gulp and felt her clutch his arm again. A quick glance showed that Dan was openly holding her other hand. 'We won't let them trap you here again,' he repeated in a low voice. 'I've promised you that, haven't I?'

'You might not be able to stop them.'

Dan squeezed her hand. 'Don't worry, lass. We'll think of something.'

Fred handed over his horse to the yardman, who was gaping at Ismay, and told him curtly to, 'See to their horses as well as mine.'

The front door opened and Peggy stood there, a look of satisfaction on her face. 'Where did you find her? That brother-in-law of hers is going to be delighted about this.' Ismay gasped and turned chalk-white. Malachi had to hold her upright.

*   *   *

Mark and Theo sat having a final drink together in the hotel bar.

Theo raised his glass. 'Keep in touch and let us know where you settle down.'

'I will.'

'And if you're ever in the west again . . .'

'Or if you ever come back to Victoria . . .'

They let the words trail away and each stared into his glass, not seeing the rum but the memories. They had become good friends over the past few months.

Theo took another sip. 'Keara's trying to hide it, but she's deeply upset. She'd hoped—well, we'd both *expected* to find her sisters.'

'I still can't believe we missed Ismay by so little.'

'Yes. Terrible luck, that. And the way she completely vanished doesn't bode well, does it? She's gone into hiding, I reckon, or worse. Not that I've admitted that to Keara.'

'It's not looking promising.' All Mark could really offer was, 'You can rely on me if there's even the slightest sign of either of them. I'll keep in touch with the police.'

'I know. The fact that you're here in Victoria is one of the reasons Keara feels she can go back to Western Australia. We both trust you absolutely.'

After another silence, Mark lifted his glass to his lips. 'Here's to raising good horses.'

'And babies. Much more important.' Theo lifted his own glass.

When he got back to their room he went to stand over the small bed in the corner where Nell slept so peacefully, then turned to see Keara staring at him from the big double bed. Knowing how upset she was, he got undressed quickly and took her in his arms, a comforting clasp, not the usual flare of passion. 'Do you want to stay here, darlin'? If so, it's not too late to change your mind.'

'No. We might—' a sob shook her '—never find either of them again and we don't want to waste our own lives or those of our children.' Then her voice broke and she wept against him, muffling the noise in his chest but shaking with the depth of her emotion.

He held her close, kissing her damp cheek and stroking her hair, all the time thinking murderous thoughts yet again about his wife in England. Lavinia had been the one to send all three of the Michaels sisters to Australia, the selfish bitch! He

230

was glad he would never see her again.

Eventually Keara slept, but he lay awake for a while longer, wishing there were something else he could do to ease her sorrow. But he racked his brains in vain.

*   *   *

Ismay pulled herself together and looked at Peggy. 'What did you say?'

'I said: that brother-in-law of yours is going to be delighted that you've been found.' As the girl continued to goggle at her, she added impatiently, 'I'm talking about your sister Keara's husband. He was here looking for you just after you ran away.'

Ismay's expression grew set and chill. 'Then I'm glad he didn't find me.' She turned away, not wanting to look at anyone as she tried to take in the information that Keara was here in Australia. Not only here, but married. Who to, for goodness' sake?

Peggy answered her question before she could ask it. 'Your sister's done well for herself. He's a real gentleman, that one is.' She clicked her tongue in exasperation as Ismay moved across to stand by the kitchen window. 'Don't you even want to know who he is, where he's staying?'

Ismay didn't even turn round. 'No, I don't. I never want to see *her* again as long as I live and I don't care who she married.'

Her voice was sharp, but to Malachi's ears there were tears being held back. He went across to put one arm round her shoulders and she threw him a quick suspicious glance, then let the arm stay there, glad of its comforting warmth.

231

'Mr Mullane explained what had happened to you two,' Peggy went on. 'He said his first wife had—'

'Mr Mullane?' Ismay swung round, mouth agape. 'She's never gone and married the master?'

'Yes. Am I not telling you?'

'Well, I don't want to hear anything else about her because now I know *exactly* why she got rid of us.' Mrs Mullane must have died in childbirth and Keara had seized her chance to grab him. He'd always had an eye for her, anyone could see that. But knowing why her sister had abandoned them didn't make things any better. They owed years of suffering to her selfishness. They'd been torn away from their home and country, separated, and Ismay had no intention of being reconciled now. She'd meant exactly what she said. If forced to see her elder sister again, she'd spit in her face, so she would. If she didn't scratch Keara's eyes out first.

She realised that Peggy had stopped talking and they were all looking at her. What else had the woman said? What did they want? 'I'm not going to discuss Keara,' Ismay said coldly. 'Not now, not ever. As far as I'm concerned, I have no elder sister.'

Dan intervened. 'Would you have a cup of tea for a thirsty man, Mrs Berlow?'

Peggy recollected her duties as a hostess and nodded. 'Yes. Yes, of course. Do take a seat.' She'd give the girl time to get used to the news and then speak to her again about her sister.

Ismay drank two cups of tea, but couldn't eat a thing. Automatically she got up to help clear the table, glad of something to occupy herself with.

Peggy looked helplessly at Fred and asked in a

low voice, 'What are we going to do about that dratted girl? I don't think she even listened to what I was telling her.'

He shook his head, as bewildered as she was.

'You're not going to try to keep her here, I hope?' Malachi said. 'She'll only run away again. And in fact, I'm not prepared to leave her here, whatever the law says about it. She nearly died last time.'

Suddenly Peggy remembered her other plan, looked sideways at him and smiled as relief coursed through her. 'It all depends.'

'On what?'

'On how well she's being looked after by others.'

'What do you mean by that?'

Peggy looked from him to Dan and then across at Ismay, who was stacking the dishes near the tin bowl they washed up in. 'It's not right a girl of that age travelling round the countryside with two men who're not related to her.'

'She's come to no harm,' Dan said indignantly. 'I think of her as a daughter.'

'Well, I'm sure *he* doesn't!' Peggy snapped, jerking her head in Malachi's direction. 'And *I* know my duty, if no one else does.'

Ismay came to sit at the table, repeating what she had said several times already, 'I'll definitely run away again if you try to keep me here.'

'She's happy with us,' Malachi protested. 'She's earning an honest living and is able to look for her little sister. Why can't you admit you've been wrong in how you treated her and leave her alone?'

'I've just told you why: it isn't *decent*, her living with you two!'

Dan hid a grin and leaned forward to ask, 'What

would make it decent?'

Peggy took a deep breath. 'If she were married. It says in her contract that we can give her permission to marry and, if so, she's free to leave our service.' She folded her arms and stared them all out. 'Since she isn't married, she'll stay here, even if I have to take her to the magistrate to keep her.'

Ismay gaped at her. 'That's ridiculous! Who would I marry, for heaven's sake?'

Dan said quietly, 'Malachi, of course.'

The silence that followed went on and on. Ismay looked at Malachi's angry expression, blushed furiously, then turned away.

He continued to scowl at Dan and when his old friend nodded encouragingly, shook his head.

Of course Ismay saw that and said quickly, out of pride, 'But *I* don't want to marry *him*.' It was a lie, of course. She did want to marry Malachi, had daydreamed about it a time or two as she sat by the campfire staring into the flames. What girl wouldn't be attracted to a man like him, so lively and clever, with such a beautiful voice and a kind nature, too? Only now he was scowling at Dan, who had dared put her dream into words and had ruined it. Even as she looked Malachi turned his scowl on her. She couldn't bear that.

'Then you'll have to stay here with us, Ismay,' Peggy said flatly. 'I'd never forgive myself if I let you do wrong.'

'You're forgetting her other sister,' Fred said mildly. 'We can let them know she's been found then she can go and live with them.'

'I'll never, ever go to *her*!' Ismay burst out. 'I hate Keara. She broke her promise and I'll never trust her again.'

'She's come looking for you, hasn't she?' Fred asked. 'That means she wants you.'

'Well, I don't want her and I'll kill myself before I'll go to her for help.' Blinking furiously the girl turned away, which brought her into contact with Malachi. She jumped back as if he were red hot, burst into tears and shoved him aside. Rushing out, she instinctively made for her old refuge near the billabong. Only at this time of year a furious torrent was pouring through it, a torrent which resembled the emotions seething inside her. She clung to a tree and leaned her forehead against its smooth bark, weeping because everything had gone wrong, every single thing she cared about.

Back in the kitchen, Dan turned to Malachi. 'Why can't you marry her, lad? You're surely not denying that you're attracted to her?'

'I don't want to marry anyone, that's why. You know I don't.'

'Then she'll have to be sent to that sister of hers.'

'She won't go. She'll just keep running away.' He remembered his own brother with equal loathing. He would hate to be in Lemuel's power, and could understand Ismay's feelings towards her sister, who sounded to be a self-seeking bitch.

Dan sighed loudly and winked at Peggy. 'Well, if *you* won't marry her, she'll have no choice about what she does, for all her angry words. I shall miss her, though. She's a grand little cook, and I could listen to her singing for hours.' He let out another heavy sigh for his young friend's benefit and added, 'Eh, she's been so happy with us.'

With a growl of anger, Malachi flung open the

door and slammed it shut behind him. He strode along the veranda, his boots echoing on the bare boards, not realising that he was taking the same route as Ismay. All he wanted was to get away from people who were trying to force him into something he wasn't ready for.

They were trying to force Ismay, too.

He stopped to frown at a shed, not seeing it, seeing instead a pair of blue eyes brimming with tears. Why didn't she want to marry him? he wondered suddenly. From her point of view it was surely the best solution?

It wasn't until he was halfway across the field that he saw her and stopped dead, wondering whether to go back. She hadn't seen him and was leaning against a tree, weeping. In spite of himself, he felt another surge of pity. For the past two years, people had forced the poor girl from one difficult situation to another. He remembered the old nun and how strict she'd been on the ship, remembered how ill Ismay had been when he and Dan first came here to Upley. And his old friend was right. She had been happy with them, travelling around. She had blossomed and grown rosy in spite of the ongoing sadness about her young sister.

Perhaps he should marry her. It'd be the kindest thing to do.

No, what was he thinking of? He had his plans made. If he'd met her later, he might have courted her, done the thing properly, but a forced marriage to a young woman at this stage in his new life—no, definitely not!

*   *   *

236

Catherine found working in the eating house chaotic at first. Her employer, Sally Grove, had little idea of how to organise things and, although she was a good cook, had no idea of catering for larger numbers. She provided too much food, so that some spoiled and had to be thrown away, and she grew visibly anxious when it was time to go through the weekly accounts with her husband.

Inevitably Catherine found herself offering to help. 'Why don't we buy less beef today? We never need as much early in the week.'

'Do you think so? But what if we ran out of food? What would the customers say? Samuel would be so angry if I had nothing to give them.'

'If we bought a big ham, we could always offer them ham and fried potatoes topped with an egg.'

Sally gave her usual answer. 'I'll have to ask Samuel.'

Her husband approved the ham and the waste was less that week.

When it came to planning the following week's meals—though really there was little to plan, because Sally always served the same things on the same days—Catherine was asked her opinion and, again, it was heeded.

At the end of the month, Sally said hesitantly, 'Would you like to take over the organising, Katie? I really do prefer doing the cooking.'

'If you're sure?'

'Yes. Yes, I am. Very sure.'

It was satisfying to be in charge of something. Catherine found herself humming as she worked, walking briskly along on market day to buy fresh food, looking for suppliers at the market who lived quite close to town and might offer them fresh vegetables at the beginning of the week as well. If she were running an eating house, she'd have her own garden and try not to rely so much on others. She missed the garden at the convent in Ireland greatly. She'd enjoyed working in it, plunging her hands into the moist black soil and seeing the fruits of her labours brought to table. Flowers weren't nearly as satisfying to grow as vegetables.

She always went early to the market, hoping to avoid Albert Bevan, but one day she was delayed and found herself face to face with him. She tried to pass but he stepped in front of her, his face dark with anger.

'Found yourself another job, have you?'

'You know I have.'

He fingered the scar on his forehead. 'You left unpaid debts behind. I'll see that you pay them, one day.'

She couldn't hide her shudder. As he walked away, grinning at her reaction, she couldn't move for a moment or two. Why? she asked herself. Why was he picking on her like this? She had never encouraged him in any way. Why had he thought he had a right to maul her around?

It spoiled the pleasure she found in her new job, knowing he was still living nearby and still threatening her.

CHAPTER FIFTEEN

JULY 1865

In England Nancy looked at Lavinia Mullane, amazed by the way her charge was blossoming. The quiet life and regular hours seemed to agree with the woman who had once been her nursling—as did Lavinia's separation from the husband she hated and release from the dangers of pregnancy. Theo Mullane was living in Australia now, and a good thing too. There could not have been a more ill-matched couple. Oh, the blue shadow was still there sometimes on Lavinia's lips, but she wasn't nearly as breathless as she had once been.

But if the younger woman was blossoming, Nancy, forty years her senior, was not. The balance of their lives had changed with Theo's departure and Nancy had *known* then, in that very special way in which she could sometimes sense the patterns of the future, that what she had seen before as most likely to happen might not now come to pass. Like a child's row of carefully balanced dominoes, if you moved one, others inevitably followed suit. She sighed and stared out of the window, wondering what to do about it all, wondering if it was even worth trying. She felt—not ill exactly, but not well, either, and knew her condition was worsening rapidly.

Lavinia breezed into the room, her plump, thirty-year-old body clad in frills more suited to a young, unmarried girl. 'Aren't you ready yet?'

'I think I'll stay home this morning. I'm not

239

feeling very well.'

'You can stay home this afternoon. I need you now to help me choose the material for my new dress.'

'We can do that tomorrow, chickie,' Nancy said mildly.

'But I want to do it today. I'd *planned* to do it today.'

Nancy pressed one hand against the pain in her side and felt her way carefully to a chair.

'I'll go on my own,' Lavinia threatened.

But for once Nancy didn't have the energy to distract her. Through a haze of pain she watched her former nursling flounce out of the house like the twelve year old she still was inside her head and wondered yet again why Lavinia's parents had ever thought her capable of marrying and producing children. They had been extremely careful to hide her shortcomings from Theo before the marriage.

Then she clicked her tongue in exasperation. What did all that matter now? The only thing that mattered was to read the tea leaves and find out if what she suspected was true.

By sheer willpower she forced the pain aside and ten minutes later sat staring into a cup, studying the patterns of damp black specks. For the third time running the tea leaves were predicting her own death. Well, she'd had over seventy years of life and done the best with it she could, so she wouldn't complain at that. But she couldn't bear to leave this life until she'd worked out what to do about Lavinia. No one else had ever cared for the poor girl and Theo had left her in Nancy's care when he went off to Australia to find Keara, believing her when she'd told him that Lavinia

240

hadn't long for this world.

She sat very still and quiet for a long time, thinking it all over.

When her nursling came home, sulky because she hadn't been able to decide between two sorts of material for the new dress, Nancy was waiting for her. She coaxed her into drinking a cup of tea, then took the cup and tipped out the residue of the liquid.

Lavinia's face crumpled. 'Don't do it, Nancy. I hate you reading the tea leaves. It frightens me.'

Nancy calmed her then read the leaves, staring down at them in shock. This was worse than she had expected, far worse. She hid her anxiety, however, and summoned up a smile. 'It only says you'll have a happy year, chickie, better than last year. Aren't you the lucky one?'

Lavinia brightened and went off to decide what to wear that afternoon when she would be taking tea with her special friends—women who tolerated her because she was 'one of them' and behaved with humble gratitude for being allowed into their circle. If you could call that friendship!

While she was away, Nancy wrote a letter to her niece, Bess, and sent the maid down to the Post Office with it. Her sister's daughter had never married. She had been a boisterous, unruly child, but had settled down in her late twenties, from all accounts, and was now in her thirties, still unmarried. Bess was the only one she could turn to for help.

*　　　*　　　*

When Bess read her aunt's letter, she did a little

241

dance. She'd been desperate to get away because she owed a few people money.

She frowned. She still needed enough to make her escape in such a way that no one would know where she'd gone.

That evening she went out with Thad Bowler again. She didn't much like him but he'd lent her money a time or two and this was the way he preferred her to pay him back. After he'd finished with her, he fell asleep as usual and she scowled at his heavy body next to her in bed. Easing herself away from him, she got dressed again.

Just as she was leaving, she saw the coins that had fallen out of his trouser pocket, hesitated, then bent to pick them up. This would help pay for a new start and to hell with her debt to him!

When she'd left, he opened his eyes and grinned. She'd soon be so deep in debt to him that she'd do anything he asked. She was a fine woman still, for all she was older than him. He reached for the bottle of gin. Nothing like a good swig or two after you'd bedded your woman.

*   *   *

Malachi couldn't bear the sight of Ismay standing there alone weeping for a minute longer. With a sigh for his own stupidity, he walked forward and laid his hand on her shoulder. She squeaked in shock and tried to push him away, but her feet slipped on the muddy ground and she'd have fallen backwards into the roaring water of the billabong if he hadn't dragged her towards him.

'Be careful, you little fool! You nearly fell in then.'

'Well, that'd have solved all my problems, wouldn't it?' Her voice was bitter, her eyes still welling with tears.

He didn't let go of her, suddenly afraid she meant it. 'Don't talk like that. You have everything to live for.'

'Do I? Tell me what?'

He couldn't think of anything but, 'You're young, you have your whole life ahead of you.'

'I've nothing.' Her voice was flat, dull, not like her usual lilting tone at all. 'No family, not even the freedom to choose my own way of life.'

'Aw, Issy lass.' And then he said it. He hadn't planned to, but the words tumbled out of his mouth before he could stop them. 'If that's the case, we'll have to give you something to live for. Let's get married and make a better life for you.'

She glared at him. 'What did they say to you after I'd left to make you change your mind about marrying me? Well, I'm *not* taking an unwilling husband. My father was forced to marry my mother when they found she was expecting and it turned him sour. She had a dreadful life with him, dreadful! He turned into a drunkard and womaniser, and he hated her.'

Again she tried to push away from him, but he was so afraid she'd throw herself into the raging water, with its broken branches and other hazards, that he wouldn't let go and began to pull her towards the house.

'Get off me!' she panted, struggling.

'Not until you promise me you won't do anything stupid!'

They both stilled for a moment, then she asked, 'Why should you care?'

243

'Because I'm fond of you.'

'Hah! Not fond enough to marry me.' She wished the words unsaid as soon as they were out and hoped the moonlight didn't show her hot blush.

'I didn't want to marry anyone yet,' he said quietly. 'That has nothing whatsoever to do with you. I'd planned to make something of myself first. It's not just the marrying, you see. If you have children, you can't go driving round the countryside selling things. You're tied to your family.' And the profits from this last journey were excellent. Feeling a sudden wetness on his face he looked up in surprise. 'It's starting to rain again. We'd better go back.'

She let him turn her round and they began to walk across the field. To her surprise, he kept his arm round her shoulders. 'You can't stop the children coming,' she said sadly.

He stopped walking to stare at her with such a strange expression that she asked, 'What's wrong now? What have I said?'

'You've given me an idea. You don't have children if you don't consummate a marriage.'

She looked at him in surprise. She didn't believe any man could manage without it, not after living in a one-room cottage and hearing how often her father pestered her mother at night.

Malachi stood there for so long frowning in thought, with the rain coming down in earnest now, that she began to wonder if he was feeling all right. Then he threw back his head and laughed. 'Issy, if we got ourselves married, you'd be free of your contract and Dan and I would still have your help with the selling. But we needn't share a bed until—

244

oh, until we're secure and settled.'

'Why bother to marry at all if you don't want me? You'll still be lumbered with me whether we go to bed together or not. What benefit would that bring you?'

'If I were ready for marriage, you're exactly the sort of woman I'd choose—or would be if you were older. Seventeen is too young for marriage and motherhood really. And this way it'd at least keep the other women from pestering me. I don't want to sound conceited, but they're a real nuisance sometimes. Mothers want daughters to find a husband, or wives want—um—little adventures, while widows want to remarry or just to have a man in their beds again.'

She looked at him doubtfully.

'Will you think about it, us having a marriage in name only—just for the time being, I mean? It'd solve your problems, and it'd not give me troubles I didn't want.'

Her voice came out surly. 'If you don't want to marry me, just say so.'

He smiled at her, his eyes gleaming in the moonlight and his skin wet with rain. 'I *am* fond of you, Issy, but I'm also fond of money, so you'd better decide whether you'll accept that sort of offer before we go back inside. They'll all be pestering us if we don't agree to do as they want.'

She shrugged, knowing this was her only way of escaping. 'Very well then, I'll marry you. Why not? I certainly don't want to share your bed or have children yet. All I want to do is look for my sister.'

But she was lying. She admitted that to herself, at least. She wished Malachi wanted her as men usually wanted women, wished he loved her. As she

245

had grown to love him and his kind ways.

*   *   *

The others were waiting for them in the kitchen, Dan leaning back and whistling tunelessly to himself, Peggy finishing the dishes, Fred reading an old newspaper for the third time. When the door opened, they all stopped what they were doing and looked expectantly at the two young people.

Malachi set his hand on Ismay's shoulder and gave it a little squeeze. 'We've decided to get wed.'

She stood beside him as the three older people beamed at them, tried to smile back at them as if she were happy and failed.

'I wish you well,' said Dan, coming across to kiss her cheek. 'It may not be how you wanted it to happen, but I truly believe you two will suit.'

She shrugged and tried to thank him, but couldn't manage that, either. Her voice seemed to have faded to nothing.

'How soon can it be done?' Malachi asked.

'We'll drive over to see the minister tomorrow,' Peggy said. 'We don't always bother out here in the bush with calling banns and such. He'll marry you there and then if he's at home.'

Ismay looked at Malachi in shock. So soon!

All he said was, 'Good. Suits me.'

Peggy bustled forward. 'We'll have to find you something pretty to wear, child. You can't get married in that old thing.'

Ismay looked down at herself. 'I don't have anything pretty.'

'I do. Come with me.' She took Ismay into her bedroom and heaved a big trunk from underneath the bed. When she knelt and opened it she had tears in her eyes. She took out the top garment and stroked the material with one work-roughened hand. 'These were my daughter's things. She died of a fever. Eighteen and engaged to be married. Eh, I miss her still, though it's five years now she's been gone.'

Ismay's anger faded. 'I'm so sorry. But I can't take them!'

Peggy looked up at her with a smile that almost twisted into tears. 'She'd want you to. We had more money in those days and I bought her a lot of clothes for her bottom drawer, more than she needed. Since then, I give them to poor girls getting married. It's good to have a pretty dress. You'll be the third I've helped.' She looked down again, her eyes blind with memories. 'She'd want you to have one of her dresses, but we'll have to take the hem up. She was much taller than you.'

She pulled several garments out of the trunk, laying them out on the bed. 'You choose.'

Ismay came forward and looked from one to the other, feeling the material and holding them against her. But it wasn't hard to choose. 'This one.' It was a soft pink muslin, made with separate skirt and bodice. It didn't ape the crinolines of richer women, but was very simple in style yet so pretty.

'She always loved that dress.'

'Thank you.'

Peggy began to put the clothes back in the trunk. 'I know you think me and Fred have been harsh with you. Maybe we have. If so, I'm sorry. We left Melbourne after Tilda died and bought this place. We didn't care about money just wanted to get

247

away. I don't mind hard work, but I hate to be without another woman here. Oh, goodness me! I nearly forgot. You'll need these as well.' She pulled out a petticoat and tossed it to Ismay, then some white stockings.

As she stood up she said, 'Malachi's fond of you, you know, watches you all the time.'

'But he doesn't want to marry me. What if he grows to hate me?'

'It'll be up to you to make sure he doesn't. You love him, don't you?'

Ismay stared down at the pile of soft material in her arms and nodded slowly. 'I do, yes.'

'I thought so. Well, it's always chancy how it'll turn out when you marry, even if you're mad for one another. There's a lot as don't love one another and marry for convenience, but love can grow if you feed it with kindness and don't try to force it.' Then she shook her head and reverted to her usual brisk tone. 'Well, talking won't fix that hem. Try the dress on and we'll see how much to take it up.'

*   *   *

One morning in August, Sally Grove tripped and fell down the stairs that led from their quarters above the general store to the shop itself, breaking her leg. The first Catherine knew of it was when the Groves' yard boy came and banged on the door of the eating house next door and yelled out that she was needed next door, quick. The missus was hurt.

Without waiting to explain, he hared off down the street and Catherine rushed next door.

Sally Grove was still lying where she'd fallen, and refused to let them even try to move her. Her husband was kneeling beside her, only half-dressed.

Strange, Catherine thought, how ordinary Samuel Grove looked in shirt sleeves with his braces dangling over the sides of his trousers. Then she forgot everything in the need to comfort Sally, who was moaning and in great pain.

The doctor arrived soon afterwards and insisted on them carrying Mrs Grove to her bedroom. Moving made her first scream then faint, after which Samuel stopped dead in his tracks. Catherine had to nudge him and suggest they get his wife to the bedroom quickly before she regained consciousness.

'I have some chloroform in my rooms,' the doctor told Samuel. 'It's more expensive to use that, but it kills the pain. I'd take her there to set the leg but I fear the journey would hurt her too much so I'll have to set it here. I shall need some assistance, because my usual nurse is attending a childbirth.'

'I can help,' Catherine offered. 'I've had some experience of nursing.' She looked at Samuel. 'We won't be able to open the eating house today, though.'

He waved one hand dismissively. 'What does that matter?'

It pleased her to see how much he cared about his wife when previously she had thought him rather an arrogant and pompous fellow.

She watched with interest as the doctor administered the chloroform and set Sally's leg without the screaming and pain usually associated with broken limbs.

249

'You did well,' he told Catherine afterwards.

'I was glad to help. I've never seen chloroform used before though I've heard of it, of course.'

'It's a wonderful discovery. One of the marvels of modern medicine. I pride myself on keeping up to date with such things.'

'I'd have thought you'd do better to practise in the city, then,' she said absent-mindedly.

'My wife and I prefer the clean air of the country, especially with four children to raise. Besides,' he grinned at her, suddenly boyish, 'as the only doctor round here, I get a wide variety of cases and that's very interesting. No sending them to hospital or calling in a famous surgeon. There's just me.'

After he'd gone, Catherine went downstairs, waited until Samuel had finished serving a customer then asked in her usual quiet way, 'What do you want to do about the eating house while your wife's recovering?'

'Can you run it for me?'

'Yes, but I'll need some help. I can't cook *and* serve.'

He sighed. 'That's the trouble in a small country town: where to find help. I wonder . . . would you mind working with a native woman? Kalaya's worked here before and she's very clean and sober. She and her husband are both well thought of in the town, don't cause any trouble, or get drunk. If all the natives were like them, life would be a lot easier.'

'I'd be happy to work with her.'

He frowned. 'I'd better go and see her myself. Can you mind the shop for me?'

He was gone before she could answer him. She

hoped he wouldn't be long. She knew little about the goods on sale.

The week which followed was one of the busiest of Catherine's life. Kalaya came to work at the eating house but had to bring her new baby. She was the first native Catherine had had any close dealings with and at first she watched her carefully, knowing how important it was to keep things clean and tidy in the kitchen. But she needn't have worried. Kalaya was quiet, but neat and clean in her habits. She already knew the main things about the job and adapted to Catherine's ways with little fuss.

At the end of the first day, Catherine thanked her for her help, which seemed to surprise Kalaya, then offered her some left-overs to take home.

'Are you sure, missus?'

'Of course. This stew is best eaten today. You can bring the bowl back tomorrow.' It was another of Sally's miscalculations about quantities.

'Thank you, missus.'

Catherine lingered. 'Your baby's lovely, so quiet and well-behaved.'

Kalaya's solemn expression lightened. 'She's the easiest of them all. I'll find someone to look after her tomorrow but they'll still have to bring her here so that I can feed her.'

'That's all right.' Catherine watched the other woman stride along the back street with the baby in one arm and a basket on the other. She locked the rear door carefully then went to give the takings to Samuel and enquire about Sally. By the time she got to bed she was exhausted, but admitted to herself that she had greatly enjoyed being in sole charge.

Mark left Nan and little Amy in the lodgings he had occupied when he first came to Melbourne. The same elderly couple was running the place and they were still as friendly as he remembered. They promised to keep an eye on Nan and his daughter while he was away.

It felt strange to board the stage coach on his own. He'd spent almost two years caring for his daughter following Patience's death in childbirth, living first at the country inn he'd run for a time in Western Australia, then back in Melbourne while helping to search for for the Michaels sisters. He wondered briefly how Maggie was doing in her new job as a barmaid—no, Maggie would be all right. She was sharp enough to take care of herself.

As the rattletrap of a coach took him out into the countryside, he could see that the city had spread further since he'd last been here and that made him wonder if things had changed much in Rossall Springs. Until his father-in-law, who had been mentally unstable, had made it impossible for him to live there, he'd thought himself settled in Rossall for life. Then he'd tried and failed to settle in Western Australia: now he was adrift again.

He didn't know why it felt so important for him to go back to Rossall, but it did. He had grown stronger in himself since his young wife's death and wouldn't run away from anything now. The pity of it was that he'd sold the eating house to his neighbour, Samuel Grove. It was exactly the sort of business Mark wanted and his sort of town, too. He didn't aspire to be rich, like his sister Annie, just to make a decent living, look after his family and enjoy the company of a few friends.

When Mark got off the coach, it seemed for a moment as if nothing had changed in the town then, as he looked round, he noticed several new buildings along the street. The man at the livery stables, where the coach stopped, was a stranger so Mark didn't stop to chat. Taking his bag, he strode off down the street to confront his past.

* * *

A week after Catherine took over at the eating house Albert Bevan walked in and stood before her, running his eyes up and down her body in a very offensive way. She forced herself to move forward to take his money, but had to struggle to pull her hand away from his because he held tight.

'Don't do that!' she snapped, taking a step backwards.

'Why not? We still have unfinished business, you and I.'

He tapped the scar on his forehead as he had done at the market and she said coldly, 'Here's your money back. Please leave. You're no longer welcome here.'

His expression turned vicious. 'I'm not moving. I have as much right as anyone else to buy a meal.'

Not knowing how to deal with him, she walked out and hurried next door to seek Samuel's help.

'Can you not cope with him?' he asked with an aggrieved sigh. 'You're imagining things, Katie. Albert Bevan wouldn't behave like that.'

She felt outraged that he could doubt her word. 'I'm not imagining anything and if you won't help

253

me in this, I'll not be able to continue working for you.' As he stared at her in shock, she added quietly, 'I'm afraid of him. Really afraid.'

'It's not good to alienate a customer. He'll talk to other people, put them off.'

'I'm not serving him, now or any time.'

'Oh, very well. I'll come and talk to him.'

They went into the eating house the back way, just in time to see Kalaya carry in a plate of food for one of the customers and Albert, who had not noticed their arrival, stick out his foot to trip her up. She went sprawling, the plate smashed and the food splattered across the floor.

'Stupid black bitch!' he jeered. 'I don't know why they allow dirty natives like you near our food.'

The women in the ladies' room stopped eating to stare anxiously out into the main area.

Samuel strode forward, face red with anger. 'I saw what you just did. Get out of my eating house, Bevan, and don't come back!'

Albert looked round in shock, then blustered, 'What do you mean? I did nothing.'

'I saw you trip her up.'

Kalaya was picking up the pieces of plate and food, avoiding everyone's eyes. When Albert stood up she jerked backwards, as if expecting him to hit her.

'She'll bear witness that I did nothing,' he said loudly. 'Did I touch you, girl?'

Catherine stepped forward. 'Go back into the kitchen, Kalaya. You don't need to say anything. Mr Grove and I both saw what happened.'

A man stopped in the doorway as she spoke, a tall, quiet-looking fellow with dark hair. He was neatly dressed and carrying a holdall. She would

254

have liked to go and greet him but didn't dare until Samuel had dealt with Albert.

'I'm not leaving this place until I've been served,' Albert blustered, 'and not by a blackie, either.'

'You won't be served here today or any other day,' Samuel snapped. 'Get out, Bevan!'

Albert grinned and sat down again. 'I don't think you're man enough to make me, Grove. And it won't do you any good to get on the wrong side of me because I have plenty of friends in this town.'

Out of the corner of her eye, Catherine saw the stranger put down his holdall and start moving forward.

'Need any help, Samuel?' he asked in a level tone.

'Mark Gibson!' Samuel looked at Albert and sighed. 'I'm afraid we do. This man is causing trouble.'

Catherine watched as the stranger stopped in front of Albert. 'I heard Mr Grove ask you to leave. Please do so.'

There was an air of quiet confidence about him that impressed Catherine. For a moment Albert hesitated, then he stood up. 'You won't always have someone to help you,' he snarled at Samuel, then looked beyond him to Catherine. 'And our business is only postponed.'

He sauntered out, taking his time, with everyone in the eating house watching him nervously.

Not until he was out of sight did Catherine say in a low voice, 'It's me he wants to hurt. I'd better leave town or he'll cause trouble for you, Mr Grove.'

Mark couldn't help saying, 'Running away never really helps, as I've found to my cost, Miss—'

'Mrs Caldwell,' Samuel supplied. His shoulders sagged, he let out a groan and then ran one hand through his thinning hair. 'I'll tell you frankly, Gibson, I should never have taken this place on. It's too much for my Sally and now that she's broken her leg, I don't know how I'm going to manage.'

Mark's face lit up. 'And I've always regretted selling it. Perhaps we can help one another?'

Samuel brightened. 'Perhaps we can. Of course, I've made some improvements and there are more people in town now so the business is more valuable than when I bought it.'

Mark grinned and stared round. 'It looks like it needs a coat of paint to me and those tablecloths are definitely getting worn. I'll give you the same price as you paid me and not a penny more.'

Samuel groaned aloud, then as his assistant from the store came to the doorway, and beckoned, he turned to Mark. 'We'll discuss the details later. But you're only getting it so cheaply because Sally's broken her leg and I'm run off my feet. Are you all right now, Katie?' When she nodded, he hurried out.

Mark looked at Catherine. 'You work here?'

'I've just started but Mrs Grove is hurt so I'm in charge for the moment.'

'I'm going to need help. So if you want to keep your job, I'd be happy to have you go on working for me.'

'But you don't know me.'

He grinned. 'Samuel wouldn't keep you on if you weren't a good worker.'

She bit her lip, worrying about staying in Rossall at all with Albert Bevan so hostile.

256

'Don't leave,' Mark said softly. 'I won't let that man eat here and I'm not afraid of him.'

'Well, I'll try it out, if you like. Better if we both see how we go working together before we make a final decision. Did you want a meal?'

'Yes, please.'

She smiled. 'I don't think I should charge you.' Then she hesitated and said, 'There's another problem, though. I have a room here. If you're coming back to live, it wouldn't be proper for me to stay and yet . . .' Her voice faded.

'My wife died when Amy was born, but my mother-in-law and daughter will be living here with me, so it'll be perfectly respectable.'

'Oh. Well, then, I'd—um—definitely like to try it.'

She watched covertly as he ate his meal. He was good-looking in a quiet way, tall and clean-shaven, tidily but not expensively dressed. But how was anyone going to keep Albert Bevan in order? Her former employer had one or two friends in the town, she now knew, men of the same ilk. She didn't want to bring trouble to someone with a small daughter to raise.

CHAPTER SIXTEEN

JULY–AUGUST 1865

When Ismay came out of Peggy's bedroom the next morning she was newly bathed and wearing the pink dress. Malachi stopped dead at the sight of her. He had never seen her look so attractive, wasn't sure he felt easy with the transformation. The vibrant colour of the material brought out the dark gleam of her hair and lent warmth to the creamy softness of her skin so that he had the sudden urge to touch her cheek. He did indeed take a step forward, hand outstretched, then stopped and contented himself with saying in a throaty voice, 'You look really pretty, Issy.'

Colour flared in her cheeks and for once she was lost for words, could only give him a shy smile and stay near Peggy, as if for protection.

Dan filled the awkward silence by stepping forward and claiming the honour of kissing the bride. As he pressed his leathery old lips to her cheek, he whispered, 'He's fond of you, lass, more than he knows. This'll work out right, I'm sure.'

He was the second person to tell her that Malachi cared for her, but she wouldn't believe it unless he told her himself. Didn't dare. She blinked up at Dan uncertainly. Had he guessed how she felt? Was it so obvious? She hoped Malachi hadn't.

He came to stand in front of her, nudging the old man aside. 'Am I not allowed to kiss my bride as well?'

Peggy put up one hand to stop him and said briskly, 'Not till you're wed, lad, so get yourself outside and find out where that husband of mine is with the cart.'

He looked at her in annoyance, hesitated but did as she asked.

Peggy turned to Ismay. 'Never give in too easily to a man. If he gets kisses for nothing, he'll not work to win your affection.'

The girl didn't know what to say to that. Peggy had given her several pieces of advice about married life as she helped her dress. Was she right? Ismay didn't know, didn't feel certain of anything this morning, she felt so strange and unlike herself. She couldn't stop looking down at the dress and stroking it with her fingertips, though. She had never in her life owned anything half as pretty and was terrified of dirtying it.

'He's looking smart, that man of yours,' Peggy said grudgingly. 'That's one of the new lounge jackets, isn't it? It looks a sight comfier than my Fred's best jacket. Malachi should have asked me to press it for him, though. I could soon have got the flatiron hot last night.'

There was the sound of the cart drawing up outside and Fred yelled, 'Aren't you ready yet, Peg? We don't want to take all day about this.'

'Come on,' she said, brisk again after her momentary lapse into softness. 'Put that cloak on and let's get you married, girl.'

It was raining lightly and cold. As they drove along Ismay huddled beside Malachi in the back of the wagon under the hood, trying to make sure she kept her lovely new dress covered and away from the dirty floor of the cart. The bench along the side was hard and the roads rough, so she was jolted against him every now and then, even though she tried not to touch him. He sat easily, his legs apart to balance himself. She liked his wiry body and his lean, intelligent face. She wouldn't want to marry a great muscular lump of a man like Fred Berlow.

At one stage Malachi winked at her and whispered, 'Dan insisted I got out my best clothes, but they're a bit crumpled. Sorry about that.'

She couldn't think what to say so held her tongue, but couldn't help stealing the occasional glance at him. She was glad he didn't wear a moustache like Dan or droopy side whiskers like Fred. His skin looked lovely, not ruddy-cheeked like some of the men in her Irish village back home, just nicely tanned.

From time to time she would catch him looking at her, then they would both look quickly in another direction. Once she saw him open his mouth as if to say something, then shake his head and snap his lips shut. Well, she could keep silent, too, she thought, and vowed not to look at him again.

She didn't keep that vow, couldn't.

And he kept looking at her, too.

It took them two hours to drive to the nearest church and as they drew up outside it the rain eased off. Malachi jumped down and turned to help Ismay. When their hands touched, she froze and so did he. As they stared at one another she forgot about the rest of the party.

Peggy nudged Dan and smiled. He nodded in approval. Fred was putting nose bags on his horses and noticed nothing. No one broke the silence until Malachi said something quietly to his bride.

Ismay wasn't sure she'd heard correctly. Had he really told her how beautiful she looked? It was the dress, that was all. She wasn't beautiful, not like Keara. She was too thin and bony, and always had been. But still, it was nice to know she was looking her best on her wedding day. That gave her the courage to hold her head up.

They found the minister at home and when he spoke about waiting to call the banns, Peggy cut him short. 'There's not time for all that fuss. Do you think we can spend three weeks driving to and fro? Take one of those marriage licences out of your drawer and let's get them wed now.'

'Is there any reason for the hurry?' He looked at Ismay suspiciously.

'Not the sort you're thinking of,' snapped Peggy. 'But Mr Firth has a travelling shop to run, with folk waiting for his goods, so he can't stay round here doing nothing for three weeks.'

With a sigh the minister led the way across to the church and threw open the door with a bang. It was small, no bigger than a house, with one big room inside. It had ten plain wooden benches facing the far end, five on each side. There was no stained glass, no fancy altar, very little to remind Ismay of the churches she had known in Ireland. In fact, it didn't feel much like one to her.

The minister disappeared through a door to one side but Malachi hesitated just inside the building until Dan gave him a shove.

'You go and wait for her at the front, lad.'

With a quick glance at her as if to check that she was all right, Malachi did as he was told, his footsteps echoing on the bare floorboards.

Dan took off his hat and set it carefully on the nearest bench, then bowed from the waist and offered his arm to Ismay. 'I hope you'll let me give you away, lass?'

She nodded.

'Just a minute.' Peggy took off the girl's cloak, straightening the pink folds of her skirt, then hesitated before giving Ismay a quick peck on the cheek. After that she took her husband's arm and led him to the front of the church, where they sat down.

Ismay missed the warmth of the cloak, but

wanted to look her best so tried not to shiver.

The minister came in from the side and stood looking down the central aisle. He cleared his throat to gain their attention. 'Will everyone please rise?'

The Berlows were the only ones sitting and as they stood up, they turned expectantly to look at Ismay.

'I don't know what to do,' she whispered to Dan. 'I don't know how people get married in Protestant churches.'

He whispered, 'It's not hard. We walk slowly to the front, you stand beside Malachi and then the minister tells you exactly what to say and do.' He drew her forward and when they got to where the groom was standing, winked at them both and stepped to one side.

As they reached the part of the ceremony where he was supposed to produce a ring, Malachi looked at Ismay in dismay. 'I was so busy getting dressed in this lot, I forgot to bring a ring. Issy, I'm so sorry.'

'I didn't forget, lad.' Dan fumbled in his pocket but didn't produce one of the imitation gold rings they sold in their travelling shop. Instead he pulled out a slender band which looked like real gold and offered it to Malachi. 'It was my mother's. They sent it out to me when she died. She said I was to have it.'

'I can't take your mother's ring,' Ismay whispered.

'Yes, you can. It's my wedding present to you. We're doing this properly.'

The minister 'ahemmed' and the service continued.

It seemed as if fate was smiling on them, for the

ring fitted Ismay's finger perfectly. As Malachi slid it on, she looked up at him, unguarded for once, her eyes brilliant with pleasure.

He swallowed hard. He hadn't realised when he'd offered her the strange bargain that she could be so pretty. He'd only ever seen her in dull clothes, her hair tied severely back, her face often gaunt with worry or sadness.

If she continued to look so lovely, how the hell was he going to keep his vow that nothing would happen between them? He was a normal man and she *was* his wife now! He took a deep breath, then another. But it didn't help much.

*　　　*　　　*

After the wedding they all drove back to the Berlows' farm and by mid-afternoon Dan, Ismay and Malachi had set off again on their travels.

Before they left Peggy gave Ismay a big hug and whispered, 'Mind now, don't make things too easy for him.'

Not used to such treatment from her former employer, Ismay could only nod. She felt shy as she climbed up to sit on the driving bench of the big wagon between Dan and the man who was now her husband. Nothing had changed, really, she tried to tell herself. But it felt like it had, inside her own head if nowhere else.

After three hours they came to a farm where Dan knew the owners and stopped to see if they wanted to buy anything. He went to the door, leaving Ismay and Malachi sitting together on the wagon.

'It—um—went quite well today, didn't it?'

Malachi said.

'Yes.' She looked down at herself. 'I'd better change out of this dress, though. I'm going to keep it for best.' Again her lingers betrayed her, caressing the soft fabric.

'Keep it on for tonight,' he said impulsively. 'You look lovely in pink and it *is* our wedding night. We must get you some more pretty clothes. The things the nuns gave you aren't . . . well, they're not flattering.'

'I know. But they were all I had. I've never had nice things because we've always been poor.'

He laid his hand over hers. 'You and I will make a lot of money together and one day you'll have nothing but pretty clothes, I promise you.'

She considered this, head on one side, then shook her head. 'I can't imagine that and anyway, I don't need fancy clothes to make me happy.'

'What do you need?'

She looked at him, stared into the distance and said, 'To find Mara and then, if we can manage it, for you and me to make a happy family life together.' She could feel herself flushing, but made herself say the words. 'I don't want you to be regretting our marriage.'

'I'm sure I shan't.'

She wished she could feel sure of that. She kept thinking of her father and how unhappy he'd made her mother. She had never understood why Mam put up with such treatment. Ismay wouldn't let anyone, not even Malachi, use her as a doormat.

Dan came out of the house just then with the owner of the farm and his wife.

'You stay here,' Malachi said quietly. 'Keep your dress out of the mud. I can show them what they

264

need.'

So she marked her wedding day by sitting like a lady for half an hour, then got thoroughly fed up of it and would have jumped down to help if it hadn't been for the dress.

After the owners had finished making their leisurely purchases, the woman clearly enjoying the novelty of being able to 'go shopping', they invited everyone to come and share their evening meal.

'Mr Reddings tells me you two got married today,' the woman said. 'We must celebrate that. It's lucky I baked a cake today.'

As they were finishing the meal, the rain came down again, thundering on the roof and making the path to the wagon a quagmire.

When it was time to go to bed, there was a lot of teasing which had Ismay blushing again. Dan said he'd sleep on the veranda and leave the young couple to enjoy the floor of the wagon in peace so they went outside.

She looked in dismay at the muddy path. Malachi, who understood how much the new dress meant to her, picked her up in his arms, making her squeak in shock. He found her lighter than he had expected. When he'd set her down on the back step of the wagon he jumped up quickly after her.

'I'd leave you to get undressed in peace, but it's too wet,' he said. 'I'll just make a light. Thank heavens for safety matches. What would we have done otherwise?' He lit the lamp and hung it on its usual hook. 'I'll turn my back while you put your nightdress on, shall I?'

She got out her nightdress and fumbled with the fastenings of her dress, but couldn't manage the many small buttons down the back. 'Malachi, could you help me, please?' she asked hesitantly. 'I can't get it undone.'

He took a deep breath and went to work, making heavy weather of the tiny buttons because the soft white flesh of her body and the sight of her new, lace-trimmed underclothing were both affecting him. 'It's going to be harder than I'd expected,' he said hoarsely when he'd finished. He took a step backwards, which was all the space there was.

'What is?'

'Not—making you my wife.'

'Oh.'

He reached out and took her gently in his arms. 'I do insist on a wedding kiss, though.' She looked up at him, her face solemn and apprehensive. 'Eh, I'm not going to hurt you, Issy love.' He bent his head and kissed her lips. They were so soft he lingered on them, then suddenly pushed her away and stepped backwards again.

'What did I do wrong?' she cried, not wanting him to take his arms away.

'Nothing. It's just—we daren't *start* the loving or we'll never keep our bargain. One thing leads to another, you see.'

'Oh.'

'I enjoyed the kiss, though.' An understatement, if ever there was one.

'It was my first proper kiss,' she confided.

'I'm glad. And one day, I'll love you as you deserve, make you my wife properly.'

She nodded. 'We have to be—sensible.'

He didn't let the groan escape him, but sensible was the last thing he felt. When he turned his back, his voice came out more harshly than he'd meant.

'Hurry up now and finish getting undressed. I'm tired, if you're not.'

She was tired, but she didn't want this night to end. When they were ready he blew out the lamp, but she could tell he was awake in the darkness. He didn't speak, so she didn't either. But he was there with her, and that felt good.

Her last thought was that now she belonged to someone again. She only hoped the people who had taken Mara were being kind to her little sister.

*   *   *

After making sure the new maid had plenty to eat for breakfast, which was served at eleven in the morning in this late-rising household, Dolly concentrated on her own food and chatted with her 'girls'. The three of them were yawning and still wearing their nightdresses under their loosely tied house gowns, but they smiled at Mara and said they hoped she'd be happy at Dolly's.

Mick and Gil came downstairs even later than the girls. They were both strapping young fellows who, as Dolly had explained, were necessary to keep order in the brothel, but it was she who was the owner and as she confided, 'Those two are always ripe for trouble, especially Mick. I try to keep 'em out of it, but I can't always manage it. You're not to do anything they tell you without checking with me first. Promise me that!'

'Yes, Dolly.'

After the convent and then the icily correct atmosphere at the Hannons' house, Mara enjoyed the friendly atmosphere here, working willingly in the kitchen but strictly forbidden to enter the brothel itself after nightfall.

'You're too young,' Dolly said flatly, 'and there's them as like young girls so it's easier if we keep you out of sight. You can help clean the front in the daytime, but under no circumstances are you to go in there at night. Not for any reason. Is that clear? You've your bed off the kitchen and a lock on the door. Use it. Always.'

'Will I work in the front when I grow older, become one of your girls?'

'Whatever put that idea into your head?'

'Mick. He said I was getting pretty now you're feeding me up and one day I'd be a big draw.'

'Oh, did he? We'll see about that.'

There was another row between Dolly and Mick the next day. Gil was more easy-going, but Mick resented the fact that his elder sister, and only a half-sister at that, called the tune in the business.

'That girl's not going into the trade and that's flat,' Dolly yelled. 'If you don't like it, you can leave and find yourself another job—and other lodgings.'

'Without a family she'll fall into it one way or another. Better here, where you can look after her properly, than in some of the other places. And someone would pay a lot to be first with her.'

'You're a rotten bastard, you know that? But get this straight: she's innocent and she's staying innocent.' Dolly looked so fierce he held up his hands in a gesture of defeat though it didn't stop him looking at Mara assessingly when his sister wasn't there. Such looks made her shiver but this was the only problem about working here so she tried to ignore him.

If only Ismay were here, she thought, they might have made some sort of life for themselves in

268

Melbourne. She'd seen lots of advertisements for maids in the newspapers and she was thirteen now, nearly a woman, even if she still looked like a child. She felt sad sometimes, wondering where both her sisters were, because unlike Ismay, she could never hate Keara, never.

As the weeks passed, she came to realise that she couldn't stay here for too long because although the people were kind, especially Dolly, it was not a good sort of place and Mick was still eyeing her. But where she'd go or what she'd do, she couldn't work out. Most days she was too tired by nightfall to think of anything but her bed.

She never forgot to lock the door of her little room, though. A couple of times she heard the handle turn and that only made her more careful.

*　　　*　　　*

Bess replied to her aunt's letter by return of post. Yes, she would be happy to give up her present job as a housemaid, which didn't entirely suit her, and come to help Nancy with Mrs Mullane. The wages offered would be very acceptable. She'd be there in a couple of days.

Nancy hoped she had done the right thing. The tea leaves had deserted her recently, mocking her with meaningless swirls of black dots, and the pain in her side was increasing all the time. So quickly . . . too quickly for her to do all she needed in the weeks or months left to her.

'I've sent for my niece Bess,' she said abruptly as she and Lavinia sat finishing dinner that evening.

'Oh?' Lavinia eyed the bowl of trifle and looked at her pleadingly. 'I think I could fancy another helping tonight.'

Normally Nancy would have told her she'd eaten enough, but she wanted her charge in a good mood. 'Why not? If you can't have a treat once in a while, what's the point of it all?' She ladled out the trifle with a generous hand, but pushed the rest of her own serving to one side. Food was starting to make her feel nauseous.

'I've something to tell you,' she said when they'd settled themselves in the parlour afterwards.

'Oh?'

'You know I've not been well these past few days?'

Lavinia looked at her in puzzlement.

'Well, I'm not going to get any better, I'm afraid.'

It took a while for the implications of this to sink in, then Lavinia's face crumpled and she burst into noisy tears. 'I don't believe you. Say it's not true!'

'I haven't long to live, chickie, so we have to face up to that and decide what to do about you.' But she had to go and cuddle Lavinia before the younger woman would stop her noisy, childish sobbing.

'What'll I do without you? Who's going to look after me?'

Why did I expect her to care about me? Nancy wondered wryly. She can't think about anyone but herself. It's the way she was made.

When the tears had died down, she said quietly, 'I have a niece, Bess. I've sent for her to see if she's the right one to look after you.'

Lavinia's mouth dropped open then some of the panic left her eyes and she said hesitantly, '*Your* niece?'

'Yes.'

'Does she look after people like you do?'

'I don't know. I think she could learn. She doesn't like her present job.'

'When can she come?'

'In a day or two.'

'I'd rather have you. Much rather. Don't leave me.'

Which surprised Nancy, but pleased her greatly. It was more than she'd expected from Lavinia. Much more.

In bed that night she lay staring at the darkness, praying that there would be enough time to do what was necessary for her girl.

CHAPTER SEVENTEEN

NOVEMBER 1865–FEBRUARY 1866

Keara's son was born in early November. The birth was as straightforward as Nell's had been and she managed perfectly well with the assistance of Noreen, wife of Theo's cousin Caley, and that of the half-aboriginal girl who acted as general help. Theo was still angry that they couldn't get other servants, but Milack was a good-natured girl who would do anything if you treated her kindly. Clearly she hadn't met with much kindness in her short life.

After it was all over, Theo came and sat on the bed and Keara passed him the bundle containing their baby. 'What do you want to call our son?'

'Devin, if that's all right?'

'That's fine.' She leaned back, tired but happy.

'You make it all seem so easy,' he said in

wondering tones.

'What?'

'Having babies.'

Keara chuckled 'It's hard work, but not too hard. I would like a rest now, though. Put him in the cradle and leave me in peace.'

'Shouldn't someone sit with you?' he worried.

'Not unless you want to keep me and Devin awake. Go away now, will you!' She flapped one hand at him.

Theo went outside and blew his nose hard, then looked up to see Noreen smiling at him. 'She's wonderful,' he said simply. 'And so is the baby.'

'Then maybe you'll get back to work and leave us women to clear the place up?'

He gave her a mock salute and went outside, whistling. But before he'd gone very far he stopped and wiped away a tear. After all the disappointments with Lavinia he'd never expected to have both a son and a daughter. It was enough to make you believe in miracles.

*   *   *

Maggie Brett hummed to herself as she cleaned the shelves behind the bar. She was really enjoying her new job. She'd have called this place a pub but in Australia it was called a hotel, which still seemed strange to her. The most important thing, however, was that it was a decent place and the landlord kept good order. He and his wife employed only respectable barmaids and treated them well because the clients were respectable too, artisans and shopkeepers mostly in the best bar at the front, and their employees in the back bar.

272

Best of all for Maggie was the constant company. In Western Australia she had lived with her friend Keara in a tiny country inn, and it had been so quiet there she'd nearly gone mad sometimes— when she wasn't in fear for her life. She missed Keara, though, had never had such a close woman friend in her life. But she hoped to see her other friend Mark Gibson occasionally. He'd said he'd look in on her when he came up to Melbourne. Funny to consider a man a friend, but there had never been any spark of attraction between her and Mark—or between him and Keara either. He was too serious-minded for her, too quiet in his ways.

That afternoon she had a couple of hours off so went for a stroll round the local shops, enjoying the warmth of the late spring day. She didn't spend much because not only was she careful with her money, she had a new ambition: to run her own hotel one day. It probably wasn't possible but she intended to try for it.

When she saw the girl across the street from her she stared in surprise, thinking for a moment it was Keara. Before she could get closer, the girl turned off down a side street and when Maggie followed there was no sign of her. Which probably meant she'd gone down one of the alleys which marked the boundary between respectable and not so respectable businesses in this part of Melbourne. There were brothels down there, Maggie had been told, and who knew what else? She certainly wasn't going to investigate.

Still, it had been an uncanny resemblance.

It couldn't be one of Keara's lost sisters, could it?

When she got back to her room, she took out the

poster Theo had had printed, which offered a substantial reward for information leading to the finding of Ismay or Mara Michaels. As she studied it, she nibbled at her forefinger, eyes half-closed, as she tried to remember exactly what she had seen today. The girl had definitely resembled Keara and therefore the drawing on this poster. And from her age, she'd have to be the younger sister, Mara. If it was her.

Maggie decided to keep her eyes open in future when she went out. Surely if the girl had been shopping nearby today she'd come again? She didn't think the girl had noticed her—and anyway, neither of Keara's sisters had ever met her, had they?—but Mara might run away if she thought someone was following her.

Maggie wondered about writing to Keara, but didn't want to raise false hopes until she was sure it was her little sister.

Then she frowned. The girl had disappeared into one of the alleys. Did that mean she was living immorally? Thieving or whoring? Maggie hoped not. Keara had had enough trouble, didn't deserve more.

*   *   *

Nancy's niece Bess arrived three days later, having simply walked out on her former mistress and got to Ellerdale by a roundabout route, going first to Manchester by train, thanks to the money she'd stolen from Hal. When the maid showed her into the small sitting room where Nancy usually sat when she wasn't in attendance on Lavinia, the two women eyed one another in silence before Nancy said, 'Come in then, and close the door.'

Bess sauntered in, determined not to show too much awe. 'Nice house.'

'The mistress is out. Have a cup of tea with me and I'll show you your room later.' She studied her niece as they sipped the fragrant liquid. Bess looked very like she herself had as a young woman: dark crinkly hair, brown eyes and a sharp knife of a nose. That resemblance reassured her and she wondered if her niece also had the gift of second sight. Not everyone in the family had it, or wanted it.

'It's nice to be waited on for a change.' Bess leaned her head back and stared round the room.

'Well, you'll be waiting on Lavinia from now on, so don't get too used to being idle.'

'Do you call her by her first name, then?'

'Of course I do. I raised her from a baby. But you'll call her Mrs Mullane.'

'Mrs Mullane,' Bess repeated obediently.

Nancy lowered her voice. 'She's slow-thinking but very stubborn. You'll have to guide her without her realising it. *I* can order her around, but she won't take that from you.'

'What does she think about me coming here?'

'She's relieved. Can't manage on her own.' Nancy didn't miss the gleam in Bess's eyes and for the first time a tiny frisson of worry ran through her. What if her niece was not to be trusted? How did you tell for certain in such a short time? 'You'll need to stop her making a fool of herself.'

'Why do you keep saying *I'll* need to stop her?'

Nancy sighed. She wouldn't be able to hide how weak she was growing. 'Because I'm dying. I've enough time left, I hope, to show you how to

275

manage things. And if you learn quickly, you'll be all set for a very comfortable life after I'm gone.'

Bess looked down, hoping she'd hidden the satisfaction she felt about that. They all knew how strict Aunt Nancy was, how rigid in her ways. She'd bet this poor Lavinia couldn't call her soul her own, let alone have a bit of fun. But if her aunt only had a few weeks to live, Bess could wait patiently for her turn.

'I'm grateful to you for thinking of me,' she said—humbly, she hoped. She'd never been good at being humble or quiet, but she'd have to manage it until her aunt was gone. The prospects were far better here than she would ever have guessed.

Nancy lifted her head. 'Ah, there's the front door. She's back.'

Lavinia bounced into the room, petulant and fussing because a lady she knew hadn't noticed her and stopped the carriage to chat. 'We should have our own carriage. I keep telling you that, Nancy. It's not suitable for someone of my station to hire one from the livery stables.'

'We don't go out often enough to make it worthwhile and it's such a short walk into town, you'd not need it for that. But if you want to stop buying so many clothes we can afford a carriage. It's up to you to choose.'

'I don't know what Theo did with all the money my father left,' Lavinia grumbled.

Nancy sighed. Lavinia had never understood money, but no matter how often she explained that the money had been lost by her girl's father, not Theo, it didn't sink in. And they had had this discussion about the carriage several times. She watched her charge look down and pat the fine lace

276

at her wrist, already thinking of something else.

'I suppose you're right about the carriage, Nancy. It would be a waste of money and I do like to look nice.'

Bess watched this incident with interest. Lavinia had done as Nancy wanted without any fuss or protest, too stupid to see that she was being manipulated.

'This is my niece who's come to see if she suits you.'

Bess got up and bobbed a quick curtsey. 'I'm grateful for the chance to work for you, ma'am, and in such a lovely house. I'll do my very best to give satisfaction.'

Lavinia studied her. 'You look like your aunt.' Then her face crumpled. 'But I'd rather have Nancy.'

We'll have to change that, Bess thought.

*   *   *

Mara often ran little errands for Dolly and the girls, enjoying going out to the shops and market stalls. Having grown up poor, she watched the pennies carefully and was praised for her astuteness and the bargains she drove.

She first noticed the woman staring at her on market day. About thirty, fresh-faced with dark hair, no one Mara knew. Her first instinct was to run away but she hadn't done the shopping yet. Was it someone who had visited the Hannons? No, it couldn't be. This wasn't a lady but an ordinary woman with a cheerful face. Oh, dear. What should she do? She didn't want anyone recognising her and sending her back to the nuns. Life with Dolly

277

and the girls was far preferable to that.

When she found the same stranger standing next to her in a queue the following week, she began to feel suspicious but that faded when the woman smiled at her and said, 'I noticed you last Thursday. Such pretty hair you've got. Reminds me of my niece back in England. Eh, I do miss her.'

Mara nodded but didn't reply, just got on with her shopping, glad to have the staring explained.

Maggie watched her go, certain now that this was Keara's younger sister. The resemblance was too marked to be a coincidence and the age seemed right. Only she needed to find out where the girl lived. She beckoned the lad next door whom she'd brought with her. 'That's her. A shilling if you can find out where she lives without her noticing you.'

Jimmy grinned. 'Easy. No one notices lads like me. They're all over the place.'

Maggie watched him go. He was right. And you had to wonder how many of these lads were fending for themselves because most of them looked scruffy and uncared for.

She made her way to the hotel and went back to work. Half an hour later Jimmy came in and winked at her, waiting at the end of the counter till she was free to talk to him.

'What's *he* doing here in the best room?' the landlord grumbled. 'Tell him to get out, Maggie.'

'He's brought a message for me. I'll send him away as soon as I've heard what he has to say, I promise.'

'Nothing wrong, is there?' He looked sharply at her, 'We don't want to lose you. You're a good worker.'

She was delighted at the compliment. 'Thank you. No, there's nothing wrong. It's something personal, that's all. I really enjoy working here, you know I do. Won't be a moment.' She went along to the end of the counter. 'Well?'

Jimmy grinned. 'Easy money.' He held his hand out.

'After you tell me what you found.'

'She's living at Dolly's.'

'Dolly's?'

'A whorehouse down Goat Lane. Hey, you all right? You've gone pale!'

Maggie clutched the counter. 'It's not a place where they sell children, is it?'

'Nah. Dolly's a good sort. Everyone likes her. She's got three regular girls and the young 'un works in the kitchen.'

Maggie let out a long sigh of relief. She couldn't have borne to tell Keara that her sister had fallen into that terrible trade. Bad enough for grown women to go whoring, but the use of children sickened her and every decent person. She'd have had to bring the police in straight away if there was any possibility that such a thing had happened to Mara.

'You're sure about that?' she asked. 'That she's just the maid there, I mean?'

'Yes.'

'Good lad.' She went to find the glass in which she put her tips and gave him two shillings. 'There's extra for finding out so much, and if you happen to hear anything else about the girl there's more where that came from. But I don't want her to know she's being watched, think on.'

He tapped his nose with one finger and

279

sauntered out, grinning.

For all his reassurances she couldn't stop worrying about Mara.

* * *

Mark brought Nan and little Amy to Rossall Springs as soon as he and Samuel had concluded all their negotiations. He was in a hurry so hadn't called in to see Maggie in Melbourne this time. As they reached the little town, he felt a sense of homecoming and beamed round.

'You're happy to be back, aren't you?' Nan asked as the cart hired to bring them and their things to Rossall trundled slowly along the main street.

'Very happy, even though it has some sad memories.'

'Eh, bad things happen everywhere. But it'll please me greatly to be able to tend my Patience's grave and to lie beside her myself one day.'

'Not for a long time, we hope,' he said at once. 'Amy and I both need you too much.'

Nan's eyes were over-bright, but her smile was warm. 'Who'd have thought things would turn out like this after what Alex did?'

'Your husband wasn't responsible for his actions. He had lost his mind and—' Mark interrupted what he was saying to call out to the driver, 'It's over there on the left, just after the grocery store.'

At last they were home. Mark looked up at the sign which still read: S. Grover, Proprietor. He'd get that changed to M. Gibson as soon as he could. The eating house looked to be doing a steady trade. Even as he watched a man went inside. He looked at the empty block of land next to it and wondered if he could buy it from the owner. He had big ambitions for this place now.

He suddenly realised the driver was looking to him for instructions. 'Sorry. I was just thinking about something. If you turn left at the next side street, you can get round to the back. We'll carry everything in that way so that we don't disturb the customers.' He waved to Katie, who had come to the front door and as she waved back, he signalled where they were going. She nodded and disappeared. He was glad she was staying on. She seemed a capable woman with a pleasant manner. Strange to see a woman with such short hair, but hers was a lovely colour, brown with red-gold glints where the sun shone on it.

Then he forgot everything but the need to get settled. Neither he nor Nan stopped working until it was time for bed. Luckily Amy was so tired that even that lively young miss went to bed early without any fuss in the room she would be sharing with her grandmother, and fell straight asleep.

Which was more than Mark did. He lay wakeful with plans buzzing round his brain. When he heard a noise, he didn't register what it was for a minute. Then he realised that what he'd heard had been glass breaking and it sounded as if it had come from downstairs. Jerking upright in the bed, he tossed the covers aside and flung on his dressing gown.

He tiptoed down the stairs, trying not to wake Nan and Amy. When he got to the bottom he went straight through into the dining room and found that someone had thrown a rock through the window, scattering shards of broken glass everywhere. He was about to go and look out on to the street when he heard a noise behind him. For one heart-stopping moment he thought it was the intruder and swung round, fists raised protectively. But it was only Katie. He let his fists fall with a sigh of relief.

She moved towards him quietly. 'What's happened? I thought I heard glass breaking, then I heard you going down the stairs.'

'Someone's thrown a rock through one of the windows.'

Her shoulders sagged and she looked at him in dismay. 'It can only be *him*. I'm bringing trouble on you already.'

'Look, we can't talk here or we'll wake the others.' He drew her into the kitchen. 'I don't know about you but I'm not sleepy. I think I'll get the fire going and make some cocoa. Do you want a cup?'

She hesitated, then reminded herself that she wasn't a nun any longer—something she still had to do regularly—and nodded. She could talk with anyone she wanted any time of the day or night. 'That'd be nice. I'll make it, though.'

'I'll go and put something across that broken window then.' He used a spill to light a lamp and vanished into the public area again.

While he was gone she got the embers blazing and set a pan of milk over the front cook hole of the stove, setting out cups and spooning cocoa and sugar into them. He came back before the milk had boiled, looking thoughtful.

'I think I'll bring my mattress down and sleep in the dining room, just to make sure no one breaks in.'

'Will you be safe? And what about the pieces of glass?'

He shrugged. 'I'll sleep at the other side of the room, and as for safe—I have a revolver which I used in the goldfields and it's the intruder who wouldn't be safe if he came back, believe me. I'd never thought to need a gun here in Rossall but I'll load it and keep it by me tonight. In the day I'd best make sure it's ready for use in my bedroom, where Amy can't get at it.'

The milk boiled and Catherine tried to concentrate on making the cocoa rather than the fact that a man was sitting there so close to her in his nightshirt and dressing gown. She glanced sideways as she passed him his cup and thought he looked a lot younger with his hair rumpled, younger and more appealing. 'Would you like a piece of cake as well?'

'Why not?' He grinned at her. 'A midnight feast, eh?'

When the cocoa was ready, she hesitated to join him at the table. 'Perhaps I'll take mine upstairs.'

He gave her a long, level look. 'I don't bite. Do join me.'

Swallowing hard, she took a place opposite him. After all, she told herself, she was as much covered up as if she'd been fully dressed. Only she didn't feel covered up. She felt—vulnerable. To hide her confusion she took a sip of cocoa, but it was too hot, so she set the cup carefully down again.

'I can't tell you how happy I am to be back in Rossall,' he said suddenly. 'It's the place in Australia where I feel most at home.'

'I like it here, too. Tell me about Western Australia. Is it very different?'

'Yes.' He described the great forests of the south-west and the country inn he'd run there for a

283

while. It was when he mentioned Keara and Theo that she stiffened. 'Not—Keara Michaels?'

'Yes.'

'I came out to Australia with her two sisters,' she said without thinking, then clapped her hand to her mouth and looked at him in dismay.

He frowned. 'I thought you and your late husband came out here earlier than that?'

She bowed her head, praying for guidance, and suddenly realised that she didn't want to lie to him. 'I think I'd better tell you the truth about myself, Mr Gibson. Then if you want me to leave, I will.'

He leaned back and studied her as she explained. Her face was shadowed with sadness as she spoke of how hard it had been to leave her order.

'I'm sorry to have lied to you,' she wound up.

Who was he to judge anyone else? he thought. 'I can see why you would need to conceal the truth. But there's surely no need for you to leave Rossall, is there?'

She looked at him doubtfully. 'I thought you'd prefer it. Especially if it was Albert Bevan who threw the rock.'

'Katie, we've all done things we regret. I ran away to Australia rather than marry a girl I'd got in the family way.' He saw the shock on her face and added hastily, 'I did leave her well provided for but I simply couldn't marry her. She was such a foolish and spiteful creature behind her pretty face. But she died a few months after she'd borne the child and I've always felt guilty for that—though I wasn't the first with her, for all that her family was strict. Anyway, I now have a daughter in England whom I've never met and that upsets me. I also have an

284

elderly father whom I love dearly and,' he grinned, 'eight brothers and sisters from my father's three marriages.'

'Goodness!'

He let silence fall again, not rushing to fill it with words, and this time it felt more comfortable between them.

When she yawned, he said, 'Go to bed now, Katie. I'll fetch my revolver and keep watch.'

'My real name's Catherine. Do you think we could use it from now on?'

He tried it out. 'Catherine. I like it. It suits you more than Katie somehow. And you must call me Mark, not Mr Gibson. I'm not the sort of person to stand on ceremony.'

'Mark, then.'

She felt happier as she went upstairs. She'd hated lying to decent people like him and Nan.

CHAPTER EIGHTEEN

MARCH-JULY 1866

Mick watched Mara carefully, sometimes touching her to feel the softness of her skin and laughing when she tried to avoid him. After Dolly saw that happen a couple of times, she told him in no uncertain terms to leave the child alone, so he followed the young maid one day when she went out shopping, wanting to watch her and study men's reactions to her budding womanhood. But some damned woman kept talking to her so all he could do was brood about how best to profit from her.

His sister's scruples made him angry. It stood to reason that if you had something of value, you should use it for your own gain. And with good food and happy working conditions, Mara was rapidly becoming valuable, growing fast and looking extremely pretty now, with a rosy complexion and budding curves. There were rich men who'd pay twenty guineas for the right to spend the first night with a young virgin like her and Dolly could give Mara a share of the money so the girl wouldn't lose out on the bargain. Why, they could pretend she was a virgin more than once if they taught her well.

Dolly was being very stupid about it all.

He brooded on this waste and became even surlier than usual. One evening he broached the idea again to his sister, using all his persuasive powers as he begged her to have a bit of sense. Why, if this worked with Mara, he could scout around for other young girls and who knew where it'd lead?

Her reply was acid sharp and she was suddenly glad he wasn't her full brother. 'Your mother must be turning in her grave at what you're saying, for she was a decent soul and always kind to me. I'm feeling sick to my stomach listening to you, I am so.' When he scowled at her, she shouted, 'Mick Brogan, how can you even *think* of using young girls like that?'

'Others do it, and make good money.'

'And hurt little children.'

'It's no different from what you do with your whores.'

'It's *very* different. My girls are old enough to

286

know what they're doing and we give honest value at Dolly's so I'm not ashamed of what I'm offering.' She was making good money, too, though she'd not told Mick how much and took care to keep her savings in a bank, not under her mattress.

As she stood up, her disgusted expression made him furiously angry and he burst out, 'Don't you be looking down your nose at me, Dolly Brogan. You're nothing but a whore, when all's said and done.'

There was dead silence in the kitchen and as she drew herself up and glared at him, he knew he'd gone too far this time.

'You'd better leave then, Mick. You wouldn't want to dirty your hands with such as me, even though I am your half-sister.'

He shrugged and stood up, not willing to grovel and plead with her to let him stay. In fact, he was fed up to the back teeth with her ordering him around as if he were still an inexperienced lad. 'Gil? You coming?'

His younger brother, who'd been sitting hunched up listening in dismay to Mick ruining their comfortable life, looked up, his eyes going from one to the other, then shook his head slowly. 'I'll stay with Dolly and so should you. She's the brains of this family and always was. We're better off here with her running things.'

'Suit yourself. But you'll be sorry. You'll *both* be sorry.'

'Sorry for what?' Dolly snapped. 'It's you who's been tossing around insults, not us. You who should be apologising.' But she knew he wouldn't.

Mick scowled at her and went upstairs to pack his things, pausing to nip into Dolly's room and take a valuable bracelet someone had once given her and of which he knew she was fond. That'd serve the bitch right, and anyway he'd earned more here than the miserable wages *she* gave him. He had a right to something extra.

Whistling cheerfully, he passed through the kitchen again.

Dolly stood up and blocked his way. 'Key.' She held out one hand.

'I've lost it.'

'I don't believe you.'

'Are you strong enough to hold me down and search me for it?' he asked in a voice little more than a growl.

Shocked, she stepped backwards and let him go. After the door had closed she turned to Gil. 'Thanks for staying. I'll make sure you don't regret it.'

'I like working here. But I'm sorry Mick's gone all the same.'

'I am too but I've seen it coming for a while.' She wondered whether to get the locks changed but decided against it. Even Mick wouldn't rob his own sister.

But when she found the bracelet missing, she went storming downstairs, shouting, 'Fetch the locksmith, Gil! At once. That sod's taken my bracelet. I'll make sure it's the last thing he ever steals from me. I've a good mind to report him to the police.' But she didn't, of course she didn't. He was still her brother, after all.

*   *   *

When Thad Bowler stepped out in front of Bess

one day in the lane behind Lavinia's commodious villa, she let out a cry of shock and tried to run away. But he caught her before she'd gone more than a few steps and slammed her against the nearest wall.

'Thought you'd got away from me, didn't you?' he growled. 'Well, no one gets away from me.'

'I got the chance of a new job, that's all.'

'And took some money from me to pay for your escape.'

She tried coaxing. 'Aw, Thad, don't be like that.'

He slammed her against the wall again. 'Just listen, Bess. As it happens you weren't the only one who wanted to get away, but you still owe me, so what are you going to do about it?'

'I'll get the money and pay you back, I promise I will!'

'I need somewhere to stay.'

'You can't stay here! My aunt's still alive. She knows who you are.'

'There's a shed and a summer house that no one uses. I can bed down there while you're finding the money.' He grinned. 'And you can come out to warm that bed.'

'Thad, I daren't!'

'Bess, you daren't refuse me. And if there's any booze in the house, bring me out a drink. I've a dreadful thirst on me.'

She sighed. He always did drink heavily. When he was sober, though, she sometimes thought she was fond of him, but at other times she hated him. And she was never quite sure how he felt about her. He kept coming back to her, that was sure, and he lent her money when she needed it. But he had other women too—and he always wanted his money paying back.

'Oh, very well!' she said crossly. 'I'll see what I can find.'

'That's my girl.'

*   *   *

It took several weeks for Nancy to realise she'd made a mistake about Bess who was inciting Lavinia to spend more money, toadying up to her new mistress and coaxing presents out of her.

Worst of all, Bess was starting to speak down to her aunt as if Nancy's brain had softened as her body deteriorated.

That was bad enough, but worst of all was the feeling Nancy got when she contemplated Lavinia's future. She knew something was about to go wrong, could sense it. Only the tea leaves wouldn't speak to her any more and she saw no pictures in her mind except for grey, heaving water every time she focused on Lavinia.

When she saw Bess sneaking out of the house one night the old woman felt extremely uneasy and suddenly she *had* to see where the younger woman was going. It took all her will power to summon up the strength to follow her niece because the pain was bad now, really bad, and she was very weak.

Luckily Bess only went as far as the summer house where a man was waiting for her. As soon as he spoke Nancy recognised his voice. Thad Bowler, a really bad lot whose family had lived across the street from her own. He'd run off to Manchester then come back, still a ne'er-do-well. She hadn't realised Bess knew him well enough to meet him at night like this. They'd be plotting something, up to no good, she was sure of that.

A white-hot spear of pain made her double up, gasping, then she pulled herself upright and moved forward until she could listen to them.

The first thing she heard was a kiss and a groan from him. 'I've needed you, girl.'

'I've brought you some food, Thad. And a bottle of her wine.'

Bess sounded nervous. Now why?

'It's not food I need most.'

More kissing and the rustling of clothing.

'We'd better talk first,' Bess said with a throaty laugh. 'Once you get me going I can't think straight.'

He sighed. 'All right, talk. But make it quick.'

'It can't be long before my aunt dies. She's looking worse every day. Once she's gone I'll get you a job here and there'll be rich pickings for us both—as long as you can learn to flatter my dear mistress.'

He chuckled. 'I can flatter with the best of them. Maybe I'll even flatter myself into her bed. Some ladies like a bit of rough stuff.'

'You'd not do it. She hates that sort of thing, likes compliments and fussing, patting and little touches, nothing more.'

'Well, then, let me know when the old hag's six feet under and I'll come to visit you openly. In the meantime I've found myself lodgings nearby and a job of sorts.'

'Yes, that'll be best. We'll say you're my cousin and you're looking for work. The mistress will let you stay, I'll make sure of that. The house is full of valuable stuff and you'll know better than me how to sell it.'

They talked for a while longer then the noises began again.

Nancy decided to make her way back while they were coupling out there like the animals they were. She moved so slowly now that she didn't want to give herself away. She was in her bedroom before Bess came back but didn't sleep for the rest of the night as she lay planning what to do.

In the morning she waited until her niece was closeted with Lavinia then went to the kitchen and handed the cook a letter. 'Go and post this now, will you, Etty love?'

'I'm going shopping later. I'll do it then.'

'Do it now, Etty, while Bess is out of the way.' She took a risk. 'Unless you want her lording it over you when I die?'

Etty looked at her in surprise. 'I thought you brought her here to do just that?'

Nancy shook her head. 'I brought her here to look after Lavinia, but I don't think she's going to do that. Not properly anyway. Do you?'

'No. I was going to give notice as soon as she took over. I want no truck with her. She's got trouble written all over her, that one has.' Etty took off her apron. 'It'll be my pleasure to put a spoke in madam's wheel. You've allus been good to me, Nancy. I can't believe she's *your* niece. You know she's meeting a fellow in the summer house at night? Thinks I'm too stupid to notice.'

'Yes, and a bad lot he is, too.' The old woman clutched her side. 'If she asks, tell her I sent you in to get me some more laudanum. In fact, you may as well get me another bottle while you're in town. Tell the chemist to put it on our account.'

She sat there when Etty had left, feeling

desperately sad. Nothing was going right lately, nothing. Was her life's work to be wasted and Lavinia left in the hands of a young woman who had no morals and was in league with a thieving boyfriend? Nancy moaned in her throat as the pain bit into her again. But it was no sharper than the emotional pain of finding out what her niece was really like.

And she was so weak now she didn't dare challenge Bess outright.

*   *   *

Catherine looked out of the window and sighed to see how heavily it was raining. She'd waited to go to the market, hoping the rain would ease off, but it showed no signs of abating and she couldn't delay any longer.

'I'd better go and buy the vegetables now,' she said to Nan. 'Can you keep an eye on the stew and see it doesn't burn? Kalaya will have finished cleaning the bedrooms soon.'

'Of course I can, love.'

Mark came in just as Catherine was putting on her outdoor things. 'You need a warmer coat than that,' he said, frowning.

'Oh, I'll be all right,' she said lightly. She did need a new winter coat, but didn't dare spend the money until she had a bit more saved.

He looked at her as if he could guess what she was thinking. She felt her face flushing, snatched up the umbrella and basket and hurried towards the door.

He barred the way and took the basket from her. 'I don't like to see you carrying such heavy loads.

293

I've been meaning to come with you to the market and get to know the traders there again. I can start doing that today. Will you introduce me?'

'Yes. Yes, of course.' She wasn't sure she wanted him to come with her, but couldn't refuse. He was, after all, her employer, and though he never ordered her around or treated her like an underling, she tried always to bear in mind her new role in life.

In spite of the inclement weather the market was as crowded as ever. Normally she loved coming here, as long as she could come early enough to avoid Albert, but having Mark beside her made her feel self-conscious, especially as she caught one or two women exchanging knowing smiles.

She introduced him to the growers she usually patronised and found he knew one or two of them already. As he lingered to chat to an old friend, she wandered on, wanting to see if there were any second-hand clothes for sale.

Suddenly she felt a hand clamp on her arm and tug her towards the temporary alley at the rear of the stalls, a place hidden by the canvas protecting the stallholders and their goods. She tried to get away but Albert was stronger than she was and she was too embarrassed to call for help as she struggled against him.

When the arm clasping hers suddenly let go she staggered backwards in time to see Mark punch Albert in the face, sending him sprawling in the mud.

'If I ever see you attack her again, I'll make you sorry.'

Albert leaped to his feet, fists raised, which was usually enough to make men back away. But Mark

294

stepped forward with his own fists raised and said in a low, angry voice, 'I learned to defend myself on various goldfields. I reckon I can give you ten years and ten pounds too. You're out of condition, Bevan, and I'll be happy to prove that.'

There was a heavy silence, punctuated by the calls of vendors on the other side of the makeshift canvas wall, then Albert took a step backwards.

'She's been egging me on. They deserve all they get, women like her.'

'You know nothing about her.'

'And you do?'

'Yes.'

'She's been lying to you.'

'She hasn't. And what's more,' Mark went on, 'if you do any more damage to my eating house, I'll not rest until I have you arrested for it.'

Catherine had never thought Mark could look so menacing, and couldn't help gazing at him in admiration.

Albert swelled with indignation, opened his mouth, then shut it again. 'I don't know what you're talking about and I've better things to do than listen to your nonsense. You're besotted with her but I'm warning you, she's a tease.'

'I hope you're not going to repeat that anywhere?'

The silence was heavy with antagonism.

'I shall be accompanying Miss Caldwell to market every week from now on.'

Making a scornful noise in his throat, Albert turned round and began to walk away, glancing back over his shoulder a couple of times as he did so, as if afraid Mark might still attack him.

When he'd disappeared from view, Catherine

drew in a shaky breath. 'Thank you.'

'Has he been bothering you?'

She nodded.

'You should have told me.'

'I didn't want to cause any more trouble.'

'*You* haven't caused any trouble. It's Bevan who's done that. Now, are you well enough to continue or do you want to go back?'

'I'll be fine.'

He gave her a warm smile. 'Then we'll continue with our marketing. I think the rain has stopped now. Yes, see. There's a bit of blue in the sky.'

But it wasn't the improved weather that had cheered her up; it was the way Mark had protected her. She stole a glance at him and found him gazing at her. He smiled again and offered her the arm not carrying the basket. After a moment's hesitation she took it, feeling her face heat up again.

'I think we'll keep this incident to ourselves,' he said quietly as they made their way back to the eating house. 'I don't want to alarm Nan.'

'All right. But I do want to thank you. I'm so grateful for your help and support.' Oh, heavens, she was blushing again! What had got into her lately?

*　　　*　　　*

It didn't take much thought for Maggie to decide that her best course was to send a message to Mark and let him know about Mara. She had neither the money nor the authority to deal with this. He could arrange to send the girl across to Keara in Western Australia. She smiled even thinking about this.

296

Keara would be so happy.

She wondered where the other sister had got to. How sad that those nuns had split them up! Something must have gone very wrong, though, for Mara to end up working in a brothel. She hoped the older girl was not in similar straits.

*   *   *

Ismay wasn't in any straits at all. They had returned to Melbourne soon after the wedding, and it was easier sharing lodgings with Malachi than it had been living in such close quarters on the wagon. She slept in one corner with a sheet hung across it so could be perfectly private if she needed.

Dan found her and Malachi a job singing in a hotel and they also took a stall at the market.

'No rest for the wicked,' he said cheerfully.

She thought the old man was tiring more easily these days but didn't say anything, just tried to prevent him from overexerting himself. One Sunday when the sun was shining and she was tired of being indoors, she persuaded him and Malachi to take her out for a walk, but at the last minute Dan said he didn't feel up to it.

'You take her, lad. It's about time you showed her something of Melbourne.'

Malachi looked at her questioningly and Ismay smiled back, suddenly pleased with how things had turned out. Although they were married, they rarely spent time alone together. He made sure of that if circumstances didn't.

As they walked along, he said abruptly, 'Dan's looking tired lately.'

'Yes. I'm a bit worried about him.'

'He's over seventy, you know. Should be resting now.'

'He doesn't want to.'

'No.' He dug his hands into his pockets. 'We should be setting off on our travels again soon but I'm wondering if he's up to it.'

'I think he'd rather die on the road than fade away in his little room. I know I would. I love it when we're travelling.'

They might have missed the piece of paper nailed to a tree if the dog hadn't rushed up to them, snapping, so that Malachi had to chase it away. She watched as the animal hesitated, growling and advancing a pace, then locked eyes with the man and hesitated. Another minute and it gave up the struggle, slinking away down the street. She leaned against the tree, laughing, and it was then she saw the poster, gasping in shock.

She tried to hide it from Malachi, but you could rarely fool him.

'What is it?' he demanded. 'You've gone white.'

'Nothing.'

He tugged her to one side and studied the poster. 'Hell, it's about you and Mara. Your oldest sister's still looking for you.'

'She can look all she wants, I'm not going near her.'

'Surely you ought to hear her side of things?'

'No! I hate her!'

He sighed. 'You're a stubborn wench, do you know that?'

'What difference does it make to you whether I contact my sister or not?'

'I just think it's the right thing to do. Why, these posters may even have helped her find Mara by

298

now, then you'd all three be reunited.' He pulled the faded poster carefully off the tree.

'What are you doing that for?'

'In case you change your mind.'

When she tried to snatch it from him, he held her off. 'Issy, stop that.'

Tears came into her eyes. 'You're going to betray me and let her know where I am, but I warn you: if you do, I'll run away again!'

'I'll not contact her without your permission, Issy, but this is the only way we have of finding her. We'd be fools to lose it.'

'Promise!'

'Eh, lass, how can you be so sensible sometimes and then so stubborn about this?' He put one arm round her shoulders and they set off walking again. 'What am I going to do with you?'

'Nothing. Just continue as we are and keep looking for Mara.' And pray that they found her before Keara did.

Ismay lay in bed that night worrying about the poster, worrying that he'd change his mind. The next day, while Malachi was out, she searched through his things, found the tattered piece of paper and burned it.

That evening when she went to bed he stayed chatting with Dan. She fell asleep to the sound of their voices.

The next thing she knew someone was shaking her awake. She jerked into consciousness to find Malachi sitting on her bed, and by the light of the candle he had set next to her could see that he was furiously angry.

'Did you go through my things today?' he demanded.

She guessed then what had upset him and tried to find the words to calm him down.

'*Did you?*'

'Yes.'

'Where is it?' When she didn't answer straight away he gave her another shake, not enough to hurt but enough to remind her that he was waiting for an answer.

'I burnt it!'

'You stupid fool! What did you do that for?'

'I didn't want you contacting her.'

'I promised I wouldn't do anything without speaking to you first.'

'But you didn't promise not to get in touch with her.' She gulped back tears, not sure whether they were of anger or the pain that sliced through her every time she thought of Keara.

'Don't you ever dare do such a thing again!' he said in a low, angry voice. 'Because if you touch my things and destroy anything of mine, I'll walk out and leave you, wife or no wife.' He sat back and folded his arms, staring at her. 'I know the address on the poster by heart, actually, and I can still contact your sister any time I want.'

She could only stare at him in horror. 'You won't. Malachi, you won't! *Please!*'

He stood up and leaned forward to pick up the candle. 'Same conditions as before. I won't do anything without telling you first.'

The sheet dropped into place as he turned and left. She heard him getting ready for bed, blowing out the candle, making himself comfortable on the narrow mattress that they pushed under Dan's bed during the daytime. He tossed and turned for a few minutes, then she heard his breathing slow down.

It was a long time before she fell asleep, though. She was upset that he'd remembered the address because she hadn't realised he'd studied the poster so closely. But she was even more upset at his threat to leave her.

What would she do if he carried it out? She clapped her hand across her mouth to hold back the sobs. She didn't think she could live without him now.

CHAPTER NINETEEN

JULY–AUGUST 1866

While Catherine and Nan prepared the food for the eating house Amy played in a corner, building up the bricks and wooden shapes Mark had made for her into towers and then knocking them down again, chuckling as she did so.

'She's a good child.' Catherine paused to watch the game with a smile.

'My Patience were just the same,' Nan said placidly, placing another peeled potato into the bucket of cold water.

'I've not had much to do with small children.'

'Is that why you don't pick her up and give her a cuddle?'

'Yes. I'm—well, afraid I'll do something wrong.'

Nan laughed gently. 'Nay, she just likes being held, our Amy does. She has a right loving nature. Go on, try it. She's fond of you.'

Catherine hesitated, then gave way to temptation and knelt to hold out her arms to the

301

child, who immediately held out her own. Picking her up, so small and trusting, sent a warmth through Catherine's body and she held the child close, rocking her to and fro instinctively. Amy put out one hand to touch the short hair, then her own short locks, after which she laid her head against the softness of Catherine's breast, putting her thumb in her mouth, a smile curving her lips.

Mark came to the doorway and stopped, staring at the sight of his daughter cuddled up close to Catherine, both of them looking blissfully happy. He stepped quickly backwards before they saw him, not wanting to intrude on the moment. But the picture stayed with him for a long time—and pleased him greatly.

'She's getting tired and wants to be laid down now,' Nan coached. 'Take her through to the sitting room. She'll sleep on the couch and we'll hear her when she wakes.'

Catherine did so, stroking the hair back from the child's forehead then giving in to another secret wish and bending to kiss her cheek. Oh, but she wanted a child of her own. Desperately. Surely it wasn't too late?

When she went back into the kitchen, Nan said, 'Eh, our Amy's really taken to you. It's a pity you and your husband never had any childer. They'd have been a great comfort to you after he died.'

Catherine murmured something, wishing Nan wouldn't keep referring to her mythical husband. She hated deceiving the kindly old woman, but was afraid of telling anyone else about her past. She didn't know why she trusted Mark to keep her secret, but she did. Colour flared in her cheeks as she admitted to herself that she did know why.

Because he was—special. Very special to her. The first man to whom she had been really attracted, the one she'd like to father her children.

As a young woman she had been her father's closest companion and had needed no one else, then the years in the convent had kept her away from other men. Now potential suitors seemed to be popping up all over the place, men who came into the eating house regularly and treated her courteously while still showing their interest. If she'd given one or two of them any encouragement she knew they'd have come courting. Only they weren't Mark.

She sighed, afraid he wasn't attracted to her. After the incident at the market he'd been withdrawn for a day or two, as if annoyed about something, and that had upset her greatly. It wasn't her fault that Albert Bevan had such a fixation about getting even with her, after all.

Mark had already said a couple of times that he didn't intend to marry again because he felt two women had died because of him and that would haunt him for the rest of his life. Yet Catherine couldn't help hoping he'd change his mind, fool that she was. And even if he didn't, he had become such a good friend that she couldn't bear to think of losing his friendship. Not yet, anyway. She didn't have any other real friends now.

Every day she looked forward to the hour they spent sitting chatting after they closed the eating house, sometimes with Nan there, other times the two of them staying for a while after she had sought her bed. Mark lent Catherine books and they discussed the latest news for they both read *The Age* newspaper avidly, and she thoroughly enjoyed keeping up with what was happening in the world after her years of seclusion.

If only . . . No, she mustn't think about that. It was too much to hope for.

*   *   *

The letter from Maggie arrived the following day. Mark read it, stared at it as if it would bite him, then re-read it carefully.

When he looked up, Catherine couldn't help asking, 'Is it bad news?'

'No. It's good news. Well, it could be. Maggie's seen Mara in Melbourne. Only,' he hesitated, then lowered his voice to add, 'the girl's working in a brothel as a maid, so I need to go up and get her out of there as quickly as possible before anything happens to her.' He began to pace up and down, frowning, then asked, 'Will you be all right if I leave you in charge for a day or two? Can you manage without me?'

'Of course I can. You've got everything well organised now and the place is so much easier to run than when Mrs Grove was in charge.'

'Thank you.' He felt pleased at her compliment. He did pride himself on having a skill for organising things, and he particularly valued her good opinion because she was such a competent woman herself. All the customers liked her, as did Nan and Amy.

'If it is Mara, you'd better tell her about me being here before you bring her back,' Catherine added quietly.

'Yes. Yes, of course. I'll go and tell Nan what's happened.'

Which meant, Catherine decided, that she had better tell Nan about herself before Mara arrived.

Mark left early the following morning and the place seemed very quiet without him. Too quiet.

When Catherine steeled herself to explain her situation to Nan, the older woman stared at her in shock. 'Well, I never!'

'I'm sorry for lying to you.'

'Well, it's not something you'd tell every stranger, is it?' She frowned. 'I don't know what to say and that's a fact. I've never had owt to do with nuns, you see. My husband reckoned the Pope and the Catholic Church were in league with the devil.'

It was Catherine's turn to stare in shock. 'Why on earth would he think that?'

'He thought a lot of stupid things about religion, and I never said no to him when I should have which I'll always regret. Is that why your hair is short?'

'Yes. Nuns have to shave their heads.'

'*Shave them!* Eh, whatever for?'

'It was the rule.' Sometimes Catherine had wondered about it, though. In fact, the further away she was from the ritual and rules that had filled her life for several years, the more ridiculous some of them seemed to her. Not the praying, never that, for she had not lost her faith, but the petty restrictions like not touching other people.

'Are you happier now, love?'

'Yes. Much happier.'

'That's all right then.' Nan realised how anxious the younger woman still looked and patted her hand. 'Well, all I can say is: you're a nice lass, nun or not.' As she saw tears well in her companion's eyes, she added bracingly, 'Eh, give over. What's there to weep about? Your past doesn't matter to me, it's what you're like now as counts.'

Nan had a sudden thought as she went on with her work. Did Catherine's past matter to Mark? Was that what was holding him back? She suspected he was attracted to his employee, as Catherine clearly was to him, and couldn't understand why he was making no attempt to court her. She'd have to ask him. Or did he think she'd object because of Patience? If so, she'd soon set him straight.

She smiled. In fact, she might even give him a nudge or two in the right direction. Men needed that sometimes. It'd be nice for Amy to have brothers and sisters, and she liked Catherine very much, finding her easy to live with.

*   *   *

Mick walked along the street, kicking rubbish out of the way, feeling furious at the world. Suddenly he saw Mara with a shopping basket over one arm, strolling towards the market. She looked dainty and happy, but he'd now persuaded himself that she was the cause of his losing his comfortable job and home so the sight of her did not please him. He'd found himself a job of sorts, as a guard in another brothel, but it was a much rougher place and they didn't allow him to sleep on the premises so he had to spend part of his wages on a tiny box of a room, a place filthy with the dirt of years.

Maybe he should have kept his mouth shut a while longer.

Or maybe—his eyes lighted on Mara again—it was time to do a little business on his own behalf. If

306

Dolly wanted to be stupid, he needn't follow her example, need he? He knew that the man who owned the brothel where he worked would welcome a pretty child like Mara, but what he didn't know was how much Mr Kellagh would pay to the person who brought such a child along.

He went back to his room in a very thoughtful mood and that evening, during a quiet patch, asked to speak to Mr Kellagh about 'a matter of mutual interest'.

'Why didn't you offer to sell this child to your sister?' Kellagh asked suspiciously.

'I did, but Dolly's too stupid to see where her best interests lie. That's why we parted company.'

'And you're sure the child has no family to interfere or make a fuss?'

'I'm certain.'

'What about your sister? Would she make a fuss if the girl vanished suddenly?'

Mick shrugged. 'Who'd listen to a whore like her?'

'Hmm. And the child is pretty, you say?'

'Very pretty. Dark hair and blue eyes. And not too well grown, if you take my meaning. Only just starting to get her titties.'

Kellagh pursed his lips, then said, 'Five guineas.'

'I was thinking of—'

Kellagh's expression grew chilly. 'I don't bargain with such as you.'

'No, sir. Sorry, sir.'

'Can you get the girl tomorrow? I have a client who's always interested in such—ah—titbits. There might be an extra guinea for you if we please him.'

Mick grinned. 'I'll try, sir.'

The next day Mara set off for the shops at her usual time, feeling happier now that Mick wasn't around. Without his brother egging him on Gil was pleasant enough, a bit lazy but not willingly unkind to anyone, so life in Dolly's kitchen was very enjoyable.

She was walking past one of the alleys on her way home when someone pounced on her and dragged her backwards, putting a hand across her mouth. The basket fell out of her hand and she tried to struggle but the man holding her was too strong.

When he stopped in a doorway and removed his hand, he stuffed a handkerchief into her mouth before she could do more than gurgle and as he did so, she saw who it was—Mick!

He grinned at her. 'You're too tasty a morsel to leave in my sister's kitchen.'

Terror slicked Mara's skin with cold sweat as she tried desperately to jerk away. Surely someone had seen what was happening to her? But no one came to her aid and he finished tying her up before wrapping her in an old overcoat and slinging her across his shoulders. She could see nothing, hear nothing, and the jolting made her feel sick. When she tried kicking her feet, he simply grasped them firmly and walloped her backside hard.

'Stop that!'

Despair filled her. 'Too tasty a morsel!' he'd said. She was no longer a naïve village girl and could not fool herself about what that meant: he was going to sell her into a brothel. She'd heard him and his sister arguing about doing that to her.

308

She couldn't scream, only whine in her throat in panic as she realised that by the time Dolly missed her, she'd be hidden somewhere, if not already being used. At the mere thought of that an oily, sick feeling settled in her belly.

*　　　*　　　*

Mark arrived in Melbourne that same day around noon, taking a cab from the coaching inn to the hotel where Maggie worked.

She shrieked at the sight of him and rushed from behind the bar to give him a hug. 'I didn't think you'd come so quickly.'

'We don't want Mara to slip out of our hands, do we? Can you tell me where she works?'

'I'll do better than that! I'll get an hour off and come with you.' She went across to a portly man who stood watching them and explained, arms waving as she spoke.

In spite of the seriousness of his quest, Mark couldn't help grinning and could see her employer watching her indulgently, too. Same old Maggie.

She came back. 'You can leave your bag behind the counter. It isn't far.'

They walked down the street in silence. As they turned into the alley, Maggie edged closer to him and he glared at a furtive-looking fellow who had started following them. 'I don't like the looks of that fellow.'

'I don't like the looks of this whole part of town yet you can see for yourself how close it is to the more respectable places. Jimmy said the brothel was halfway down here on the left. Yes, look!' She pointed to a sign saying simply 'Dolly's'.

309

Mark knocked on the front door and when a man opened it, asked to see Dolly.

'We don't open till the evening.'

'It's not about that sort of business. It's about Mara.'

'Oh. Well, you'd better come in then, I suppose.'

*   *   *

In Ireland on the Ballymullan estate Dick Pearson opened the letter quickly when he realised it was from Nancy. She only wrote when there was something wrong. He quickly scanned the single page of wobbly writing, then read it again more slowly, such dismay on his face that Diarmid O'Neal, who was helping him open the estate mail, asked, 'What's wrong?' Numbly Dick held out the letter.

Dear Mr Pearson

I'm writing because I'm dying and desperate to find someone to look after Lavinia. You know as well as I do that she's not capable of running her own life. She's fallen into the hands of two scoundrels, my niece Bess, I'm sad to say, and a man friend of hers called Thad Bowler.

They've already persuaded Lavinia to overspend her allowance for this quarter and to borrow more money from the bank. They've cheated most of this out of her and I'm too weak now to prevent them for I can't leave my bedroom.

When I die, Theo will be the only one who can manage Lavinia. She's still legally his wife and his responsibility after all. He must make

310

some provision for her or there will be trouble.

If he doesn't intend to return to Ireland, you must send her to him in Australia. That'd get her away from those two. You'll have to do this forcibly, though, because she won't go back to him willingly. My nephew Fred still lives nearby and will help you if you pay him.

Much as I love Lavinia, I can do no more. Don't delay but come at once. I haven't long to live.

Nancy

The two men stared at one another in horror.

'Dear God, I thought we were shot of that stupid bitch!' Diarmid said. 'What the hell are we going to do?'

'I'll have to think about it. I'll come down to your place this afternoon and we'll discuss it again.'

Dick thought long and hard, but Theo was his half-brother and needed help. There was no time to send messages to and from Australia, so this fell to Dick. He grimaced. He'd never wanted to leave Ireland, but it looked as if he was in for a long sea voyage to Australia. A wry smile twisted his lips for a moment. Well, he'd have to travel cabin class to keep an eye on Lavinia so at least he'd go in comfort.

Diarmid would have to manage without him for the year or so this would take, but he was a capable man. When Theo had discovered what the rest of them had long realised, that he and his valet shared the same father, he'd made the two of them jointly responsible for the estate.

Dick set off for England the next day, grimly determined. He hated the thought of how this

311

would affect Theo who, from his letters, had never been so happy in his life as he was with Keara, even though they were having difficulty finding her two sisters.

However, Dick would first give Lavinia a chance to dismiss this Bess and settle down with some sensible older companion. He could take his time to find a reliable woman.

But the more he thought about that, the more he doubted Lavinia would agree. She took violent fancies to people and if this female was her latest, she'd dig in her heels. He winced as he remembered her temper tantrums, not sure he could deal with them adequately.

Only how was he to get her to Australia if she refused point-blank?

*   *   *

Jimmy saw a man snatch Mara off the street but when he got close enough to recognise Mick Brogan, slipped hurriedly to one side and hid. Mick was a nasty sod and didn't mind who he kicked and thumped. Jimmy didn't want to be the butt of his anger. What the hell was he doing with Mara?

Picking up the basket she'd dropped, he watched Mick tie up the poor girl and stride off with her slung over his shoulder. He saw a couple of other people watching, too, but nobody interfered with such a big fellow.

When Jimmy followed them down an alley, he was dismayed to see them go into Kellagh's brothel. With a shudder to think of a nice kid like Mara trapped in that place, Jimmy turned to leave and tell Dolly.

'Why were you following me?'

He gasped as he found himself confronted by Mick who had come out of the side entrance. Before he could turn and run, the man grabbed him by the scruff of the neck and frog-marched him inside.

The door shut with a great bang behind him.

Out in the street the contents of the basket vanished quickly, but the basket itself, broken now, was kicked aside.

*   *   *

Nancy felt so ill she didn't get up that day. She called Lavinia into her bedroom and patted the bed beside her. 'Come and talk to me, chickie.'

'You look dreadful.' Lavinia stayed where she was.

'Sit down here!'

A sulky expression on her face, the younger woman did as she was told.

Nancy took her hand and kept tight hold of it. 'I've not got much longer to live.'

Lavinia's lips wobbled. 'You're very selfish to leave me like this.'

'I have no choice, you know that. I want you to do something for me before I die. Will you?'

'What?'

'Send Bess away. We'll find someone else to look after you, someone much nicer. Bess isn't a good woman.'

Lavinia gaped at her, then pouted. 'I like her. She's fun.'

'She'll get you in trouble, chickie. I've seen it in the tea leaves.'

'Bess says the tea leaves are rubbish and I don't like it when you talk of them.' Lavinia dragged her hand away from Nancy's and stood up. 'I don't want to stay here. I don't want to see you die. Bess says it's horrible when people die.'

She was nearly at the door when Nancy pointed her finger at her and said in a strange, loud voice, 'If you don't send Bess away, I'll come back and haunt you both. I promise you that.'

Lavinia burst into tears of sheer terror and ran from the room to seek shelter in Bess's arms, then allow herself to be petted and cosseted till she had recovered from her shock. Except that she couldn't quite get Nancy's strange tone of voice out of her mind.

When the mistress was settled by the fire with a plate of small iced cakes and a glass of brandy, Bess went to see her aunt.

She found Nancy gasping for breath, her face white and pinched and one hand clutching her throat.

Bess leaned against the door post. 'Lavinia won't get rid of me, you know.'

'Then—I'll haunt—you both.' Suddenly it seemed to Nancy as if she could see into the future once more.

Bess jumped in shock as her aunt spoke in that strange sing-song voice, her eyes seeing things that were kept from others.

'You'll not find what you want if you stay with Lavinia, Bess. You'll never find what you want with her.'

'You're just making that up.'

'You'll see whether I am.'

Even as her niece took a step backwards,

Nancy's hand dropped and the room fell silent.

'I don't believe it,' Bess muttered, then said it again, more loudly, '*I don't believe in your stupid tales!*'

But the corpse continued to smile at her from the bed and in sudden fright she ran screaming for help.

*   *   *

Dick Pearson arrived the next day to find the house in chaos. The undertakers had removed Nancy's body but Lavinia was still weeping hysterically and would not be comforted. She was also drunk and he noticed a half-empty decanter of brandy on a small table nearby.

There was no meal ready because the cook, Etty, had left the minute she knew Nancy was dead and no one knew where to find her. A man called Thad was making himself a sandwich in the kitchen. Dick took an instant dislike to the fellow who at first tried to bluster and insist he was part of the household then turned surly when ordered to leave. 'You'll need me if you want to keep Mrs Mullane in order, sir. She won't listen to anyone except me and Bess. You'll see.'

'If you don't leave, I'll fetch the constable.'

When he'd got rid of the fellow, Dick tried to talk to Lavinia about what she wanted to do, but she insisted on ringing for Bess and referred every decision, large or small, to her new companion. As he had taken as much of a dislike to the woman as to her man friend, he said curtly that Bess would not be staying, upon which Lavinia had hysterics.

After the maid had helped her recover, she lay

315

looking so white and exhausted that he grew quite worried for her.

'You can't send Bess away,' gasped Lavinia. 'She's *my* servant and you're not my husband. Once the funeral's over you can just go away again, back to your horrid, rainy old Ireland.'

That night Dick sat in the parlour after everyone had gone to bed and acknowledged that Nancy had been right. Only Theo could sort this mess out.

The following day was the funeral. Lavinia at first refused to go, but Dick insisted everyone in town would be scandalised if she didn't attend her old nurse's funeral and might never speak to her again. Even Bess agreed with him, so in the end Lavinia gave in. He refused point blank to let the maid accompany them in the carriage but sent her separately in a cab, thinking the less she had to do with Lavinia henceforth the better.

He almost felt sorry for Theo's wife, so white and afraid did she look, but then he remembered how many times she had behaved cruelly to others, what she had done to Keara and her sisters, and hardened his heart.

Nancy's nephew Fred turned up at the funeral and seemed to be the only one who genuinely regretted the strange old woman's passing.

Afterwards Dick stopped him and said, 'I need to talk to you without Bess or Mrs Mullane finding out. There's a little job your aunt asked me to do before she died and I'm prepared to pay you well to help me. Will you meet me at the Tanner's Arms later and let me buy you a drink while we discuss it?'

Fred nodded.

Bess came up just then so Dick said loudly,

'Thank you for coming. Your aunt was a good woman.'

Fred nodded then stared at his cousin. 'I see you've wormed your way in.'

'Aunt Nancy sent for me to look after Lavinia.'

'Biggest mistake the old lady ever made,' he said. 'Even I know you're not to be trusted.'

With a scowl she flounced back to Lavinia's side and by the time Dick reached the carriage, she was inside with her mistress. He debated hauling her out again but decided it'd cause too much gossip, so got in and drove back with them, sickened by the way Bess was patting Lavinia and even wiping her eyes for her.

CHAPTER TWENTY

AUGUST–SEPTEMBER 1866

Ismay was glad to get out of Melbourne and into the countryside again. The tension between her and Malachi since their discovery of the poster had made things so difficult that now she tried to think carefully before she said anything to him—which didn't make for long conversations. She was still worried that he would try to get in touch with her sister.

One day, however, when Dan was drowsing in the back of the wagon and the horses were clopping gently along an easy track, Malachi said abruptly, 'Why are you so furious with Keara? Why won't you even try to find out her side of the story?'

Ismay looked down and shrugged. 'Because she

promised.'

'Promised what, Issy?'

She clenched her hands and tried to hold back the tears that would well in her eyes, but failed. 'We had a talk one day, just before Mam died. Keara promised me faithfully that if anything happened to Mam, she'd leave the Mullanes and look after me and Mara. We'd get work in a town somewhere, share a room, be happy. I was relying on that. *And she didn't even come home for Mam's funeral! Didn't even write!'*

She tried hard to hold them back but sobs erupted from her, so violent that her whole body shook. When Malachi took her in his arms and held her close as she wept, she could do nothing but sag against him.

With the weeping showing no signs of abating, he looked down at her slight figure and his heart went out to her. He began to murmur meaningless phrases against her damp cheek, anything to offer her comfort. Then, as the sobs slowly began to subside, he held her away from him so that he could look into her eyes and smooth back the damp strands of hair from her flushed forehead.

'Have you ever cried over that before?' he asked gently.

She shook her head. 'No. I c-couldn't. I always had to be the strong one, for Mara's sake.' She laid her head on his shoulder with a ragged sigh.

'You should have talked to me about it.'

'I knew I'd weep if I tried. I didn't want you to see me—like this.'

He curved his forefinger and used it to push her chin up and kiss her on the lips, not a passionate kiss but a loving one. 'Issy, you can always talk to me. I'm your husband now.'

The look she gave him was still shadowed with unhappiness.

'What's wrong? No, don't pretend! I can feel it in your body as well as see it on your face.'

So the other grief burst out too. 'But you didn't want to marry me! And . . . you're not really my husband. Sometimes I feel as if no one in the whole world wants me.'

More sobs shook her and he wrapped his arms round her, making shushing noises. When she didn't stop weeping he bent his head and kissed her again. As he muffled her sobs with his lips, he felt the softness of her body against his and desire throbbed suddenly through him. He had experienced many sleepless nights because of her closeness.

'How can you think no one wants you?' he scolded, though his voice came out soft and loving, not angry. 'There's Dan treating you like a daughter, smiling whenever you turn to him, proud as anything about how well you do in the shop and how prettily you sing. And there's me—' he hesitated, then admitted '—nearly bursting my trousers sometimes from wanting you.'

She stared at him open-mouthed, tears caught on the long dark lashes of her beautiful eyes 'You—do want me?'

'Of course I do, you fool!' His voice was rougher now. 'You have a mirror. You must know how bonny you are. If I'd not wanted you, I'd not have married you, whatever anyone said or did.'

'But you told me—'

'I said this wasn't the time for me to be setting up a home and family. And it isn't.' He gestured

319

around them. 'How could we bring up children and run a travelling shop? It's hard enough to keep ourselves clean. And who'd help you birth a baby when your time came if you were living like a gypsy? I want better than that for my wife.'

She swallowed hard, hope welling in her painfully as if it had to force its way up through the hot anger.

'One day, Issy love, when we can settle down, we'll be a proper man and wife, I promise you. But I don't want my children to live roughly, don't want to risk your safety. Having a baby is dangerous enough for a woman when she has a house and people to help her.'

'It'd be a better life than we had, my sisters and I, even so,' she said, with a sad, distant look in her eye.

He couldn't resist kissing her again but when the kiss deepened, he pushed her to arm's length, breathing deeply. 'I'm a dreadfully stubborn fellow,' he said apologetically. 'So we'll stop the kissing now.'

They travelled along for a while then he said, almost to himself, 'There's another thing driving me on. My brother prophesied I'd fail here in Australia but I'm determined to make something of myself—more than Lemuel will back home for he's a right old stick-in-the-mud and coopering's not the trade it was. And if I do succeed—well, maybe I can go home and bring my mother out here to live with us. It's one of my dearest wishes, that is. I hope there'll be a letter from her waiting for me in Melbourne. I wrote before we went out travelling the first time but she hasn't written back and that's not like her. I did write again though, in case my first letter went astray.'

Ismay watched a smile crease his face when he spoke of his mother, such a tender, loving expression that she wished it was for her.

'Eh, you'd like my mother,' he went on, not noticing her reaction. 'Hannah, she's called. She's not old like other folk's mothers. Her hair's still as dark as mine and her face is all rosy. Folk say she's a pretty woman still and—well, she is. When I was little she used to sing to me and dance me round the kitchen if my father wasn't at home—she has a lovely voice. It's from her I get the love of music. And we could always talk about things, she and I, talk about anything.'

He paused to frown at a less pleasant memory. 'Lemuel is like my father, scornful of such foolishness. Only it's not foolish to talk to one another—well, I don't reckon it is. But then,' he gave her a boyish grin, 'I've always been able to talk the hind leg off a donkey. You could work next to Lemuel all day and not get twenty words out of him.'

A moment later he added, 'I've never understood why Mam married a man like my father, though he was fond of her in his own way—and proud too, because she's a fine housewife. But she was only sixteen when they wed and he was nearly forty.'

'Your mother sounds lovely. I hope I shall meet her some day.'

'I do too. In fact, I'll make certain you do. I often think of her.' He gave a wry smile. 'Her and her dreams.'

'Dreams?'

'Yes, when I was a kid we had a game of

321

dreaming. Little dreams were worth a penny, big important dreams were worth threepence. I always wanted to be rich and carry her away to a life of comfort. That was my threepenny dream.'

'What did she dream of?'

'She wanted me to be happy.'

'But for herself?'

He shook his head. 'When I look back, her dreams were all for me. I don't think she was unhappy, exactly, because she's not the sort to pine about what can't be helped, but she and my father were chalk and cheese. She'd never speak disloyally about him, especially to one of her children, so I suppose she kept her threepenny dreams to herself, but I'm sure she had some. I'd see her look into the distance sometimes and her eyes would go all soft. Now, well, I dream of bringing her out here to live with us, which is another reason for being careful.'

In the rear of the wagon Dan nodded silent approval and wiped a tear from his own eye with one rough fingertip. Things were looking up. They were talking to one another now, his lad and lass as he thought of them, and Malachi kissed her regularly. Yes, he reckoned it was going to be all right for them.

He grinned. And he'd bet ten guineas they didn't wait much longer to consummate the marriage, human nature being what it was. And why should they?

*   *   *

Dolly came into the front parlour, looking puzzled as she assessed her visitors. Respectable, the woman as well as the man, so what were they doing here? 'How can I help you?'

'We've come about Mara,' Mark said. 'Her sister Keara's looking for her, been looking for a while.' He passed the poster to her and watched as she read it carefully.

'What's *your* connection to Mara then? Are you after the reward?'

'No. I'm a friend of Keara and Theo's. They live in Western Australia so I'm acting as their agent over here in Victoria. I can direct you to Theo's lawyer if you want confirmation of that.'

Dolly grinned. 'He'd not allow a woman like me across his threshold, let alone tell me anything.' The amusement faded from her face and she sighed as she added, 'I'm going to miss her but it's maybe for the best. She's growing fast now she's eating properly and I don't want her attracting the wrong sort of interest.' She looked them in the eye. 'I don't believe in children being used in my trade. I run an honest house here where the girls are treated well and looked after, so I'm not ashamed of what I do. But children—that's wrong.'

Mark nodded, waited a moment, then asked, 'Is she here? Can we speak to her?'

'She's out shopping but she'll be back soon. Will we have a cup of tea while you're waiting?'

'I'd love one,' Maggie said.

Dolly nodded. 'Won't be a minute, then. The kettle's always on at this time of day.'

Maggie looked at the fussy, tawdry room and pulled a face. 'I'd probably be happier sitting in the kitchen.'

'Me, too.' Dolly led the way out to the back, gestured to some plain wooden chairs and set about making a pot of tea.

Maggie looked round, approving of how clean the kitchen was and how unexpectedly homely, too. Mark sat quietly, looking forward to meeting Keara's sister.

Suddenly there was a hammering on the back door. 'Missus! Missus!'

Dolly threw it open. 'Not now, Pete.'

A thin old man in ragged, filthy clothing stood there, swaying from side to side, a look of great anxiety on his face. 'Missus, they took the lass. The little 'un.'

Mark stood up so quickly his chair fell over behind him and strode to join Dolly at the door. 'Does he mean Mara?'

She nodded and said in a low voice, 'Move back and leave this to me. He's a bit simple and if you frighten him, he'll run away.'

'But—'

She turned a steely gaze on him and he did as she asked, but didn't sit down again.

The man was still rocking from side to side, wringing his hands.

'You did the right thing, coming to me, Pete,' Dolly said in a loud, slow voice. 'We're all very pleased with you, and after you've told me everything I'll give you some food.'

His face brightened and he nodded several times.

'Who took Mara?'

He looked over his shoulder.

She put one hand lightly on his arm. 'Whisper it to me.'

He leaned forward.

Mark watched a spasm of pain cross her face as Pete spoke.

'Where did he take her?'

Again, a terrified glance over his shoulder, then he shook his head. 'Daren't say.'

She took a deep breath, holding her impatience in check.

'Food?' Pete asked. 'Give me food now?'

She nodded, turned abruptly and sawed him off a thick slice of bread, buttering it liberally. As she held it out to him, she repeated her question. 'Where did he take her? Won't you whisper it to me?'

But he grabbed the bread and ran off down the alley.

With an exclamation, Mark tried to push past her and give chase, but she held him back.

'It wouldn't do any good. He's a very fast runner. It's saved his life a few times.'

'But if someone has Mara and he knows . . .'

A man came into the kitchen, yawning as if he'd just got up though it was well into the afternoon. 'Oh, sorry, love. Didn't know you had visitors.' His eyes were on the teapot. 'You haven't got a spare cuppa, have you?' he wheedled.

'Yes. Sit down and I'll pour you one.' She turned to Mark and Maggie. 'This is my brother Gil. He works here. I have another brother, Mick who left recently. He's the one who took Mara.'

Breath whistled into Gil's mouth and he looked at her in shock. 'He never?'

She nodded. 'Pete just came to tell me, but he ran off when I asked where Mick took her.' She looked hard at Gil. 'Where is he working?'

He hesitated.

Her voice suddenly turned harsh. 'If you don't tell me, you'll be out of here before you can blink.

I'm not having that little lass hurt.'

'He's at Kellagh's.'

'No!' Her voice rang with anguish. 'How the hell are we going to get into that place, let alone find her?'

'Who's Kellagh?' Mark asked.

'He owns a big brothel and specialises in . . . satisfying the wilder tastes. He's also got several strong fellows working there. Needs them too sometimes.'

'Money is no object,' Mark said quickly, glancing sideways at Gil as he spoke. 'Mara's sister will pay handsomely to anyone who rescues the girl.'

Gil was chewing one side of his lip. He put his forefinger to his mouth and chewed some more.

Dolly gave a little sign to Mark to keep quiet so he held his impatience in check again.

'How much?' Gil asked at last.

'A hundred pounds.'

'And you'd need to pay a few of the lads to help us get into Kellagh's.'

'I'll pay whatever it takes.'

'You could be in danger yourself if you were seen to be part of this, Gil,' Dolly said, torn between worry for her brother's safety and fear for the girl.

'Doesn't matter. I've been thinking of leaving Melbourne anyway.'

'You never said! Why?'

'Because Mick's being a bloody nuisance, always on at me to join him at Kellagh's and I'm not working for that bastard, but mainly because I don't like living in the city, never have.'

'My client breeds horses in Western Australia. He'd find you a job, I'm sure,' Mark promised.

'And pay me fare across?'

'Yes.' He looked sideways. 'What about you, Dolly? Will you need to move?'

She shook her head. 'No. I'm well in with the local police and I have one or two customers who'd have a word with Kellagh if he tried to annoy me. I'll be all right. Though I'll hire more guards for a time. Anyway, Vincent Kellagh never holds a grudge for long and I'm no competition for him, nor ever like to be.'

'Look, can't we discuss this afterwards?' Mark exclaimed. 'Heaven alone knows what they're doing to that child!'

She gave him a wry smile then nudged her brother. 'You go and set things up, Gil.'

'Right, then. Give me an hour. I'll be back with some fellows I know.' He went and gave his sister a quick hug, drank the remains of her cup of tea, then hurried out of the back door. He left it swinging open, creaking slightly, showing the wind blowing rubbish to and fro against the fence.

After a minute or two Maggie broke the silence. 'An hour's a long time to wait.'

Dolly looked up. 'If we went in after her now, on our own, Kellagh would just get her out the back way.' As they both sighed, she added, 'It's in God's hands, so it is. And our Gil's.'

Mark began pacing up and down the kitchen.

Dolly moved across to a cupboard. 'I don't know about you two, but what I need right now is a dash of rum in my tea.'

They both shook their heads. She shrugged and poured a liberal splash into her teacup, topping it up with stewed tea. 'Ah, that's better.' She sat sipping it, not attempting to make conversation.

The clock seemed to be ticking more slowly than usual, and each of them glanced at it often.

*   *   *

Dick strolled down to the Tanner's Arms and found Fred waiting for him. He explained the situation and Fred frowned. 'You'll not get Madam Lavinia to go willingly and the trick we played with Keara, pretending she was drunk when we carried her on board, won't work with a cabin passenger. Ladies don't get drunk in public.'

'But I *have* to do something! We can't just leave her here. Lavinia can no more look after herself than a child can.'

'What if there was no more money?'

'I'm authorised to pay her more in an emergency.'

Fred screwed up his face in thought. 'But they don't know that. I've dealt with Bess afore. She's a mean bitch, clever at looking out for herself, but money never sticks in her pocket long so she's allus after more. She's never had much to do with the nobs, though . . .'

'And?'

'Well, if she thought it was *her* idea to send her mistress to Australia, that the only way to get more money out of that husband of hers was to visit him in person, she might persuade her to go.'

'Bad enough having to take Lavinia to Australia. I'm not taking that bloody maid of hers as well!'

Fred grinned. 'That's where I come in. I'll nobble Bess just before the boat sails. You can get Mrs Mullane on to the ship and say Bess is following with the luggage. Mind, you'd better find

328

her another maid for the journey. She won't be able to look after herself.'

Dick beamed at him and shook his hand. 'You'll not regret this.'

Fred smiled complacently and when he left pocketed the three gold sovereigns Dick had given him to start things rolling.

*   *   *

While they were at the pub, Thad came to the back door of Lavinia's house. When Bess saw him she tried to slam the door in his face, but he put one foot inside and grinned at her. 'None of that, now. That Irish sod who chucked me out isn't here today, I made sure of that.'

Scowling, she led the way inside.

'Wouldn't mind a cup of tea and summat to eat, Bess lass.'

Still silent, she slid the kettle to the hottest part of the hob and took out a fruit cake.

'Got any money?'

'No. I spent it.'

'You always were a stupid bitch where money's concerned.' He ate the cake and gulped down a cup of tea, not seeming to notice how hot the liquid was. 'Well, I'm sticking with you and once he's gone, I'll expect you to find me a job here. I wouldn't mind a soft life like yours.'

When he'd gone she sighed. Was she never to be rid of him?

*   *   *

Dick arrived back for dinner, by which time Bess

had had a little chat with her mistress.

'Before you leave tomorrow,' Lavinia told him, nose in the air, 'you must give me more money. I've none left.'

Bess, who was serving them, lingered to listen.

Dick let the maid stay. If he was lucky she'd help him in this. 'The money's always lasted before and you're not paying Nancy's funeral expenses. What have you spent your allowance on this time?'

Lavinia shot a quick, uneasy glance at Bess. 'I've had—special expenses. Theo has all my father's money and can easily pay me more.'

'You know your father lost much of his money before he died, I keep telling you that.' But she kept refusing to believe it. She had that stubborn look on her face now. 'I could let you have ten pounds to last till next quarter, if that'll help, but I'm not authorised to pay you more money regularly.'

Bess moved to stand behind her mistress. 'Mr Mullane wouldn't leave his wife wanting and in debt, surely?'

'No, of course not. If you're having trouble, you can always come back to Ireland with me, Lavinia. There's plenty of room and it'd cost you nothing to live there. There's a girl in the village who could act as your maid . . .' He stole a glance at Bess and was delighted to see a look of fury on her face at those words.

'I'm not going back to that place!' Lavinia shrieked, bouncing to her feet. When Bess laid one hand on her shoulder she took a deep sobbing breath and calmed down, after which she looked round. 'I'll have to sell something, then.'

'You can't do that. An inventory has been taken

of every single item in this house. It's all the property of Mr Mullane and if anything goes missing,' he looked at Bess as he spoke, because she was gaping at him in shock, 'then I'm authorised to prosecute whoever's responsible. There's a detailed inspection held every year.'

Bess turned to Lavinia. 'You said nothing about an inventory. He's making it up, isn't he? These things are yours, aren't they?'

Lavinia looked at her like a dog cringing before its master and the sight of that made Dick even more determined to get rid of this horrible woman. 'Mrs Mullane wasn't involved in the inspections. They were all conducted by Nancy and a man from the lawyer's office.'

'How can she get more money, then?' Bess asked bluntly. 'You can't expect a lady like her to live in poverty.'

'From her husband. Only he's in Australia so she can't see him. She'll have to write to him, I suppose. But it'll take six or eight months for a reply to get back. She'll have to go to Ireland in the meantime if she can't manage.'

Lavinia thumped the table. 'I won't go to Ireland and I hate Theo. I don't want to see him.'

Dick nodded. 'I wasn't suggesting you went out to Australia, just wrote to him there. It'd be very—um—inconvenient if you turned up there. I think, from the sounds of it, you'd better come to Ireland until we get a reply.'

Bess had been looking thoughtful. 'What if she wanted to go and see him in person?'

'But I don't!'

She patted Lavinia's hand absently. 'Shh, love, it might be worth it. Your husband pays you a measly amount now. What if we could get him to raise that amount?'

'I don't want to see him and I don't want to go *anywhere* by ship.'

'It'd not be convenient,' Dick said quickly. 'He's—um—got another woman living with him out there.'

Bess smiled. 'Then he'd do anything to get rid of us quickly. It'd definitely be worth the trip. Anyway, sea air's good for you.'

'But I was always seasick going to Ireland,' Lavinia protested.

'That was in cold weather. It's nice and sunny going to Australia, everyone knows that.' Bess had answered an advertisement for maids to go out to Australia once when she was desperate and had almost gone, except that she'd got hold of some more money so it hadn't been necessary. 'You'd enjoy yourself. There are concerts and people to talk to and games to play. I've read about those ships.'

Dick held his breath. Was it going to be this easy?

Bess turned to him. 'Would you be able to find the money to send her to Australia? They say a sea voyage is good for the health and she's a bit run down. I'll look after her and it'll take her mind off losing my poor aunt.'

Dick frowned. 'Why bother? She can come to Ireland and wait for a reply there.'

But as they argued Bess became more and more certain that he was just putting them off and they'd get far more money by going to Australia and confronting this mean sod of a husband. Only she was going with her mistress cabin class, not

332

steerage. Lavinia's companion, that's what she'd call herself. She'd be living with the nobs and she'd get right away from Thad and never come back to this part of England again, if she could help it.

'Let me talk to my mistress,' she said to Dick.

He pretended reluctance and left them alone.

'You don't want to go to Ireland, do you?' Bess asked.

Lavinia shook her head.

'Then you'll have to go to Australia to see Theo. He has your money.' It took her a while, and she had to repeat things several times, but she managed to lodge the idea firmly in Lavinia's head that they had to go to Australia.

In the end Dick agreed to find the money for their fares. He didn't tell them he'd be going to Australia with Lavinia. Or that he was arranging to prevent Bess from going at all.

*   *   *

Dick called upon Lavinia to make the final arrangements for the voyage to Australia. She was still insisting on taking Bess with her in cabin class as her 'companion', so he pretended to go along with it. He would have been mildly pitying of how reluctant she was to make the journey had he not seen the debts which had piled up in the last few weeks. That annoyed him. He was sure many of the clothes recently purchased had been for Bess, who dressed far too finely for a maid, but Lavinia too was wearing some very fancy new garments.

Grim-faced, he took the latest batch of bills away with him to arrange for payment.

The next day he escorted Lavinia and Bess to

Liverpool where he settled them in a small hotel near the port.

When he called for Lavinia two days later to take her to the ship with him, he told Bess to follow them with the luggage.

'I'm supposed to be her companion,' she protested, smoothing the full skirt of the new dress she was wearing.

'Yes, and companions are the ones who always deal with the luggage and such details,' he told her.

She glared at him.

Lavinia looked from one to the other, mouth trembling. 'I don't want to go. I don't.'

Bess went to put her arm round her mistress. 'Yes, you do. You know you like warm sunny weather. We're going to have lots of fun, you and me.' And a certain fellow wouldn't be able to pursue her to Australia. She'd make sure Lavinia settled in the south of England when they came back, a place where no one knew them.

Lost in her dreams, she took her mistress out to the carriage, waved a cheerful goodbye then went to get the hand luggage down. In the bedroom she found Thad waiting for her and gasped in shock.

'Trying to give me the slip?' he asked mildly.

'I've no choice about what I'm doing. She has to go to Australia and I'm her maid.'

He grinned at her. 'Well, it's a good job I'm coming with you on the same ship then, isn't it? Got a job as a steward, haven't I, because one of 'em fell ill. Had a nasty accident, poor fellow.' The smile faded. 'You didn't think you were keeping this little goldmine to yourself, did you, Bess? If we play our cards carefully, that stupid woman is the key to a good life for you and me.'

She bit her lip but could see no way of preventing him from travelling to Australia. 'I thought you didn't like sea voyages?'

'I don't. But I do like money. And it'll suit me to get away for a time. Besides, stewards get to handle the nobs' wine and rum and stuff. I shall enjoy taking my share of that.'

'You're not starting drinking again! I thought you'd given it up.'

'What else will there be to do on a long voyage?'

As they were getting ready, there was a knock on the door. Thad slipped behind it as she answered.

'Ah, there you are, Bess,' said Fred. 'Mr Pearson's asked me to take care of you. He doesn't want you going to Australia.'

As he entered the room, Thad hit him over the head with the heavy iron doorstop and Fred fell like a log. Chuckling, Thad tied him up then turned to Bess. 'Now, let's get on board. By the time they find this fellow, we'll have sailed.'

CHAPTER TWENTY-ONE

SEPTEMBER 1866

Albert took his wife to market, told her he had to see a fellow and left her. He walked along to the back of the livery stables. 'There you are, Ned. Any news?'

'He's gone rushing off to Melbourne so she's got no protector at the moment.'

'What about the old lady?'

'She's still living there.'

'We'll have to see if we can separate 'em then.' A coin exchanged hands and Albert walked away. It suddenly occurred to him that *she* might be at market and he walked briskly back, to find her talking to his wife of all people. At the sight of him, Catherine nodded farewell to Olwen and walked away. He watched her go, mouth pursed in thought.

'She's looking well, isn't she?' Olwen said wistfully.

'Who is?'

'Katie.'

'Cheating bitch! Letting us pay her fare here then waltzing off to another job. She has no *right* to look well.'

Olwen sighed. 'Leave her alone, Albert.'

'What did you say?'

For once she didn't flinch. For once she held her ground. 'If you think I don't know when you sneak out at night, then you're fooling yourself.'

He'd hit her across the face before he could stop himself.

Someone nearby muttered, 'Shame.'

He swung round, but couldn't work out who it was.

Olwen stared at him, cheek red, tears welling in her eyes, then turned and walked away without a word.

'Where are you going?' he yelled, and chased after her, grabbing her arm.

She stopped and stood perfectly still. 'I'm leaving you.' Then she began walking again.

Several people overheard this and someone called, 'Good for you, Olwen! Need any help?'

'Stupid bitch!' he yelled. 'I'll give you one hour

to get back to the cart.'

She didn't turn, didn't so much as twitch, just continued walking steadily away.

An hour and a half later he was still waiting by the cart and a small crowd had formed to watch him, consisting mainly of people who had known Olwen before he married her. The looks they kept giving him were not friendly. It had been a mistake to hit her in public, he acknowledged. He should have waited until he got home.

A small boy came up to him with a note, looking nervous. He took the note, wondering where she was. But it didn't come from her.

Yore wife left town on the Melb'ne coach half hour ago.

Albert cursed and tore the note into shreds, then clambered up on the cart and drove off. What the hell had got into Olwen today? It was all that bitch's fault, giving his wife silly ideas. Women should do as their husbands told them and keep their bloody mouths shut.

But Olwen would be back, he knew. She'd be going to her sister's but she'd never leave her things behind. She was fond of her ornaments and mementoes. Yes, she'd be back for them and when she came, he'd make sure she stayed.

*   *   *

In Melbourne Olwen used the last of her market money to take a cab to her sister's house. There she fell into Nesta's arms and sobbed out her woes.

'I'm not going back to him, I'm not! Even if I get none of my things back.'

A little later, she said bitterly, 'You were right. I

337

should never have rushed into marriage so quickly, but I was desperate.'

As the tears began to dry up she admitted, 'Albert hits me. He likes hurting people.'

Nesta hugged her all over again. 'Well, you can stay here as long as you like, *cariad*. There's always a place for you in my home, and my Ennis will say the same. Hitting you, indeed! What sort of man is he? If I ever see him again, I'll give him a piece of my mind.'

*   *   *

As the ship left Liverpool, Dick stood by the rail, feeling homesick already. It would never have been his choice to leave Ireland, and only for Theo would he have done this.

Lavinia was sitting on the upper deck, looking terrified. With a sigh he went across to her. 'How are you?'

'Where's Bess? I need a maid to help me in case I'm sick.'

'You won't be sick if you stay in the fresh air. And you'll do better if you stop thinking about it.'

'You don't know anything! Go and find Bess at once. I wish to retire to my cabin.'

He decided to fetch the new maid he'd hired and introduce her to Lavinia before he explained that Bess wouldn't be joining them on the voyage. There were bound to be hysterics and he wanted help in dealing with them.

He walked along the deck, scanning the crowd, but couldn't see Clemmy, the sturdy, sensible girl he'd hired, anywhere.

He made his way towards the entrance to the

steerage passengers' cabins and found a steward he could ask about Clemmy. For a consideration the man agreed to find the Matron and ask her because of course Dick wasn't allowed into the single women's quarters.

A few minutes later the steward returned with a stern-faced woman. 'Are you the one who brought Clemmy Martin on board?'

'Yes. She's the maid to my brother's wife.'

'And what about this Bess person?'

'What do you mean, "Bess person"?'

'I have another woman on board also claiming to be Mrs Mullane's maid and had to prevent her from attacking Clemmy who seems to me a decent young woman—which is more than I can say for the other one.'

Dick stared at her in horror. 'Bess is on board?'

She nodded.

'But I made arrangements to stop her . . . how did she manage that?'

A voice said, 'By force. Your friend Fred is nursing a broken head, I'm afraid.' Bess came up from behind the Matron and smiled at Dick, not a nice smile. 'Now I'll go and see to my mistress, if you don't mind. *You* can do something about the other woman.'

'Tell Clemmy I'll be back to speak to her in a few minutes,' Dick told the Matron hastily and rushed off after Bess. He wasn't cut out for intrigue, but how could he have known that Bess would prove stronger than Fred—or had she had help?

He found Lavinia clutching Bess's hand and listening to the tale of how Mr Pearson had tried to separate them. He could only admire the way Bess managed to keep her mistress from hysterics,

339

something Lavinia was an expert in, and yet continue her tale with a few discreet sobs.

'You must arrange for her to travel cabin class,' Lavinia told him in the end.

'No. I'm not spending the money on her.'

'If you won't, I will.'

'Do you have enough money? Won't you need some when we arrive in Western Australia?'

She glared at him. 'You know I have no money! I have to go to Australia to get some from Theo.'

Her voice had risen to a shrill pitch, attracting glances from people nearby, and again Bess shushed her.

Dick looked at the two of them, sick to the soul to think he'd be spending over three months travelling with them. And when they arrived, he'd have to find a way to warn Theo that Lavinia had followed him to Australia while at the same time conveying the two of them safely to his brother. He'd also have to make sure Clemmy was all right.

When this was over, he was going back to Ireland and never setting foot off its shores again. Not even for Theo.

He went back to sort things out for Clemmy, who said comfortably that he wasn't to blame and she had seen at a glance the sort Bess was.

The Matron agreed to find Bess a berth, telling him sourly that he was lucky there were a couple of spares. 'But that young madam will get no better treatment than the rest of the women under my protection,' she finished with a sniff.

Clemmy looked at him more sympathetically. 'It's a right old mess, isn't it?'

He nodded. 'I'm not cut out for this sort of thing.'

'Then you'd better leave the two of them to themselves and just enjoy the voyage.' She grinned. 'If I've no work to do, I'll surely be doing that.'

'You have every right to be furious with me,' he admitted.

'What good would that do?'

But he had, he admitted to himself that night in bed, made a right old mess of it, he had so.

*   *   *

Ismay woke up to hear the patter of rain on the hood of the wagon. She sat up, pulling her blankets round her, but as the rain turned rapidly into a downpour, called out to the men camping outside, 'Dan! Malachi! Hadn't you better take shelter in here?'

'It just woke me. I don't think Dan's awake yet,' Malachi called.

Ismay turned towards the end nearest the driving seat, expecting them to tumble, laughing, into the wagon as usual. What was taking them so long tonight?

Malachi called out, his voice urgent and with an undertone of fear. 'Can you come and help me, Issy? There's something wrong with Dan. He's not moving and he's breathing funny.'

She cast off the covers and decided against a shawl, which would only need drying afterwards. As she slipped down from the wagon, barefoot, rain pounded down on her and she shivered as she ran across to where the men had been sleeping under a nearby tree. Malachi was supporting the old man, his face a pale blur in the darkness.

'What shall I do?'

'Take his feet. We'll have to carry him.'

Dan seemed to be only semi-conscious and it was with difficulty that the two of them managed to lift him on to the tailboard. Panting from her efforts, Ismay clambered up beside him.

'Put him in my bed, Malachi. He'll be warmest there.'

By the time they'd done that, she was shivering.

'Get out of those wet things, love. I'll just go and fetch our bedding.'

He went out again into the wet, windy darkness and was back a few minutes later, tossing a pile of soggy blankets into the back of the wagon. By that time she'd got the lantern lit, but its light seemed to be sucked up by the darkness and the wagon kept swaying as the wind buffeted it.

'The blankets are wet through. We can't use 'em.' He started unbuttoning his shirt, then stopped to look at her. 'I thought you'd have got out of those wet things by now. You'll catch your death of cold.'

'I've been looking at Dan. His mouth's pulled down at one side. I think he's had a seizure. What shall we do?'

'There's nothing much we can do till it's light, then we'll go and find the nearest doctor. In the meantime we have to find ourselves some dry bedding.' Malachi began unbuttoning his trousers. 'If you don't get those wet things off quickly, my lass, I'll take 'em off for you.'

Blushing, she did as he suggested, avoiding his eyes as she rubbed herself down with a towel. She was shivering even harder by the time she took a blanket from the stock and wrapped it round herself. She watched him doing the same and

342

couldn't take her eyes off the lean muscular body she'd admired once or twice when she'd caught him washing in a stream.

'Do you have a dry nightdress handy?'

'Yes.'

His voice was suddenly harsh. 'Then put it on, for heaven's sake. I'm only human and the sight of you without clothes is giving me ideas.'

She scrambled into her spare nightdress, wrapped her old grey shawl round her shoulders, then the blanket on top of that. He slipped on a pair of underdrawers and a flannel vest, then got out some more blankets from their stock. He hesitated as he looked at her. 'We'd be best sharing a bed. We'll get warm quicker.'

'Yes.'

He moved to kneel beside her and study their old friend. Dan was still breathing but there was no more they could do for him. Blowing out the lamp, he got down into their nest of blankets.

She hesitated to lie down beside Malachi, though. It felt different tonight, as if things had changed between them.

His voice grew softer in the darkness. 'Come on, love. You're still shivering.' He pulled the covers over them, spreading a tarpaulin on top of that because rain was blowing into the wagon. As they wriggled into position in the cramped space, they were pressed close together. When she shivered again, he said in her ear, 'We'll soon warm up now.'

'Yes.' But she had never lain in a man's close embrace before, feeling the soft warmth of each of his breaths on her face, feeling the hardness of his body against hers.

'Are you feeling better now, Issy?'

'Yes, thank you. And you?'

'I'm fine.'

After a few minutes, she ventured, 'I don't feel sleepy though.'

'Nor me. Eh, I'm that worried about Dan. I do hope he'll be all right. I've grown fond of the old fellow.'

They dozed, jerked awake and dozed again. It seemed a long time until dawn filled the clearing with grey light and she was able to see Malachi's face so close to hers. When she looked at him, he gave her a half-smile, then kissed her, a kiss that went on and on.

'Issy, you'd tempt the devil himself!' he muttered.

'I don't want to tempt the devil, only you.'

He looked at her very solemnly. 'One day, love . . .'

Dan groaned and that broke the spell. She wriggled round to check on the old man but he still seemed only half-conscious, not aware of his surroundings. 'Is it light enough to set off?' she asked.

'Yes.'

She thought she heard Malachi mutter, 'And a good thing too!' as he pulled on his trousers.

*   *   *

They didn't find a doctor until mid-morning. After he'd clambered on to the wagon to examine Dan, he took them into his consulting room and said bluntly, 'I'm afraid there's nothing I can do for your friend, Mr Firth.'

Issy clutched Malachi's hand.

344

'He may have another seizure and go like that.' He snapped his fingers. 'Or he may linger like this for days, weeks, even longer. He's in no fit state to travel round the countryside, though.' He looked disapprovingly at their wagon, standing outside his house.

Malachi sighed. 'He'd hate to be shut up indoors.'

'You don't have a proper house to take him to?'

'No. The wagon's as near a home as he's had for a long time. We'll look after him as best we can, then.' Malachi paid the doctor, angry that he was so disapproving. He listened impatiently to some more advice then went to stand beside the wagon, fists clenched, his expression bleak.

'What are we going to do?' Ismay asked when he didn't speak.

'I'm not sure. He's not fit to travel, but there's nothing for us in Melbourne. Or for him.'

'He does have a house,' she said softly. 'And there's even a healer there. We can afford to stop selling and look after him for a while, can't we?'

Malachi nodded. 'Of course we can. We've been making good money.'

'Well, then, let's take him home and ask Wilya to help us care for him.'

He stared at her for a minute, then a smile dawned. 'Good idea, love. You won't mind nursing him till we get there?' Already she had cleaned the old man, working tenderly on his limp body.

'Of course I don't. I nursed Mam when she was dying. I'm not afraid of people's bodies.'

'Good lass! I'll help you in every way I can, with the lifting and such, but I don't know much about caring for sick folk.'

345

'I know a little.' Her face was sad.

It took them a week of gentle travel. Dan seemed to regain a form of consciousness, for his eyes followed them round, but he couldn't speak or move much. When Ismay told him where they were taking him, he relaxed visibly and she knew then that they were doing what he wanted.

Malachi watched her in admiration. He had thought her too young to marry, but now she seemed older and more capable. Perhaps a hard life did that to you, and she'd had a very hard life indeed.

'You're marvellous with him,' he said one night as they sat by the camp fire. 'I don't know what I'd have done without you.'

'I'm very fond of him.'

'Me, too.'

They looked at one another sadly.

'He won't get better, will he?'

Malachi shook his head.

Each stretched out their nearest hand instinctively and the human contact and warmth was a comfort. He looked at their joined hands, then at her face, lit by the flickering flames. 'I'm glad I married you, Issy.'

'Are you really?'

'Yes.'

'Well, that's something, anyway.' But she wanted to be his wife not a nurse.

*   *   *

Gil strode back into the kitchen. 'We're ready.' He looked at Mark. 'You coming?'

Mark nodded.

346

'Know how to handle yourself in a fight?'

'I lived on the goldfields for a while. I can hold my own against most men, though I'm a bit out of practice.'

Maggie clapped one hand to her mouth but said nothing.

Dolly raised her second cup of rum-flavoured tea to them. 'Here's luck to ye.'

When Mark followed Gil into the side alley, he was pleased at the sight of six tough-looking men waiting there.

'They want their money first,' Gil said. 'You can trust them to earn it. My life on it.'

When the payment had been made, he sent three men off to secure the rear of Kellagh's, waiting five minutes by Mark's big silver watch, which his companion held open in his hand, then nodded. 'Right. Let's get it over with.'

Mark turned to hand his watch to Maggie, then followed him along the alley.

When they arrived at Kellagh's, Gil hammered on the door. As it opened, he simply punched the man in the face and knocked him flying. Pouncing on him, he shook him by the jacket front. 'Where's the new lass been put?'

A voice from the back of the hall said, 'If you're not out of my premises in two minutes flat, I'll start shooting.'

Gil threw the man he'd punched aside and growled something angry under his breath.

Mark, who gone to stand behind a pillar the minute they gained entry, gave no warning but took aim and fired.

The other man cursed and dropped his revolver, cradling the bloody hand that had held it as he

347

turned to run.

Gil took him down before he'd gone three paces, making him scream as the injured hand was slammed down on the floor. He looked up at Mark who had followed him. 'Good man! Meet Vincent Kellagh, the owner.'

Mark picked up the other's revolver and stared at the man on the floor, one gun in each hand. 'Where's Mara?'

'Don't know who you mean.'

'I think you do. The new girl is the sister of a very good friend of mine, and her brother-in-law is a landowner of means who'll leave no stone unturned to find her. Give her up now and if she's unharmed, we'll say no more about this.'

A voice from above yelled, 'Gil Brogan, you're a bloody traitor an' I'll make damned sure you regret this!'

Gil looked up to see his brother Mick's angry red face leaning over the banisters. 'What I regret most of all is having a brother who preys on children,' he replied.

*   *   *

Upstairs, Jimmy heard the commotion and gun shot. He was in an attic, supposedly locked in, but had already made sure he could pick the simple lock on the door and did so now, assuming his captors would be too busy to check on him if there was a fight going on.

As he crept along the corridor, wondering where Mara was, the other doors along it opened and some of the house's girls looked out.

'If anyone wants to escape, now might be the

348

time,' he suggested.

Most of the girls immediately went back into their rooms and shut the doors, but two of the younger ones stayed out in the corridor.

'Where will they have put the new girl?' he asked them.

'I'll show you,' one said.

The other said nothing, but continued to follow them, her eyes huge and shadowed in her thin, white face. They were so young his heart bled for what they must have suffered here.

The door the girl indicated was solid and when he rattled it, didn't give. 'Are you there, Mara?'

'She'll be drugged,' his guide told him. 'They always drug the new ones.'

'Where's the key?'

'*He* keeps it on him.'

Jimmy fiddled with the lock, but it was a good one. 'Sod him! I'm not strong enough to kick the door down. We'll have to see what's happening downstairs. Tread softly and stay behind me.'

On the landing below they nearly bumped into Mick who was still staring impotently down into the central hall. Jimmy put one finger to his lips and looked round for something to smash over Mick's head. He found a large vase, picked it up and thumped it down.

With a roar, the man spun round to confront him, staggering a little, but not rendered unconscious even by such a blow.

'Help!' Jimmy called out, suddenly terrified. 'Someone help me!'

Gil gestured and one of the men who'd come with him ran up the stairs just as Mick started to try to choke Jimmy. The two girls were nowhere to be

349

seen.

With a grin, the man grabbed Mick's shoulder and dragged him round, aiming a punch at his chin. The punch never landed, but it served to free Jimmy and the two men began to struggle, getting nearer and nearer to the top of the stairs and eventually rolling down, bouncing and grunting and yelling.

At the bottom Mick lay groaning while the other man got quickly to his feet, wincing in pain. With a snarl of anger, Gil stepped forward and kicked his brother hard in the side.

Two of Kellagh's men came in from the rear and Vincent grinned at Mark. 'The advantage is on my side now, I think.'

'I think not. If you look behind them . . .'

Kellagh snarled in anger at the sight of Gil's three friends who'd entered the brothel by the back way. 'What the hell do you want?'

'The new girl.'

'You're too late. She's gone.'

'Then you're all going to explain that to the police.'

'Gil, she's still up here!' Jimmy called. 'Only he's got the key.'

'Good lad!'

Mark levelled the revolver at Kellagh again. 'Give us it.' His face was cold rather than angry, the face of a man who would not be afraid to shoot again.

Kellagh growled under his breath then fumbled in his pocket with his uninjured hand.

Gil stepped forward to take the key off him. 'You keep the gun on him, Mark, and I'll go and find the girl.' He passed Kellagh's gun to one of his friends. 'You know how to use one of these, don't you, Ted me boy?'

The man grinned, nodded and examined it quickly, then held it ready.

Upstairs Gil found Jimmy, and behind him two girls hiding round the corner where they couldn't be seen from downstairs.

'They want to escape from here,' the lad said.

Gil tried to hide his shock at how young they were. 'All right. We'll take you with us. Wait here.'

When they opened the locked door they found Mara inside, tied to the bed and only half-conscious.

'She's still wearing the clothes she was captured in,' Jimmy whispered.

'Let's hope she's not been used,' Gil said. They untied her and he picked her up, anger on his face. 'That bloody brother of mine was born to hang and I want nothing more to do with the sod.'

He carried Mara downstairs, nodding to the two girls to follow.

At the sight of them Kellagh roared, 'What are you two doing out of your rooms? Get back upstairs at once!'

The girls cringed but Jimmy gave them a shove forward. 'Don't listen to him. He can't hurt you now.'

'They seem to be unwilling guests,' Gil said mildly. 'And they look rather young to me. Do you really want the police involved?'

Kellagh breathed deeply but didn't answer.

Jimmy guided the girls towards the front door and Gil signalled to his men. 'We've got her. You can get out now.'

Mark emptied the ammunition from Kellagh's

revolver and tossed the gun down into the basement entry as he left.

They moved through the streets in a group, with two men staying behind to watch for anyone trying to follow them. Gil was still carrying Mara and a grim-faced Mark had his revolver handy in his coat pocket.

As they entered the house, Dolly jumped to her feet, gaping at them. 'Three girls! I thought you only wanted Mara.'

'They wanted to escape.'

'Hell, you'd better get them out of town quickly then. Kellagh will be furious.'

Mark interrupted. 'I'm taking Mara back to my hotel. Will you and the lads come with me, just to be sure we're not attacked?'

'Aye.'

He looked at Jimmy and the two girls. 'What about them?'

'Ah, I'll see to them,' Dolly said, her voice a little slurred and her face flushed.

'Not by using them here!'

'What do you think I am?'

'A good-hearted woman, that's what. Here, take this.' Mark pressed some coins into her hand. 'If you need any more, let me know. This trade in children sickens me.' He turned to Jimmy. 'You did well, lad.'

Dolly put one arm round each of the girls and studied Jimmy. 'Want a job here, young fellow?'

He brightened. 'Yes.'

She looked at Gil. 'Still leaving Melbourne?'

He nodded.

'Well, you're not going till you've found me a couple of tough lads to work as guards. Reliable ones, mind. And you'll take a message from me to the Chief Constable, too. I've met him once or twice.' She winked.

'I'll have to get back to work now,' Maggie told Mark, relieved that it had all gone well.

'I know. Thanks for your help.'

'How are you going to manage with her?'

'My landlady will help. I've known the Parkers for years and always stay there when I'm in Melbourne. You sure you'll be all right?'

'I'm fine. I've never had a job I liked half as much.'

Which was one worry off his mind, at least.

CHAPTER TWENTY-TWO

SEPTEMBER–OCTOBER 1866

Dick scanned the groups of passengers on the deck and waved when he saw Clemmy. She greeted him with her usual smile and he could think of nothing to say, could only stand there and smile foolishly.

'Isn't it a lovely day?' she said in her soft, slow voice. 'I never knew there could be so much sunshine.'

'It is. Are you all right?'

'Yes, of course. I've never had a holiday like this one. But you look worried.'

He shrugged. 'Lavinia again, and that Bess. They seem to enjoy plaguing the life out of me.'

'Well, you just stand by the rail with me. You'll soon calm down.'

But it was her presence that calmed him, not the

sight of waves sparkling in the sun, her presence that he sought every time he could. 'I like being with you, Clemmy.'

She went a little pink. 'Well, I like being with you too, Dick.'

'You do?'

A young man came up just then and scowled at him. 'Are you coming to listen to the story, Miss Lowe?'

'Not today.'

'You'll not find out what happens.'

'I can guess.'

With a frustrated sigh he walked on.

'I'm keeping you from your friends,' Dick worried.

'You're not.' The pink in her cheeks deepened. 'I'd rather be with you.'

'You would?'

She nodded.

Feeling bold, he took her hand. 'And I'd rather be with you than with anyone else.'

After that, they spent every moment they could together.

*   *   *

Mara lay feeling heavy-headed. But if she didn't get up and start work, Dolly would shout at her. She raised one arm to push the covers back, but the arm didn't seem to have any strength and with a sigh she let it fall again.

'Mara? Are you wake?'

She jumped in shock and opened her eyes quickly because it was a man's voice and she never let men into her tiny bedroom off the kitchen. Only

354

this wasn't her room and the man sitting by the bed watching her anxiously was a stranger.

Memories came flooding back and she panicked, somehow finding the strength this time to scrabble at the covers and try to roll away from him.

'You're safe, Mara,' he said quietly. 'I'm a friend of Keara's. Your sister Keara.'

She stilled, mouth half-open in surprise, then closed her eyes for a minute as the room wavered round her.

'She's been looking for you,' he went on. 'She had to go home but I said if you were found, I'd help you get to her. I'm Mark Gibson, by the way.'

Without opening her eyes, Mara said sadly, 'Keara sent us away. Why would she be looking for us now?'

'She didn't send you away. She didn't even know about your mother dying until months afterwards.' The girl absorbed this information with a frown and he waited a moment to see how she'd react.

She opened her eyes and stared at him. 'How could she not know? Diarmid sent her a letter.'

'Mr Mullane was away from home. Mrs Mullane got hold of the letter and she didn't tell Keara.'

Mara could not hold back an unhappy noise in her throat as the memories flooded back. 'Mam was calling for her, right until she died. Calling her name, even when she could only whisper it.'

'That must have been dreadful to see.'

Mara nodded. 'Me and Ismay, we did our best but Mam knew Keara hadn't come and she kept crying for her. Ismay got so angry.' The frown returned. '*Mrs* Mullane did it, you said?'

'Yes.'

'She's a dreadful woman, that one, always

355

screaming and yelling at folk.' Then something occurred to her. 'Did Keara come all the way to Australia to look for us?'

'No. Mrs Mullane had her kidnapped and sent to Australia as well—only she sent your sister to Western Australia, which is a long way from Melbourne.'

'But Keara did come here, you said?'

'Yes. She spent several months over here in Victoria, searching for you, but she's expecting another baby and had to go home.'

Mara struggled to sit up but when he came to help her with the pillows, she flinched back, so he sat down again. When she was sitting comfortably she said doubtfully, 'You don't look like a liar.'

'Thank you. I'm definitely not lying to you.'

'Ismay said Keara must have known about us being sent to Australia, but I always did wonder.'

He nodded. 'She'd never, ever have sent you away. She loves you very much.'

Silence greeted this, then a sigh. 'She's married, then? Who did she marry?'

'She isn't married. Keara loves Mr Mullane and he adores her. They can't marry but he treats her just like a wife. They've had a daughter called Nell, which makes you an auntie, and there was another child due in November.'

She gaped at him. 'Keara and Mr Mullane?'

'Yes. They live as man and wife, and Theo loves her very much indeed.'

'But what about Mrs Mullane?'

'She's still in England. Theo's bought a farm in Western Australia. He and Keara want you to go and live there with them.'

'What about Ismay?'

356

'They want her too, but we have to find her first.'

'Don't the nuns know where she is?'

'Not now. She ran away from the people she was working for. And the convent burnt down.'

'It never did!'

There was a knock on the door. 'Is she awake, Mr Gibson?'

He went to open it and an older woman came in to stand at the foot of the bed and smile at Mara.

'This is Mrs Parker, our landlady. I always stay with her when I'm in Melbourne.'

She smiled at him then turned back to the girl in the bed. 'You'll want a wash before you have something to eat, dear. Go away, Mr Gibson, and leave me to help this young lady.'

'All right. I'll see you later, Mara.'

It was a big effort to move about and do everything necessary so when Mrs Parker tucked her up in bed again afterwards, the girl didn't protest.

'Mrs Parker, have you known Mr Gibson for long?'

'Bless you, dearie, yes. He always stays with us when he comes to Melbourne and a more decent fellow you couldn't hope to find. His wife died, but his mother-in-law lives with him and looks after his little daughter.'

Mara sighed in relief. You couldn't doubt a woman with a face as open and honest as this one.

'Don't go to sleep yet. I'm bringing you a glass of milk and a piece of cake.'

The girl slid down in the bed, her main worries dispelled. This man wasn't like Mick. She shuddered at the memory of how he and that horrible man he worked for had prodded her body

357

and planned to use her.

By the time Mrs Parker returned, however, her guest was fast asleep, so she put the milk and cake next to the bed, tucked the covers securely round Mara and went back to her kitchen.

*   *   *

When they turned the wagon off the main road, Dan began to get agitated, rolling his eyes and looking fixedly at Malachi.

'I remember, old man. You want me to hide our tracks.'

There was the barest softening in those faded eyes.

When he had finished, Malachi clambered aboard and took up the reins again. 'Our tracks are hidden now, Dan. No one will follow us.'

'I don't remember the journey here before,' Ismay said softly. 'Only being in the hut with Wilya—and the scent of eucalyptus.'

When they got to the clearing Jack was waiting for them.

'Dan's not well,' Malachi said. 'I think he's dying so we brought him here.'

'Good place to come. He's an old man. Had a hard life. Been happy sometimes. Can die on his own land.' Jack went to feed some more wood to the cook fire, leaving Malachi to unharness the horses.

A few minutes later Wilya slipped out of the woods as quietly as she did everything else. She studied Ismay in silence then said, 'You look better. Still not happy, though. But those sisters are waiting for you.'

'Well, Keara can wait for ever, as far as I care. We've got Dan here—he's bad.'

Wilya laughed softly. 'You'll find them sisters again.' She went to look at Dan, climbing on the wagon as nimbly as a young woman but shaking her head at what she saw. 'Let's make you comfortable, Dan.'

He tried to smile at her and she patted his shoulder.

Ismay expected Wilya to take him into the hut, but she didn't. Instead she gave various orders to her husband who began to build a kind of shelter on the other side of the clearing. When Wilya saw them looking at her, she gave one of her mysterious smiles. 'He say long ago, he don't want to die shut up in a room, want to die with the sun on his face. Now, I have to get things ready before you bring him to me.'

She worked for quite a while, scraping lines in the dirt around the area where Jack was building the shelter, then smoking the area by burning gum leaves and wafting the smouldering branches around. Only then did she allow them to lift Dan into the shelter.

After that, Wilya took over the nursing and Ismay was at a loss as to what to do with herself.

'Come and sit down by me,' Malachi said. 'We'll sing to him later. He always loved to hear us singing.'

When the shadows lengthened he brought out his guitar. As they got ready Dan's eyes were almost smiling again. Malachi strummed a chord, then turned to Ismay. 'We'll sing "The Last Rose of Summer",' he said. 'It was always one of his favourites.'

They began to sing softly, but gradually lifted their voices until the clearing seemed to be filled with music. Both lost themselves in the singing they loved and forgot about the others. When they had finished they stared at one another as if they were strangers who had only just met, a pretty young woman and a thin, energetic young man, then Wilya's voice recalled them to the present.

'You made him very happy,' she said quietly. 'His spirit went home gladly.'

'Dan's dead!' Ismay gasped. 'Oh, no!'

Wilya's hand grasped hers. 'He was glad to go,' she repeated. 'It was his time. He gave you this.' She gestured to the wagon. 'And he gave you one another, too.' Her expression grew sterner. 'Now see you don't waste his gifts.' She went into the little shelter Jack had built and drew away the blanket as she tended Dan's body for a final time.

When she was ready, she looked at the young couple. 'We tell him stories now, dreamtime stories, so he knows we send him away right.'

It was a while before she had finished and although they didn't understand her language, they sat quietly, out of respect. Then Malachi told his own story of meeting the old man.

The following morning they buried the body in a place Dan himself had chosen years before.

'I'll miss you,' Malachi said as he made his final farewells, standing by the grave.

'I'll miss you too, Dan,' Ismay echoed, tears trickling down her face.

Wilya nodded as if she approved of what they'd said.

When they got back to the clearing, she looked at Malachi. 'You want me an' Jack to leave now?

360

You going to live here?'

'No, I want you to stay. It's your home too now.'

She nodded, didn't thank him but raised her hand in farewell as she walked off into the forest again, carefully avoiding the area with the painted lines. Jack vanished behind the hut.

Malachi turned to Ismay. 'Dan left a letter for us.' His voice was thickened with tears and he had to swallow hard before he could continue. 'He gave it to me when we got married and told me to read it after he died.' He got up and went into the wagon, coming back with a large envelope. He took out a piece of paper.

> *Dear children, for so I think of you*
>
> *I'm so glad you got wed. I'm sure Ismay's the right lass for you, Malachi lad. I've left you everything, the land and house and wagon, all tight and proper. I arranged it last time we were in Melbourne. Go to Mr Bessing the lawyer who has offices just off Collins Street, near Beemy Lane, and he'll see you get it all. There's a bit of money saved in the bank, too.*
>
> *Don't grieve for me. I've had some good years lately, more than I deserved perhaps, but the best were with you two.*
>
> *See you look after one another.*
>
> *Written for Dan Reddings by J. Lanton, clerk, at the chambers of J. Bessing and Sons*

There was a squiggly cross at the bottom of the page, and next to it in brackets 'Dan Reddings, his mark'.

Ismay felt sad, but didn't cry. They'd known Dan was failing for a while and he'd died as he wished, in the open air, not locked away from the world. When Malachi put his arm round her, she leaned against him.

'We'll finish selling the stuff on the wagon,' he said. 'Then we're going to find your sister Mara somehow. After which we'll go and see Keara.'

'No!' She tried to pull away, but he wouldn't let her.

'Yes,' he said in a decisive tone of voice she'd never heard him use before to her. 'You have to find out what really happened, Issy. You're living with anger and that's no way to build a good life.' He hesitated then added more gently, 'I want us to have a happy life together, you and me. I don't want to be married to a bitter, unhappy woman.'

She was shaken by his words. She wanted to find Mara again, of course she did. But she definitely didn't want to confront Keara.

Maybe something would happen to stop the meeting. It must. She just couldn't trust Keara again, didn't dare.

*   *   *

Mara didn't wake again until that afternoon, by which time the effects of the drug Kellagh had given her had worn off. She was so ravenous she ate the piece of cake and drank the glass of milk, then wondered if she should get dressed.

There was a knock on the door and Mrs Parker poked her head round. 'I thought I heard you stirring. We're going to have tea in a few minutes. Do you want to come and join us?'

'Yes, please. I'll just be a minute.'

In the dining parlour she sat shyly beside Mark,

listening to him chat to the Parkers. She made a hearty meal then ventured to ask, 'What's going to happen now?'

'We're going to Rossall Springs where I live with my mother and baby daughter. You can stay with us until we can make arrangements for someone to take you by coastal steamer to Western Australia.'

'Oh. I thought you'd be taking me?'

'I have a new business to run and my daughter to look after, I'm afraid. I'll write a letter to your sister before we leave Melbourne and make inquiries on your behalf about sailings. Better to let Keara know in advance that you're coming, don't you think? You'll need someone to meet you at the port.'

She nodded. 'I wish Ismay was with me. I'd not be as nervous of seeing Keara again if she was here. What can have happened to her? What if we never find her again?'

'You've nothing to be nervous about. Keara's your sister and she wants very much to find you. She'll be overjoyed when she receives my letter. And we'll try our hardest to find Ismay. She can't have vanished into thin air.' As an afterthought, he added, 'And I hope you'll write Keara a note, too? It'll make her very happy.'

The thought terrified Mara, because Keara was sure to show it to Mr Mullane and he'd think she was a poor writer, she was sure. Well, she'd never been as good a scholar as Ismay and Keara. 'I shan't know what to say.'

'Tell her where you've been since you left the convent, what you've been doing.'

'What, even about Dolly's?'

He shook his head in warning, his eyes going to

363

the Parkers, and she didn't pursue the point.

After the meal was over he asked Mara to stay downstairs for a few minutes as he had something else to tell her. When their hosts had left them, he told her about Catherine.

Her face lit up. 'Oh, I'm so glad she'll be there. I really liked Sister Catherine.'

'She's not a nun any more and no one knows she used to be one so you mustn't call her that. But she's looking forward to seeing you again. Now, about this note to Keara . . .'

He wrote his own letter quite quickly, but Mara sat and nibbled her pen, sighing and crossing words out, then suddenly screwing up the first piece of paper.

'Is something wrong?' he asked.

'I don't know what to say. I've been feeling angry at her, mostly. I can't just undo it all in a minute. Will I not be better waiting till I see her?'

'I think you should write something.'

With a sigh she scribbled a few lines then handed the paper over to him. 'You can read it if you like.'

He looked down at the round, childish handwriting.

Dear Keara

Mr Gibson says you didn't know we were coming to Australia and I'm glad of that. Ismay and I were very upset about coming here, but I like it now, especially the sunshine.

I don't know what else to say. It'll be easier when we see one another, I think. I'm all right, though.

Mara

It wasn't much to bridge the gap of several years between the sisters, but he supposed it would have to do. 'I'll put it in with my own letter,' he said.

When she went up to her bedroom, Mara leaned on the windowsill watching light rain pattering down. It stopped then started again, warring with the sun which was still trying to shine. When a rainbow appeared, she wasn't surprised. It was only small, a penny rainbow, she thought with a smile, but it made her feel better, less alone.

'Are you there at the other end of it, Ismay?' she whispered, wondering if her beloved sister had changed much since they last met, wondering where she was this night. Somewhere nicer than this, Mara hoped. She was tired of city streets and narrow alleys. Mark said Keara lived in the country and she was glad of that.

She couldn't imagine what she would say to Mr Mullane and was still a bit shocked that Keara had children now without being married. Their mother would have thrown a fit at that. Mara didn't know whether she was dreading the reunion or looking forward to it, only that she was tired of moving all the time, living a few months here and a few months there.

'If I don't like living with them, I can go for a maid again,' she decided at last and on that comforting thought she got ready for bed.

In the next room Mark lay wondering what Mara was really thinking. She was such a solemn child, her face like Keara's and yet not like it. She was thinner and very slightly built, but her eyes had a deep sadness in them that sometimes made her look older than her fourteen years.

He hoped Catherine would do better at talking

to her. He was finding it very difficult. In fact, he'd be glad to be done with all this and be at home again. Most of all, he wanted to see Catherine, be with her again. He'd missed her greatly while he'd been in Melbourne. Nan was a dear and he loved his little daughter, but he needed someone to talk to—another adult, a woman of his own.

He wasn't going to let Albert Bevan drive Catherine away from Rossall. He wanted . . . His mouth fell open in shock as he admitted something he'd been trying to avoid thinking about: he'd fallen deeply in love with her. So quickly, too! The smile hovered on his lips as he thought of her and when he saw the rainbow above the trees outside, it seemed an omen, somehow.

He hadn't really prayed for a long time, but he prayed now. *Please let her love me, want me. I can't imagine life without her.*

But in the morning he remembered how two women had died from loving him and wondered if it would be best for her if he did not speak about how he felt. He had never forgotten how Patience had died, the blood that had poured from her after she'd borne their child. He didn't think he could face that again.

CHAPTER TWENTY-THREE

OCTOBER 1866

Albert found life without a wife very difficult indeed. He ordered one of his men to do the cooking, but the results were barely edible and the

366

other man grew sulky. None of them had any idea how to wash clothes and Albert wasn't going to clean the house, which was women's work, so the place soon looked as if it had never seen a duster or broom.

It made him so angry that one day he decided to go after Olwen, who would no doubt be at her sister's because where else could she go? He'd demand that she return with him. She was his wife, after all. No doubt that uppity bitch had planted ideas about independence in Olwen when she was working for them. It was another thing he'd make Katie pay for, if he had to wait years to do it.

He set off very early, taking the coach into Melbourne then a cab out to his sister-in-law's house. More expense!

He hammered on the door, but although he was sure he saw the curtains move, no one answered him. 'I know you're in there!' he yelled.

Inside the house Nesta exchanged frightened glances with Olwen, then went out the back and sent the lad from next door with a note to fetch her husband. Ennis came hurrying home from their little drapery shop to find the brother-in-law he had met only once sitting on his doorstep, arms folded, anger radiating from him.

Albert stood up. 'I was wondering when someone would come.'

'What do you want, Bevan?'

'I want my wife back.'

'She doesn't want to go back and I won't make her.'

'Let me speak to her.'

'I'll find out if she wants to see you.' Ennis used his key to open the door, but when he tried to close

367

it, Albert put one foot in the entry.

'Aren't you going to invite me in?'

'No, I'm not. Get out!'

'Well, I'm coming in anyway.' Albert shoved the door back and clumped into the hall without attempting to wipe his muddy boots.

Ennis backed away from him, suddenly afraid of this large well-muscled man who was more than a match for a plump shopkeeper.

In the kitchen Olwen clutched her sister's arm. 'What are we going to do?'

Nesta realised that her sister was trembling and even paler than usual. She would never be able to stand up to her bully of a husband. 'You slip out the back way and nip along to the Powells'. I'll come and fetch you when it's safe.'

Olwen did so and Nesta closed the back door quietly then picked up a spoon and began stirring the cake mixture she'd abandoned earlier to send a note to her husband. Ennis came in followed by Albert Bevan.

'Where is she?' he demanded at once. 'Don't you dare hide my wife from me!'

'She's not here. And mind how you speak to me. The cheek of it! Coming pushing your way into my clean kitchen with those dirty boots.'

He thumped his hand down on the table. 'She must have come to you, there was no one else, so you have to know where she is.'

Nesta shrugged, then as he made his way round the kitchen table towards her, a purposeful look on his face, she shrieked and fled to her husband's side.

'Get out of my house, Bevan,' Ennis said, but his voice quavered.

Albert gave a scornful snort. 'I'm not leaving till I've checked whether you're lying or not. And if Olwen's here, she's coming with me if I have to drag her. A woman's place is with her husband and you have no right to come between us.'

'Well, a woman wouldn't leave a husband who treated her decently,' Nesta threw at him, anger overcoming prudence.

Albert's face went puce with rage. 'What's the bitch been saying to you?'

As he glowered at her, fists clenched, she decided she'd throw the heavy earthenware mixing bowl at him if he came any closer, then run outside screaming. But after a minute he grunted something and went back into the hall. They heard him searching the house, banging doors open on each side of the central corridor.

'He's gone mad,' Ennis whispered. 'But he's a big strong fellow so if he attacks us, you run outside and I'll try to hold him back.'

She looked at her short, plump, middle-aged husband, prepared to take a beating in her defence and love filled her. How lucky she was to have him. 'If he attacks us, we'll both fight back. We'll stand more chance then. I'm not letting him hurt you.'

'No, I have a better idea . . .'

When Albert had searched the house and was certain his wife wasn't hidden anywhere, he went back to sit in the kitchen, arms folded.

Nesta was no longer there.

'Where's she gone?'

'Shopping.' Ennis took a chair at the other side of the table and waited.

Half an hour later Nesta returned with two policemen, and though Albert blustered and insisted he had a right to see his wife, they escorted him off the premises and took him to the coach depot. Within minutes he was sitting on the coach back to Rossall, seething with fury.

Women! It was a pity you needed them, by hell it was! From thinking angrily about his wife, he went on to consider the other woman who'd been occupying his thoughts lately. That bitch of an ex-maid of theirs. *She* was still in Rossall. Still within reach. And after he'd allowed himself the satisfaction of dealing with her, he'd go back and fetch his wife. Only this time he'd be a bit more cunning about it, go at night, pay someone to help him.

*   *   *

As Ismay and Malachi drove away from the cabin in the woods, she sighed to think of Dan lying in the earth on his own. She stole a glance sideways at her husband, finding him looking back at her, very solemn and yet with a hint of a smile behind that serious expression. 'It feels strange, doesn't it?'

She had no need to ask what he meant by that. 'Yes. I miss him already.'

'I'll look after you, Issy.'

'That's not what I meant.'

'It's what I intend, though. I take a husband's duties very seriously.'

'Not all of them,' she muttered.

'Yet.'

The word seemed to hang in the air between them.

At the next settlement they were warmly welcomed. Folk sent messages to neighbours further afield and more came in to inspect the stock and buy carefully. No one seemed to have a lot of money in the country, Ismay thought, but everyone needed the basic necessities like sewing needles and pins, or cooking utensils and knives, because however careful you were, things wore out or broke and had to be replaced.

They stayed on and an impromptu party developed in one of the houses, something that happened regularly. It was another thing she had noticed in the country. People seized every opportunity they could to socialise, even when they couldn't afford fancy refreshments and half the guests had to sit on planks laid on boxes, or bales of hay covered with blankets. She liked that villagey feeling.

Of course someone had noticed the guitar hanging inside the wagon and she and Malachi were persuaded to sing. Their voices blended so perfectly that when they were singing all their other cares and worries seemed to drop away. Sometimes when they were driving along one or the other of them would start humming and before they knew it they'd be singing away.

Afterwards Malachi stayed to drink beer with a group of men and Ismay went to bed in the wagon which was standing at the rear of the house. When he joined her, she pretended to be asleep. It seemed the easiest thing to do. Who would have thought that not having Dan with them would make for so many small awkwardnesses?

Malachi lay down near the rear flap and was soon asleep. She kept her breathing slow and regular, but it was a long time before she could follow his example.

The following morning they had intended to set off early, but their hosts insisted on feeding them an enormous breakfast and it was well into the morning before they were on the road.

'Do you know where Dan intended to go?' she asked.

'Only vaguely. He was always going to explain his itinerary to me so that I could write it down but never got round to it.' He pulled a wry face. 'I think he knew it by heart, but couldn't always put a name to places, or remember where to turn until he saw the road again. So I thought we'd just find our own way round till the stock runs low, then head back to Melbourne.' He looked at the horses with a frown. 'I don't want to go too far off the beaten track. That left horse isn't as strong as the other one. I think we were cheated with him. The two we had last year were a much better matched pair only it'd have cost a fortune to keep them in feed and stabling for the months we were in Melbourne. Dan said one horse was as good as another but I don't reckon that. I'll be more careful next time.'

They didn't do too badly, always asking at each settlement where the best place to go next would be and finding people generally helpful.

Then there came a night with a bad thunderstorm. Ismay huddled in her nest of blankets, wincing as lightning flashed, rain drummed on the canvas hood and thunder rumbled. It seemed so close overhead.

His voice was gentle in the darkness. 'You don't like storms, do you?'

'No. But I can manage. I don't give in to my fear, so you've no need to worry about me having hysterics.'

372

He chuckled. 'I'm more likely to worry about you throwing something at me when you get angry.'

She smiled. She'd been very sharp with him earlier because he hadn't said a word for miles. 'I've never thrown anything at you.'

'Yet.'

The minute he said that word, it took her back to their first real conversation after they'd buried Dan. She let out her breath in a puff of exasperation. She was tired of pretending to understand what the other married women talked about when they were alone—tired of feeling uncertain about how Malachi really regarded her. Maybe he was just being kind. Well, she didn't want treating like a child. She wanted to be treated like a woman, to belong to him properly. Oh, she wanted it so much!

A particularly loud rumble of thunder was followed almost immediately by a blinding flash of lightning and she couldn't hold back a squeak.

'Would it help to cuddle up to me?' he offered.

'Yes, please.'

She tripped as she was trying to get closer to him and landed squarely on top of him. The next bright flash showed his face, the face she had grown to love, only inches away from hers. She could have wept when he didn't take advantage of the moment to kiss her but helped her to lie down beside him. But he did put his arms round her and that felt so good she sighed and wriggled closer.

'I used to cuddle up with Mara and Keara in bed,' she confided. 'We would whisper and laugh, and even in the coldest weather we managed all right. Keara got some sacks from one of the fanners and we had those on top of the blanket.'

373

He couldn't imagine a childhood so impoverished that sacks would be regarded as good bed coverings. 'What was it like, your childhood?'

So she told him about the single room with its earth floor, then the proper cottage—which they'd only had after Keara left to work for Lavinia Mullane. Inevitably she mentioned her da and never in terms of warmth or approval. But she'd loved her mother dearly, that was obvious. And her sisters. The more she talked about them, the more certain he became that if Keara were at all as Issy described her now, she would never have deliberately abandoned the other two. And that only made him more determined to reunite the sisters.

In the meantime his resolution of not making love until they were better set up to cope with a family was receiving its hardest test. He'd grown fond of Issy, more than fond, and she was altogether too pretty to ignore now that she was eating properly and enjoying life.

After a while she fell asleep in his arms, as soft and trusting as a kitten, but he lay there for a long time, too uncomfortable with his need for her to sleep easily. It was far more difficult than he'd expected to avoid consummating their marriage

*   *   *

When Mark and Mara got off the stage coach, they saw Catherine on her way back from market. He pointed out the tall, rosy woman with the short hair and gentle smile on her face as the former nun and Mara stared at her in amazement.

'I'd never have recognised you,' she said shyly

when Catherine joined them.

'I'd have recognised you anywhere, even though you've grown a lot since I last saw you.' She hesitated then stepped forward to hug the girl, who clung to her convulsively.

Albert, watching them from a distance, because he'd been following that bitch, scowled and spat to show his disgust. Everyone was a-hugging one another while he had no one, not even to clean his house, let alone warm his bed. As he looked at the woman and girl, who were laughing and chatting animatedly like old friends, it occurred to him that this might offer him a way to get back at Katie bloody Caldwell. His first wife had done anything he wanted when he threatened the children— though thank God they'd grown up and left home now, for a more ungrateful pair than his sons he'd yet to meet. But Katie was clearly very fond of this girl so if he had her in his hands, that bitch was stupid enough to sacrifice herself for another, he was sure, just as his wife had been.

But it'd have to be well planned. He wasn't having Mark Gibson interfering again.

Thoughtful now, he went along to the nearest bar and bought himself a beer, sitting frowning into it while he considered and discarded ideas. Couldn't even go to the eating house and buy himself a decent hot dinner now on market days, could he now, because of *her*!

After he'd paid her back—and he'd threaten to attack the girl again if she told anyone—he'd fetch Olwen home where she belonged. But not until he'd had his revenge here. He finished his beer and called for another glass, smiling into it when it arrived.

In fact, it was useful to have Olwen away at the moment or she'd be trying to interfere. You couldn't very well have your way with another woman when your wife was watching, could you? Or could you? He sniggered at the thought and called for more beer. Whatever Olwen said about not drinking in the daytime, beer quenched your thirst like nothing else and stayed your hunger too.

*　　　*　　　*

Mara was so tired she went to bed early and Nan pleaded exhaustion in order to allow Mark and Catherine some time together.

They lingered over a final cup of cocoa, chatting comfortably about how things had gone in the eating house and about Mark's plans for the future.

But he didn't say anything personal and Catherine had no idea how to lead him on. She had no feminine wiles, she decided sadly as she got ready for bed, though she had strong feelings for him. Such a quiet, caring man. And so good-looking.

Ah, she was probably fooling herself when she read more into his behaviour than mere friendship. Only . . . he did look at her warmly, he did sit and chat to her many an evening, just the two of them, and he did discuss his plans with her, always including her in them.

What was a woman to do?

She only wished she knew.

*　　　*　　　*

Ismay and Malachi were camping rough that night,

heading back towards Melbourne to restock. They sat and chatted easily over the camp fire, discussing the goods they'd need for their next trip. They could always talk about their work, if not about themselves.

'Don't you ever wish to settle down and run a shop in a town?' she asked idly.

'You know I do, but this is the best way to make money quickly.'

'How much more do we need? You never talk of it in detail, so I don't understand.'

'Are you good with figures?'

'I don't know.' She pulled a rueful face. 'I've never had much money to count.'

'Well then, perhaps I'd better teach you.' And for the first time he told her how much money he had saved and how much he thought he'd need for a shop, even about the sort of small town in which he'd like to settle and run a proper general store.

'You sound very rich to me,' she said, awed. 'I've never had even a pound of my own, and my poor mother had to make every farthing count. Many a night I've gone to bed hungry. It's not right, is it, that some are rich and some poor?'

'I'm not rich!'

'You are to me.'

'Well, it's *your* money as well, now we're married, so that makes you rich too.' She stared at him, sitting so close he could see the flames reflected in miniature in her eyes.

'I don't have anything,' she said flatly.

He was surprised. 'Of course you do. You're my wife.'

'You could still get rid of me. We haven't consummated the marriage.'

He saw the sadness on her face and took her hand. 'I'd never do that, Issy.' The hand felt warm in his, a little roughened, the hand of a hard-working young woman. Without thinking he raised it to his lips and kissed it.

She gasped and half-closed her eyes.

Desire rose in him like a high tide, overflowed and he was lost. He pulled her to him and said in a voice that was rough with suppressed passion, 'What if I were to make you my wife? Would you feel you had something then?'

'Yes. Oh, yes.' She swayed towards him. Stars twinkled down on them, flames crackled merrily, and suddenly he could hold out no longer. He pulled her into his arms and kissed her with all a young man's long-repressed hunger. She clung to him and kissed him back, murmuring his name over and over again.

'Oh, Issy, I can't wait any longer.'

Her voice was fierce. 'I don't want you to. I've never wanted you to!'

He pulled her to her feet, swept her up in his arms and carried her to the wagon, setting her down gently on the tail flap. Leaping up lightly beside her, he said quietly, 'Let me love you, then, Issy.'

Gently, he unfastened her clothing, smothering her with kisses till she felt as if the world was spinning around them. When she plucked up the courage to kiss him back, heat seemed to flow between them.

He held himself carefully in check, knowing enough about women to understand that he must make this first time good for her if he wanted their loving to be satisfying for the rest of their lives.

Which he did.

Behind him he seemed to hear Dan's soft chuckle. Before him, his wife's slender white body was silvered by the moonlight and her shy smile drew out the tenderness in him as well as the passion.

They caressed and loved and at last moved together into the slow dance of love. The night was filled with moonlight and their cries of joy in one another.

After it was over, he lay with his head on her breast and whispered, 'I love you, Issy. And now you're my wife truly.'

She tried to hold back the tears, but couldn't.

He was devastated. 'What's wrong? Have I hurt you?'

'No. Never that, Malachi. They're tears of happiness. I feel as if I've come home at last.'

'We're both home, then.' He kissed away the tears and wrapped her close in his arms. He wanted her again, but knew she was exhausted after their hard day's work. When he looked down she was asleep, nestled against him with a faint smile on her face, a tear still glistening on one cheek. He brushed it away with one fingertip, but she didn't stir.

His only regret now was that he couldn't yet afford a proper shop, that he had to keep dragging her round the countryside like a vagabond. One day, he promised silently, you'll have your home and family and everything else a woman wants, Issy my darling girl.

And in the meantime, we've got one another.

He, too, fell asleep with a smile on his face.

One night as the ship ploughed on through the water and the warm air made the cabins feel even smaller and more airless, Dick gave up the struggle to sleep and went outside to stand by the rail, lost in thought. The gentle motion of the waves was very soothing and for once there was no one nearby to interrupt his ruminations.

He still didn't see what else he could have done, but he was dreading telling Theo that he'd brought Lavinia to Australia, absolutely dreading it. She hadn't improved over the years, was still stupid beyond belief: encouraged in her silly ideas by Bess, laughed at by the other cabin passengers behind her back, taken advantage of by all and sundry when left to live alone. At the moment his daily confrontations with her were wearing him down.

Something warned him of a presence beside him, some instinct honed while shooting in the woods around Ballymullan, and he swung round just as a dark figure wearing some sort of mask tried to push him into the water. He yelled for help as he struggled against being tipped overboard, but the man was bigger and stronger than him. Desperate fear for his life added to Dick's efforts, but he was fighting a losing battle and knew it. He continued to yell, not even aware of what he was yelling, only that he didn't want to die.

Then shouts and pounding footsteps made his assailant curse and suddenly the hands holding him were gone. Too relieved even to try to give pursuit, Dick moved quickly away from the rail, sobbing for breath. A hand on his shoulder made him realise that one of the crew members standing night watch was speaking and he tried to pull himself together.

'What's wrong, sir?'

'Someone just—I can't believe it!—they tried to push me overboard!'

'*What?* Are you sure?'

'Of course I'm sure.'

'Did you recognise him?'

'No. He had his face covered. But he was taller than me and heavily built, much stronger. If you hadn't come, he'd have succeeded.' Dick began to shake as reaction set in.

The man looked round, seeing nothing untoward. 'There's not much I can do at present, sir, but I think you'd better speak to the Captain about this tomorrow. I'll escort you back to your cabin. For tonight you'd better stay inside and lock the door. In fact, if we don't catch the fellow, you'd better make a practice of doing that every night.'

'I will, I will.' Still shuddering, Dick made his way back to bed. He lay there for a while, thinking furiously. They'd not been long under way when he'd seen Bessie's friend Thad, working as a steward. He'd not forgotten him from the time they'd met just after Nancy's death. He'd guessed she and this Thad meant to cause trouble when they got to Australia, but it had never occurred to him that his life might be in danger before then.

It was undoubtedly Thad who'd tried to tip him overboard, but he could prove nothing. There were still weeks of the voyage to go. How was he to keep himself safe?

He said as much to the Captain the following day.

'Is there anyone you suspect, Mr Pearson?'

381

After a moment's hesitation, he gave the man's name and the Captain frowned at him, tapping his fingers on his desk. 'Hmm. I'll ask about the fellow and let you know what my officers say.'

They all agreed that Thad Bowler was surly, always trying to avoid work, and made a poor steward. They also agreed that Pearson was a decent fellow, not the sort to make up tales.

Proof or not, the Captain's suspicions were aroused and he transferred Bowler to other duties, ignoring the fellow's protests and making sure the officers kept him busy all day. At night he slept with the other crew members, not the stewards, and one or two of them were asked to make sure he didn't wander around the ship after dark.

After that, Dick saw Thad a few times on deck and on each occasion was offered a black glare and once a muttered, 'I'll get you yet.'

Nothing had prepared him for this. He wasn't a violent man, was slightly built and just wanted to live peacefully in Ballymullan. One day, maybe, he would marry and have a family, but he hoped to stay at Ballymullan ever afterwards. It was his true home and no other would suit him.

CHAPTER TWENTY-FOUR

NOVEMBER 1866

The letter from Mark arrived in Western Australia but took several days to reach the south-west, and even then languished in Bunbury until the weekly mail service brought it to the small hamlet of

Hesley Brook where Theo had bought land. Keara recognised Mark's handwriting on the envelope and didn't wait for Theo to come in from the fields but tore the letter open at once. When she read that Mara had been found, she burst into tears and wept so long and hard that the maid gave up trying to soothe her and went running out to fetch the master.

Theo was kneeling by Keara's chair with his arm round her before she even realised he'd come in. 'What's wrong, my love?'

'Mara's been found.' She indicated two crumpled pieces of paper on the table and watched as he read them.

'That's wonderful news, not something to cry about, you eejit!' He took her in his arms and she sighed against him.

'I know. But I'd begun to think we'd never find them.'

'We must write back straight away.'

'It'll take ages. Can't we go to them?'

'I think not, my love. For the children's sake.'

She knew he was right, really, but oh, how she wanted to set off this minute and go to her little sister. Or not so little now. Mara would be fourteen, almost a woman. That was hard for Keara to imagine. What would she look like? Keara tried to remember Ismay at the same age, but Ismay had always been sharper than Mara and somehow she couldn't imagine her little sister's expression as anything but gentle.

Theo's voice recalled her to the present. 'If you get the letter written, I'll ride into Bunbury and put it in the post there this very day.'

'Thank you.' She gave him a tremulous smile

and went into the dining room to find the writing materials.

When he joined her a few minutes later, there was a screwed-up piece of paper beside her.

She looked up, her eyes rueful. 'I'm terrible with the writing, Theo. Can you help me with this?'

Together they wrote a note in which they asked Mark to send Mara across to them as soon as possible and to make sure she understood that Keara had had no hand in sending her sisters to Australia. He'd better send them a letter first and then wait for the next steamer so that somebody would be there to meet Mara. Keara also wrote a short note to her sister, saying there was a home for her with them and that she was longing to see her. Her dearest hope now, she added, was that Ismay would be found.

As she watched her husband ride away, she prayed the letter would bring Mara across to Western Australia as soon as possible. Only it'd be a two-week journey for it to reach Victoria, on the other side of Australia, then another day or two to reach Rossall Springs which wasn't as isolated as the place where she now lived, thank goodness. Even then Mark would have to make all the preparations, send a letter and wait for the departure of the next coastal steamer. Would he bring Mara himself or would he just send her across in the care of some other travellers?

With a sigh, she went to consider the spare bedroom. It always stood ready for unexpected guests, so there wasn't much to do to prepare it for Mara. She wished there were.

Then she heard little Devin wake up and start crying for her, so hurried to pick up her baby son and feed him.

She'd have to be patient, but it was so hard.

*   *   *

It was the silliest accident, really. Ismay was coming back to the wagon after a trip into the woods to relieve herself when she slid on a muddy patch and fell with a bump that knocked the breath out of her. Pain shot through the arm she'd used to try to save herself and it took her a few minutes to pull herself together. When she tried to use her left arm, it hurt so much she let out another cry of pain.

'Issy? Are you all right?'

She gave a sob of sheer relief and yelled, 'Malachi! I've fallen and hurt myself.'

'Keep talking and I'll find you.'

Making no further attempts to get up, she waited for him to reach her.

He knelt beside her, his expression anxious. 'What happened? Where are you hurt?'

'I slipped and fell. It's my left arm. It hurts so much I daren't move it.'

He sat her up gently, examining the arm as best he could and looking at her anxiously as she cried out in pain at the slightest movement. 'You may have broken it. Not badly, or it'd be a lot worse. I think I'd better get you back to the wagon and then we'll go and find a doctor.'

'Ah, don't move me yet,' she begged. 'It'll kill me for sure if you do.'

He studied her, frowning. 'I think it'll be best if I bind the arm in place before I carry you back. Will you be all right for a minute if I go and find something to bind it with?'

'I will, yes. I'm sorry.'

'Whatever for?'

'Being so clumsy, such a nuisance.'

He smoothed back the hair from her forehead, worried at how pale she was. 'Darling Issy, you didn't do this on purpose. I'm only sorry you're in such pain.'

When he'd gone she lay there, comforted by the way he'd called her 'Darling Issy'. It was almost worth getting hurt to hear that, because he was usually sparing with endearments.

He was back quite quickly, carrying a torn sheet. But when he lifted her to wrap the sheet round her, she couldn't help crying out again.

Trussed in the binding, she let him lift her into his arms, closing her eyes and digging the fingernails of her right hand into her palm in an effort not to cry out.

He walked back slowly and carefully, murmuring to her as he did so. The sound of his voice was soothing and she held on to that.

'It's a good thing you're so light.'

'And that you're so strong.'

'It makes you strong, this sort of life. I think my mother would be surprised to see me now.' If she was all right. He hadn't heard from her before he left Melbourne but hoped to find a letter waiting for him there once they returned.

He laid Ismay on the back of the wagon, then climbed up and moved her on to her sleeping things, which he'd already spread out.

'You've thought of everything.'

'I tried to. Will you be all right here while I drive, love?'

'Yes, of course.' She made a vow not to let him

hear her moan or cry out, though it was hard to keep silent when the wagon jolted on particularly bad stretches.

When they came to a house, he asked directions to a doctor and was told the only one in these parts was in the town of Rossall Springs, five miles down the road. There was nothing for it but to continue. When the track became a well-defined dirt road the ride was a little smoother, but it still hurt because there were ruts where heavy wagons had passed. He was so thankful it wasn't winter when the journey would have taken three times as long.

Even before they got to the outskirts of the town, Issy was weeping silently from the pain and trying to hide it from him.

It nearly tore Malachi's heart in two every time he glanced back at her, but he knew the best way of helping her was to get this journey over with as quickly as possible so didn't stop. This was why you didn't want to try running a travelling shop when you had a wife and children to care for. He was prepared to take risks with his own health but not with Issy's. Maybe he had enough saved to open a small store somewhere? If not, he'd have to find employment until he'd saved more, though he didn't fancy working for others, not after being his own man. He wondered how much money there was in Dan's bank account. 'A bit saved' Dan had said in his will. Well, every bit would help from now on.

He stopped the wagon again to ask directions to the doctor's house and continued in the direction indicated. To his enormous relief, the doctor was home and came out at once to see Ismay before they even tried to get her out of the wagon.

'We'll give her a dose of laudanum first,' the doctor decided. 'It'll dull the pain. There's no broken bone showing so it may be only a fracture. If so, putting a splint on it may be enough.' He smiled down at Ismay. 'I know it hurts, Mrs Firth, but it could have been worse.'

She didn't see how. She'd spoiled things for Malachi. They wouldn't be able to trade while they were in a town with its own shops and they wouldn't be able to travel on until she was better— and even then she'd not be much help. She was just costing him money. She was a liability. No wonder he'd not wanted to get married. That thought made her want to weep, but the medicine the doctor had given her was making the world seem very blurred and she couldn't seem to raise the energy to do anything but lie there and close her eyes.

When the doctor examined her arm pain lanced through her again, but Malachi held her still and spoke soothingly and at last it was over.

'Just a fracture,' the doctor told her.

She tried to understand but it was all too much. She closed her eyes.

Malachi looked at him anxiously. 'What do you need to do? It doesn't matter what it costs, I want the best treatment for her, the very best.'

The other man smiled. 'I always try to give my patients the best treatment, Mr Firth, whether they can afford to pay me or not. I'll have to put a splint on that arm, then we'll strap it to her chest to keep it immobile. Do you have someone to look after her?'

'I'll look after her. There's only the two of us and we travel around in the wagon so we don't have any close friends. But whatever you tell me to

388

do, I'll manage it.'

'It'd be better to find a woman to help her with the more delicate things.'

Malachi's jaw set into a determined jut. 'I can do everything a woman can.'

'Perhaps you should move into a hotel? Though the one we have isn't very fancy, I'm afraid.'

'No. If we can find somewhere to put the wagon and a field for the horses, we have our own home.' And a poor place it was for a sick woman, too, but he'd make her as comfortable as possible.

The doctor pursed his lips in thought. 'The Johnsons live on the edge of the town and they've a bit of land. They'd be glad of some extra money, I know. They even have a spring of good clean water in one corner of their field. Maybe they'd let you stay there—if you don't mind the fact that they're natives? Well, half-native. They're a decent couple though. Give no one any trouble and clean-living.'

'I'd be the last person to mind that. When we were out in the bush, a native healer saved Issy's life.'

'Did he now?'

'She.'

The doctor raised his eyebrows in surprise. 'You must tell me about it sometime. I believe they have some interesting practices.'

Malachi followed the directions to the Johnsons' house and explained what had happened. Kalaya came out to the wagon to speak to Issy, then showed him where he could stand it.

'The horses will be all right in the field,' she said. 'There's good grazing and we've some stones you can use to make your fireplace.'

'How much do you want for this?'

389

'You'll have to ask Billy when he comes home from work.'

'All right. And thank you.' He unharnessed the horses, made the wagon secure for a few days' stay and set about building a fireplace then preparing tea for them both. But Issy was still only semi-conscious so he had to drink it all himself. He felt very alone.

When he next looked up, he saw a man with dark skin coming towards him.

'Anything I can do to help, Mr Firth?'

'Just letting us stay here is a big help.' Malachi held out his hand and saw the man's surprise and momentary hesitation before he shook it.

After they'd agreed terms, his companion said thoughtfully, 'One of your horses doesn't look so good.'

'No. It's been struggling for a while. It seemed all right when we bought it, though.'

'Not strong enough for pulling heavy loads. You should sell it and get another one.'

'I will as soon as I get back to Melbourne.'

'My boss breeds horses. He'd do a deal with you. That one might be all right for riding, but it's not got the heavy muscle for pulling a loaded wagon.'

'When my wife's a little better, perhaps you'd introduce me to your boss? Thanks for your advice.'

Malachi helped Issy as necessary then sat by the fire. The doctor had given him some laudanum and he was to give her another dose or two until the worst of the pain had gone. He got out his guitar and began strumming it, singing softly to himself.

You never knew what life would dish out to you next. He was just glad it'd brought him Issy.

He gave a wry smile. She was sharp-tongued sometimes and still full of anger, but she was his Issy now and he loved her dearly.

*   *   *

Kalaya proved very kind and helpful with Ismay so Malachi left her keeping an eye on his wife while he went into town to stretch his legs, look round and make a few purchases. Sitting around doing nothing fretted him. He bought some fruit at the market, knowing how much Ismay would enjoy it, then wandered down the main street. He was, of course, drawn to the grocery and general store and couldn't resist going inside.

Ah, this was what he wanted! A fixed store, his family living above it with him, neighbours he could get to know and people coming in and out all day.

'Can I help you, sir?'

He turned to see an older man with a proprietorial air to him and guessed it was the owner. 'How do you do, sir?' He stuck out one hand. 'I'm Malachi Firth. I run a travelling store and was just admiring your premises. One day I hope to have a fixed place of my own like this one.'

Samuel smiled at him. 'You're the one whose wife has broken her arm?'

'Yes. The news has spread quickly.'

'It's a small town. We've nothing better to do than gossip about our neighbours.'

They fell into a discussion about the goods Malachi carried and trading generally then he took his leave. At his companion's urging, he promised to pop in again.

'Nice young fellow,' Samuel told Mark that

afternoon. 'Very devoted to his wife, too. I wish he were further on in his career. He wants a settled store and I'm considering retiring.'

'You are?' Mark was surprised.

'Yes. Since Sally broke her leg she's lost heart. Wants to go and live in Melbourne near our daughter, see more of the grandchildren. And we can afford it if we get a decent price for the store.'

'Then you might also consider selling me the block next to the eating house, perhaps?'

Samuel was all attention. 'I might. If the price is right. What do you want it for?'

'I want to build a boarding house or hotel, somewhere for folk to stay in comfort, somewhere ladies and families will feel comfortable rather than staying over a public drinking house. I think the town's grown big enough to need a small hotel.'

'I like to see young fellows investing in the town's future.' Samuel sighed. 'I'd have liked to stay here myself when I retired, but my son didn't want to take over the shop and my daughter moved to Melbourne so it wasn't to be. Now, about that block of land. Let's take a stroll round it and discuss the price . . .'

When Mark had closed the eating house, he turned to Nan and Catherine and let out the excitement he'd been reining in ever since his discussion with Samuel. 'Today I agreed to buy the block of land next door. I've nearly enough saved to build a boarding house. If I had more, I'd make it a family hotel.'

Now, surely, he'd propose to Catherine? Nan thought, but still nothing happened.

*   *   *

As the voyage continued, Dick knew he couldn't let Clemmy go once they arrived in Western Australia. 'Did you have any plans for when we arrive?' he asked cautiously one day.

She looked at him sideways as if puzzled by his question. 'Not really. I suppose I'll have to look for work. I've never had trouble finding a job before and I don't suppose I will in Australia.'

'Sure, I envy you your optimism.'

'My mother once said I'd still be hoping for the best as they drove me to the gallows.' A rare frown pulled her brows together and she looked into the distance, twisting one strand of fair, curly hair around her finger. When he didn't speak she looked up at him again. 'Tell me about this Ballymullan of yours that you're so eager to get back to. It sounds a lovely place. I worked with an Irish girl once and she was allus wanting to go home.'

'It is lovely, yes. So green and beautiful. Only for Theo would I leave it, let alone come so far. I'm a home body at heart.'

'Well, he'll no doubt be grateful. The two of you sound to get on better than most full brothers.'

'We do, yes.'

He almost asked her then but his courage failed. Why should such a lovely girl agree to marry a man like him, a man who couldn't even arrange a journey on a ship without things going wrong? But he continued to seek her out and she continued to smile at him, and lean on the rail next to him. She was so warm and uncomplicated, and after a fraught session with Lavinia, who wasn't looking very well, he found the sheer sanity of Clemmy

393

soon drove away the anger and frustration.

One night, a week or two before they were due to make landfall, he screwed up his courage and while most of the passengers were enjoying a concert, asked if he could speak to her instead.

'Eh, I'll be sorry to arrive,' Clemmy confided as they went to one of their favourite places by the rail. 'I've enjoyed the journey so much and met so many pleasant folk.' She looked up at him, hesitated then added, 'I'll miss you, too, Dick.'

'There's no need to,' he said in a voice made scratchy by nerves. 'What I mean is, we could— well, get married if you like?'

Clemmy smiled up at him in that comfortable way she had. 'I can't deny I've thought about that.' Her smile faded. 'It's just—a maid like me is a bit beneath a man like you and I don't want you to— well, regret it afterwards.'

'You're not beneath anyone, Clemmy. You're honest and pretty and fun to be with. I've seen you with children sometimes and I'm sure you'd make a fine wife and mother, too. It's proud I'd be if you took me as your husband. Oh, Clemmy!' He put his hands on her shoulders and when he heard what sounded like a sob, turned her towards the light from a nearby lantern. Tears were sparkling on her lashes and her lips were trembling. 'My darling, you're crying? What's wrong? What have I done?'

'There's nothing wrong, I'm just so happy.' She brushed away a tear with the back of one hand. 'Now kiss me, you fool, or I'll think you don't love me.'

It was as easy as that. Everything seemed easy and pleasant when he was with her. He liked to think Clemmy was his reward for accompanying

Lavinia and Bess to Australia. The only thing he regretted was that they both felt it wiser not to announce their engagement to anyone. He was still worried about what Bess and Thad intended to do after they arrived in Australia. Very worried.

CHAPTER TWENTY-FIVE

NOVEMBER–DECEMBER 1866

As Malachi walked into town another day he thought about his and Issy's future. He liked Rossall and intended to learn as much as he could while he was here about shops in small towns. But how to do it? He called in at Samuel Grove's busy store and observed what was going on, as he always did, but didn't like to linger too long without buying something.

Tempted by the wonderful smells from next door, he bought his midday meal at the eating house and arranged to take a dish of food home for his wife, which would be far better than his inexpert cooking.

As he walked slowly back to the wagon, carrying the dish they'd lent him, it suddenly occurred to him that he could ask to work in the store for a few days until Ismay was fit to travel. Even if Samuel didn't pay him, he'd learn so much by being there from dawn till dusk. Would Samuel allow it? And would Issy mind?

When she woke, he explained and asked about leaving her in Kalaya's charge.

'I don't need much help now but if she's nearby

395

I'll feel better.' Issy considered his idea in that serious way of hers, head tilted to one side, eyes half-closed. 'I'd like to stay in one place, I must admit. Yes, you do that, Malachi. I can already walk around a bit so I may even come into town to see you.'

'No.'

She looked at him, puzzled by his emphatic tone. 'Why not?'

'You're not to do that unless I'm with you to offer you my arm and see that you don't get too tired. I know you, Issy. You rush into things without thinking of the consequences.'

She would have been offended by this, if it hadn't been for his fond smile and obvious concern for her welfare. Feeling her face grow warm, she shrugged her shoulders and said, 'Oh, very well. But you'll have to find me a book to read or I'll go mad with boredom. There's so little you can do with only one arm. It'd be better to have broken my leg and then at least I could have done some sewing.'

'I'll bring you back something to read.'

When he made his request to work at the store, Samuel looked at him thoughtfully then nodded. 'All right. I'll pay you normal wages if you're a good worker—'

'I am.'

'—and I'll teach you what I can. It's a pity you can't afford to buy the place because I'm intending to sell.'

'How much are you asking?' Malachi sighed regretfully when he heard the sum. 'I don't have nearly that much.' Swallowing his disappointment, he started work, rushing home at lunch time with

396

another dish of food for Issy and a book for her to read. He'd borrowed it from Miss Caldwell who worked in the eating house. Her face seemed vaguely familiar, but he couldn't quite place where he'd seen her before. And it had seemed to him that she looked at him strangely the first time he went in for a meal, as if she recognised him, too. But she hadn't said anything so he didn't like to pry. Perhaps she'd been a passenger on the ship coming out to Australia? Yes, that was probably it.

When he took the dish back to the eating house he got the shock of his life because he thought for a moment, that Issy was standing in the kitchen. Then he realised this girl was smaller and younger than his wife. It was—it must be Mara! The dish fell from his hands and smashed to the floor unheeded as he called her name.

She turned, gaped at him, then yelled, 'Malachi!' and ran towards him, arms outstretched.

He gave her a cracking hug then stepped back, still staring at her. 'I can't believe it's you. You've grown so much.'

Nan appeared in the doorway, drawn by the sound of something breaking, but when neither of them noticed her, she remained where she was.

Mara was laughing and crying at the same time. 'What on earth are *you* doing in Rossall, Malachi? Have you—did you come to find me?'

'No. At least, I would have if I'd known but I didn't.' He took a step backwards and something crunched under his feet. 'Oh, dear, look at this mess I've made.'

'Never mind that. I'll clear it up later. Tell me what you're doing here.'

He opened his mouth to explain then caught

397

sight of the clock. 'It's too complicated so I'll have to tell you later. I must get back to work now. I'm working next door temporarily. Are you living here?'

She nodded. 'I am, yes, with Catherine and Mark. Oh, and Nan. This is Nan.'

He nodded in the direction of the older woman standing watching them, a small child in her arms, but could not take his eyes off Mara. After all their searching, just to run across her like this!

She tugged his sleeve to get his attention. 'I'll be leaving in a few weeks to go to my sister Keara in Western Australia. Malachi, you haven't seen Ismay, have you? She disappeared from the place where she was working and Keara's been looking for her everywhere.'

He had been turning to leave, but spun round again. 'You've been in touch with Keara?'

'Yes. We wrote to let her know Mark had found me. He's a good friend of hers. She's living in Western Australia and he's arranging for me to travel over there to join her.'

He thought rapidly. He'd have to prepare Issy for this. 'You'll be here this evening?'

'Of course.'

'I'll come and see you then. But I do have news of Ismay. And don't worry, she's fine.' Another glance at the clock and he hurried out, calling over his shoulder, 'I'll be back later!'

Mara gaped at him, then looked at Nan and gave her a wobbly smile. 'He said he had news of Ismay. Oh, Nan, I've been so worried.' Then she was sobbing in the older woman's arms until little Amy, also caught up in the embrace, began to wriggle and protest.

In the store next door, it was only by exerting the strictest self-control that Malachi kept his mind on the customers he was serving. When the shop was quiet, however, he couldn't help thinking of this amazing coincidence and trying to work out how best to break the news to Ismay. She'd be overjoyed at seeing Mara again, but how would she feel at the thought of seeing Keara? He didn't want her upsetting Mara with her anger, for she still seemed convinced, against all reason, that Keara could have done something to help them after their mother died.

In one of the more peaceful periods of the day he realised suddenly that Mara had called Miss Caldwell 'Catherine' and another possibility occurred to him. There had been a Sister Catherine on the ship. He closed his eyes and brought her face up in his memory. Was it possible? Was Sister Catherine no longer a nun? That would explain why he'd thought he recognised her. He'd never seen her hair, and of course she'd usually had her eyes downcast and kept her distance from people, but it could have been her.

Why had she said nothing to him, though? He might not recognise her without the cumbersome black habit and wimple, but she would surely have recognised him?

As soon as the shop closed for the night he'd talk to Mara, then perhaps both of them could go and see Ismay. Well, he was sure Mara would insist on that as soon as she found out that her sister was so close. But he'd tell her to wait near the Johnsons' house until he called her across to the wagon. Yes, that would be best.

And then somehow he would persuade Issy to go

and see Keara, to give her elder sister a chance to explain what had happened. Issy wouldn't run away now that she was his wife, would she? No, she wouldn't be able to, not with her arm still in a splint. And anyway, he'd make sure she didn't. She was his and he loved her dearly, wanted only the best for her—and to be rid of the anger that was still eating at her, however much she tried to hide it.

Only as the day was ending did he wonder what he would do about his business if they had to travel to the other side of Australia.

Well, family came first. His mother had taught him that, though his father and Lemuel had treated him sometimes as if he wasn't really a member of the family. He'd make sure all his own children were loved and knew it, by hell he would. No playing favourites like his father had.

*   *   *

Mara went to find Catherine who was clearing tables in the eating house as the main rush of lunchtime customers slowed, mostly single men working in various trades around the town or visitors passing through. Eagerly she told her about meeting Malachi. 'Didn't you recognise him when he came into the eating house earlier?'

'Yes, but he didn't recognise me,' Catherine admitted, 'so I wasn't sure whether to tell him who I was or not.'

'Oh, you should have done. And he says he has news of Ismay. Isn't that wonderful? If we can find her, then we can all three be together again, just like we were in Ballymullan.'

'Things can never quite be the same again, you know.'

'But we're still sisters, aren't we? And surely when Ismay knows Keara didn't send us here, she'll stop being so angry at her? She wouldn't even mention her name when we were at the convent.'

'You can never tell what people will do,' Catherine cautioned. She knew Ismay had a hot temper and did things without thinking out the consequences sometimes, like when she'd cut up the new clothing at the convent. She would hate Mara to be hurt because the younger girl was so gentle and loving that it made her more vulnerable than other people.

When Mark came in, Catherine told him what had happened.

'Maybe I should go and see him, ask about Ismay,' he worried.

'He said he'd come here after he'd finished work,' Mara said. 'He'll tell us then.' But as the afternoon passed she kept looking at the clock and sighing.

*   *   *

Malachi left the store early, as soon as it went quiet, and hurried to the eating house where he found everyone waiting for him.

'Come in,' Mark said. 'We'd be really grateful if you'd come straight to the point. Do you know where Ismay is? We've all been worried sick about her.'

'Yes.' He hesitated then confessed, 'She's here in town, actually. She's my wife and she's broken her arm so she's staying with the wagon at the

401

Johnsons'.'

Mara's eyes filled with tears. 'Oh, why didn't you tell me that earlier? I'd have gone to see her straight away.'

'It's a bit more complicated than that, I'm afraid. She's so filled with anger at Keara that she won't listen to reason about your sister. We found one of the posters a while back and she burned it. Then our partner Dan fell ill and it wasn't the time to force things. He died a few weeks ago. I was going to do something about contacting your sister when we got back to Melbourne, because I remembered the address to write to, only Issy broke her arm and that's how we wound up in Rossall instead, looking for a doctor.'

'You must bring her here and let us look after her,' Nan said. 'Surely she'll be more comfortable in a house?'

'We manage fine in the wagon and Kalaya has been helping Issy. I just—I think I should go and prepare her first. It'll be such a shock and she's not quite herself.'

Mara looked at him, her face white and eyes brilliant with tears. 'I have to see her tonight.'

Malachi couldn't deny her. 'Of course, but still, you'll let me go and see her first, won't you?'

'I'll come with you,' Mark offered.

'No!' Mara looked at him. 'Just me this time. Please. I want to speak to her on my own.'

Catherine looked from one to the other. 'It might be better, Mark. Otherwise, we'll seem a crowd, almost as if we're there to bully her.'

'I'll come over to pick Mara up in an hour's time, then,' he told Malachi. 'It's a fairly peaceful town but I still don't want her walking round the streets on her own after dark.'

So Malachi and Mara walked slowly along the back road and he left her sitting on the grass just outside the Johnsons' garden fence. As he walked across the field behind, he prayed he'd be able to explain tactfully, not make Issy fire up and do something silly.

She was waiting for him, sitting on a stool gazing into a small fire. 'No food tonight?'

'I forgot. I have some news for you. Let's go and sit in the back of the wagon together and I'll tell you.'

'You look very solemn. It's not bad news, is it?'

'No, it's good news, wonderful news.'

When they were comfortably settled in one of their favourite positions, sitting on an old patchwork quilt and leaning against a box of goods, with his arm round her shoulders and their feet dangling over the back edge of the wagon, he said gently, 'Issy love, I've been trying to think how to break the news to you, but there's no easy way. Mara is in Rossall and—'

'Mara! Why didn't you bring her back with you, then? Doesn't she want to see me?'

'I wanted to speak to you first. There's more, you see. Sister Catherine is here too, only she's not a nun any more, and there's a man called Mark Gibson, who's a friend of your other sister.'

She stiffened against him. 'I don't want to hear about *her*. And if she's in town as well, I shall refuse to see her.'

'She's not. She's living in Western Australia—as the wife of Theo Mullane. Though of course she can't really marry him because he's married already. They have two children and—'

'So she did all right for herself by abandoning us,' Issy said with great scorn.

'Not exactly. Mrs Mullane had her kidnapped and sent out to Australia, too. Theo came after her . . .'

'*What?*'

'. . . and Keara didn't know about your mother being ill, or even dying, until months later. Truly she didn't.'

'I don't believe that! Letters were sent. More than one letter.'

'Which Mrs Mullane kept from her.'

'But Keara must have guessed something was wrong. She knew Mam was ill!'

He couldn't think how to counter that because there was some truth in it. He let silence flow around them for a minute or two, then asked. 'So— shall I go and fetch Mara? She's waiting just down the road.'

'Yes! Only tell her not to talk to me about Keara. Not tonight. Just about us.'

'If you insist.'

'I do.'

*   *   *

As Mara sat waiting two men came stumbling along the road from Rossall, rather the worse for drink. She shrank back into the shadows, but there was enough moonlight for them to see her.

One of the men nudged the other and began to smile. 'Look who's waiting for us.'

'I'm not waiting for you,' she said clearly, and stood up, intending to run after Mark.

But Albert was too fast for her. He grabbed her

404

arm and as she tried to scream, clapped one hand across her mouth.

Terrified, she began to struggle, but he just laughed and said to his companion, 'Have you got something to tie her up, Ned? I've been wanting to catch this little pigeon for a while.'

'She's too young to bed. Let her go.'

'I don't want her in my bed. I want to use her as bait. I have plumper prey in mind.'

'Well, all right then.'

They trussed up Mara and carried her along the road to the rickety wooden house on the edge of town where Albert's friend lived, their steps wavering more than once. Partway there they laid her down so that they could rest and take a couple of pulls from a bottle of rum.

When they arrived, they dumped her on the veranda and Albert saddled his horse then wrote a hurried note to 'Katie' to be given to her in two hours' time by his friend.

'And you're to have a horse waiting here for her, Ned lad, so that you can bring her to me,' he wound up as he mounted his own animal and set Mara across the saddle in front of him. 'I don't want her trying to wake folk up at the livery stables. I'll bring it back to you afterwards, don't worry. Or she will.'

Laughing aloud at his own cleverness, he set off for home with the girl. Fate was being kind to him at last. That bitch would soon be in his hands and if he didn't have her grovelling to him within a very short time, his name wasn't Albert Bevan.

*   *   *

405

Malachi went back to the road, but couldn't find Mara. Worried, he searched a little way in each direction. Surely she wouldn't have returned to the eating house without seeing her sister?

In the end he ran back to the wagon and told Ismay.

'I'm coming with you into town,' she insisted at once. 'Something must be wrong. Mara wouldn't run away just when she was going to see me again, I know she wouldn't.'

At the sight of her determined expression, he said only, 'Very well.' He knew if he didn't take her, she'd follow him.

They knocked on the door at the back of the eating house and when Mark opened it, Malachi asked, 'Did Mara come back?'

'No, of course not.'

'Then something's happened to her.'

'Come in and tell us, quickly.'

Catherine went to hug Ismay and then sat with her on the sofa while Malachi explained.

The men went out again to scour the streets. While they were away, Catherine left Nan to keep Ismay company and went into the scullery to wash the dishes, unable just to sit and wait. While she was there she heard a tapping on the window. Looking out, she saw the faint outline of a man. He put his finger to his lips to indicate she should be silent and she guessed he was here in connection with Ismay. She went quickly towards the back door, her only thought to find out what had happened to the girl.

The minute she opened the door, he grasped her arm and said in a hoarse whisper, 'Keep quiet if you want to save your young friend.'

Shocked, she stared at him, smelling the rum on his breath and seeing that he was swaying. He had a silly grin on his face as if this was just a game to him.

'Which friend would that be?' she asked cautiously.

'Mara, isn't it?'

'Ah.'

'I'll take you to her, but only you.' He put one finger to his lips again and made a shushing noise.

Anger surged up in her at the thought that some drunken louts like this one had kidnapped and no doubt terrified Mara. With a ferocity she hadn't known she possessed Catherine clouted him on the ear, sending him reeling backwards, then seized the yard broom from near the back door, belabouring him about the shoulders as he tried to get up. Shrieking for help at the top of her voice, she kept him trapped in a corner of the back yard until Samuel Grove from next door came running towards them and Nan came out from the kitchen brandishing the frying pan.

'Good thing he was drunk,' Catherine panted as they tied his hands behind his back with her apron strings and hauled him, struggling, kicking and swearing, into the kitchen. There, Samuel helped her tie him more securely to a chair with the clothes line.

Just then Mark and Malachi returned.

'Do you know him?' she asked as they all stood staring down at their captive.

Samuel answered, 'Yes. He's called Ned Lindon and lives on the edge of town. He scrounges a living any way he can and spends most of what he earns on drink. Used to be married but his wife ran

407

away with someone else.'

'Will you go for the constable while we talk to this rat?' Mark asked.

Samuel grinned. 'Pity to miss the fun, but all right.'

Mark stood over Ned, fists bunched, looking furious, and beside him Malachi radiated just as much anger. Faced with the two of them, their prisoner didn't take long to admit that Albert Bevan had Mara and that they had snatched her on impulse.

'It was to get at you,' he told Catherine, giving her a dirty look. 'You shouldn't have treated Albert so badly. It's *your* fault. You women are all as bad as one another.'

'*Treated him badly!* The man tried to rape me.'

'You'd been leading him on. He told me all about it.'

She opened her mouth to refute this hotly, but Mark laid one hand on her arm.

'Where's the girl now?'

'Albert took her home with him.'

From across the room Ismay looked from one to the other, desperate for them to do something to help her sister instead of just talking. If she'd had her way, she'd have thumped this man good and hard.

'How does kidnapping Mara get back at Catherine?' Mark asked, puzzled.

Ned cast another surly glance in her direction. 'I was to give her a horse and send her out to the farm. Because she cares for the girl, we thought she'd do what Albert wanted. They could've been back by dawn and no one would have been any wiser.' He sniggered. 'She probably slips out quite often.'

Mark's expression was so dark with fury that Ned cowered back and indeed he was very close to being punched, would have been if Malachi hadn't stepped between them.

'You'd better be careful what you say,' he warned their captive. 'My friend can get rather impatient, then he hits out.'

Ned shut his mouth tight, though he cast them another angry look.

Mark took a deep breath. 'We'd better get some horses then and ride after them.'

'He's still got the girl,' Ned reminded them. 'You'll not persuade him to give her up till he's had what he wants out of this one.' He jerked his head in Catherine's direction. 'Most stubborn man I've ever met, my friend Albert.' He smiled at them triumphantly then yelled, 'Get him off me!' as Mark shook him like a rat and flung man and chair sideways on to the floor.

The constable arrived just then, hair still tousled and clearly not fully alert yet.

'Keep them off me!' Ned yelled.

The constable ignored him and looked at Mark. 'What's going on?'

When they explained he turned to glare at Ned. 'Didn't I warn you last time about getting into trouble again?'

'Aw—it was just a bit of fun.'

'Kidnapping a girl isn't fun. You're under arrest and I for one will be glad to see you locked away.'

'Constable, I think we'd better get out to the farm at once,' Mark prompted.

'I've got to lock this rascal up first, then call out my deputy.'

'We'll go ahead of you then. I'm not leaving that child in Bevan's hands for a second longer than I have to. I'll rouse the fellow at the livery stables, tell him to have your horse saddled and ready. You can follow us as soon as you've dealt with this wretch.'

'All right. But go carefully.' The constable grinned as he added, 'Don't do anything I wouldn't.'

As Mark swung round towards the door, Catherine grabbed his arm. 'I'm coming with you. In fact, when we get there, why don't I pretend I'm alone and keep Bevan busy while you two get inside the house and find Mara?'

'Good idea,' said Malachi at once.

'Not a good idea. I'm not having you risking yourself, Catherine,' Mark snapped.

'If you don't take me with you, I'll follow. Anyway, she may need a woman's help afterwards and Ismay can't go.'

Ismay looked down at her arm. 'Why do I have to be so helpless when I'm needed? Please go with them, Catherine.'

*   *   *

They rode out by moonlight. Mark had his revolver and Malachi had borrowed Nan's rolling pin. It was slung at his waist now, bobbing against his thigh. It must look ridiculous, but he didn't know anything about guns and didn't want to. If he needed to defend himself, this would make a good weapon. He was determined to get in at least one good punch at this fellow who had kidnapped his little sister-in-law, quite determined about that. More,

410

maybe, if Bevan had harmed Mara in any way.

When they were getting near the farm Catherine reined in and said, 'He'll hear the horses if you come any further and realise that I'm not on my own.'

'You ride on then, but slowly. We'll tie our horses up here and go the rest of the way on foot,' Mark said. 'You're not going in there on your own.'

'When we get there, delay him as long as possible,' Malachi advised. 'Keep him talking.'

Once they arrived at the farm, her two companions stayed back in the shadows while Catherine rode forward.

Mark's eyes followed her and his mouth was set in a grim line of determination. If Albert Bevan hurt one hair of her head . . .

She rode up to the front door quite openly, making as much noise as she could. She had no idea what her friends were doing so concentrated on distracting Albert.

The door opened and he came out to lean against the door frame, one hand grasping Mara by the hair, the other brandishing a big knife. He grinned at Catherine. 'Stop right there.'

She did as ordered.

'You're not coming any further till I'm sure you're not carrying a weapon. Take your clothes off.'

She gasped. 'You can't mean that! I give you my word I'm not concealing anything.'

'You're not coming in unless I'm sure. You had a stone in your pocket last time.' He scowled at her. 'If you were a man, I'd kill you for what you did to me.' He flapped one hand at her. 'Well, get undressed. After all, if I don't have you to distract

411

me, I may hurt the girl.' He tugged Mara's hair sharply backwards and put the knife to her throat.

Catherine hesitated, not knowing whether she could take her clothes off in front of a man, she who had not even looked at her own body for so many years.

'Your choice.' He deliberately pushed the tip of the knife into Mara's throat and a drop of blood welled slowly from the pierced skin and then ran down her throat.

He was drunk and she was terrified that he might let the knife slip more than he intended so Catherine forced herself to start removing her clothes, all the time conscious of his eyes on her. She couldn't help blushing hotly and hoped the lamp on the veranda wasn't bright enough to show that.

But he let out a raucous caw of laughter. 'What have you to blush for? You were a married woman, and don't tell me you haven't been sweetening your boss at the eating house because I won't believe you.'

Even though she knew Mark was nearby, the way Albert stared made Catherine shudder. She removed everything except her chemise and one petticoat and she simply could not take those off.

'Get the rest off,' he ordered.

'I can't do it. I just can't.'

He scowled, looked at the knife and then back at her, a nasty smile curving his lips. 'Well, it'll be fun ripping them off you. Now, move forward slowly.'

She didn't move. 'There's one more thing . . .'

'Who do you think you are to order me around? I'm in charge now.'

'I'm not doing anything until you've sent Mara

away.'

'You'll do as you're bloody well told!'

'No. I don't trust you to let her go.'

He stared at the girl, then back at Catherine. 'Come into the kitchen first. I'm not having you run away once I've let go of her.

Keeping one eye on her as she advanced slowly, he backed towards the kitchen, dragging Mara with him. When they got there, he waited till Catherine was inside and kicked the door shut. 'Over here.'

She moved towards him.

He let go of Mara and gave her a shove in the direction of the back door. 'Out, you!'

Then he turned to Catherine and said with a leer, 'Now, Miss Katie bloody Caldwell, come here and start behaving yourself. First, we'll get the rest of those clothes off you and . . .'

CHAPTER TWENTY-SIX

DECEMBER 1866

When Catherine vanished inside the house, Malachi whispered, 'She's a brave woman.'

Mark wanted only to rush after her. 'If he harms her, I'll kill him!'

As the two men moved quietly round the house, Malachi found a bedroom window open and whispered, 'I'll go in this way.'

Mark nodded and made his way cautiously round to the rear where he was able to watch what was happening in the kitchen and listen to Catherine arguing with Bevan. He was only waiting

413

for Mara to get clear before acting.

When the girl came outside and saw him standing there, she let out an involuntary squeak. Mark stepped out into the light, one finger on his lips, and she quietened, sagging in relief.

Inside the kitchen, Albert grabbed Catherine and brandished the knife close to her face.

'You'd better not have brought anyone with you, you bitch, or I'll mark you so that no man will want you again. Hoy, you, Mara! What did you cry out for?' he shouted.

An involuntary shiver passed through Catherine and he laughed before saying loudly, 'If there's anyone else out there, this one will regret it, I promise.'

Mara called quickly, 'I nearly trod on a snake, Mr Bevan. I'm frightened of them.'

Mark nodded at her encouragingly.

'Where did it go?'

Mark pointed towards the far end of the veranda.

She nodded her understanding. 'Along to the end of the veranda.'

'Damned snakes, can't stand the things,' Albert muttered. 'Still, it probably won't come inside. They don't usually.'

Mark gestured to the girl to move away and found a spot from where he could see through the window what was happening inside without being seen himself.

Catherine knew Mark would be unable to get inside and rescue her if Albert kept the knife at her throat. She didn't even know for certain that he was there, but had to trust that his presence was why Mara had exclaimed. With a long sigh, she

414

sagged against Albert. 'Put the knife away. I won't struggle any more. I've never met a man as strong or daring as you.'

He smirked at her. 'That's because you're working with the fellow at the eating house and he's too soft for his own good. What sort of job is it for a man, cooking meals for people?'

His face was so close she could feel his hot breath on her skin, but the knife was still too near for her to make a break. She tried to smile at him, but wasn't sure she succeeded. 'You shouldn't have frightened me like that. I'm still all a-quiver.'

The knife dropped a little further.

She raised her hand slowly and pretended to caress his cheek though she hated to touch him, absolutely hated it.

As the knife wavered and he began to breathe a little more deeply, she thrust him suddenly away and lurched towards the kitchen door. With a speed she hadn't thought him capable of, he raised the knife and slashed out at her, catching her on the arm.

Mark erupted through the back door and as he shoved Catherine behind him, Malachi slipped in through the hall door and jumped on to Albert from behind, carrying him to the ground.

Mark stamped on the hand still holding the knife and as Bevan yelled in pain and let go, it skittered across the floor. Catherine picked it up quickly and put it on a shelf, then looked for something to hit Albert with, finding only a stew pan.

The kitchen erupted into violence as the three men rolled to and fro on the floor, knocking chairs out of the way. Bevan fought like a madman, trying to gouge out Mark's eye then biting Malachi's hand.

She raised the heavy iron pan, determined not to let him escape. But Mark had learned a few tricks of his own on the goldfields and managed to knee Albert in the groin. With a scream, he jerked away and she used this opportunity to swing the pan down as hard as she could.

There was a sudden end to the yelling as Albert stopped struggling and sagged on to the floor. The near silence that followed was filled only by the panting of the other two men. Malachi was the first to get up, then Mark, who had been underneath their opponent.

Catherine let the pan fall with a clang. 'I haven't killed him, have I?'

As she began shaking and covered her face with her hands, Mark took her into his arms and cradled her against him.

It was left to Malachi to check that Bevan was unconscious and then, with a wry smile, he went outside again, to find Mara standing on the veranda weeping. Still keeping an eye on the figure on the kitchen floor, he put his arm round her and said quietly, 'It's all over now and I'll make sure no one ever kidnaps you again, little sister.'

Inside the kitchen, Mark had realised suddenly that Catherine's arm was bleeding. 'He did hurt you!' He looked round. 'We need something clean to staunch the blood.'

'Tea towels. In the dresser.'

He set her down on a chair and went to the dresser, but there were no clean tea towels only a large tablecloth. He shook that out, using the knife to cut the hem so that he could rip off a strip, then knelt beside her and bound up the cut.

416

As she looked at him, her face so trusting and full of love, he couldn't hold his own feelings back any longer. When he'd finished binding the wound, he took her face in both his hands and gently kissed the streaks of tears. 'My love, my dear, dear love, you were so brave!'

'Oh, Mark.' She forgot everything then: her state of undress, the pain of the cut, even the other people nearby. She had never realised before that a man's lips could be so soft while his arms were so firm around her.

When he pulled away a little, he said, 'I love you very much, Catherine,' in a low voice.

'I love you, too, Mark.' She tried to smile at him, but was still shaking. 'I'll be—all right—in a minute. It's just—reaction to everything.'

'You were so brave.'

'Mara?'

He glanced towards the door. 'Malachi's with her.' Taking a deep breath, he looked at Catherine very solemnly. 'Do you think you could marry me?'

Joy spread across her face. 'Oh, yes! Yes!'

As her love shone in her face, he raised first one hand then the other to his lips and beamed back at her.

There was a groan from the floor. Outside Malachi cleared his throat loudly. Neither of the lovers even noticed him, so he came in and rummaged around for something to tie up Bevan, ending up ripping another strip off the maltreated tablecloth.

As he finished knotting it carefully, he saw Mara staring across at Mark and Catherine in open fascination and winked at her. 'That's what it's like to be in love.'

417

She looked at him, still child enough to ask, 'Is that how you feel about Ismay?'

'Oh, yes. I love her very much indeed, even though she's sometimes a real crosspatch.'

A smile dawned slowly on Mara's face. 'It's wonderful, isn't it? Seeing them like this helps make up for what *he* did.'

His voice grew suddenly sharp. 'He didn't hurt you?'

'Not in the way you mean.'

'You understand what I'm asking?'

She nodded. 'Yes, I do. I was a kitchen maid in a brothel in Melbourne for a while.'

He hated even to think of that. 'You and Ismay have both been through some very difficult times. I'm sorry I let Bevan capture you. I shouldn't have left you on your own when I went to tell Ismay.'

'You weren't to know he'd come along.'

'Well, I'll take better care of you from now on, I promise, you and Ismay both.'

There was the sound of hoofbeats outside. She looked at the two lovers and whispered to Malachi, 'I think Catherine had better put her clothes on again before the constable comes in, don't you?'

'Hell, I'd forgotten about that!' Grinning now, he went to shake Mark's arm. 'Better let Catherine get dressed again. The constable's just arrived.'

Blushing hotly, she realised where she was and how lightly clad.

'Go into the bedroom,' Mark said. 'I'll send Mara in with your things.'

By the time Catherine emerged, she was fully clad again, though still with a heightened colour and with one sleeve unbuttoned and rolled up.

The constable looked at the woman and girl. 'I

418

hope you're not hurt, ladies?'

'She is,' Mara said. 'That man cut her with a knife.'

'*What!*' He glared down at the semi-conscious man. 'Then I can promise you he'll be spending an even longer time in prison.'

'We'd better get them home now,' Mark said. 'I don't think Catherine should even try to ride. All right if we borrow Bevan's cart?'

'Of course. Leave it at the livery stables. But don't leave town,' the constable warned. 'I'm going to need you as witnesses for the preliminary hearing.'

'I wouldn't miss it for anything!' Catherine said from the shelter of Mark's arms.

The constable watched them go, smiling. Nothing like a bit of danger to bring out the love. He'd seen it before. His wife would be very interested to hear about Mr Gibson and Miss Caldwell.

A cough nearby made him swing round.

The farm hands were standing there. 'Is it all over?' one of them asked.

'Yes. Why didn't you help them?'

The man looked uncomfortable. 'He's our employer—and anyway, they didn't need any help.'

'Well, it's Mrs Bevan will be your employer now, so if you two want to keep your jobs, you'd better make sure you run this place properly until I can let her know it's safe to come back.'

And in the meantime—he scowled down at the recumbent figure—he and his deputy had better get this villain back to town and lock him up.

There'd be a few people glad to see the back of that one.

419

As they drove home, Catherine sat next to Mark on the driving bench and leaned against him. She was exhausted, her arm was throbbing but she was feeling happier than she had for years. The riding horses were tied to the rear of the cart and trotted along quietly, as if they knew the excitement was over. Malachi and Mara sat in the back, talking quietly. He was telling the girl about the travelling shop and her sister's broken arm.

They took Catherine and Mara back to the eating house, then Mark drove the cart and horses across to the livery stables.

As the three of them went into the house, Malachi slipped his arm round his young sister-in-law's shoulders because he could see how nervous she was feeling. 'Issy will be delighted to see you,' he whispered. 'I know she will.'

'Eh, thank God you're back safe!' Nan said as they went into the kitchen, then looked behind them. 'Where's our Mark?' She heaved a gusty sigh of relief when they explained, then smiled at Mara. 'Your sister's waiting for you in the parlour. She was tired out so I made her lie down for a bit.'

Mara drew in a shaky breath. 'I don't know why I'm so nervous of meeting her again.'

Malachi took her to the parlour door and gave her a push. 'Tell her I'll be with you in a minute.' He closed the door gently behind her and returned to the kitchen. 'Any chance of a hot drink and something to eat, Mrs Jenner?'

'I've got the kettle just coming to the boil. Sit down and tell me what happened.' Then she saw

Catherine's arm. 'Eh, what did he do to you? We'll have to wash that cut and bind it up properly.'

'I think it'll need the doctor to stitch it together,' Malachi said. 'It's a nasty one.'

'We'll fetch him when it gets light but we'll still wash it now. You unpin that bandage and I'll go and find some clean cloths while this kettle is boiling.'

Inside the parlour the two sisters stared at one another, then with a sob Mara flew across the room to hug Ismay and sit beside her, clasping the hand that wasn't in a sling.

At first they simply studied one another, taking in all the changes the years had made. 'You've grown so much taller,' Ismay said wonderingly. 'All that time they kept us apart I used to imagine what you'd look like. Did you miss me?'

'Every single day.' Mara gave her a tearful smile. 'And I thought of you most of all whenever I saw a rainbow.'

'Me, too.'

'Tell me what hap—' they both began at once, stopped and laughed.

'You go first,' said Ismay.

Malachi peeped into the room, saw them sitting close together, blew Ismay a kiss and backed out again.

A little later, while Nan was finishing tending to Catherine's arm, he took in a tray with cups of tea and pieces of cake, kissed Ismay on the forehead and then kissed Mara's cheek for good measure. But he didn't stay—and they didn't ask him to.

Only as the room grew fully light did Mara touch on the subject they'd avoided so far.

'I'm going to see Keara,' she said abruptly. 'I

421

want to hear from her exactly what happened.' As Ismay opened her mouth to protest, she raised her voice to add, 'And you're coming too.'

'I can't think straight about her,' Ismay confessed. 'They tell me she knew nothing, but I can't help feeling she should have *guessed* because she did know Mam was ill, and then I get so angry. It's the not seeing Mam before she died that hurts most of all, even worse than her letting them bring us to Australia.'

Mara looked at her, opened her mouth then closed it again. She wouldn't push matters further at the moment. The main thing now was that they were together again.

'I think it's wonderful that you've married Malachi!' she exclaimed. 'I liked him from the first time I met him on the ship. Remember how he danced with us both, even though I was only a little girl?'

'I do, yes. And I liked him then too,' Ismay confided. 'He's a lovely fellow. I don't know what I'd do without him now.'

*   *   *

Mark came back from the livery stables feeling tired but elated. He waited until Nan had finished tending the cut, then said, 'Catherine and I have some news for you.'

She looked up, glanced from one to the other, saw Catherine's blushes and guessed at once. 'You're going to get wed.'

'I'm sure you'll be happy,' said Malachi. 'Your love for one another shines out.'

Mark nodded, but it was Nan that he was

looking at, as if he half-expected her to protest.

Instead she beamed at him. 'And about time too! I was despairing of you.'

'You were?'

'Yes. There were the two of you were, looking at one another all soppy like, but nothing was happening. I was going to give you a good talking to soon if you didn't look sharp and ask her to wed you.'

'You don't mind then?'

Her expression softened and she gave him a hug. 'No, Mark love. Why should I mind? You loved my Patience while she was alive, but now you have a new life to build. All I ask is that you let me be part of it.'

'You *are* part of it, Nan. What would Amy do without you?' He hugged her back and kissed her cheek for good measure, smiling as she stood on tiptoe to kiss him back.

Catherine looked at them wistfully. Other people seemed to hug and kiss one another so often and she was hungry sometimes for a human touch.

As if she'd guessed, Nan came across and hugged her like a daughter. 'I couldn't be more pleased, love.'

'I can't quite believe it's true. For so long I cut myself off from a normal life and now—now I have everything I could wish for. Or I will once we have children.'

A shadow crossed Mark's face and she said firmly, 'Life and death are in God's hands, not yours, Mark. You're wrong to blame yourself for what happened to Patience. Or what might happen to any of us at any minute.'

The silence went on for a while, then he said, 'I suppose you're right, but I don't have your faith. I never did have.'

'My faith is still part of me, even now.' She hesitated then went on, 'After we're married I want to go to the Bishop and tell him what's happened. I'll ask him to write to the order for me. They should give me my dowry back. I don't want to come to you penniless, Mark, not when there's money due to me.'

'I know nothing about Catholics,' he confessed. 'My father is a Methodist. His chapel means a lot to him. He was one of the group who helped found it and raise money to build the church. I think he'll be a bit shocked that I'm marrying an ex-nun.'

'Some Catholics think it's wrong to marry outside our church,' she said, 'but I've come to believe that since we all worship the same God, it's not so important. As long as I can go to a church regularly.'

'Every day if you want to. How soon can we be married?'

Her smile was a glory of happiness that brought a lump into Malachi's throat. He wished he could make Issy smile like that, but there was always something tight and hard underneath her smiles. He didn't think she'd be truly happy until she'd seen her sister and realised that Keara hadn't abandoned them and wasn't the monster Ismay had built her into during her years of unhappiness.

'We can be married as soon as you like,' Catherine said. 'I just need one pretty dress to wear, then I'll be proud to become your wife.'

'Then you and I had better start sewing,' Nan said. She couldn't hold back a yawn. 'Now, I think

424

it's time some of us went to bed or we'll be good for nothing tomorrow.'

To give Mark and Catherine some time together, Malachi pretended to be tired and said he'd go and lie down in the eating room while his wife talked to her sister. He'd take the kitchen rug, if they didn't mind, to soften the floor a little.

They didn't even notice but sat on, holding hands, not speaking much, just enjoying the comfortable feeling of being together.

*   *   *

When it was fully daylight Malachi came into the parlour. 'I don't know about you, wife, but I need to sleep. I've been lying down on the floor of the eating house, but our own bed is a lot more comfortable so if you've not finished talking now, it'll have to wait until later.'

Ismay immediately yawned, which set Mara off yawning as well, then the two of them started giggling.

'We'll see you this afternoon, lass,' he told Mara. 'I need to get to know you properly now we're related. Oh, and Issy, did you know Mark and Catherine got engaged last night?'

She gazed at him in surprise.

'I forgot to tell her about that,' Mara admitted.

'I'm glad for them,' Issy said softly, then allowed her husband to pull her to her feet and escort her back to their wagon.

*   *   *

Rossall was buzzing with the news the following

425

morning. As soon as they could decently expect the doctor to be awake, Mark sent Nan to wake Catherine and took her to have the cut stitched. The doctor complimented her on her fortitude in enduring this and went off to tell his wife the news.

Mara woke with a start, jerked to a sitting position, realised she was safe at the eating house and let out a long, low groan of relief before snuggling down again. But the sound was enough to alert Nan, who came up with a cup of tea.

The business of the eating house couldn't wait. As soon as he got back Mark went into the kitchen, followed by Catherine, who might be forbidden to use one arm but was sure she could be of assistance.

'I'll send for Kalaya,' he said firmly. 'She knows what to do.'

Catherine looked at him so uncertainly that he whisked her into the store room to kiss her and ask, 'Surely you're not doubting me?'

She blushed. 'It's just—there are so many prettier and younger women and . . .'

'But there's only one Catherine.' He smiled at her. 'Never doubt my love for you, dearest one.'

*   *   *

When the eating house closed that night, they all gathered there to eat a late meal together and make plans for the future, tired but buoyed up by their happiness.

'Catherine and I intend to marry as soon as we can,' Mark announced. 'We're going to Melbourne to buy the ring, then we'll come back and get wed.'

'We'd better start on your dress afore you go,

426

love,' Nan said, patting Catherine's arm. 'Then I can sew for you while you're away. I'm a fine needlewoman, if I say so myself.'

'Can you run the eating house for me?' Mark asked Malachi. 'I'll leave detailed instructions and we'll plan the menus in advance.'

'Why not?' He grinned at Issy, who was fully aware of how little he knew about cooking.

'I'll help him,' she announced. 'My arm's getting better every day.'

'And while we're there, I'll book your passages to Perth,' Mark went on. 'Theo left me enough money for that.'

'I can pay our way,' Malachi said with a frown.

'Theo isn't wealthy but he's comfortably circumstanced. Let him pay for this,' Mark insisted.

Only when they were on the coach riding towards Melbourne did he say to Catherine, 'And we'll go and see this Bishop of yours while we're there. I'm not afraid of him.'

'But he might try to keep me there.'

'He won't succeed, I promise you.'

*   *   *

Two days later, he escorted Catherine into the Bishop's palace, feeling her arm quivering on his and seeing for himself how pale she was. But he was determined to sort everything out properly before they were married.

The Bishop tried to insist on her staying with the order until she was formally released.

'Impossible,' said Mark. 'We're getting married in a few days' time. This visit is a mere courtesy to you—and we'd also be grateful if you'd set matters

427

in train for the return of Catherine's dowry.'

The Bishop looked at her sternly. 'Is this really what you want?'

'Oh, yes. I turned to the order in grief, which is not a proper reason for becoming a nun.'

'Very well, then. On your own head be it.' His expression was chill and disapproving. The meeting terminated soon afterwards.

When they got back to Rossall the dress was ready for its final fitting and only needed the lace Catherine had bought in Melbourne to be sewn on.

'I'll need to leave my wagon somewhere while I take Issy and Mara to see their sister,' Malachi told Mark that night, the two men having become close friends. 'Eh, I wish I had more money saved. Samuel Grove wants to sell his store and I'd love to buy it. Let alone it's just the sort of place I want, it'd be nice to have friends already in the town.'

The wedding took place two days later, a private affair just for family and close friends. But many of the citizens of Rossall found an excuse to linger outside the church and greet the bride and groom with cheers and hearty good wishes.

'So,' said Malachi next morning as he saw his wife and sister-in-law into the coach, 'we move on to the next adventure.'

His remark was greeted by Ismay with a scowl. 'I only hope it's worth it. It's costing someone a lot of money to send us to Western Australia.'

She had been very grumpy for the past few days. Malachi didn't try to argue. He knew his Issy. He winked at Mara and studied the scenery till his wife had recovered a little, then discussed what they'd do in Melbourne.

He almost forgot about Dan's legacy but Issy

428

reminded him and so they paid a visit to the bank. There they found that Dan had left them five hundred pounds, enough for them to be able to buy the store in Rossall after all.

A letter was sent to Mark explaining and asking him to tell Samuel Grove that he had a customer for the store, so not to sell it till they returned, then at last they boarded the coastal steamer for Perth. They hadn't had time to write and let Keara know that they were coming, but Malachi was sure he could find a way of getting to her, hire a vehicle and horses maybe.

'Things are going better now, aren't they?' Mara said, as they stood by the rail watching Melbourne fade into the distance.

'Wait till we see how we get on in Western Australia,' Ismay chided. 'There's such a thing as counting your chickens before they're hatched.'

'Oh, you're such a cross-patch sometimes!' Mara exclaimed, and went to stand further away.

'Well!'

Malachi grinned at his wife. 'She's right. You are a cross-patch—or maybe a hedgehog, all spikes. But I still love you.' Then he became more solemn. 'I know you're nervous, love. But Keara is your sister and I'm sure she won't have changed that much.'

'You're too good to me,' she said gruffly, staring across the water and seeing nothing for the tears in her eyes.

'I love you,' he said simply.

CHAPTER TWENTY-SEVEN

JANUARY 1867

For most of the journey Lavinia had looked puffy and unwell, but had behaved fairly normally. However, as the ship drew closer to Fremantle and the weather grew warmer again, she began to spend most of the day on deck, lying on one of the wooden deck chairs, hardly saying a word and only moving when she had to. The colour the sun put into her skin looked like badly applied paint and beneath it was the greasy pallor of ill health.

Dick kept an eye on her and wondered about calling in the ship's doctor, but when he suggested this to Bess she vetoed it, saying her mistress didn't want 'mauling about' and would get better as soon as they arrived on dry land. Even though he knew it was mainly out of self-interest, he couldn't fault the way she was looking after Lavinia, so he let matters stay as they were.

Another worry to him was Thad Bowler. Inevitably he saw the fellow working around the ship and noticed that he spent a lot of time with an ugly man who had lost most of one ear. The two seemed as thick as thieves and that worried Dick. What if Thad was planning something for after their arrival? It sometimes seemed that both Thad and Bess regarded him with sly amusement as if they knew something he didn't, as if they felt themselves to be cleverer than him.

A little judicious questioning of the Chief Steward revealed that One-ear was called Bin and was not well thought of. He was considered lazy and suspected of theft, though no one had been able to prove anything against him.

Of far more concern was the fellow's physique. Bin looked strong and well-muscled and Dick knew he would be no match for two such burly men.

Even sunny-tempered Clemmy was starting to worry about their arrival because Thad had started muttering about 'folk as are going to get their comeuppance' whenever he passed her.

Dick consulted the Captain, but although he could guarantee their safety on board ship, he had to admit he would be powerless to help them once they disembarked—though he promised to keep Bin and Thad on board until the others had had time to get to Perth.

'There'll be no keeping our whereabouts a secret with Bess in the party,' Dick said gloomily. 'Ah, ye're marryin' a poor sort of fellow, Clemmy love. I should be able to do better than this.'

'You're exactly the sort of fellow I like,' she insisted.

But although that pleased him and lifted his spirits temporarily, it didn't stop him continuing to worry.

*　　　*　　　*

Keara beamed at Theo. 'It shouldn't be much longer before Mara arrives. I can't wait to see her again. She must have grown so much. She'll be nearly a woman now.'

He put his arm round her. 'I'm glad for you, darling. Glad for me, too. I feel that at last we are starting to make up for what Lavinia did to your sisters. And I shan't stop looking until we find Ismay as well, I promise you.'

The following day a letter arrived by special messenger from Perth, such an extravagant way of communicating that Theo knew even before he tore it open that something was wrong. He read it rapidly, cursed and read it again more slowly.

'What is it?' Keara demanded, and when he didn't seem to hear her, twitched the piece of paper out of his hand and read it herself while he began to pace up and down.

My dear Theo

This will no doubt come as a great shock to you, but I'm here in Western Australia and have had to bring Lavinia with me.

Nancy died a few months ago, but warned me before she passed away that Lavinia had got into bad company with a new maid. Bess is Nancy's niece but she is a bold piece, and, I believe, a thief and opportunist. Under her influence your dear wife got into serious financial difficulty and would heed no one but this Bess.

I could see no way out of this other than bringing Lavinia to you, for she refused point-blank to go to Ireland. I was even ready to kidnap her, but Bess seemed eager to leave Lancashire and come to Australia so she persuaded Lavinia into the venture.

I tried to have Bess prevented from coming on board and hired another maid to replace her after we sailed but Bess was too clever for me. She has a man friend who is a rough sort and he must have helped her overcome the fellow I sent to prevent her leaving England because after we set sail I found that Bess and Thad were on the ship.

Lavinia is still clinging to the woman and I fear what Bess and her man friend are planning. Someone tried to push me overboard on the voyage.

Please come to Perth immediately, Theo, and bring a gun. Lavinia isn't looking well and I'm worried about the man friend and my own safety, as well as that of Clemmy, the woman who was to be Lavinia's maid and who is now betrothed to me.

I'm sorry to serve you so poorly, my dear brother, and regret the way this is going to disturb your happiness with Keara. But there was no other way out: you are the only one left who has the authority to deal with Lavinia.

Dick

They looked at one another and Theo shook his head helplessly. 'It's taking a few minutes for this to sink in, Keara.'

'Lavinia coming here!' Her voice was full of loathing and she looked round the home she loved, already hating the idea of Theo's wife taking it over. But that was the sort of thing that happened to people living in sin, so she could hardly complain.

'No. That at least I'll not have.'

'She'll have to live somewhere and she *is* your wife, after all.'

'You feel more like my wife than she does. Ah, Keara, come here.' He pulled her into his arms, feeling how upset she was by the rigidity of her body, 'It'll make no difference to us, I promise you.'

She sighed, unable to believe that.

'I'll ride across to speak to Caley and Noreen. Maybe they'll agree to let Lavinia stay with them until I can make other arrangements for her—and the arrangements I have in mind are a passage straight back to England without her maid.'

She threaded her arm through his, trying not to add to his worries by letting him see how upset she was. After fighting a battle for self-control, she said more calmly, 'You can't send her straight back if she really is ill. You can't impose on your cousins, either. You know how awkward Lavinia is. And Theo—she *is* your wife, your responsibility, however you feel about her. Or me.'

He let out a heartfelt sigh. 'Well, I'm still not having you and the children thrown out of your home. Oh, hell, Keara darling, what am I going to do with the stupid woman?'

He went to see Caley and Noreen that evening and came back to say they'd have Lavinia, who could stay in their overseer's cottage with her maid if she grew too troublesome, since they were temporarily without domestic help.

Keara nodded, but privately wondered for how long Lavinia would put up with that. As Theo's legal wife, she had a right to live with him whereas Keara had no legal standing. If anything happened to him, she didn't know what she'd do. He said he'd made a will, left money to her and the children, but that meant nothing. She loved him so much. He was the centre of her life.

*   *   *

434

Thad watched *them* leave the ship and when an officer came to chivvy him into doing some work, went off whistling. It wouldn't be long now before he was released from this damned prison. He well knew who he had to thank for being moved to the crew from being a steward and had added it to the list of scores to settle against Mr Dick bloody Pearson.

Bin said it'd be easy to find them again in Perth because it was a small place even if they did call it a city. When he was paid off Thad took his money, waited for Bin, and then the two of them went upriver to Perth on the paddle steamer.

They spent the first night getting drunk because it'd been a long time. The second day they found where the sods were staying and Thad went inside to ask for Mrs Mullane's maid.

The woman at the hotel counter asked, 'Your name?'

'None of your business.'

She drew herself upright in disapproval. 'Then I can't tell her you're here.'

'Thad Bowler.'

She consulted a list. 'Sorry. Mr Pearson made a particular point of asking that you be kept away from his party. You'll kindly leave the hotel, Mr Bowler.'

He crashed his fist down on the counter, enjoying the way she jerked backwards and the fear that came into her face. 'I'm not going until I've seen Bess.'

She rang a bell and a man came through the back door, a fellow as big as Thad himself.

'This is the man Mr Pearson warned us about.

435

He refuses to leave.'

The man eyed Thad with anticipation. 'Will you leave now or must I make you?'

He looked so bursting with strength and energy that Thad decided not to press the point. He was a big man himself, but this fellow was bigger. He strolled to the door and went to wait opposite the hotel.

He waited in vain that day, so went back the next and was rewarded by the sight of Bess coming out of the front door.

When he called her name, she ran across the sandy street to join him, relieved to have his help again, however much he annoyed her at times.

'We'll go somewhere and talk,' he said.

'I can't be long. She's not well.'

'She's never well, that one.'

'She's our way to more money so I'm looking after her carefully. She frets if I'm away for too long.'

'How long are they staying in Perth? It'd be easier to deal with them in the country. My friend Bin says there's a lot goes on in the bush that folk in the city don't know about, and no police to spoil the fun. Sounds like a good place to live to me.'

'Mr Pearson sent a message to her husband as soon as we arrived. They're waiting for him to come and collect her.'

'It's taking him long enough.'

'He has two days' riding to get here. There isn't even a proper railway.' Bess looked around with loathing. 'You might like this place but I hate it. I never thought it'd be like this. The streets are more like sandy tracks and I loathe this heat. They might have a few decent buildings in this town—and how

436

they can call it a city, I don't know—but most of the houses are no bigger than cottages.'

'Well, hate it or not, you're here now.'

'But we're going back to England as soon as we've got the money, aren't we?' When she saw him shrug, her mouth fell open. 'Thad, you can't mean to stay!'

'I'm not working as a sailor again. Bloody slave labour, that is. I hate climbing up that rigging.'

'You can buy a passage back, have an easy time of it as a passenger,' she said impatiently. 'It's me that will have a hard time looking after *her.* Then, when we're home again, we'll take the money off her and start enjoying ourselves.'

'Let's hope dear Mr Mullane is eager to get rid of his wife again, then.'

'If he isn't at first, I'll make sure he is later. She'll do anything I ask and she enjoys upsetting folk.'

'You're a right little bitch, you are.'

Bess smiled, taking it for a compliment—which was how he'd intended it.

He looked at her assessingly, wondering if she meant to cheat him out of his share of the money when they got back. Well, he'd stopped her running away from him and he'd stop that, too. Which was why he was thinking of staying here. Though she was right, it was a poor sort of place.

But the rum was cheap and plentiful—and he'd drink to that any day.

*   *   *

Lavinia lay on her bed, hating the heat. She fanned herself briefly, then let her hand fall and the fan

437

drop off the side of the bed because it was too much of an effort to move. Why had she allowed Bess to persuade her to come here? The voyage had been dreadful, the company most unpleasant, and she had suffered several bouts of seasickness during rough weather. But she'd endure it all over again to get back home. She wasn't staying here, she definitely wasn't! Once they got the money out of Theo, she was going straight back home to England and never leaving it again.

She turned her head suddenly, thinking she had seen Nancy come into the room, something that had happened a few times lately. More tears overflowed at the thought that her dear old nurse was dead. At first it had been fun with Bess, but now she was tired of her new maid. Bess was no comfort when you were unwell. She tried to jolly you out of it when you wanted only to sleep, and she was always asking for money—money you didn't have.

On that thought Lavinia sighed and turned over, kicking the bedcovers aside and trying in vain to find a cooler spot on the bed.

What was she going to say to Theo? Bess had said she was to demand more money and refuse to be put off, but Theo was a stingy creature and always had been. He'd taken all her father's money then given her a pittance. Nothing would persuade her that he hadn't kept her dowry for himself.

*   *   *

Theo took his fastest horse, leading another behind it to spell them both, and pushed them hard. His cousin Caley did the same. Theo wanted to reach

Perth and get the confrontation with Lavinia over. Poor Dick! Theo's wife was enough to try anyone's patience, but to say he feared for his life was surely exaggerating? Why should anyone want to harm a kind fellow like Dick?

'Better give the horses another rest,' Caley said from behind. 'You're riding as if all the devils in hell are after you.'

Theo reined in. 'Sorry. I'm a bit upset.'

'I know, I know.' As they sat by a small fire and made themselves some pint-pot tea, Caley repeated what he had said several times before. 'I can't believe that Lavinia would come all this way and endure the discomforts of a long voyage. Her of all people!'

'I can't either. It's this new maid of hers. Dick says my dear wife won't heed anyone else. Well, I'll be dismissing the woman for a start.'

Caley looked at him. 'Might not be advisable. You remember how hard Lavinia is to manage.'

Theo's shoulders drooped. 'I do indeed. How can I ever forget? Oh, hell, was there ever such a mess?'

*   *   *

The coastal steamer arrived in Perth the same day as Theo set off there. Malachi, who'd learned a lot from his fellow passengers, shepherded Ismay and Mara off it and into the town of Fremantle, though it looked more like a hamlet to him. They found a clean lodging house and set about making travel arrangements.

Since none of them was used to riding, they had already decided to buy a small cart and drive down

439

to Bunbury. It sounded straightforward enough. You simply headed down the coast till you got to a small town called Mandurah, then headed inland to another place called Pinjarra, then headed south-west towards Bunbury. When he'd worried about taking the wrong turning, the man advising him had roared with laughter. The only turnings from the road were, it appeared, farm tracks.

'There are no other towns,' his mentor said simply when he had stopped chuckling.

It all started well. Malachi knew enough about horses and carts by now not to be cheated, and the two sisters went shopping for supplies, blankets and cooking implements. On one shopkeeper's advice they bought wide-brimmed straw hats and sent Malachi out again to find one that fitted him.

Within two days they had set off, travelling early in the morning, resting for the hottest part of the day and moving on again until the light faded at night. At this time of year it rarely rained and heat was more of a problem than cold.

They were lucky to be offered accommodation the first night, and the young son of the household, shyly admiring of Mara, named the native birds for her. She was fascinated by everything because she'd never travelled round the Australian countryside before.

Listening to what they were saying, Malachi decided that it was a bit different here from the eastern side of the continent, though not that different. There were parrots flying round, with green plumage so shiny it gleamed in the sun. The lad called 'twenty-eights' because of the sound they made. There were dainty little birds called honey eaters in a variety of striking shades, and his own

440

favourites, cheeky black and white birds called willy wagtails whose tails never stopped wagging and whose song was beautiful.

As they drove on the following day Malachi watched indulgently as Mara exclaimed at her first sight of a kangaroo with a baby in its pouch and marvelled at the bleached look of the countryside, for at this time of year, in the full heat of summer, the grass in the fields looked more like straw.

Sometimes they would pass a huge tree and the whole road would make a detour round it. As they got further south they passed small farms and found a welcome any time they cared to stop and ask for water or eggs or milk.

'I wish it wasn't so hot,' Ismay grumbled. 'Sure I'm near to melting.'

'I like it.' Mara held her face up to the sun, her skin already tanned after the sea voyage.

'It's a good thing you got the hats, Issy,' said Malachi, giving her a quick hug. When she refused to be cheered up, he asked bluntly, 'What are you getting grumpy for?'

'Grumpy? *Me?* I'm not grumpy, am I, Mara?'

Her sister grinned. 'You are, yes, just a bit.'

Ismay scowled from one to the other. 'Well, I didn't want to come, so I have a right to be grumpy.'

'Or is it that you're getting nervous about meeting Keara again?' he asked gently.

'Of course I'm not!'

But she was. She didn't know what to say to her sister, how to talk about what had happened, wasn't even sure she could try.

When they got to Bunbury, she stared around angrily. 'Why, it's hardly more than a village!'

Malachi asked the way out to Theo Mullane's property, which was apparently some distance inland.

'I heard he'd gone up to Perth,' one man told them. His face was so brown his skin looked like tanned leather, and the sun was so bright he squinted at them as he talked from eyes set deep in wrinkles. 'Your ladies wouldn't be relatives of his wife, would they? They have a look of her. Nice woman, she is. Always got a pleasant word for you.'

'Yes. They're her sisters.' Malachi shook his hand and drove on. At least they'd found a bridge or two here and not had to travel across fords where he worried about getting bogged down, though the rivers they crossed were quite low because it hadn't rained for months.

As the sun was sinking in the sky and long shadows banded the road they found the turn signposted to 'Ballymullan'. Ismay gripped Mara's hand and sat very upright, tension radiating from every inch of her body.

'You'll be all right, love,' Malachi said gently.

She didn't even try to deny her nervousness. 'How will I know what to say to her?'

The other two exchanged glances.

'She's just Keara still,' Mara said.

Ismay breathed deeply and scowled at her.

'If you can't think of anything, squeeze my hand and I'll think of something,' Malachi offered.

She made an angry little sound and that was the last noise she made until the house came into sight at the end of a long dusty avenue bordered by young trees wilting in the heat.

*   *   *

442

Theo arrived in Perth and made his way straight to the hotel. When he asked for Dick he was directed to the residents' sitting room and stopped in the doorway at the sight of his half-brother in earnest conversation with a plump, fair-haired young woman. This would be Dick's betrothed, he guessed, from the looks on both their faces. Theo didn't speak for a moment while he studied her. He didn't want some maidservant marrying his half-brother just for an easier life. But to his relief she had a sweet expression and the sort of face you'd trust instinctively.

When he cleared his throat they both turned round and Dick's face lit up. He hurried across the room to clip Theo in a hug and then hold him at arm's length. 'Look at you! You're so brown-skinned now! And I'd swear you've grown.'

'Grown broader, perhaps. I work outdoors most of the time and love it.' Theo laughed. 'I wasn't cut out to be a gentleman of leisure and go to social functions. I'm so much happier now.'

A shadow crossed Dick's face. 'And I've brought you trouble you didn't need.'

'Not only trouble. Aren't you going to introduce me to your friend?'

Dick turned round and beckoned to his companion. 'Clemmy darlin', I'm sorry, I'm neglecting you. This is Theo.'

'It's not neglecting me to go and greet a brother whom you haven't seen for a year or two.' She walked across the room, not appearing at all nervous and shook Theo's hand. 'I'm pleased to meet you, Mr Mullane.'

'Theo.'

'Theo, then.' She turned to her betrothed. 'I'll leave you two to talk. I think I'll go for a stroll now the heat of the day is past.'

When she had left Theo said, 'She seems pleasant.'

'She's wonderful, so calm and sensible and yet fun to be with. But we ought to talk about Lavinia.'

'Yes.'

They sat down and Dick sighed heavily. 'She's not well, but she's as awkward and irritating as ever.'

'I'm not looking forward to meeting her again, I must admit.' Theo thrust his hands in his pockets and stretched out his legs in front of him. 'But I'm not going to let her hurt my Keara.'

Dick stared down at his feet, quite sure Lavinia would upset everyone. She had a talent for it.

Theo stood up, as if unable to sit still. 'Let's be getting the first meeting over with, then.'

They went upstairs and Dick knocked on a bedroom door. When Bess opened it, he said, 'This is Mr Mullane. He's here to see his wife.'

'And about time, too.'

Theo studied her, astonished that she'd greet him so impertinently and not liking what he saw. With her bold, dark eyes, she looked like a caricature of a young Nancy, but there was something sly about her that there had never been in her aunt.

'I'll find out if Mrs Mullane can see you,' Bess said and turned away, beginning to close the door.

Theo put out his hand to stop her doing that and said sharply, 'You can make yourself scarce! I don't need an audience when I see my wife.'

'Don't leave me, Bess!' a voice quavered from

444

inside the room.

She stepped back and Theo, annoyed that she was not even attempting to do as he'd told her, pulled her out of the room and moved quickly inside, shutting the door on both her and Dick.

Bess glared at Dick and then looked thoughtfully at the door.

He guessed that if he moved away, she'd be back eavesdropping within seconds so stayed put. 'You may as well go and wait until your mistress rings for you.'

'Ah, you're nothing but a pet dog to him,' she said, for once not even trying to hide her spite. 'Pity you didn't fall overboard that time! Maybe on the way back . . .'

She walked away laughing, but he stood there, shaken. After a moment or two he went to sit on a chair at the end of the corridor to make certain she didn't come back to eavesdrop. Sure enough, she peeped round the corner a short time later, scowling when she saw him still there.

He inclined his head to her with a half-smile.

*   *   *

Inside the room Theo walked slowly over to the bed, shocked rigid at the sight of Lavinia. She had grown very fat and her complexion was muddy and unhealthy.

'If you touch me, I'll scream my head off!'

'And why would I want to touch you?'

She gave a sniff.

'I'm your wife. I'm entitled to live with you. But I'll still scream if you touch me.'

She sounded as if she'd learned the words by

heart.

'You may be my wife, and I'll make sure you're looked after, but you're *not* coming near Keara and the children. Anyway, you won't be staying here in Australia for long if I can help it.'

She opened her mouth to say wild horses wouldn't persuade her to stay in this dreadful hot dusty country, then remembered what Bess had been saying to her and changed it to, 'I might want to stay.'

'Why the hell did you come here, Lavinia? Of all the foolish things to do! Why could you not have written to me?'

'Because you'd just have said no. I need more money, much more, and I have to have it or Bess will leave me. I have a *right* to more money. It was my father's.'

'He lost a lot of his money. There isn't a great deal to spare, Lavinia. I'll find a little more for you, but you'll have to be careful with it when you go back.'

'I knew you'd be mean to me! You're a dreadful man. Well, I'm *not* going back until I have the money.'

'And how much do you want?'

She tried hard to remember the amount Bess kept telling her but had forgotten, so took refuge in tears. 'Ask Bess. She'll know.'

When he came across to the bed, she whimpered and tried to move away from him, but when she sat up she felt dizzy and fell back against the pillows with a muffled cry.

'You don't look at all well. I think we'll have the doctor in to see you before we go any further.'

'I don't need a doctor. All I want is my money

446

and to go ho-o-ome!'

Then she clutched her chest and moaned, going so chalk-white he was afraid for her. He set the bell pealing for the maid and when she came, snapped, 'Look after your mistress. I'm calling in a doctor.'

*   *   *

After he'd examined Lavinia, the doctor joined Theo in the room he'd taken for himself and Caley.

'Well?' Theo asked impatiently as the man hesitated.

'I'm afraid your wife is very ill.'

'I can see that.'

'She shouldn't have made the journey to Australia, and from now on, you'll have to ensure that she doesn't exert herself in any way. And she mustn't be upset. Over-excitement could be fatal. Even with the greatest care, I don't think she'll last much longer.'

Theo paid him, took the medication and listened carefully to the instructions for using it, then walked down to the lobby with the man out of courtesy. Back in his bedroom, he thumped one fist on the bed, then thumped it again.

The last thing he needed was to nurse a dying wife! And with Lavinia in this condition he couldn't ask Noreen and Caley to house her. Which meant he'd have to seek somewhere else for Keara and the children to live until he could see his way clear to finding a permanent solution.

Groaning, he rested his head on his hands and muttered, 'Hell, Keara, I never meant it to come to this. Who'd ever have thought she'd come out here?'

CHAPTER TWENTY-EIGHT

JANUARY 1867

Keara had been unable to sit still all day. The children picked up her mood and neither would settle for an afternoon nap. She put them down on their beds anyway. When she heard the sound of a vehicle approaching, she frowned. It couldn't be Theo, not yet. Could it be Mara? She stilled and one hand went up to her throat as if to protect herself, then she shook her head. No, they were going to write and let her know when her sister would arrive.

'You're just being stupid,' she muttered. 'Go and see who it is. Guessing gets you nowhere.' But for some strange reason she couldn't force herself to walk towards the door at more than a slow shuffle by which time the vehicle had stopped outside.

When she opened the door, she gasped and stumbled forward to clutch the veranda post, unable to believe what she saw.

No one spoke, not a word.

No one moved.

Time itself seemed to be waiting for something to happen.

That something was Nell, who came toddling through the open door and beamed at them all with her usual sunny good nature. 'Horsey.' Totally unafraid, she would have walked out towards the two tired-looking animals had not Keara suddenly come to her senses and scooped up her little daughter. 'I'm sorry. I was just—shocked. It's

448

wonderful to see you again. Come in, won't you?'

Mara tumbled off the back of the cart and went racing to hug her sister and niece, weeping and laughing at the same time.

'You see,' Malachi said in a low voice, nudging his wife, 'It's not so difficult. Go and join them.'

But Ismay couldn't move, could only stare to see Keara looking so like her old self except for the tanned face and arms. It wasn't fair. So much had happened. Something had to show in her sister's face, surely?

With a click of exasperation Malachi looped the reins over the holder and jumped down, going round to the other side to pull his wife down too.

'I can't!' she hissed.

'You can!'

By this time Keara had stopped hugging Mara for long enough to stare across at Ismay, who was scowling at her.

'Dear God, you're a woman grown!' was all she could think of to say. She set Mara aside, put Nell down and walked down the veranda steps towards her other sister. As she pulled Ismay into an embrace she felt her stiffen, then shudder and hug her briefly before pulling back. So this one has been the most damaged by it all, she thought, as she turned to look questioningly at the man. Well, they'd all been hurt by what Lavinia had done, that was sure.

'I'm your brother-in-law,' he said quietly. 'Malachi Firth.'

He held out one hand but Keara used it to pull him towards her and give him a kiss on the cheek. 'Then you're too close a relative for hand-shaking.' She glanced sideways at Ismay then back at him,

449

liking his open, friendly smile.

'I hope so.'

'And this is my daughter, Nell. I have a son, Devin, but he's asleep—at least, I hope he is.'

Malachi smiled down at the tiny girl-child whose dark wavy hair reminded him of her mother and his wife. Nell had turned shy now and was clinging to her mother's skirt and hiding her face in it. 'She's a bonny lass.'

'You speak a bit like my mother,' Keara said.

'I'm from Lancashire, too.'

'I'm glad you still remember her,' Ismay said, a sharp edge making her voice shriller than usual.

Malachi looked at her and shook his head warningly, but she tossed her head at him.

Another awkward silence, then Keara said as lightly as she could manage, 'I don't think any of the men are around. Would you mind taking your horses round to the stables at the back and seeing to them yourself, Malachi? Just help yourself to feed.'

'Not at all.' With another warning glance at Ismay he turned and climbed on the wagon and told the horses to move on.

'Will we go and make a cup of tea?' Keara asked her sisters. She didn't wait for an answer but put an arm round each of them, intending to walk with them into the house. But Ismay shrugged her arm off so she led the way with Mara, shooing Nell in ahead of them. 'Theo is away from home just now. He had to go up to Perth.' She closed her eyes, imagining yet again what it would be like if he returned with Lavinia, if she had to move out of this house, what all the neighbours would say when they found she wasn't really married to him. She realised Mara was speaking.

'We've driven down from Fremantle. People were so kind. We slept on one family's veranda and they cooked a meal for us. It was such fun.'

'You must be tired, though you don't look it. It's not easy travelling in such heat. Come and sit down on the back veranda or would you like to have a wash first?'

'Have a wash,' Mara said at once. 'Wouldn't we, Ismay? I feel to be covered in dust.'

Keara showed them into the bedroom she'd prepared for Mara. 'I'll get another ready for you and your husband, Ismay.' There was no answer. She was getting more and more worried about those stiff silences. Surely her sister didn't think she'd deliberately abandoned them?

In the kitchen Keara looked for something to occupy Nell while she made the tea, but her daughter grizzled, wanting to go to the visitors, so she sat her on a chair and when she tried to wriggle off it, shouted at her to sit still. Which didn't make either of them feel any better.

In the bedroom Mara glared at Ismay. 'You might say something to her! She keeps looking at you and you just go all wooden. You haven't even given her a chance.'

'I—can't. I just can't.'

In the kitchen Keara got things ready then listened for the sound of footsteps on the bare boards of the corridor which would herald the return of her sisters. When they came, she turned to face them, determined to clear the air. 'What's wrong?'

Ismay took a deep, shuddering breath. 'You knew Mam wasn't well. Why didn't you come back to see her?'

'Mrs Mullane wasn't well, either.'

'What did *she* matter?'

'I hoped Mam was hanging on. She'd been ill for so long and hung on against all the odds that I was never quite sure how bad she was.' Keara dropped the tea towel and buried her face in her hands. 'Heaven help me, I thought she must be managing and that you'd let me know if I was needed.'

'We *did* let you know. Father Cornelius wrote to you—more than once! He wrote about your old friend Arla too.'

'Mrs Mullane intercepted the letters. I never did see them. She was—is—a very selfish woman.'

'Well, I think you were too busy making friends with her husband to think about us or Mam!' Ismay yelled. 'And I'll never forgive you for that.'

Malachi came into the kitchen and grabbed his wife's arm. 'Don't say something you'll regret, Issy. You can't know how it was for your sister.'

'I know how it was for us, though, taken forcibly from home and sent out to Australia, then separated.'

She was sobbing wildly now, losing control in a way he'd never seen before. He pulled her into his arms and tried to shush her but she continued weeping, clearly beyond reason. 'Is there somewhere I can take her?' Malachi asked.

Keara, who had been standing frozen with shock, nodded and moved to show him to a bedroom. Ismay seemed blind to what was happening around her, sobbing so hard her whole body was shaking. As Keara opened the door, Malachi picked his wife up and carried her through to lay her on the bed.

When Keara moved to leave them he came across to the door with that swift, neat stride of his, saying gently, 'She's never really been able to grieve. She always had to be strong, to cope. First for Mara, then for herself because she was on her own and there was no one who cared about her. I don't know if she'll even recover enough to talk to you again tonight. But I'm glad we came, believe me.'

Then he patted her on the shoulder, shut the door and went back to his wife. He had hated to see how ravaged Keara's face looked, but Ismay came first and her sobs were tearing at his heart. He lay down beside her on the bed and pulled her into his arms, letting her weep against him, weep and weep until surely there were no more tears left.

He found himself weeping too, tears flowing for what she had suffered, was still suffering, because she was his Issy and he loved her more than he had ever thought possible.

Dusk had fallen by the time she quietened a little. When he thought she might be able to speak again, he brushed the damp hair from her flushed forehead and kissed it. 'I'll go and get us something to eat and drink, love.'

'I don't want anything.'

'Well, I do.'

'I don't want to see anyone.'

'I know. For tonight it'll be just you and me, and if you want to weep all over me again, I'll be here.'

'I never thought I'd love anyone as much as I love you.' She looked at him and her mouth fell open in wonderment. 'You've been crying too.'

He had great difficulty holding back more tears of his own. 'Of course I have. Your pain is my pain,

453

and you've had a hard time of it these past few years. But I intend to make sure things are never that bad again. Now, let me go and get some food before I shrivel up and die next to you.'

She managed a watery smile and lay there feeling his love still wrapped around her as his arms had been a short time before. Something hard inside her melted a little.

*   *   *

When Keara returned to the kitchen she looked at Mara. 'Do you think she'll ever forgive me? I truly didn't realise how bad Mam was, wouldn't have thought even Lavinia Mullane capable of such unkindness.'

'I'm sure Ismay will forgive you. She's just—a bit sharp. But Malachi's lovely with her. If anyone can make her happy again, properly happy, it's him.'

'Tell me what happened to you.'

Keara listened in dismay to her younger sister's story. They had none of them had an easy time of it, she realised.

*   *   *

By the time Malachi joined them in the kitchen they'd had something to eat, fed Nell and Devin and put them to bed, feeling more like sisters by the minute.

Keara looked at him anxiously. 'How is she?'

'Utterly exhausted. Not in a fit state to see anyone. But I'm hungry and if I take some food into the bedroom, she'll maybe have a bite or two with me.'

454

'I'll get you something.'

As Keara finished loading the tray, she asked him the same question she'd asked Mara. 'Will Ismay ever forgive me?'

'I hope so. Because if she doesn't, she'll never be truly happy.'

He went back, to talk lightly of how tired he was and how hungry. Ismay drank two cups of tea and ate a bite or two at his urging. She looked so wan he set the tray on the dressing table and came back to the bed when he'd finished. 'I'll go and bring our clothes in, then we'll go to bed.'

'Won't she mind?'

'She knows you're exhausted.' He turned to leave then swung round. 'She asked me if you'd ever forgive her. I said I hoped so because if you don't, Issy, it'll sour you and I want us to have a *happy* life together.'

'I can't think about it now,' she said in a thread of a voice.

When he came back she was asleep so he undressed quickly and climbed into bed beside her, expecting to lie awake worrying but falling asleep almost immediately.

*　　　*　　　*

Bess didn't manage to get out to speak to Thad until much later that night. He was waiting for her outside the hotel, pacing up and down on the other side of the street, radiating impatience.

'Well?' he asked before she'd even finished crossing the road.

'The doctor's given her something to make her sleep, but she told me what Mr Mullane said:

there's not much money left—he must have spent it all on his whore—and he can't afford to give his wife much more than he does now.' Bess scowled into the distance, thinking hard. 'We have to do something to convince him to pay more, but the trouble is *she* really isn't very well. The voyage tired her more than I'd expected.'

'Hell, I hope she doesn't die on us! That'd really ruin things.'

'I know. I was thinking that myself.'

'Where's his whore living then?'

'At his estate near Bunbury. He calls it Ballymullan, after the place in Ireland.'

'Is she there on her own?'

'She's got two children. I was listening to him telling Pearson about them. Talk about proud father and besotted lover! She must be good in bed.'

Thad snapped his fingers. 'That's it!'

'What do you mean?'

'That's how we get at him. If me and Bin go down there ahead of you lot, we can capture them, take them away somewhere and use them to bargain with him. We might not even have to take *her* back to England with us at all.'

Bess looked at him, her upper teeth digging into her lower lip as she thought this through. 'Or he might set the police after us.'

Thad laughed. 'Bin's been telling me about this place. There aren't so many police, especially in the country. He says if you go out into the bush you can find deserted huts where you can live for a bit. He knows how to drive a damned horse and cart, I bloody don't, so we'll have to take him with us and cut him in for some money but I reckon we can still

456

do well out of this. And we'll take one of that fellow's kids with us to England. He won't do anything to get at us then. We can ditch the brat when we get back to Liverpool.'

'Dare we?' she breathed, much taken by the idea.

'It's do it or be stuck in this place for ever.'

'I thought you liked it here.'

'I do. But home is best—especially if you have some money behind you.'

'We'd better think carefully about it.'

'You do too much thinking. It's action we need. You just carry on looking after that stupid woman and we'll go on ahead of you. He's bound to take his dear wife down there because there isn't a ship leaving Fremantle for another couple of months and he'll have to do something with her. We'll be waiting nearby—but his whore and children will have vanished.'

'Well, be careful what you do, and don't touch drink when you're working.'

Bess went back inside the hotel, worrying about what Thad had said. He always did rush into things. But on the other hand Bin knew what it was like here, so maybe it'd work. She brightened. And if it didn't, she could deny knowing anything about his plans. Yes, that was what she'd do. So she had nothing to lose.

As she was crossing the road she could have sworn she saw her Aunt Nancy standing further along the street near a lighted doorway, and stopped in shock. Then she blinked and the figure vanished. 'You're getting too fanciful for your own good, you fool,' she told herself and went back into the hotel.

457

But she didn't sleep soundly. She couldn't get rid of an uneasy feeling. Thad could be violent. She didn't want him killing anyone, least of all a kid. She liked kids, always had. They were funny creatures, especially the little ones. And what did they really know about Bin? He might be planning to kill both of them and steal the money.

*   *   *

The following morning Ismay felt utterly washed out but Malachi persuaded her to get up and join the others in the kitchen, saying she couldn't hide in the bedroom all day.

She smiled a greeting at her sisters and sat down at the table. The little girl immediately came over to stand beside her.

'You're my Auntie Ismay.'

'Yes.'

'I've got an Auntie Mara too now.' With a smile, she wandered across the room to plump down on the floor and start playing with a kitten.

'What can I get you for breakfast?' Keara asked.

Ismay didn't answer so Malachi filled in for her. 'Anything will do, but I warn you, I'm a hungry fellow.' He looked sideways at his wife. 'What about you, Issy?'

'Just a piece of bread.'

'And how about a bit of ham to go with it?' Keara coaxed.

Ismay shrugged.

They made stilted conversation over the meal. Keara was in despair about Ismay when she heard the sound of horses ride up. She looked out of the window and smiled. 'It's Noreen. She's the wife of

Theo's cousin. You'll like her. They live just down the road.'

Noreen's arrival filled the room with conversation. 'I heard you had visitors, didn't realise you'd got *both* your sisters back!' She went to hug Mara then Ismay and hesitated in front of Malachi.

'You can hug me too if you want,' he teased.

So she did.

Mara helped Keara and the native maid but Ismay spent most of the day sitting on the veranda, sometimes with Malachi beside her, sometimes on her own. The arm she'd fractured was aching and she felt so tired she could hardly keep her eyes open and indeed did fall asleep for an hour or two in the afternoon. She couldn't understand what was wrong with her.

Keara was grateful for her brother-in-law's help in maintaining some sort of conversation during the evening meal. She was even more grateful when Ismay went to bed early.

'She was a bit like this once before,' he confided in Keara after his wife had left them. 'Nearly died on us, would have done if it hadn't been for a native healer.' He hesitated then said, 'Your hired hand has to go to Noreen's house with a mare tomorrow morning and asked if I'd like to ride over with him. Is that all right with you?'

'Yes, of course.'

'I think it might help if I left Issy on her own with you.' He gave her a wry grin. 'On the other hand, it may make things even more difficult. You never know with my Issy.'

'Whatever she does, she's still my sister.'

459

The trip down to Bunbury didn't go well. Bin had borrowed a horse and trap from an old friend, who lived in Fremantle, but they'd had to leave some money behind as surety, which would be refunded when they returned the creature.

'Doesn't your bloody friend trust us?' Thad demanded.

Bin grinned at him. 'No. Would you?'

'I would if I called myself a friend. How long will it take us to get to this Bunbury place?'

'Couple of days.'

'Funny sort of place that doesn't have railways. Give me England any day.'

'Shouldn't have come here, then. And if you don't stop grizzling, you can count me out. I'm fed up of your moaning.'

'I'm glad I bought that gun.' Thad cast a mistrustful glance around.

'I've got a knife and that'll do me.' Bin grinned again. 'Good thing we bought the rum. Can't go on a long journey without refreshment, can we?'

On that they were both in complete agreement.

As a result of the rum, the journey took them three days.

In Bunbury they purchased some more bottles and got instructions for finding the property of Mr Mullane. They decided to camp outside the town overnight and then set off early in the morning. It was cooler down here than it had been in Perth, so they had a drink or two to warm them up.

In the morning, Thad noticed Bin taking a pull from a bottle and scowled at his friend. 'Lay off the booze till we've got 'em captured.'

'Ah, just a sip or two to give me a start.'

'Well, pass it over. You're not drinking it all on your own.'

Ballymullan was easy to find because there was a big sign pointing down a dusty track.

The two men sat looking at it.

'Better go past,' Bin said after sucking thoughtfully on a hole in a back tooth. 'We'll find somewhere to camp and then come back on foot.'

They found a good place by a stream so left the horse and cart there. Bin frowned at Thad who was stuffing the gun in his pocket. 'Are you sure you know how to use that?'

Thad shrugged. 'What's to know? You just point it and pull the trigger.' He suited the action to the words and a shot rang out. The recoil made him stagger back a step or two.

'That was a stupid thing to do! Now you'll have to reload it. And what if someone comes to find out who fired a shot?'

'There's no one but us in listening distance.'

'You never know.'

'And I won't have to reload the damn' thing because it's got six bullets. Anyway, I'm not going to shoot anyone. Dead people can't pay up.'

Since they were neither of them woodsmen, they went back to the road to Ballymullan Estate then slipped into the bush to one side, keeping out of sight behind the trees. They saw two men ride out, leading a horse, and exchanged pleased glances.

'Looks like we've fallen lucky,' Bin whispered.

*　　　*　　　*

Keara heard the distant gun shot and frowned.

'Who'd be shooting when Theo's away? I hope we haven't got vagrants making a nuisance of themselves. Any of your people around, Milack?'

The maid shook her head. 'No, missus.'

'Pity. We could have asked them to go and have a look round.' After frowning in thought, she said suddenly, 'I think I'll go and get the shotgun out. You can't be too careful with no men around.'

Even Ismay was jerked out of her abstraction. 'Are you after shooting guns now, Keara?'

'You have to learn when you live in the country. There's no one to help you here but yourself.' She went into their bedroom and took down the loaded shotgun from on top of the wardrobe. Some people left their shotgun standing behind the outside door in case they were attacked, but with Nell around she didn't dare do that. She frowned at her lively little daughter and said in a low voice to her sisters, 'I'll put it in the pantry. Don't leave the door open. Nell gets into everything.'

She suited the action to the words and smiled round. 'There. I'm probably being foolish but I feel better now.'

CHAPTER TWENTY-NINE

JANUARY 1867

To Theo's intense frustration there weren't any ships sailing for another few weeks and Lavinia was getting no better. The hotel owner had already intimated that he wasn't running a hospital, and today he'd asked—not as politely as before—how much longer they'd be staying. Afterwards Bess came to complain that she received only grudging help with her mistress from the hotel maids, who seemed to resent any extra chore.

'I can't ask Noreen to look after Lavinia while she's so ill,' Theo said in frustration over the evening meal. 'I think I'm going to have to take her home.'

Caley whistled and rolled his eyes. Dick said nothing, but guilt was written all over his face.

Theo clapped him on the shoulder. 'You were right to bring Lavinia to me, given that she had refused all other options. There's no easy way out and she *is* my responsibility. But I'm worried about Keara. At the very least I'll need to give her warning.' He turned to his cousin. 'When we get closer, would you ride ahead and let her know what's happened, why I have to do this?'

Caley nodded. 'Of course. And if she and the children want to move over to our house, then they can. I know without asking that Noreen will be happy to have them.'

Theo nodded. 'I'm grateful. Thank goodness Keara's sister hasn't arrived yet so we'll have plenty of bedrooms to spare. Mark said he'd let us know which steamer she would be taking. We'll get nearly two weeks' notice.'

'And if you need someone to meet her, I'll do that too,' his cousin offered.

'You're a good fellow. Thanks for that.'

After dinner Theo went to see his wife.

Lavinia scowled at him from her bed. She had tried refusing to see him, but he just pushed his way into her room. For once, however, he didn't send Bess away so she felt a little safer.

463

'I've decided to take you home with me till the next ship sails for England,' he said abruptly. 'This hotel is no place for a sick woman. We can make you much more comfortable at home.'

'*We?*' she asked, roused out of her lethargy. She buried her face in the sheet and began to sob. 'I'm your *wife*! It's an insult to take me to your mistress's house.'

Bess was at her side instantly, patting and soothing. 'Now, now. You know how much worse you feel if you get agitated.'

'But you heard what he said!'

'I know, I know. But I don't think you have much choice, Mrs Mullane dear. It's not like England here. And this hotel is not good enough for you, it really isn't.'

'Oh, Bess, not more travelling!'

Her plea was so heartfelt and she looked so white and ill that even Theo was touched. 'We can make it easy for you this time, Lavinia, hire a big wagon and put a bed in the back for you. It'll be like having your own travelling bedroom. And it's only a two-day journey in this dry weather, if we hire good horses and set off early.'

Her only reply was to scowl at him and cover her eyes with her arm.

Bess hid a smile. This was just what she'd wanted them to do, and if things went as she hoped the mistress wouldn't even be there when they arrived. See how he liked that, the stingy devil! He deserved all he got, that one did, the way he treated her after all she'd done for his wife. Anyone else would be giving her extra money and thanking her, but not him. He hadn't given her a farthing. She'd pay him back for that by taking

464

everything she could from him.

Well, perhaps Thad was already doing it for her. She hoped so. And hoped Bin was keeping him off the grog.

*   *   *

Milack was doing some washing for the children outside in wooden tubs set up on a bench of planks. When she heard a sound she turned and frowned because it seemed to be coming from the nearest patch of uncleared bush. When it came again she could tell it wasn't an animal. Knowing the missus was always worried about intruders when the mister went away, she slipped back inside the house to warn her. 'I think there's someone out there, missus, hiding in the bush.'

Keara felt her shoulders sag for a moment then straightened up. She didn't need any more trouble, but if it came she was the only one who could cope with it.

'Milack, is there any way you can get out without being seen and find out who it is?'

The maid nodded and slipped off her white apron and petticoat, leaving her with only a dark top and skirt.

As soon as Milack entered the bush she seemed to vanish, as if she'd become one with the trees and earth. Keara had seen her do this before and marvelled at her skill.

She came back after a few nerve-racking minutes to report, 'Two white fellows out there. No one else following 'em.'

'Thank you.' Keara bit her lip, then turned to her sisters and tried to speak cheerfully. 'It's a pity

Malachi's gone over to Caley's today, isn't it? Looks like we'll have to rely on ourselves.'

Mara shuddered.

Ismay put one arm round her. 'We'll not let anyone hurt you.' She looked at Keara. 'Tell me what to do.'

Keara marshalled her forces, hoping three women and one girl would be enough.

*   *   *

Thad and Bin crept closer to the house. Small insects bit them and the weather was hot enough to make them both sweat profusely.

'Damned country,' muttered Thad.

'Ah, you get used to it,' Bin said.

'Then why do you keep talking about leaving?'

His companion shrugged. 'Don't like to stay anywhere too long. Might try Sydney next.'

Thad clutched his friend's arm suddenly as a thin brown snake wriggled past, but it paid no heed to them. When it had vanished he let out his breath in a sour gust. 'I *don't* like snakes.'

Bin slapped in vain at a hungry mosquito. 'It's spiders I don't like. There's some as have nasty bites. They can kill you.'

Thad gulped audibly. 'You never told me that before.' He looked down at his feet then up, squeaked in dismay and edged away from a spider's web hanging from a tree.

'There's one with a red mark on its back. Lives in cracks and under things. Long as you don't go sticking your fingers into cracks, you'll be all right.' Bin chuckled at the sight of his friend's expression. 'Here, have another swig. You'll be all right. I've never been bit, not once.'

Thad took a grateful gulp of rum, then another for good measure.

'Well, how do you want to do this?' Bin asked.

'You're the one as knows how folk live here. You tell me.'

Bin scowled as he bent his mind to the problem. 'I think each of us should creep round one side of the house and get in through windows. Big place like this, they won't be able to keep watch on everything.'

Thad thought about this. The rum was giving him a warm, confident feeling, as it usually did. Ah, he and Bin would be right whatever they did. They were only dealing with a few women, after all. They'd seen two men ride away, hadn't they, and not seen hide nor hair of any other fellows? 'All right.'

They sat there, sweating and slapping at insects, taking another gulp of rum each before starting off to find the woman and her brats.

*   *   *

The women locked all the doors then Ismay went to keep watch on one side of the house, Keara on the other. Milack said she'd stay in the hallway and go to help whoever called out.

Mara stayed with the children in an inside store room, playing with them and keeping them quiet. Keara's instructions were very definite. She was to leave everything to the others. Her job was to keep the children, specifically Nell, away from the trouble.

When Thad appeared from the bush, Ismay

467

watched through the window in amazement as he simply walked towards the house without any attempt to hide himself. Was it her imagination or was the man staggering a bit? She hurried to fetch Keara and Milack and they all stared in amazement at him.

'That fellow been drinkin',' Milack said.

'I'd like to shoot him this very minute,' Keara muttered, clutching the shotgun against her chest, but making sure the barrels pointed upwards.

'Perhaps they just want a handout of food?' Ismay offered.

'Don't look hungry to me,' Milack said disapprovingly. 'Fat bugger, that one is.'

Keara hid a grin. She had given up trying to control Milack's language, which always deteriorated rapidly in times of stress. Then her smile faded as they heard a noise of breaking glass from the other side of the house. 'Oh, heavens, the other one must be getting in. I'll go and check the kitchen end. You two keep an eye on this fellow.'

She held the shotgun ready to use as she pushed open the kitchen door. There was no sign of anyone inside and no noises from anywhere else. But even as she stood there, Bin, who was a much quieter mover than his companion, crept up behind her and tried to snatch the shotgun.

She shouted involuntarily and managed to keep hold of it, but in the struggle one barrel went off, nearly deafening her. The struggle took them into the kitchen and she found it harder and harder to keep hold of the gun. She couldn't hold her own against this large man for much longer.

Suddenly from behind them came a yell, 'You let go of my sister!' and Ismay launched herself at Bin, wielding a frying pan that had caught her fancy as a weapon. She wasn't a big woman, but her expression was so fierce that in the shock of the moment the iron pan landed a blow to Bin's temple. He took a quick step backwards, blinking in shock.

Keara took the opportunity to swing the stock of the gun against the other side of his head, because she couldn't bear to shoot anyone, and he yelled in pain, his expression turning murderous.

But Ismay scooped up a broom and jammed the handle between his legs. Roaring in anger and dismay, he tried to stride forward and fell to the ground, arms still reaching out for Keara.

Steeling herself, she kicked him and the blow sent his head thumping into the heavy wooden table leg. His eyes rolled up and he stilled.

In the silence they stared at one another then Ismay whispered, 'I can't hear the other one. We'd better tie this one up quickly and go and look for him.'

Back on the other side of the house, Milack had seen Thad come creeping towards the next bedroom window and jerk it up. The catch was rusty and it gave almost immediately, allowing him to slide the bottom half up and swing his leg over the sill.

She was nervous of hitting a white fellow, especially one so much bigger than she was, so went to hide behind the door. Leaving it slightly open she watched through the crack as he began to creep along the corridor, staggering slightly. He grinned, pulled a revolver from his pocket and brandished it, then dropped it with a clatter.

Cursing, he tried to pick it up, but gave up after

469

a couple of failed attempts and took out the bottle again. After another hearty swig, he squared his shoulders and moved forward, forgetting about the gun.

Milack slipped out of the bedroom, snatched it and ran back to hide it on top of the wardrobe.

'Only a bunch of women,' Thad muttered. 'I'm stronger 'n' they are. Don' even need a gun.'

He continued to stagger along the corridor, stopping outside the room at the end, swaying slightly as he listened. But there was no sound from inside. Perhaps Bin had already dealt with the bitches. Good bloke, Bin. Taking a deep breath, Thad slammed the door open and ran inside. His rush took him across to Keara before she had a chance to aim the shotgun.

'Argh!' He grabbed her and tried to take the gun away, somehow managing to trip and pull her down to the floor in the process.

With a banshee shriek, Ismay hit him on the shoulder with the pan and her intervention gave Keara a chance to roll away. As Ismay also jumped back out of the way, he stared at them both owlishly, grunted something and made an attempt to stand up.

'Ship's rolling badly t'night,' he muttered, bracing himself for another attempt.

But as the two women watched in puzzlement, he failed even to raise his head and with a groan, he rolled over, snuggling on to his side as if making himself comfortable in bed. Within a minute he was snoring.

Milack crept across with a noose of thin rope and slipped it on one wrist. He snorted, twitched a little and let out a contented-sounding sigh. Her heart pounding, Keara knelt down and reached for his other hand, expecting him to wake up at any moment. If he was asleep. If he wasn't just pretending.

But even this didn't wake him and soon they had his hands securely tied, after which they attended to his feet.

'Ugh! He stinks of rum!' Ismay said as she pulled the rope round his ankles tight and fastened it to the heavy table leg.

Keara beamed triumphantly at the others. 'We did it, girls!'

Ismay fell into her arms and they wept and laughed together, turning to pull Milack into a slow circle-dance of joy.

When they stopped Milack stepped back and Keara looked at her sister.

Ismay smiled at her, really smiled, then flung her arms round her again. 'I thought he was going to hurt you. I couldn't have borne that!'

Keara hugged her and they held each other close. Somehow the minor battle had wiped out the years of separation and the anger. 'I'm all right, love.'

Ismay blinked at her and said tremulously, 'I didn't really hate you.'

'I know, I know.'

'Oh, I missed you so much!'

Then they were weeping together, joy and sadness mixed.

Milack watched with interest. But as they went on hugging and weeping, murmuring incoherent things to one another, she decided to go and fetch the children and get on with her work.

The other sister immediately joined in the

hugging and, with a shake of her head, Milack checked the two men again, finding them both snoring peacefully. She took the children outside to play while she finished the washing.

*   *   *

When Malachi and the stable hand came home an hour later the two intruders were still tied up, Thad smiling in his sleep and snoring manfully. Bin was glaring at everyone because Keara had gagged him after he woke suddenly and starting cursing them, but he was too securely tied to do anything else. And anyway, they had a shotgun and the older woman clearly knew how to use it.

Malachi came in and stopped dead, gaping at the disordered kitchen, the pile of broken crockery swept into a corner and the bruised faces of Keara and Ismay. 'What the hell's been happening here?'

But when he saw the way the three sisters exchanged warm glances, he didn't care what had been happening because he could tell that the ice which had held Ismay's deepest emotions frozen had melted fully at last.

'Well, aren't you going to tell me, wife!' he ordered in mock anger, and joined them at the table. All three sisters tried to tell him at once.

Only when he and Ismay were alone that night did they get a chance to talk about the other thing. She looked at him shyly as she slipped into bed 'You were right, Keara didn't know. And she's had her own troubles.' She nestled against him. 'I never thought I'd be glad that two drunken fools tried to rob us.'

He kissed her eyelids, then her soft, quivering

472

lips. 'Ah, my darling girl.' As the kisses became more hungry, he abandoned words to show her in the oldest way known how very deep his love ran.

CHAPTER THIRTY

JANUARY–FEBRUARY 1867

Caley arrived at Ballymullan Homestead two days later around noon, having set off very early carrying a letter from Theo. He'd worried all the way about how he would tell Keara.

She rushed out to him before he had even dismounted. 'Where's Theo?'

He looked down at her, seeing the stark terror in her face. 'He's fine, I promise you.'

She let out a whoosh of air in relief, then grinned at him. 'And I'm fine too. You'll never guess what's happened.' She didn't wait for him to ask what but continued, 'My sisters are here, *both of them*. Isn't that wonderful?'

'They're here?' Oh, hell, he thought, it'd be a houseful then. Dismounting, he let the stable hand take his precious horse, which normally only he would have cared for, and put his arm round her shoulders, stopping her from leading the way inside. 'We need to talk, just you and me. Something's happened. It's Lavinia . . . Theo has to bring her here.'

She stared at him in shock and echoed his last word. '*Lavinia?*'

'Yes.' He guided her across the stable yard where they stood by the fence and stared across the home

473

paddock the parched grass still beige from the dry summer, with heat rising from it in a shimmering haze.

'Tell me what's happened,' she said.

He passed her the letter. 'Read that first, then we'll talk.'

My own darling Keara

I hate to write this, but must do so. Lavinia is very ill and there's no ship leaving for England for nearly two months. Even if there were, she'd not be well enough to sail.

You know what she's like. It's impossible to care for her in a hotel, equally impossible to ask Noreen to look after her. So I must bring her back with me.

Dear God, that I should have to ask you and the children to move out! But not for long, I promise you. At the first opportunity, as soon as she gets better, I'll take her back to Perth and make sure she leaves the country.

Keara stopped reading for a moment to stare blindly across the paddock. It wasn't until Caley's voice broke into her thoughts that she looked sideways, gave him a quick half-smile that wavered near to tears almost immediately, and went back to her reading.

I know it's a lot to ask, but can you prepare a bedroom for her and her maid? Not ours, never ours! I'll sleep there alone. Then Caley will take you and the children to his house and bring Noreen back to act as hostess or housekeeper, call it what you will.

*It's all I can think of to do with her. I can't
stand that maid of hers, don't trust her an inch,
but at least she looks after Lavinia with tender
care—or rather deep self-interest.*

My love is, as always, yours,
Theo

Keara looked at Caley. 'It's a dreadful mess, isn't
it?'

He nodded.

'And there's worse to add to it.'

He stared at her in surprise.

'While you were in Perth, two men came here. I
think they intended to capture me and the children
and use us to extort money from Theo.'

He exclaimed in shock. 'What happened?'

'We captured them instead. They were drunken
buffoons, but it was still frightening. Malachi's
spoken to them—not gently—and they've
confessed that this Bess was involved in the plot.'
She paused for a moment then cut off his
exclamations and said firmly, 'So I'm not going to
leave my home. I'll stay here and run things. We'll
house Lavinia in the far bedroom and see how we
go from there.'

'Lavinia's been saying dreadful things about you.
You shouldn't have to face that, Keara.'

She shrugged. 'I *am* Theo's mistress, not his
wife. But I'm sure of his love, so whatever she says
or does won't tear me apart.'

'It's not what he wants.'

'None of this is what either of us wants.'

He shook his head, not sure what to do, then
frowned and asked, 'What about the two men?'

'Malachi and John drove them into Bunbury

475

yesterday. The magistrate committed them for trial.'

'Malachi did well to capture them with only John's help.'

She smiled then. ' 'Twas my sisters and I did the capturing, with Milack's help. Malachi and John were across at your place when they attacked.'

He goggled at her, then an answering smile crept slowly across his face. 'You're indomitable, Keara my girl. If you can do that, perhaps you can even cope with Lavinia.'

She sighed and grew solemn. 'I can but try.' And she'd have her sisters with her to do it. That gave her a lot more courage somehow.

*   *   *

Theo drove the big wagon round to the rear of his house and brought it to a halt close to the kitchen steps. He heaved a sigh of relief to be home, then glanced over his shoulder into the back of the wagon. Beside him, Dick echoed the sigh.

In the rear Clemmy watched Bess pat Lavinia's hand and then hold it in hers. Clemmy's lips tightened in disgust. The woman was shameless and Lavinia Mullane a fool, but a very sick fool, more sick than Theo seemed to realise for he was still talking about getting his wife better enough to return to England.

When Caley and Malachi came out to offer their help in getting Lavinia inside, Theo jumped down and asked in a low voice, 'Is Keara all right? Did she understand?'

Caley nodded towards the kitchen window. 'See for yourself.'

476

'I told you to get her out of here! I'll not have her exposed to insult.'

'She'll not leave, though she's sent the children across to our place. And she has some news for you.' He looked towards the wagon. 'Better get Lavinia inside before we do anything else, I suppose.'

Theo and Caley helped the sick woman down. As she tried to stand up, she swayed dizzily, her face going chalk-white and began to crumple.

'We'll have to carry her,' Caley said. 'You take her head.'

When Lavinia was settled in bed in the furthest of the bedrooms with Bess ministering to her, Theo went into the kitchen and gathered Keara into his arms. 'Dear God, why did you stay here? She'll show you no respect.'

She stepped away from him, never able to think clearly when he was holding her close. 'I need none from her. Besides, something's happened and—'

Someone cleared their throat and they turned to see Bess standing in the doorway, a nasty smile on her face. She didn't at first notice Theo.

'You must be the mistress,' she said to Keara. 'Well, *my* mistress wants some tea, so you might as well get it for her.' She sat down on one of the chairs and folded her arms.

Keara shook her head as Theo opened his mouth. She looked at Bess and said quietly, 'Thad and Bin are in prison, and if you don't want to join them, you'll keep a civil tongue in your head and do what you're employed for, which is look after Lavinia.'

Bess stared at her in shock, then noticed Theo and gasped in dismay. 'I don't know what you

477

mean,' she muttered, bitterness running through her like acid. How had Thad managed to mess this up? But she knew. Booze. He must have got drunk. And now he'd ruined everything, all her hopes for an easy life.

'You know well enough. They told the police everything.' Keara let this sink in then said briskly, 'Now, when you come into this kitchen from now on, you'll wait until I or my sisters or our maid can help you. You'll not touch anything without my say-so, let alone sit down like a guest. Is that clear? This is my house and you'll respect that.'

Bess met her eyes, read the implacable will there and stood up. There was anger on Theo's face and she shivered at the sight of it. He must love this woman very much. 'I'm sorry,' she muttered.

'Thank you. Now, you can help me prepare a tray of food for Mrs Mullane, tell me what may tempt her appetite. And until she's ready to leave her room, you'll say nothing to her of my presence here. Is that clear?'

Bess found herself nodding again.

Theo watched his beloved with admiration. Keara was a wonderful woman as well as the light of his life. Then he suddenly realised what she'd said. 'Your sisters?'

'That's what I was trying to tell you when *she* came in. Not only Mara but Ismay as well.' Tears welled in her eyes as she looked at him. 'Oh, Theo, it's all coming right again. It is.' He took her in his arms and held her close. 'I'm glad for you, darlin'. And we'll cope with Lavinia somehow.' He pushed her to arm's length and added with a chuckle, 'Or *you* will. You dealt with Bess really well just now.'

'I'm not letting someone like her speak to me

478

like that in my own home. Anyway we have a hold on her.'

He kissed her quickly then pushed her to arm's length. 'Well, where are your sisters?'

With a laugh she took his hand. 'I told them to wait outside until I'd explained to you. Come and meet them again. Oh, they've grown so much. You'll never believe it . . .'

*   *   *

Lavinia didn't leave the bedroom so didn't find out about Keara's presence. She lay in bed, staring into space, hardly rousing herself even to speak to Bess.

Worried, Theo sent for the doctor from Bunbury, agonising over how to explain to him who Lavinia was.

Keara had a word with Bess then said to him, 'Tell the doctor she's your cousin's wife who came out to improve her health. He'll be used to seeing people who've done that—and failed to thrive.'

They looked at one another.

'She's dying, isn't she?' he asked.

'Yes. You can't mistake that look. We should make her comfortable and let her die in peace.'

'You're very generous.'

She shrugged. 'I've got your love, borne your children, that's what matters most to me. I can't ever remember her being happy. It's not in her. I feel sorry for her in some ways.'

The doctor examined Lavinia who did not pay much attention to him, her thoughts seeming to be elsewhere. He went to Theo and said bluntly, 'I doubt your cousin's wife will last more than a day or two longer.'

479

'It's that close?' Theo was startled.

'I'm afraid so. She has a heart problem. The beat is very weak and irregular. No sea voyage could have helped her.'

'Perhaps it gave her hope for a time.'

'Perhaps. Who knows?'

'Thank you.'

When he'd gone, Bess came into the kitchen and looked at Keara. 'I saw the doctor's expression. She's not got long, has she?'

'I'm afraid not.'

'What's going to happen to me afterwards?'

Keara and Theo had already discussed this. 'We'll pay your passage back to England, give you some money to tide you over when you arrive and you can make a new life for yourself. Or we'll send you to Sydney and you can do the same there.'

Bess stared at her. 'You'd really do that?'

'Yes. You're no friend of ours, but I know how hard Lavinia is to care for and you've at least looked after her properly. But if we ever hear of you saying anything about us or our concerns, we may suddenly remember Thad and Bin's evidence.'

Bess stifled her anger and said with assumed meekness, 'I won't say a word.' She wondered if they'd keep their word and how much money she could squeeze out of them.

*   *   *

That night Bess was sitting by Lavinia's bed, feeling tired after a difficult day, when the lamp flickered and went out. 'Dratted oil must have run dry,' she muttered, went to pick it up, thankful there was nearly a full moon so she could still see her way.

480

But the oil reservoir was almost full still.

'Must be the wick.'

As she turned to take the lamp into the kitchen to find out what was wrong, darkness seemed to gather in one corner of the room. She jerked backwards, moving towards the window, one hand across her mouth, setting the lamp down hastily on the chest of drawers.

Lavinia, who had been drifting in and out of sleep all day, raised her head and smiled, a child's happy innocent smile, incongruous on that puffy face. 'Nancy!' she cried in a stronger voice than she had managed for days.

Bess felt a chill run through her. She could see the darkness—a black presence that had no right to be there in a moonlit room—though she couldn't see anything that looked like her aunt Nancy, and didn't want to. Her legs began to shake and she fell to her knees, trying to call for help and unable to force out a sound.

Lavinia was talking eagerly to the darkness which drifted nearer to the bed, hiding the sick woman.

Bess moaned and felt the room spin into nothingness.

When she recovered consciousness there was no darkness and the lamp was burning brightly on the chest of drawers, showing her the face of the woman on the bed. Lavinia was still smiling but she was definitely dead.

Screeching in terror, Bess ran out of the room and into the kitchen where she couldn't form a word properly, could only sob and moan in terror.

Theo took hold of her and shook her hard, but it was a while before she stopped gibbering and

481

managed to explain what had happened.

Keara ran along to the bedroom. No darkness here that she could see. Nothing to fear, either. The lamp couldn't possibly have gone out and then relit itself. But Lavinia was definitely dead.

Crossing herself, Keara said a prayer for the soul of the dead woman and turned to find Theo standing beside her.

'She's gone then?' he asked, not needing an answer but moving to stand by the bed. 'She looks happy.'

'Yes. I hope she is.'

*   *   *

It wasn't until they had buried Lavinia that Theo took Keara aside and asked, 'Will you marry me, my darling?'

She smiled serenely. 'I'd better. Am I not expecting another of your babies? Hadn't you guessed?'

'Yes, but it's wonderful to hear you say it.' His face was a glory of joy and love, and when he held open his arms, she walked into them and nestled against him. Then he moved back a little, his expression more sober, saying, 'We'll have to find a way to get married secretly. I'll not have you reviled for living in sin.'

'I don't mind what other people say about us.'

'I do. I mind very much about your good name.'

'You'll not hide it, Theo. They write down the marriages in church registers, and I want it to be properly done.' She laid one hand on his arm. 'But we'll do it quietly and I don't think people will say anything—not the people who matter to us,

482

anyway. Afterwards, we'll come home and celebrate with my sisters, your brother and your cousins.'

'It'll be the best party I've ever thrown.'

* * *

The wedding day dawned bright and sunny and they set off early, with Caley driving the wagonnette Theo had bought to transport his growing family and dependants round in.

Keara, radiant in a simple dress of blue silk that matched her eyes sat beside Theo, while Clemmy and Dick were nearby, looking equally happy, for they too were to marry that day. The rest of the family squashed in anyhow, with Nell sitting on her aunt Mara's knee, Noreen holding young Devin and the Gallaghers' sons sitting quietly at the rear.

The ceremony was short and to the point, but even so it moved Theo so much that his voice was husky with emotion as he made his responses. Keara spoke clearly and confidently. She had gone against her upbringing to live in sin with this beloved man of hers, knowing how that would have upset her mother. But now that was all over and her mother could rest easy in her grave. And ah, such a man she'd found herself!

Sunlight greeted them when they came out of the church, walking behind Clemmy and Dick. Theo had hoped when he planned this that the inevitable onlookers who always gathered at a wedding would focus on the other couple, not him and Keara. But by the time the ceremony was over, he'd forgotten that and was in a blissful daze through which he only saw his darling.

They went back to the Gallaghers' house for the wedding celebration, because Noreen had refused point-blank to let Keara prepare her own wedding feast. But truth to tell, neither Theo nor his new wife had much appetite, though they toasted one another in the wine Caley had provided.

'Be happy,' Ismay whispered as Keara and Theo prepared to go back home ahead of the others.

'I am. Oh, I am!'

They looked at one another and then hugged again, rocking to and fro.

Ismay and Malachi had to return to Victoria soon, where they would run their shop. But at least Keara had the comfort of knowing that Mara had chosen to stay with her in the west. And Ismay would be writing, keeping in touch, even visiting once in a while perhaps, if things went well. Or, Theo said, they could all go to Victoria for a visit. What was money for, after all, but to spend on your family?

Mara moved to join them, hugging both sisters indiscriminately, tears of happiness running down her cheeks.

Theo, who had been watching them fondly, judged it time to intervene and stepped forward to order with mock sternness, 'No tears on my wedding day, young woman! Now, wife, it's surely time to go home?'

All three sisters turned to smile at him.

'Look after her,' Ismay said.

'Make her happy,' Mara added.

As he and Keara drove away in his trap, Mara turned to Ismay, smiling mistily. 'He keeps saying the word "wife" all the time.'

'He loves her dearly.' Ismay linked her arm in

her sister's. 'Did you ever think we'd all wind up in Australia?'

'No. But I like it here.' She watched Malachi come towards them, smiling at his wife, his love for her showing as plainly as Theo's did for Keara. Mara wished suddenly that their mother could have been here today to see so much happiness.

Then Nell stumbled towards her, face sticky and hands held out for a cuddle.

'What have you been getting into, young woman?' Mara demanded with mock sternness.

'Cakes.' With a gurgle of laughter, Nell allowed herself to be picked up and laid her head against her aunt's shoulder.

Ismay stood beside Malachi, holding his hand and giving him a glowing look. 'Did you ever see anyone look as happy as Keara?'

He smiled at her. 'Yes, you. You *are* happy now, aren't you, my darling girl?'

'Oh, I am, yes. Very happy indeed.' She stood on tiptoe to whisper in his ear and when she had finished, he stared at her incredulously then whirled her round in a dance that made everyone stop what they were doing and stare at them.

He stopped and sketched a bow to the roomful of people. 'I've just been informed that I'm going to be a father.'

Ismay blushed a vivid pink. 'Malachi Firth!'

But she soon forgot her embarrassment as everyone crowded round to congratulate them.

Pity there was no chance of a rainbow today, Mara thought, looking at the clear blue sky. Then she smiled. They didn't need rainbows now, though she would always love the sight of one. She and her sisters were together again, wherever they lived.